KEN SANCHEZ

Light Redeemed (Shadowguards Book 2)

A Gay Urban Fantasy

Contents

Descriptions — v

Here's What Happened In The Story So Far... — viii

1 Training in Session — 1

2 Warning in Disguise — 13

3 Problematic Gods — 26

4 Looking for Clues — 38

5 Living the Music — 49

6 Raving Afterlife — 61

7 Troubles in the Afterlife — 73

8 Cursed Soul — 85

9 Rescue — 97

10 Godly Visit — 109

11 Taking in Strays — 121

12 Confusing Evidence — 133

13 The Sea God — 144

14 Leviathan — 155

15 Celestial Key — 168

16 Hole of Glory — 179

17 Jailbreak — 190

18 Art of the Deal — 202

19 Too late — 213

20 An Offer to Refuse — 225

21 Blood Is Currency — 238

22 Setting Up the Stage — 255

23 Taken — 267

24 Blood Soul   275
25 Blood Vessel   282
26 Light Redeemed   294
Thank you and Please Leave a Review!   300
About the Author   301
Also by Ken Sanchez   302

Descriptions

Characters

Eryx Ross - Musician bonded with the reawakened soul of Apollo, granting him increasing magic abilities. Has struggled coping with the revelations about his celestial heritage.

Alex Knight (Alias of Hades) - Leader of the Shadowguards organization. Romantically involved with Eryx and helps guide him in controlling his burgeoning powers.

Apollo - Greek god whose soul has been reborn fused with Eryx's spirit. Grants Eryx access to Apollo's signature music and healing based magic over time. Former love of Hades in a past life.

Ari Green (Alias of Artemis) - Member of Shadowguards, possesses nature/hunting related magic connected to her goddess domain

Dion Verdant (Alias of Dionysus) - Member of Shadowguards, wields wine and revelry related magic

Hermes - The messenger god who had deep ties with Alex and his team.

Lily Evans (Alias of Persephone) - Possesses earth magic and is skilled at sensing thoughts/emotions in others due to her goddess domain

Marcus King - Member of Shadowguards with superhuman speed/agility and is the son of Hermes

Gabe Reed - Member of Shadowguards serving as their resident witch and a skilled strategist

Emma Lock - Member of Shadowguards with ability as an enchanter (type of magic user)

Olivia Santiago - Member of Shadowguards who is an arcane mage skilled in wielding fire magic

Lucas Raft- Member of Shadowguards possessing skills as a sorcerer and technology expert

Dr. Finn Sloan - The Shadowguard's medic and healer, provides vital support with precise mastery of healing magic and advanced medical skills

Thanatos - Messenger of the mysterious Fates, tends to appear suddenly to deliver ominous warnings

Richard Lane - Famed musician who is later revealed to be a demigod

Winston Thorne (Alias of Zeus) - Ruler of the Greek Pantheon who now lives undercover on earth along with his wife Hera after past wars with Titans

Ares - God of war who attacked Eryx and the Shadowguards at

Carnegie Hall out of resentment towards his brother Hades

Morvain - Devious leader of the mysterious faction known as The Order. Known to be a sinister manipulator seeking various mythical artifacts

Sven Janssen - Works for The Order and is a powerful "mimic" with ability to copy others' magical abilities. Attacked Eryx in London and later changed shape to impersonate someone close to Eryx.

Organizations

Shadowguards - Organization led by Alex focused on protecting both human and supernatural beings from threats

The Order - Sinister organization of unknown motives that serves as a recurring antagonist in the story

HIB - Human Investigations Bureau - who is tasked with dealing with human and mortal affairs.

Other Terms

Magic - Various supernatural abilities displayed by characters in the story, often linked to their divine/mythic affinities

Shadow Wraiths - Dangerous monsters made of living shadow serving the hidden villains

Mark of Kronos - Ominous symbol associated with the antagonist faction The Order

Here's What Happened In The Story So Far…

With Apollo's god soul awakened within him, musician Eryx Ross has struggled to navigate dangerous new supernatural abilities alongside old traumas.

His nightmares and visions first escalated after an incident at an underground club. Eryx shocked himself by violently shattering a wall confronting a harasser, exhibiting inhuman strength. The dreams only compounded his lifelong struggle with haunting sleep plagued by horrific images of war and death.

That strange night made Eryx question his unexplained power and inner demons – until a fateful encounter set him on an extraordinary collision course.

While leaving a grocery store, Eryx was ambushed by vicious werewolves. The alpha's soulless eyes pierced into him with sinister intent before a swift arrow felled it. His timely rescuer was a ruggedly handsome man named Alex Knight, igniting attraction and intrigue in Eryx. The mysterious Alex diffused the bizarre attack but had to rush off, promising to meet again.

True to his word, Alex reemerged into Eryx's tumultuous life, gradually gaining his trust and offering glimpses into the secretive organization Alex led called Shadowguards. They existed to safeguard both humans and supernaturals, though Alex remained vague on many details.

Their fledgling relationship intensified upon a lavish first date together, which concluded with a passionate kiss promising deeper intimacy to come. The evening also unveiled hints of hidden threats looming over them – warnings delivered by the enigmatic Thanatos who vanished as swiftly as he appeared. With tension brewing on the horizon, Alex and Eryx found solace and comfort in each other.

Meanwhile, Eryx received a miraculous career boost: an offer from his longstanding manager Sam Mitchell to perform at the prestigious Carnegie Hall. The opportunity was a dream come true, and Eryx poured his soul into diligent rehearsals with the headliner band fronted by charismatic musician Richard Lane. After dazzling rehearsal sessions that revealed Eryx's true star potential, the band gifted him a stunning Gibson guitar in thanks.

For Alex, the inexplicable attack on Eryx stirred darker rumblings of enemies thought long defeated – the mysterious and lethal Order rising anew. His Shadowguard team's investigations into supernatural events unearthed chilling links to the Order's sinister Modus operandi. Victims and bodies discovered bore a Mark of Kronos, a terrifying and prophetic sign of what havoc the Order intended to unleash upon both the mortal and supernatural worlds.

Unbeknownst to Eryx, the Shadowguard team mobilized to Carnegie Hall upon receiving a tip-off that a disastrous assault would occur at the fated concert. With Eryx's safety as their prime directive, they entered the iconic venue, unaware that the trap was meant to ensnare them as much as the concertgoers.

From the opening notes of his world premiere performance, Eryx found himself wholly in his element. Despite the grandeur of the stage, a spark of intimate connection with one special face in the rapt audience fueled his passion. For Alex, the man fate seemed to have fated for him, Eryx gave his most heartfelt performance yet, dazzling the crowd with his soulful voice and hypnotic guitar.

Still, fate had other plans. A sinister chain of orchestrated events plunged Carnegie Hall into chaos. Explosions disrupted the concert, terrifying the audience. Eryx found his friends under attack by monsters of living shadow called Shadow Wraiths serving an unseen evil puppet master. Alex and the Shadowguards defended concertgoers, but the leader of the assault, the god Ares, unleashed a terrifying wave of conjured fire to overwhelm them.

Before Ares could deal a killing blow, a blinding radiance erupted from Eryx as the awakened god Apollo emerged. Apollo and Ares clashed as primal titans of light and war, the battle spilling into the streets of New York. The Shadowguards finally drove Ares into remission with wounds that would not swiftly heal.

Amidst the shockwave of revelations about his inborn divinity, Eryx found himself initiated into the mysteries of the supernatural and unlocking magic thought lost to humanity. The Shadowguards extended their offer of membership, welcoming him into the fold, though Eryx knew the decision would drastically alter the trajectory of his life and music career.

With Eryx now inextricably linked to both Alex and the Shadowguards, tensions rose in the supernatural world. The malevolent Order had proven themselves willing and able to strike those held most dear as weapons against Alex and his ilk. When a human detective with the initials D.C. was found soulless and murdered bearing the Mark of the Order, it suggested a gambit intended to provoke Alex by attacking his one-time ally.

Desperate for allies against the rising dark supernatural forces, Alex turned to the gods themselves. After establishing protectiveness around Eryx, Alex met with Zeus and Hera, who now lived secretly on Earth as media mogul Winston Thorne and his wife Eleanor. Long-simmering hostilities between them threatened to sabotage any chance of an alliance until Hades and Zeus managed to temper their wounded ties from broken oaths in ages past. Hera, as always, remained fiercely skeptical of Hades' intentions.

With Eryx acclimating to training and missions with his team, he received the surprising offer to join global superstar Richard Lane on tour overseas. The chance to pursue music at the highest levels beckoned enticingly, causing friction with Alex over losing precious time mastering control of his enormous powers. However, neither man could ignore the soul-deep attraction kindled between them.

Eryx eventually embarked on a whirlwind leg of the international tour with Richard's band. Alex tried not allowing his jealousy at tabloids linked Eryx with the notoriously player musician, instead throwing himself into his duties with the Shadowguards.

While overseas on tour, Eryx found himself falling into old bad habits with booze and pills meant to quiet nightmares linked to Apollo. After an explosive tabloid scandal showing him leaving a dance club kissing a pretty English boy, Eryx's troubles turned worst when a private afterparty resulted in him drunkenly burning down a mansion.

Only then did Eryx realize, with Richard's encouragement, the depths of his self-destructive issues rooted to lifelong trauma and fears of abandonment. After tearfully coming clean to Alex about the disastrous bender, he made the hard choice to cut the tour short and commit to sobriety and self-healing.

Making tough personal progress thanks to Shadowguard allies' help, Eryx still felt wracked by soul-deep doubts about what kind of man Apollo expected him to be while merging godly destiny with mortal yearning. His identity crisis came to a head when Alex revealed critical secrets kept from him for protection.

Eryx discovered truths about his celestial reincarnated spirit and sacred bond to Apollo that left him emotionally shattered. Coping with the revelation that he was never fully in control of his fate, Eryx fled the outpouring of support from those around him. He withdrew into isolation to process this radical reframing of his very existence, with only Mr. Whiskers as comfort during a depressive spiral.

With Apollo's voice maddeningly silent in his darkest hour, Eryx felt haunted by perceived expectations to be a flawless savior fused to the golden god. He longed bitterly for the simple life of obscurity, but with music career and heart in tatters, he saw no way out of the gilded cage his reborn divinity had become.

Only after feeing lost in darkness did Eryx receive his sign. A once beloved song emerged on the radio singing his own secret mantra - "No Light, No Light." Finding strange solace in resonant words of Florence and the Machine, Eryx emerged from hiding.

With fresh eyes unclouded by self-loathing, Eryx now grasped how his loved ones held no grand designs upon him, only affection for whoever he chose to be. Rejoining the Shadowguard team with Alex patiently waiting, he embraced the facets of himself both mortal and divine. Eryx soon astounded allies and enemies alike how fiercely his reborn will to live burned when stoking his merged soul to furnace temperatures.

For the enigmatic group known as The Order still lurked in the night, their dark schemes churning inexorably toward an apocalyptic endgame fated to shake the foundations of magic, gods, and human empire alike...

The stage had been set for Eryx and Alex to stand united against the oncoming tempest. But could their bond survive the ultimate trial by fire? And would Eryx finally find the belonging and purpose the reborn sun god inside him craved? Their fates shall soon converge under ominous heavens as the next chapter begins...

1

Training in Session

Eryx

The clang of metal against metal reverberated through the training room as Eryx parried Olivia's fiery strike. Sparks flew from the point of impact, illuminating the determined set of Eryx's jaw. Sweat trickled down his brow and stung his eyes, but he blinked it away, unwilling to give ground.

He retaliated with a blast of blinding light, pouring all his focus into the attack. Golden radiance exploded from his palms with a concussive whoosh of displaced air. But Olivia was ready, bringing up a simmering shield that absorbed the energy with a crackle and hiss.

Across the room, Alex watched the exchange intently, arms crossed over his broad chest. His stormy grey eyes tracked Eryx's every movement, analyzing his form and technique. When Eryx successfully deflected another volley of fireballs, Alex gave a nod of approval, pride tugging at the corner of his mouth.

"Good, Eryx. You're anticipating her attacks better," Alex called out, his deep voice cutting through the sounds of combat.

A grin flashed across Eryx's face at the praise, there and gone in an instant as he refocused on his opponent. Validation from Alex never failed to ignite a warm glow in his chest. More than anyone, he craved making his mentor proud.

Not just your mentor, but your partner. Your equal, Apollo chided gently in his mind. The god's presence was a steady thrum beneath Eryx's skin, ancient power intertwined with his mortal soul.

I know that, Eryx argued back silently even as he ducked under a searing lash of flame. *But I still have so much to learn. Alex has been doing this for centuries.*

As have I, Apollo reminded him, mental voice warm with affection and gentle reproach. *Our bond is a gift to you, not a crutch. Time to spread your wings and fly.*

Eryx set his jaw and nodded slightly, accepting the wisdom of the god within him. Drawing a centering breath, he extended his senses, tapping into the well of radiant energy singing through his veins.

He let Apollo's essence guide his movements, limbs suddenly feeling feather-light and fast as quicksilver. The bow materialized in his hands in a flash of shimmering gold, perfectly balanced and thrumming with potential.

Olivia's eyes widened as Eryx nocked an arrow of pure light to the string in one fluid motion. She hastily reinforced her shield, but it was too late. Eryx loosed the projectile with a musical twang, its blazing head punching clean through her defenses to strike her square in the chest.

Olivia flew backwards with a startled shout, hitting the padded wall and sliding down it with a faint groan. Instantly, Eryx allowed the bow to dissolve and rushed to her side, worry and guilt warring on his face.

But Olivia waved away his apologies with a rueful laugh even as she accepted his hand up. "Damn, Sunspot. Guess I need to up my game if I'm gonna keep pace with you."

"I got lucky," Eryx demurred, cheeks flushing at the new nickname. He still wasn't used to the easy camaraderie of the team, the way they celebrated each other's victories as if they were their own.

"Wasn't luck," Alex said, striding over to clap Eryx on the shoulder. "Your instincts are getting sharper, your connection to Apollo's power more intuitive."

The open approval in Alex's gaze made Eryx's heart flutter, a different kind of exhilaration from the rush of battle. He basked in the rare, unguarded smile on his lover's face, a sight that never failed to steal his breath.

Some of his awe must have shown, because Alex gave an almost imperceptible shake of his head, eyes openly fond. "Don't look so surprised. Even before Apollo, your potential was clear as day. I'm just glad you're finally seeing it for yourself."

He's right, you know, Apollo said, smug satisfaction coloring his mental tone. *I chose you for a reason. You are a worthy vessel for my light.*

Our light, Eryx corrected, something fierce and proud kindling in his chest. He was slowly growing into this destiny, remaking himself into someone new. Someone stronger.

As he stood there, surrounded by the people who believed in him most, Eryx finally let himself imagine a future where he stood tall at their sides. Not just a mortal muse playing at godhood, but a true guardian in his own right.

There would still be stumbles and doubts, insecurities to overcome. But with Alex's unwavering support and Apollo's ancient wisdom, he would face them head on. He had something precious to protect now, and powers to forge into a weapon for good.

Eryx squared his shoulders, meeting Alex's eyes with a determined nod. "Again," he said simply.

And in his mind and heart, three voices spoke as one - mortal, immortal, and the sweet spot in between.

Again.

After training, the team hit the showers, steam billowing as hot water soothed aching muscles. Playful banter echoed off the tiled walls, punctuated by laughter and the occasional yelp of indignation.

"Yo, who used up all the good shampoo?" Marcus griped, glaring at the empty bottle. "My hair needs the premium stuff!"

Olivia snorted, flicking suds his way. "Oh please, like your buzz cut needs delicate treatment."

"Hey, this is a precision look," Marcus huffed, running a hand over his close-cropped hair. "Takes effort to maintain, thank you very much."

Eryx chuckled, shaking his head as he rinsed the last of the conditioner from his own unruly locks. These silly, mundane moments with the team were a balm to his often overtaxed mind.

His gaze strayed to Alex, as it so often did, drinking in the play of water over toned bronze skin, the corded strength of his back. Even in repose, his lover exuded controlled power, a jungle cat at rest.

Careful, you're staring, Apollo teased, a smile in his voice. *Don't want to scandalize the children.*

Oh hush, Eryx shot back, cheeks warming. *Let me appreciate art in peace.*

The god's rich laughter reverberated through his mind, edged with wistful fondness. *He is rather breathtaking, isn't he? Hades was always the most striking of his siblings. Those brooding good looks turned many a head in Olympus.*

Eryx bit his lip against a sudden swell of anxiety in his chest. *I still don't know what he sees in me.*

Apollo's presence grew serious, a steadying hand on Eryx's metaphorical shoulder. *He sees your heart, dear one. Your courage, your resilience, your capacity for love. In you, he has found a home.*

Eryx swallowed against the lump in his throat, eyes stinging from more than soap.

As if sensing his turbulent emotions, Alex turned, brow furrowing in concern when he noticed Eryx's subdued demeanor. With a few quick strides, he crossed the room, strong hands coming up to cradle Eryx's face.

"Hey," Alex murmured, stormy grey eyes searching Eryx's own. "What's going on in that head of yours?"

Eryx almost deflected, pasting on a smile. But here, with Alex's thumbs gently stroking his cheekbones, honesty rose to his lips unbidden.

"Just…it's been a lot lately," he admitted quietly. "The new powers, the constant attacks… sometimes I wonder if I'm really cut out for this hero thing."

Alex's gaze softened, an ocean of understanding in those pewter depths. "Oh, Eryx. You're already a hero, in all the ways that matter."

He brushed a tender kiss to Eryx's brow, as if he could physically soothe the doubts whirling beneath. "Do you think any of us knew what we were doing at first? Godhood doesn't come with an instruction manual."

A huff of laughter escaped Eryx at that, some of the tension easing from his shoulders.

"Even I had to learn as I went," Alex continued, a rueful quirk to his lips. "Made my share of mistakes, questioned my worth. But I kept going, kept trying to do better. That's all any of us can do."

He tilted Eryx's chin up, holding his gaze intently. "You're not perfect, love. None of us are. But you're brave, and kind, and so damn determined to do good. That's what makes a true hero."

Eryx let the words wash over him, a balm to his bruised spirit. He surged forward, capturing Alex's lips in a fierce kiss, pouring all his gratitude and love into the slide of their mouths.

Distantly, he registered the team's good-natured whistles and catcalls, but he paid them no mind. Right now, his world narrowed to the heat of Alex's body against his, the thrum of their bond in his veins.

When they finally broke apart, both were flushed and slightly breathless. Alex's eyes glittered with mischief, thumbs rubbing distracting circles on Eryx's hips.

"What do you say we get out of here?" Alex murmured, voice pitched low and intimate. "I'm thinking milkshakes at Crave, extra whipped cream. Then maybe we can continue this back at home…"

"Oh god, please don't traumatize the kid!" Olivia groaned theatrically, chucking a loofah at Alex's head. "Save the bedroom eyes for behind closed doors, yeah?"

"Alright, alright, show's over," Alex said, smiling despite the gruff words. "Everyone get dressed. Those milkshakes aren't going to drink themselves."

The promise of a sweet treat worked like a charm - the team scrambled to throw on clean clothes, playful pushes and genial ribbing resumed.

Eryx and the team walked into Crave, the comforting scent of fried food and coffee enveloping them like a warm hug. Eryx inhaled deeply, a grin spreading across his face at the familiar aromas.

"Smells like heaven," Emma sighed happily as they wove through the crowded tables.

The retro décor was all chrome and red vinyl, vintage music posters lining the walls. Servers bustled to and fro balancing trays laden with towering burgers and thick milkshakes. Laughter and chatter provided a lively soundtrack to the cozy chaos.

"Hey kids, your booth's ready in the back," Dion called out with a welcoming smile, appearing from the kitchen.

"No way!" Eryx rushed to embrace his old friend, a grin splitting his face. "D, what are you doing here?"

Dion laughed, returning the hug with equal enthusiasm. "Well, someone's gotta keep an eye on you, kid. Figured I'd set up shop close by, make sure you're not getting into too much trouble."

Eryx pulled back, raising an eyebrow. "Let me guess - you own this place?"

Dion's eyes twinkled with mirth. "You know me, always loved playing host. Now come on, I've got your favorite booth open in the back, away from prying eyes."

As they followed Dion through the diner, Eryx felt a rush of gratitude for his loyal friend. Even now, Dion was subtly protecting him, ensuring a place where Eryx could relax and be himself without the constant scrutiny of the public eye.

Sliding into the corner booth, Eryx breathed a sigh of relief. The worn vinyl seats and familiar scent of greasy comfort food were like a balm to his frayed nerves.

Once they were all settled, Dion passed out menus, his gaze lingering on Eryx. "I know it's been a rough go lately, kid, but it's good to see you still smiling. You've always been resilient. Whatever comes next, I know you'll rise to meet it."

Eryx swallowed down the sudden lump in his throat, touched by Dion's unwavering faith in him. He hoped his friend was right - that with the support of his loved ones, his resilience would carry him through the trials ahead.

Under the table, Alex gave Eryx's hand a gentle squeeze, a silent reassurance that he wasn't alone. Eryx glanced over at his boyfriend, a small smile tugging at his lips. How did Alex always seem to know exactly what he needed?

As the group settled in, Eryx's mind couldn't help but wander to the chaotic media circus that had been surrounding him and the Shadowguards lately. Ever since news broke about his involvement in the supernatural attack at Central Park a couple of months back, the press had been hounding him relentlessly.

Paparazzi followed him everywhere, shouting questions and snapping photos. News outlets speculated endlessly about his connections to the mysterious Shadowguard group. Some even accused him of staging the Central Park incident as a PR stunt, which made Eryx's blood boil.

He missed the days when he could grab a coffee or take a walk without being mobbed by cameras and microphones. He had never wanted fame for fame's sake - music was his passion, not the circus surrounding it.

But there was no going back now. His life would never be strictly private again, his every move scrutinized under the public eye. The thought made Eryx's skin crawl, but he knew he'd have to adjust to this new reality.

For now, though, in the refuge of Dion's diner, Eryx could relax and enjoy time with his loved ones, away from the prying eyes of the world.

"Wait a minute," Eryx said, turning to Alex with a raised eyebrow. "Did you already know Dion owned this place?"

Alex's smile widened, a mischievous glint in his eye. "I may have had an inkling, which is why I suggested we come here."

Eryx chuckled, shaking his head. "Should've known you two were scheming together."

"Only for your benefit, babe." Alex leaned in, pressing a chaste kiss to Eryx's cheek.

Olivia groaned playfully, rolling her eyes. "Ugh, get a room, you two."

Marcus pretended to shield his eyes, peeking through his fingers. "The PDA is blinding!"

Eryx tossed a balled-up napkin at them, laughing. "You're just jealous."

Their teasing banter was interrupted by Dion's return, a notepad in hand. "Alright, kids, enough gossip. Who's ready to order?"

As Dion took their orders, Eryx felt surrounded by warmth - the comfort of old friends and new, a refuge from the chaos awaiting outside. With Alex's hand clasped in his beneath the table, he breathed deep, cherishing this momentary peace.

After a few more minutes, Gabe and Emma arrived at the diner and slid into the corner booth to join the group. Gabe's striking silver hair and sharp green eyes always made him stand out, and Eryx couldn't help but feel a little intimidated. As a skilled magic user and strategist, Gabe was someone you definitely didn't want to mess with.

The conversation flowed easily as they caught up on lighter topics, everyone grateful for a brief respite from the supernatural drama that constantly swirled around them. Marcus took some good-natured ribbing about his new pet dog keeping him up at night.

"At least I don't stay up moping and listening to emo music," Marcus shot back with a grin, his eyes twinkling mischievously as he looked at Alex.

Alex rolled his eyes, but Eryx could see the hint of a smile tugging at the corner of his mouth. "I seem to recall someone being a bit of a grump before a certain pop star came along…" He nudged Eryx playfully, their shoulders bumping together.

Eryx laughed, warmth blooming in his chest at the easy affection. "Yeah, yeah, we all know I'm the charm that keeps you smiling."

As the laughter died down, Alex's expression grew more serious. "Any updates from your contacts, Gabe? We're still largely in the dark about Sven and The Order's plans and next moves."

Gabe shook his head apologetically, his brow furrowing. "Unfortunately, my sources have been unusually silent as of late. I don't like it - feels like there's a storm brewing just out of sight."

Eryx frowned, unease prickling along his spine. He hated this feeling of waiting for the other shoe to drop. "So what do we do? Just sit and wait for them to make the first move?"

"For now, vigilance and patience may be our best options," Alex said, his voice steady and reassuring. "Better to gather our strength and let things unfold than act rashly."

Olivia grumbled, sparks dancing across her fingertips in agitation. "Easier said than done."

Gabe nodded solemnly. "I understand the desire for action, but we must be strategic. When my contacts resurface, hopefully we'll gain more insight into Sven and The Order's plans."

Eryx bit his lip, trying to tamp down the frustration simmering in his gut. He knew Alex and Gabe were right, but the lack of intel made him feel like they were flying blind. He glanced at Alex, their eyes meeting in a silent vow to protect each other through whatever uncertainty lay ahead.

As the conversation drifted back to lighter topics, Eryx let himself relax, buoyed by the comfort of friends and good food. Laughter flowed freely, and for a little while, the weight of the world didn't feel quite so heavy.

But the reprieve was short-lived. Just as they were lingering over coffee and dessert, their SHDs (Shadow Holographic Devices) began buzzing with an alert. Eryx jumped, still not fully accustomed to the futuristic tech that let the Shadowguards communicate and monitor supernatural threats. He much preferred his vintage guitar and notebook to these glowing holographic screens.

Alex checked his device, his brow furrowing. "It's Lily. She says we need to get back to HQ ASAP."

They quickly wrapped up, saying their goodbyes to Dion. Eryx embraced his old friend tightly, a lump forming in his throat. "Stay safe, kid," Dion murmured. "Call me if you need anything."

The streets were a blur of neon as they hurried back to headquarters.

Eryx's mind raced with possibilities, each more dire than the last. What could have happened to put Lily on high alert?

Upon entering the briefing room, they found Lily already standing at the central holographic display, an image of a crime scene projected above the table. Even in the midst of crisis, her beauty and grace struck Eryx. He knew that despite moving on from Alex romantically, part of her still cared deeply for him. Eryx was grateful she supported their new relationship, giving them her blessing.

"Sorry to pull you all away from lunch, but we have a situation," Lily said, her voice tight with tension. She introduced the man on the holo-screen as Derrick Green, their new liaison from the Human Investigative Bureau.

As they took their seats, Alex's expression turned serious. "Derrick, what are we looking at here?"

Derrick's face was grim. "A body was discovered on Fifth Avenue an hour ago. Our forensics team found abnormal markings that suggest a supernatural cause of death. We need you on scene to investigate further and contain it if necessary."

The team peppered Derrick with questions, trying to get a clearer picture of the mysterious murder scene. Eryx listened intently, his mind whirling with theories and possibilities.

When Derrick revealed the lack of witnesses or solid evidence, a heavy silence fell over the room. This was going to be a tough case to crack.

Alex remained stoic, issuing orders for the team to suit up while he coordinated backup resources with Lily. As they walked briskly toward the armory, Eryx glanced at him with concern. "Do you think Lily's doing okay? I know you two have a complicated history."

Alex gave Eryx's hand a comforting squeeze, his touch grounding amidst the chaos. "She's one of the strongest people I know. I'm sure this case is bringing up some painful memories for both of us, but Lily can handle herself."

Eryx nodded, letting the subject drop for now. There would be time to talk later - right now they had a job to do.

2

Warning in Disguise

Alex

Alex grudgingly admitted that the armored Bearcat transport Gabe had pushed him to acquire was coming in pretty damn handy as their mobile command center. But he'd never give Gabe the satisfaction of actually telling him he was right.

"Admit it, you've grown attached to this beast," Gabe chuckled from the driver's seat as he steered them out of the city.

Alex only grunted, arms crossed.

"Aww, no need to pout. I won't say I told you so," Gabe continued needling him.

"Keep running your mouth and I'll make you walk back," Alex grumbled half-heartedly.

Gabe just laughed as he followed the GPS directions to their destination. Alex peered over his shoulder to the back, where Eryx was chatting and joking around with the rest of the team. His boyfriend's smile made his heart swell, even as his protective instincts kicked in.

As if reading his mind, Gabe spoke up. "Eryx is gonna be fine, you know. Kid can handle himself."

Alex sighed, dragging a hand down his face. "I know, it's just…I worry about failing him. That someday I won't be enough to keep him safe."

Gabe's expression softened with understanding. "You really love him, huh?"

"More than anything," Alex admitted. "I've never felt this way about someone before. The thought of losing him…"

"Hey, you can't think like that," Gabe said firmly. "What matters is the here and now. And right now? You two are solid. So stay focused on the present and you'll be alright."

Alex nodded slowly. Gabe was right - he had to trust in the strength of what he and Eryx had built. And have faith in his boyfriend's skills and tenacity.

"Thanks man," Alex said gruffly. "I appreciate the pep talk."

"Anytime, boss man," Gabe replied with an easy smile.

The Bearcat rolled up to the taped off crime scene on fifth Avenue, just in time by the looks of it. Alex surveyed the situation as he stepped out of the vehicle.

A crowd was starting to form around the alley's entrance, held back by barriers and uniformed officers. Forensics techs were working under floodlights while detectives took statements from potential witnesses. It was controlled chaos.

Alex spotted their HIB liaison, Derrick, heading their way. The man's athletic build and sharp golden-brown eyes marked him as more than just your average agent, which made sense given Lily's connections. Alex guessed cheetah shifter based on the subtle predatory grace in his stride.

They shook hands firmly when Derrick reached them. "Thanks for getting here so quickly," he said. "My superiors are anxious for your take."

"No problem. What's the status?" Alex asked briskly.

"Detective Turner is running point inside the scene. He's waiting for you. And I believe your, uh, consultant Leo is already examining the body," Derrick answered.

Alex nodded. Having their resident necromancer Leo on the case was a fortunate bonus. Though the detective kept his true nature secret from his HIB colleagues.

"Good, we'll start there," Alex decided. He directed the team to fan out through the scene, trusting Derrick to smooth things over with the human authorities.

Passing under the police tape, Alex spotted Detective Turner conferring with a CSI team near the mouth of the alley. The grizzled veteran detective managed a terse greeting before returning to barking orders at his techs.

Alex left them to it and continued on to where Leo was crouched beside the body, eyes closed in concentration as he communed with the lingering essence of the deceased.

Eryx was speaking with a shaken witness, coaxing out any small details that could be relevant. Though clearly uneasy, he listened intently and offered the woman kind reassurance. Pride swelled in Alex's chest at seeing his boyfriend's compassion.

Marcus and Emma were combing the periphery of the scene for physical evidence or magical traces. But as expected, it appeared the cunning killer had covered their tracks.

Gabe conferred with CSU techs to review their findings, though the lack of telling forensic clues had him shaking his head. Meanwhile, Olivia closed her eyes, mentally scanning the area for any residual supernatural imprints.

After checking on his team, Alex approached the detective in charge, who was barking orders at some uniforms securing the perimeter.

"Detective Turner?" Alex extended his hand. "Alex Knight, Shadow-guard special investigator."

Turner shook briskly, sizing Alex up with sharp grey eyes. "Right, the spook squad. You got an ETA on your people?"

Alex had to resist bristling slightly at the detective's flippant "spook squad" remark. He knew they still had a ways to go in getting local law enforcement to fully accept and cooperate with the Shadowguards. Old prejudices died hard.

Sizing up Detective Turner, Alex reminded himself to be patient. The man had sharp, insightful eyes that suggested competence, despite his apparent wariness towards the supernatural. Alex imagined Turner was simply guarded after encountering something so far outside his experience and understanding. It would take time to earn his full trust.

In the meantime, Alex resolved to remain professional and helpful, providing whatever expertise and resources the Shadowguards could offer. He sensed Turner's bleeding heart motivation in pursuing justice for the victim. In that, at least, they were aligned.

With time and successful collaborations, Alex hoped to show the detective that the Shadowguards were valuable partners, not meddling "spooks." It would be a gradual process, but Alex was prepared to weather the scrutiny and skepticism. Winning over local law enforcement would make protecting the city far easier.

"They're already here examining the scene," Alex nodded over his shoulder. "What can you tell me so far?"

Turner sighed, glancing down at his notes. "Victim is a Jane Doe, mid-thirties, average height and build. No ID on her. ME's en route to transport the body."

Alex's jaw tightened. "Any clues on how she was killed?"

"Exsanguination by the looks of it," Turner said. "But no murder weapon found, and no blood trail leading to or from the body. It's like she was just dumped here."

Alex surveyed the alley. Nothing seemed amiss besides the dark pool of blood under the victim's slumped form.

Turner shook his head, clearly rattled. "In all my years, I've never seen a scene this clean with such violence. It's unnatural."

Alex's gaze landed on some indentations in the brick wall. "She wasn't just dumped. I think your victim was lured here."

He gestured for Turner to follow him. Crouching by the marks, Alex traced the claw-like gouges.

Turner frowned. "Those look like shifter scratches, but something's off. The spacing and depth…"

"You're right, these weren't made by shifter claws," Alex said grimly. "But something wanted us to think they were."

Turner paled at the implication. They were dealing with a supernatural killer trying to mask its tracks. And whatever it was, it would strike again if not stopped.

Alex stood, resolution steeling his features. "I give you my word, my team will uncover the truth. And the monster that did this will be brought to justice."

Turner nodded gratefully. "Any help you can give to solve this, I appreciate it. Just keep me informed, yeah?"

After his conversation with Detective Turner, Alex returned to where the victim's body still lay, Leo crouched beside it checking it all over.

Over the past few months, Alex had grown to deeply appreciate Leo's skills and discretion as a necromancer operating within the HIB. Leo drew on his occult gifts subtly to aid investigations, while keeping the full extent of his powers concealed from his mundane colleagues. Alex was grateful to have him collaborating on this troubling case.

Kneeling across from Leo, Alex spoke quietly to avoid attracting attention. "Were you able to pick up on anything further from the body?"

Leo didn't look up, brow furrowed in concentration as he hovered a palm over the victim's pale throat. "There is indeed a faint bite mark here, suggesting a vampire's involvement."

Alex frowned. "But that doesn't track with the blood spilled at the scene. A clean vampire kill wouldn't leave that behind."

"Precisely," Leo murmured, still focused on his reading. "I believe whoever did this wanted to deliberately give the impression of a vampire attack, while exercising less...restraint."

"A frame job," Alex growled. "Someone's trying to ignite tensions again."

Leo nodded grimly. They both knew violent ripples from this would extend far beyond this one murder.

Alex's hands tightened into fists, angry at the turmoil this would incite across supernatural factions. He ached to reach out with his powers and read the psychic imprints left on the victim's essence. But with it being a human death, direct infernal contact could corrupt crucial evidence.

Alex stood tense, hands fisted as he resisted the urge to unleash his powers. This killing was meant to unleash chaos, and he refused to corrupt the evidence needed to stop it.

Suddenly, his comm crackled as Lily's urgent voice came through. "Alex, we have a situation developing nearby. Possible related disturbance at the park on fifth and Elm."

Cursing under his breath, Alex tapped his earpiece. "What are the details, Lily?"

"Several civilians reporting shadowy creatures emerging from the pond, attacking park-goers. The energy signature appears similar to..."

"Shadow wraiths," Alex finished grimly. Of course that menace would rear its head now. He switched channels to alert his team.

"Wrap up here and converge on the park ASAP," Alex ordered tersely. "We've got incoming wraith activity."

The team immediately moved to follow, while Detective Turner approached Alex. "What the hell's going on now?" he demanded.

"A possible related incident - we're on our way to contain it," Alex explained hurriedly.

Turner's eyes widened, but he nodded. "Got it, just keep my people out of your freaky business with those monsters."

"Will do. Stay safe, Detective." Alex took off after his team, Eryx falling into step beside him.

"You good?" Eryx asked, sensing Alex's barely contained fury.

Alex gave a taut nod. "I'll feel a lot better when we end those damned wraiths for good."

Eryx offered a supportive hand squeeze as they ran.

Alex harbored a deep hatred for the wraiths that had caused so much past misery.

They arrived at the park to find it overrun by spectral entities emerging from the murky pond - shadow wraiths in all their malevolent glory. People fled screaming as the wraiths attacked, leaving smoky trails of terror.

Near the epicenter stood a lone figure holding a twisting black staff, energy rippling out to unleash more wraiths. Alex's eyes narrowed - that was no Staff of Umbra, but dark magic nonetheless.

"Marcus, Emma - evacuate the civilians," Alex barked out. "Gabe, Olivia - suppress those wraiths. Eryx, with me to take down whoever the hell that is."

The team leapt into flawless action. Emma's shields covered fleeing bystanders while Marcus whisked people to safety with enhanced speed. Gabe and Olivia released blasts of light and flame to dissipate oncoming wraiths.

Shadowy howls filled the air as Alex and Eryx fought through writhing entities towards the conjurer. Alex tore through them with hellfire, clearing a path for Eryx to take down the hooded threat with a concussive burst of light.

As they charged towards the conjurer, Alex said sharply, "Eryx, stay behind me!"

Eryx huffed in annoyance. "Come on, I can help take this bastard down!"

Alex turned and growled, "Not now! Just watch my back."

With a frustrated nod, Eryx fell in line as they slashed through oncoming wraiths. Alex could feel his boyfriend's irritation, but he refused to risk Eryx getting hurt. There would be a price to pay for his overprotectiveness later, but for now, focus was needed.

Summoning a flaming sword, Alex viciously struck down smoky wraiths as they closed in. Beside him, Eryx called on bursts of light to disintegrate the entities. They made steady progress, but more spectral foes kept pouring forth.

Ahead, the hooded conjurer grinned manically as he saw them approach, malevolent energy crackling around him. With a dramatic sweep of his staff, he tore open another writhing portal, the very air shuddering with the force of the dark magic. Shadowy howls echoed as reinforcements emerged, their twisted forms surging forward to impede Alex and Eryx.

"Fuck," Alex cursed under his breath, the bitter taste of desperation on his tongue. "Eryx, shields up!"

Eryx gritted his teeth, sweat beading on his brow as he poured every ounce of his strength into layering more protection around them. Light coalesced into a shimmering barrier, but it flickered and wavered under the onslaught of the shadowy horde.

Alex arched his sword, hellfire blazing along the blade as he sent an inferno careening toward the conjurer. But the flames dissipated harmlessly against an inky barrier surrounding the man, the dark energy seeming to devour the light. This dark mage was protected by something ancient and powerful.

"Who are you?" Alex demanded, his voice raw with fury and desperation. "Why summon these abominations?"

A chilling, disturbingly familiar laugh emanated from the figure, the sound distorted and echoing unnaturally. "Oh Hades, still so desperate for answers," the voice mocked, dripping with cruelty. "Let's call this game a warm-up."

Alex's blood boiled at the taunt, rage and frustration searing through his veins. "Show yourself and face me, you fucking coward!" He charged forward, striking repeatedly with all his might, but his blows glanced off the conjurer's shield, not even leaving a scratch.

Eryx rushed to Alex's side, his heart pounding in his ears as he watched his lover batter fruitlessly against the conjurer's seemingly impenetrable defenses. "Let me try something," Eryx shouted over the deafening shrieks of the wraiths, his voice hoarse with desperation.

Alex hesitated for a moment, his instincts screaming at him to protect Eryx, to keep him away from this madman. But he knew they were out of options. With a terse nod, he fell back slightly, allowing Eryx room to work.

Eryx closed his eyes, drawing in a deep, shuddering breath as he reached deep within himself, grasping for the searing, almost painful intensity of Apollo's essence. Light began to coalesce around his hands, growing brighter and hotter until it was nearly blinding. Complex melodic tones began resonating in the air as Eryx crafted a powerful sonic wave, pouring every last drop of his strength and will into the attack.

The vibrating discord reverberated through the conjurer's protections, the shield rippling and warping under the onslaught. For a moment, it seemed like it might hold - but then, with a shattering sound like a thousand panes of glass exploding, the barrier crumbled, leaving the mage exposed.

Alex seized the opportunity, slashing through the weakened defenses with a blast of hellfire. But their foe retaliated with a blast of shadows that knocked Alex back, sending him crashing to the ground with a sickening thud.

"Is that all you've got?" the conjurer taunted, his distorted voice dripping with contempt.

Alex snarled, staggering to his feet as he hurled a massive fireball at the mage. The conjurer barely managed to deflect it, the force of the blast sending him stumbling back.

Beside him, Eryx called down blinding rays of light, the searing radiance further wearing down their opponent's defenses. They pressed the attack in tandem, neither slowing, both driven by the desperate knowledge that if they failed here, countless lives would be lost.

"Give it up, we've got you outmatched!" Eryx yelled, his voice raw and hoarse as he deflected a volley of dark energy bolts, each one feeling like a physical blow.

The conjurer only cackled manically in response, his veil slowly shredding under their combined assault. With a nod to Eryx, Alex gathered every last ounce of his strength, unleashing a massive inferno just as Eryx struck with a final, devastating wave of resonating sound. Their joint blow shattered the conjurer's remaining protections, sending him crashing to the ground, unconscious.

Panting, his chest heaving with exertion, Alex immediately restrained their foe with magic-suppressing cuffs. The dark staff crumbled to dust now that its wielder was defeated.

With shaking hands, Alex activated his comm, updating the team on the situation. "We apprehended the summoner, but it's clearly the Order behind this. Secure the park, and let's get this bastard back for interrogation."

He turned to Eryx, seeing his own exhaustion and desperation mirrored in his lover's eyes. They had won this battle, but both knew it was only the beginning. The Order was growing bolder, and they would stop at nothing to achieve their dark goals.

With the conjurer in custody, Alex directed Gabe to update Detective Turner and the HIB about the connected supernatural threat. The rest of the team secured the park while Alex and Eryx escorted their prisoner back to headquarters.

Over comms, Lily informed them she had called in Dr. Finn Sloan to examine the captive upon arrival. Alex acknowledged, before glancing over at Eryx's tense expression. Clearly they were in for a heated discussion about Alex's overprotectiveness during the fight. He probably deserved the wrath he was about to face.

Once back at HQ, Marcus and Lucas took custody of the conjurer and headed toward the medical bay. Finn met them partway, falling into step beside Alex.

"What exactly are we dealing with here?" the doctor inquired.

Alex quickly summarized the shadow wraith ambush orchestrated by their magically disguised foe. "He was wielding some serious darkness, but we managed to subdue him. All vitals seemed stable when we brought him in."

Dr. Sloan nodded. "I'll monitor him closely and update you on any developments."

"Appreciate it, doc." Alex clapped Finn's shoulder before continuing toward his office, Eryx trailing silently behind. The tension radiating off Eryx was palpable.

The office door had barely closed before Eryx rounded on Alex, his eyes blazing with fury. "What the hell was that stunt back there about not letting me engage?"

Alex threw his hands up, frustration evident in every line of his body. "Listen, I was just trying to protect you! The situation was dangerous, and I—"

"Oh, cut the overprotective bullshit!" Eryx snapped, his voice rising as he stepped into Alex's space, their faces mere inches apart. "After all our training, after everything we've been through together, you still don't trust me to handle myself in a fight?"

"That's not it at all!" Alex shouted back, his own anger flaring hot and bright. "I just know how unpredictable these magical psychos can be! I didn't want you getting hurt!"

Eryx jabbed an accusatory finger into Alex's chest, his touch searing even through the fabric of Alex's shirt. "That's not your call to make for me! I don't need you shielding me like some fragile damsel in distress!"

Alex's control snapped, his power surging beneath his skin as he grabbed Eryx's wrist, holding it in place. "I'm trying to keep you safe because I lo—!"

"Don't you dare," Eryx hissed, his eyes flashing with warning as he wrenched his arm free from Alex's grasp. "I swear, if your next word was 'love,' I will walk out that door and not look back."

The air between them crackled with tension, their chests heaving with the force of their emotions. Alex could feel the heat of Eryx's anger, could see the hurt and betrayal simmering beneath the surface.

It was that glimpse of pain in Eryx's eyes that finally broke through the haze of Alex's own fury. He forced himself to take a deep, shuddering breath, trying to rein in his temper. Yelling at each other wasn't going to solve anything.

Slowly, deliberately, Alex unclenched his fists, running a tired hand down his face. "You're right," he said, his voice rough with emotion. "I was out of line trying to sideline you like that. I just… I worry about you, constantly. But that's no excuse for not trusting in your abilities. You can clearly handle yourself out there. I'll try to do better about not being so overprotective."

Eryx stared at him for a long moment, the tension in his shoulders gradually easing as he processed Alex's words. "Thank you," he said finally, his anger cooling to a simmer. "I know you want to keep me safe, but we're partners now, Alex. We have to trust each other in the field, no matter what."

"You're absolutely right," Alex agreed, tentatively reaching out to take Eryx's hand in his. Relief washed through him when Eryx didn't pull away. "No more benching you from the action. We're stronger together, and I need to remember that."

Eryx's fingers tightened around Alex's, a silent acknowledgment of the apology. They still had a lot to discuss, a lot of hurt feelings to work through, but for now, the worst of the storm had passed.

They were still holding hands, the argument behind them, when the air suddenly crackled with energy. A shimmering portal tore open, and out stepped a lean, athletic figure with windswept hair - Hermes.

"Hermes!" Eryx broke into a grin and rushed to embrace the god of messengers. Despite his sass and trickster nature, Hermes had a good heart under his bravado.

After Hermes affectionately ruffled Eryx's hair, he approached Alex with a serious expression. "Alex," he greeted formally. "I come bearing a message from Winston."

Alex straightened, immediately on alert. For Winston to send Hermes rather than just contacting him directly, something big must be happening.

3

Problematic Gods

Eryx

"I come bearing a message from Winston," Hermes said, his normally playful demeanor replaced by a somber gravity that set Eryx's nerves on edge.

Eryx gave Alex's hand a reassuring squeeze, feeling the tension radiating from his partner. At the mention of the king of the gods, Eryx felt Apollo's essence stir within him, a ripple of unease that echoed his own growing sense of foreboding.

What do you make of this unexpected summons, my young host? Apollo's voice echoed in Eryx's mind, a note of apprehension coloring his words.

Eryx sighed inwardly, a heavy weight settling in his chest. *Whatever it is, it can't be good. But let's find out more first.*

Outwardly, Alex was pressing the messenger god for details, his voice tight with barely restrained impatience. "Hermes, what exactly does Winston want from me? You know I have duties here I can't simply abandon."

Hermes ran a hand through his disheveled hair, looking as though he carried the weight of the world on his shoulders. "Apologies, but Winston was sparse with specifics. Only ordered me to see you promptly."

Eryx studied Hermes closely, taking in the deep shadows beneath his eyes, the slump of his normally proud shoulders. The sight of the usually irreverent god so worn down sent a chill down Eryx's spine. Whatever news Hermes bore, it was clearly grave enough to take a heavy toll.

"Hey, you doing okay?" Eryx asked softly, concern lacing his words. "Need to sit down?"

Hermes managed a wan smile, but it didn't reach his eyes. He waved off Eryx's offer with a shake of his head. "I'm fine, just one too many errands on the old man's list. Nothing some ambrosia and a nap won't fix."

Alex crossed his arms, his jaw clenched tight. "Well, once you've recovered, feel free to enlighten us about this so-called threat."

Hermes drew in a deep, bracing breath, as though steeling himself for the words to come. The air seemed to grow heavy, the very atmosphere pressing down on them with a sense of impending doom.

"One of the old gods' bodies has gone missing," Hermes said, each word falling like a stone into the silence. "From its burial vault in the fifth hell."

Eryx's blood ran cold, a shiver racing down his spine at the implications. Beside him, Alex went rigid, his expression turning stormy as the gravity of the situation sank in.

Inside Eryx's mind, Apollo's essence quaked with alarm, a surge of ancient fear and dread that left Eryx feeling dizzy. *Missing? But the only beings entombed there are...*

Apollo's voice trailed off ominously, leaving a heavy, oppressive silence in its wake.

Alex pinched the bridge of his nose, his eyes squeezing shut as though he could block out the terrible news. "The fifth hell contains the remains of the ancients, the gods of primordial chaos. If one has gone missing…"

"Someone is trying to resurrect a god on our hands," Hermes concluded, his voice bleak and heavy with dread.

Eryx swallowed hard, his mouth suddenly dry as dust. *Apollo, do you know anything about these ancient ones?*

There was a long, weighted pause before Apollo replied, his voice strained and distant. *Only old myths and legends, but nothing good. Their power was once unmatched, but also unpredictable. They had to be sealed away to restore balance.*

"Whose body is unaccounted for?" Alex demanded, his eyes snapping open, burning with a fierce intensity. "We need details before proceeding."

Hermes hesitated, as though the very words were painful to speak aloud. "The vault holding Absalom was ransacked," he said finally, each syllable dripping with dread. "He's the one missing."

The name fell like a thunderclap, the air itself seeming to tremble with the weight of it. Apollo cursed vehemently in Eryx's mind, a string of ancient oaths that sent a chill through Eryx's very soul.

Absalom? Apollo's voice was strained, edged with a fear Eryx had never heard from the god before. *If he has returned, we are all in grave danger…*

As Apollo's concern bled through their bond, Eryx felt his own apprehension growing, a knot of dread tightening in his chest. He watched as Alex and Hermes continued discussing the security of the hell vaults, their voices low and urgent, but their words seemed to fade into the background as Eryx focused inward, desperate for answers.

Who is this Absalom? Eryx asked, his mental voice shaking slightly. *Clearly not someone to be trifled with if he's got you this shaken.*

Apollo's essence shuddered, a ripple of ancient terror that left Eryx feeling cold and hollow. *Absalom was an ancient vampire god, the first and most vicious of his kind,* Apollo replied, his voice heavy with dread. *I was the one who finally struck the blow that ended his reign of bloodshed, but it nearly cost me my life. His ilk were the deadliest foes we ever faced.*

Eryx's heart stuttered in his chest, a wave of icy fear washing over him. He turned to Alex, his eyes wide and haunted. "Is it even possible to revive a dead god? Wouldn't that require an insane amount of power?"

Hermes nodded grimly, his face etched with lines of worry. "It would take immense magic and sacrifice," he acknowledged. "But the risk grows each day Absalom's corpse remains missing. His essence lingers in the ether, waiting for a host."

Alex swore violently, his hands clenching into fists at his sides. "Winston expects us to clean up his mess when we're already spread thin? We don't have the resources to hunt for one body in the underworld!"

Hermes raised his hands in a placating gesture, his expression diplomatically neutral. "All I ask is that you investigate where you can. But I understand your constraints."

With a reluctant sigh, Alex nodded, his shoulders slumping in defeat. "We'll look into it discreetly. But I make no promises of leaving here when our city still needs protecting."

"I understand," Hermes said solemnly. "I will inform Winston that you will assist where able. Hopefully, we can avert disaster."

As Hermes took his leave, Eryx reached out through their soulbond, sensing the tightly leashed emotions roiling beneath Alex's stoic exterior. He sent a pulse of calming energy, hoping to temper his boyfriend's worry for his old friend.

But even as he tried to soothe Alex's fears, Eryx couldn't shake the sense of impending doom that hung over them like a shroud. The revelation of Absalom's disappearance had shaken him to his core, and he could feel Apollo's essence trembling with dread within him.

After Hermes' ominous visit, Eryx and Alex wearily headed home, dreading the gauntlet of paparazzi likely awaiting them. Ever since Eryx's ties to the Shadowguards leaked, their building was staked out day and night by rabid photographers. But Eryx also missed their pets Mr. Whiskers and Cerebus, who had no doubt been bored all day alone.

The ride was quiet, Alex keeping a comforting grip on Eryx's hand the whole way. When they pulled into the underground garage, Eryx tensed, preparing to be bombarded. But strangely, no one was waiting.

Alex huffed in surprise. "Well, looks like we caught a lucky break for once."

Eryx laughed, the first time that tense day. "Let's get inside before they realize their cash cow is home."

They took the elevator up to their sprawling penthouse apartment overlooking the city - one of many compromises made when they moved in together. Eryx had insisted on the stylish high-rise, but Alex preferred something more low-key. Still, they'd made the cavernous space their own.

Stepping inside, Eryx immediately noted their sleek, modern decor combined with his own eclectic flair - plush rugs for lounging, walls decorated with album art and concert posters, scented candles filling the rooms with cozy aromas.

Despite its size, it felt like home. And even more so when Cerebus came galloping to nearly bowl them over, tail wagging eagerly. Laughing, they greeted the massive hellhound before his whimpering drew their attention to Mr. Whiskers winding between their legs.

Scooping up the attention-hungry tabby, Eryx nuzzled his furry head. "Sorry baby, long day keeping the city safe."

Alex slipped past them to fill food bowls, Cerebus happily on his heels. Eryx smiled as he watched Alex dote on their unique little family. No matter the craziness awaiting outside, within these walls they created their haven.

Once their pets were cared for, Alex sidled up behind Eryx, hands sliding around his waist. "Finally got you alone," he murmured, trailing kisses down Eryx's neck. "I believe some stress relief is in order…"

Alex pressed Eryx against the bedroom wall, devouring his mouth in a searing kiss. "I've been thinking about this all day," he murmured huskily.

"Oh yeah?" Eryx breathed, heart pounding with anticipation.

"Mmhmm…about all the ways I'm gonna ravage this gorgeous body." Alex trailed a hand down Eryx's chest, palming him through his jeans.

Eryx's head fell back with a groan as Alex mouthed along his neck. Clever fingers slipped under Eryx's shirt, tracing each ridge of muscle and teasing his nipples into stiff peaks.

"Someone's eager," Eryx chuckled, feeling Alex's prominent arousal against his hip.

"You have no idea, babe." Alex guided them toward the spacious bed. "I'm gonna take my time unwinding every bit of tension in that sexy body."

They tumbled onto the plush mattress in a passionate tangle of roaming hands and seeking mouths. Alex pinned Eryx's wrists over his head, grinding their hips together deliciously.

"I'm all yours tonight," Eryx panted, drunk on desire.

"Good, because I don't plan on letting you up anytime soon."

Alex trailed hot, open-mouthed kisses down Eryx's heaving chest, lavishing attention on each sensitive nipple. When he wrapped his lips around Eryx's straining arousal, clever tongue caressing in all the right ways, Eryx was reduced to wordless cries of bliss.

They moved together unhurriedly, savoring every gasp and tremor of pleasure. Alex took him to dizzying heights again and again, until Eryx was spent and quivering. Only then did Alex finally chase his own peak, burying himself in Eryx's willing body.

After, they held each other close, floating in satiated bliss. No matter what chaos awaited outside, in these moments together they had found refuge.

Coming down from their high, Eryx chuckled and poked Alex's shoulder. "Was that your way of apologizing for being an overbearing ass earlier?"

Alex grinned, pulling Eryx against his chest. "Did it work?"

"Mmm, maybe. You're forgiven, but don't pull that protective crap again." Eryx softened the reprimand with a gentle kiss.

Alex's expression turned serious. "I really am sorry. No more benching you, I promise." He brushed his lips against Eryx's, sending a warm tingle through their joined souls.

After a contented moment, Eryx brought up the ominous visit from Hermes. "So, resurrecting an ancient vampire god, huh? Just another day for us, right?"

Alex snorted. "If it's true, we've got a big headache coming. The primordial ones make Ares and Morvain look like playground bullies."

"Did you ever meet this Absalom back in the day?" Eryx asked curiously.

"Only in passing, but he wasn't social. Mostly kept to his monstrous offspring and cult followers." Alex's tone darkened. "Let's just say he didn't earn the title 'God of Vampires' being gentle."

Eryx bit his lip. "Do you think we need to get involved in this? Chase down a missing corpse?"

Alex nodded grimly. "As much as I hate dancing to Winston' tune, we can't ignore it. Too many vampires still revere Absalom in myth. If he returns, chaos follows."

"Then I guess we better find this body fast." Eryx tried to sound confident despite the daunting task.

Sensing his unease, Alex gathered him close and kissed his hair. "Try not to stress. We'll figure this out together, like always."

Curled against Alex's sleeping form, Eryx's mind spun with unease over the possibility of the vampire god's resurrection. He couldn't imagine anything powerful enough to threaten the immortals who had ruled for eons.

Apollo? he called inwardly, seeking answers from the god within. *What makes Absalom's power so much greater than the other fallen gods?*

After a weighty pause, Apollo responded solemnly. *His venom was unlike anything the pantheon had encountered - lethal even to us deathless ones. More than once I narrowly escaped his fangs, weakened to near obliteration.*

Eryx shivered, a cold dread seeping into his bones. According to myth, the gods were untouched by mortal frailties like poison or disease. To think something could bring them to the brink of eternal darkness...

If he returns at full strength, the carnage will be unfathomable, Apollo continued. *Imagine an undead army bred from his blood, beholden only to his will. It would be a scourge upon the land not seen since the days of Ragnarok.*

Burying closer to Alex's reassuring warmth, Eryx's mind swirled with horrific possibilities. He tried to cling to hope - surely their combined power could prevent Absalom's resurrection. But Apollo's grim certainty ate at his confidence.

They had overcome terrible foes before, but nothing like this primordial evil. Would even Hades' flames be enough to stop a ravenous god? The thought of Alex facing that venomous maw made Eryx's blood run cold.

Jaw clenched with resolve, Eryx swore to himself that he would do everything in his power to halt this threat. He would walk willingly into the underworld itself before losing Alex to the endless dark. They had defied death before - together, they would find a way again.

Morning sunlight streaming through the windows roused Eryx from sleep. Reaching across the bed, he found Alex already gone, which was unusual for the habitually sleepy god.

Stretching out his senses, Eryx detected two familiar voices speaking in the living room - Alex and Richard. Eryx broke into a smile, quickly showering and dressing before going to greet them.

As he caught a glimpse of himself in the mirror, Eryx paused to take stock of the subtle changes to his appearance since absorbing Apollo's essence. Gone was any last softness of youth - his physique was all sculpted muscle now, kept lean and strong from training. His facial features seemed more chiseled too, any hint of roundness in his cheeks smoothed into sharp lines.

But the most striking change was in his eyes. Outward evidence of the divine soul now sharing his mortal form.

Admiring the view? Apollo's amused voice echoed in his mind. *You wear godhood well, my young host.*

Eryx huffed a laugh as he finished dressing. *Just noticing that I'm starting to look like one of those ancient marble statues of you. All I'm missing is a laurel wreath.*

In due time. Our merging is still ongoing, Apollo replied. *You've yet to see the full extent of changes and abilities to come.*

Sobering, Eryx studied his reflection. It was true - he could feel himself aging much slower, and suspected his strength and senses would only continue sharpening. Both exciting and daunting to contemplate.

Do you ever miss your original form? he asked Apollo curiously. *Does being stuck as just a soul fragment chafe?*

Apollo's essence took on a wistful quality. *Sometimes, yes. But preserving even a sliver of myself through you was worth the sacrifice. I content myself experiencing the world anew through your eyes.*

Heart swelling with affection, Eryx sent a silent thank you to the god who had given up so much to empower him as a hero. He would strive to be worthy of Apollo's gift.

Squaring his shoulders, Eryx turned from the mirror to join Alex and Richard, leaving his musings behind for now. There were too many blessings in his extraordinary life to dwell on what was lost. He had never felt more whole.

He found Richard sitting on the couch, happily petting a purring Mr. Whiskers while Cerebus lounged contentedly nearby. Both men turned at Eryx's approach, faces lighting up.

"Morning, sunshine," Alex grinned, pulling Eryx down onto his lap and kissing him soundly.

Laughing, Richard shook his head. "You two are adorably domestic. Who knew the fearsome Hades could be so smitten?"

Eryx chuckled, leaning into Alex's embrace. "I bring out his soft side, what can I say?" He turned curiously to Richard. "So what brings you by so early?"

Richard's expression turned excited. "I actually have some big news - I've found your new manager to take the reins!"

Eryx's brow shot up in surprise. "You're tired of me already?" he joked.

"Never," Richard assured. "But there are others who can nurture your gifts in ways I no longer can. You deserve the best team possible."

Eryx nodded slowly. Richard had guided his career since the tragic loss of his first manager, Sam. Letting someone new fill that role felt momentous, but Richard would only entrust him to capable hands.

Though joining the Shadowguards had been the right call, part of him was devastated to leave his passion behind. But Alex had reminded him that his purpose wasn't either/or - he could have both.

He remembered that day when they were in the underworld, Alex recovering after his brutal fight with Ares. Eryx sat at his bedside, despairingly recounting his plans to quit music and focus solely on honing his new abilities. Sacrificing his passion felt like the only path forward.

Alex took his hand, expression earnest. "You've worked so hard to build this career. Are you certain you want to walk away completely?"

Eryx sighed heavily. "I don't see another way. My old life ended when I absorbed Apollo's soul."

"You can find balance. Your music and abilities don't have to be mutually exclusive," Alex argued gently.

Eryx fell silent, realization dawning that Alex was right—quitting fully did feel like running from himself. With Alex's steadfast support, perhaps he could have both purpose and passion.

Alex squeezed his hand. "There are still people who need your gift, now more than ever. Don't lose hope."

Eryx smiled softly, the memory of Alex's wise counsel warming him. In the present, Richard's voice pulled him back to their conversation.

"Now, I know you have Shadowguard business, but we're set to meet your potential new manager today if you're up for it?"

Eryx hesitated, glancing at Alex. "Are you sure I should step away right now?"

Alex waved a hand. "The team's got it covered. This meeting is important for your career. I'll fill you in on any developments after."

Reassured, Eryx leaned in to kiss Alex gratefully. "Have I mentioned you're the best?"

Richard coughed pointedly. "Alright lovebirds, save it for when I'm not here."

They pulled apart laughing as Richard studied his phone and frowned. "Looks like the vultures have arrived. Paparazzi lurking downstairs."

Eryx sighed, smile fading. The walls felt like they were closing in whenever the media hounded him outside his home. His newfound purpose was worth the attention, but that didn't make it less aggravating.

Alex gave his shoulder a comforting squeeze, sensing his frustration through their soulbond. "Just keep your head up and don't give them the reaction they want."

Eryx nodded, steeling himself to deal with the circus awaiting him. At times like this, he missed the relative anonymity of simply being a musician, before his life became so complicated.

Trying to balance his music career and his duties with the Shadow-guards certainly presented challenges. But Alex's steadfast support kept him going during the difficult moments of adjustment.

With a deep breath, Eryx stood and straightened his jacket. "Well, let's get this over with."

Alex gave him an encouraging smile. "Good luck. We'll debrief later on the investigation and get some takeout from that place you like."

Buoyed by the promise of comfort food and Alex's arms to come home to, Eryx steeled himself to brave the gauntlet of shouted questions and blinding camera flashes outside. As long as he had his two families - in music and in purpose - he could withstand anything.

4

Looking for Clues

Alex

Alex took Cerebus out for an early walk before heading to Shadowguard HQ. As the hellhound sniffed around trees, Alex called Lily.

"Morning," he greeted when she answered. "Got time to talk when I get in today?"

"I'm just finishing coffee, be there soon," Lily replied easily. Alex smiled - he could always count on her. Despite their messy romantic history, Lily remained his steadfast friend. Her wisdom had steered him true too many times to count.

After Cerebus finished his business, Alex gave the massive hound a scratch behind the ears. "Alright buddy, hold down the fort with Mr. Whiskers. Be good." Cerebus licked his hand before trotting back inside.

Driving to HQ, Alex was glad the media crowd that constantly hounded Eryx had finally dispersed. He hated watching his boyfriend endure their harassment. Eryx had enough to balance without vultures scrutinizing his every move. If Alex could, he'd turn them all into snakes. But for now, supporting Eryx through the adjustment was all he could do.

Arriving at the sleek downtown highrise housing their operation, Alex greeted their stalwart security guard, Mr. Evans, before heading to his office. As expected, Lily was already there making herself at home in his chair.

"You just can't resist stealing my seat, can you?" Alex teased as Lily vacated his leather office chair.

She shot him a cheeky grin. "What can I say, it's just so comfy!"

Alex chuckled as they settled on the sleek modern couches in the sitting area. His amusement faded as he met Lily's expectant gaze, knowing this conversation was no laughing matter.

"So what's so urgent you couldn't tell me over the phone?" Lily prompted.

Alex's expression turned grim. "Hermes paid me a visit yesterday. On Winston' behalf, bearing troubling news."

Lily tensed, instantly on alert. "What happened?"

"Remember the ancient burial vaults in the fifth hell?" At Lily's nod, Alex continued, "One of the entombed primordial gods has gone missing."

Sharp concern flashed across Lily's face. "Who?" she asked tersely.

Alex hesitated before answering reluctantly. "Absalom."

Lily went utterly still, the color draining from her face. Alex knew she understood the implications of that name, her horror matching his own.

"Winston commanded Hermes to retrieve me, insisting that I help them," Alex went on quietly. "But I didn't commit to anything yet, not without more intel."

Lily nodded distractedly, clearly unsettled. "Do you think the Order is involved in this? Morvain and his ilk?"

"It's likely," Alex frowned. "Either trying to tap into Absalom's power, or…"

"Or resurrect him entirely," Lily finished grimly. She began to pace, a nervous habit when her agile mind was spinning scenarios. "We have to get ahead of this, Alex, before it's too late."

Alex rose and gently stilled her with a hand on her shoulder. "We will. But there's no sense borrowing trouble prematurely. We're going to approach this strategically, like we always do."

Lily took a deep breath, steadying herself. "So what now?"

Alex crossed his arms. "We stay focused on the current murder investigation for now. If that ends up connecting to Absalom, so be it."

"Agreed, but we should also look into the missing corpse separately," Lily advised. "Quietly probe for any whispers or trails."

Alex nodded slowly. "I have an idea on where to start. But you won't like it."

Lily's eyes narrowed suspiciously. "Why do I sense you're about to suggest something reckless?"

"Because your senses are as sharp as ever," Alex huffed. "I'm considering paying a visit to Dolos. The trickster has eyes and ears everywhere."

"Absolutely not!" Lily snapped, bristling. "Dealing with him always comes at a price. Or have you forgotten what happened last time?"

Alex clenched his jaw as memories of his previous encounter with the cunning and dangerous Dolos flashed through his mind…

Centuries ago, when Alex was still known as Hades, his cherished son Zagreus was kidnapped by Kronos' forces. Desperate for any information on the boy's whereabouts, Alex sought out the trickster god Dolos in his cavern lair.

Torchlight cast flickering shadows as Dolos turned, smiling coldly. "Lord Hades. To what do I owe the honor?"

Alex stepped forward, jaw tight. "I'm told you trade in secrets. I have need of your knowledge."

"Oh?" Dolos purred. "And what price are you prepared to pay for this 'knowledge' you seek?"

"Name it," Alex growled.

Dolos tapped his chin in mock thought. "Hmm, I think your blood will do nicely. Power of an elder god's life force is so hard to come by."

Alex tensed, knowing he was bargaining with a viper. But left with no other options, he reluctantly agreed.

Alex forcibly wrenched his mind back to the present. Lily watched him with knowing sympathy, recognizing the shadows in his eyes.

"I appreciate your caution more than ever," Alex admitted quietly. "But Dolos may prove a necessary evil, as much as I hate to admit it."

Alex could see the objection burning in Lily's eyes as they continued arguing back and forth.

"There has to be another way to get information," Lily insisted.

Alex dragged a hand down his face in frustration. "Believe me, if there was a better option here, I would take it. But Dolos has eyes and ears across realms."

"And he'll use your desperation as leverage!" Lily shot back. "We can't trust anything he says."

"You think I don't know that?" Alex retorted. "But we're flying blind right now. What choice do we have?"

Lily crossed her arms defiantly. "We keep digging, turn over every stone before stooping to bargain with snakes."

Their voices rose as they debated in circles, neither willing to back down. Finally, Alex held up a hand.

"How about a compromise - we see what Thanatos can dig up on Dolos' location first. If he comes up empty, revisiting this will be a moot point anyway."

Lily considered this and slowly nodded. "Alright, that seems reasonable. It's a place to start at least."

Alex let out a relieved breath. Debating Lily's keen intellect was always mentally taxing. "Right, let's go have a chat with our inside man then."

Closing his eyes, Alex focused his power, reshaping the reality around them. When he opened them, his sleek modern office transformed into the more gothic aesthetics of Thanatos' domain in the underworld.

Heavy blackout curtains blocked any natural light, leaving the office dimly lit by iron candelabras and a glowing fireplace. The walls were paneled in dark wood, with accents of silver and emerald green. An intricate Persian rug depicted faded scenes of pallbearers and mourners.

Dominating the room was a massive obsidian desk cluttered with stacks of parchment. Shelves bore skulls of various shapes and sizes - some animal, some distinctly inhuman. The overall atmosphere was brooding yet elegant, much like its occupant.

Alex inhaled the familiar scents of parchment, candle wax, and cigar smoke. After so many clandestine meetings here over the eons, he found the space oddly comforting in its familiarity. Trust Thanatos to perfectly capture the gothic majesty of their subterranean realm, even in more modern times.

Taking in every detail, Alex felt for a moment as if he were home in his true palace of underworld stone and shadow. But the illusion faded quickly - this was but a small sanctuary Thanatos crafted and no true replacement for what Alex had lost. With a quiet sigh, he returned his focus to the dilemma at hand.

Lily lifted a brow. "Subtle," she commented wryly.

Alex just grinned and called out, "Thanatos? Got a minute?"

The god was impeccably dressed as always. "Lord Hades, Lady Persephone," he inclined his head in greeting. "How can I help?"

Alex saw through the diplomatic facade - behind closed doors,

Thanatos had no need to stand on such ceremony with them.

"You can drop the formalities, my friend. It's just us here," Alex said.

In response, Thanatos materialized one of his favored cigars and took a deep drag, leaning back casually. "Very well. What brings you both to my humble abode?"

Alex's expression turned serious. "We're looking for Dolos. I assume you've heard whispers of the missing primordial?"

Thanatos froze mid-puff, eyes narrowing. Slowly he rose and perched on the edge of his desk, studying them closely.

"So the rumors are true. Absalom's body was taken," he mused. At their surprised looks, he smirked. "Please, did you think such a disturbance would escape the notice of Death himself?"

Lily stepped forward, brow furrowed. "If you knew about this, why didn't you say anything?"

Thanatos tapped his cigar lazily. "It wasn't my place to intervene in the affairs of the pantheon. Winston' edicts have made that quite clear."

Alex crossed his arms. "Do you at least know what happened to the body? Was Absalom truly lifeless when entombed?"

At that, Thanatos hesitated, his nonchalant facade cracking slightly. "In truth, the vampire god was never fully extinguished. Apollo merely contained his essence."

Lily's eyes widened in dismay. "What? But we were told he was dead and buried!"

Thanatos shrugged. "Even gods tell lies, my queen. Absalom's followers have been trying to resurrect him ever since his downfall."

Clenching his fists, Alex began pacing as implications set in. This changed everything - the threat was far more severe with Absalom's essence still lingering.

He turned back to Thanatos. "We need to find Dolos. Can you locate the snake?"

Thanatos held up a hand. "I will try, but the Deceiver does not reveal himself easily. Give me time."

"We don't have time!" Lily snapped. "The longer that monster's spirit is free, the closer he gets to returning!"

"Peace, I shall do what I can," Thanatos said firmly, quelling further outburst. "Now if you'll excuse me, I have inquiries to make."

Alex placed a calming hand on Lily's shoulder, exchanging a silent look of understanding. Time was of the essence, but they had to be strategic.

With a nod to Thanatos, Alex said simply, "Keep us informed, old friend."

After their clandestine meeting with Thanatos, Alex focused and transported him and Lily back to his sleek modern office. He checked his watch, surprised to find they'd already lost over an hour. Time flowed differently beyond the mortal veil.

"We better get moving if we want to catch the team before they dive into the murder case," Alex said, moving briskly toward the door.

Lily fell into step beside him. "Are you going to tell them about Absalom's missing corpse and our hunt for Dolos?"

Alex shook his head firmly. "Absolutely not. I don't want them involved in this mess." His expression hardened. "They've risked enough lately because of warring immortals. I won't put them in harm's way again."

Lily nodded, squeezing his arm supportively. "I understand, and I'm sure they will too. Let's just focus on the task at hand for now."

Together they made their way to the recently upgraded briefing room. After the attack by Ares, Alex had ordered extensive renovations to improve their security and tech.

Entering the spacious chamber, Alex spotted his team already gathering around the central hologram display, files and notes spread before them. Marcus glanced up as Alex and Lily arrived.

"Morning boss. No Eryx today?" he asked.

Alex shook his head. "He's tied up with some label meetings at first, but should join us later."

Marcus shrugged good-naturedly. "More donuts for us then. Take a seat and we'll catch you up."

Alex hid a smile at the eager young hero's flippancy. Marcus' irreverence often helped diffuse tense situations. Settling in beside Lily, Alex focused his attention on the disturbing case at hand. The nexus with Absalom could wait - lives hung in the balance here and now.

"Alright team, what do we have so far?" Alex asked, entering mission-mode as the briefing got underway.

Gabe tapped the display, pulling up photos from the crime scene. "As you can see, there are some shifter-like claw marks that are clearly meant to misdirect us."

He zoomed in on the gashes in the brick wall. "But the lack of any real struggle or blood trail suggests this was staged. Our killer wanted us chasing the wrong suspects."

Emma frowned thoughtfully. "But why target this victim specifically? Was there a personal motive or just opportunity?"

"Hopefully the autopsy will reveal more about her background," Alex said. "Any indications she was supernatural herself?"

Gabe shook his head. "Nothing concrete yet, but still digging."

Marcus stood, examining the projected image. "Check out her clothes though. She was dressed for a night out clubbing."

"So likely lured there by someone she knew or trusted," Lucas suggested grimly.

Olivia leaned forward. "We need to identify her and retrace her steps that night. Friends or family might know something."

Lily nodded. "I can coordinate with the HIB on tracking down next-of-kin." She exchanged a knowing look with Lucas. "One way or another, we'll get access."

Alex stroked his chin contemplatively. "Gabe, set up a meeting with Alpha Hansen for later. The local wolf pack might have useful street intel."

Gabe nodded, already pulling out his phone. As the team continued bouncing theories and making plans, Alex surveyed them with quiet pride. Each of them brought unique skills to the table. Together, they would solve this.

As his team continued examining evidence and building their plan of attack, Alex stepped away for a moment of solitude by the large windows overlooking the city.

Staring out at the dazzling skyline, he contemplated how far this modern world still felt from the only home he'd known for eons - the sprawling palace and winding caverns of his underworld kingdom. The constant light still felt alien at times after endless nights below.

Alex pulled out his phone and dialed Eryx, frowning when it went to voicemail after multiple rings. Usually Eryx picked up immediately, their soulbond allowing him to sense Alex calling. Cold fingers of dread crept up Alex's spine.

Closing his eyes, he focused inward, relief washing over him as he felt their link still intact. Eryx's essence glowed strong, easing Alex's worry that something had happened. Likely just busy with his career responsibilities, but Alex made a mental note to check on him soon.

A hand on his shoulder made Alex turn to see Gabe. "Hey boss, the alpha called - he can meet within the hour but has another appointment later."

Pushing down his unease, Alex nodded. "No problem, I can head over to the pack headquarters now. You good holding down the fort here?"

"You got it," Gabe assured. "We'll keep digging and have updates when you get back."

After leaving instructions with Lily, Alex headed down to the parking garage. Sliding into one of their armored SUVs, he tried Eryx again during the drive over. Still no answer.

"Come on babe, starting to get worried here," Alex muttered, shooting off a quick text. He knew he was prone to mother-henning, but his protective instincts were on high alert.

Arriving at the elegant brownstone that housed the wolf pack headquarters, Alex was greeted at the door by a stoic beta who escorted him straight to the alpha's office.

Alpha Jared Hansen sat at a heavy oak desk finishing some paperwork when Alex entered. The stately suite still looked freshly renovated from the attack months prior when the alpha's mate and pack mates had gone missing.

Alex cleared his throat politely. "Appreciate you taking the time to meet, Alpha Hansen."

Hansen set his pen down and waved for Alex to take a seat. "Of course. My pack owes you a great debt. What can I do for you?"

"I'm afraid I can't disclose many details," Alex apologized. "But we're investigating a homicide possibly intended to frame local shifters."

At that, Hansen's expression sharpened, eyes glinting amber. "Explain."

Alex passed him the photos showing the gashes on the alley wall. "These claw marks were left to misdirect blame towards your kind. But the actual murder was…too meticulously executed for a shifter in beast form."

Hansen examined the photos, nostrils flaring. "These were certainly made by one of our claws. But I've heard no whispers of such an act among the packs." His brows furrowed. "You believe someone is setting up shifters to take the fall?"

"It seems likely," Alex confirmed grimly. "Have there been any recent tensions or incidents that might provide motive?"

The alpha leaned back with a weary sigh. "Nothing specific comes to mind. But there is something you should know…"

He met Alex's gaze. "There are whispers of a drug called Moonblood have been resurfacing and it brings out violent instincts in shifters. Could explain these fabricated claw marks if someone is peddling it."

Alex tensed. He knew that street drug all too well, along with its destructive effects. "If Moonblood has resurfaced, it would give our perp easy access to involuntary shifter muscle."

Moonblood was developed illicitly using a rare flower that only bloomed beneath the full moon. When ingested, the drug caused a partial shift in shifters, making them more aggressive, violent, and susceptible to suggestion.

In beast form, inhibitions were lost, making Moonblood users easy puppets for someone's violent bidding. There were always those willing to exploit shifters in that induced state, using them as involuntary muscle. Alex had seen the carnage from Moonblood overdoses and deaths firsthand.

If their suspect was somehow behind Moonblood's re-emergence, they'd have ready access to shifters to do their dirty work then frame. It was insidiously brilliant - using the drug to create the violent claws marks as shifter misdirection. This tied into the murder all too neatly.

Hansen nodded. "I pray you are wrong, but the timing aligns too well." He stood, jaw set firmly. "You have my pack's support tracking down whoever committed this murder. Moonblood's return cannot be tolerated."

Alex rose and shook the alpha's hand gratefully. "Your assistance is invaluable as always." donning his jacket, Alex strode out with fresh determination. This killer had crossed the wrong predators. The hunt was on and they are running out of time.

5

Living the Music

Eryx

Riding to the label offices with Richard, Eryx gazed out the tinted window, mentally prepping for meeting his potential new manager. Richard glanced over from the driver's seat.

"So, how are things going with the Shadowguard crew lately?" Richard asked. "Surviving all the training and missions?"

Eryx chuckled. "What, you wanna join up now too?"

Richard laughed. "Tempting, but I prefer leaving the hero stuff to you young guns." His expression turned serious.

That question made Eryx realize there was still much he didn't know about his manager's past and powers. "Hey, are you some kind of demigod or something? I don't think I ever asked."

Richard hesitated briefly before replying. "Well…not exactly, but it's complicated. I promise I'll explain everything when the time is right."

Eryx nodded, curiosity piqued but sensing Richard's reluctance to elaborate further today. He had proven trustworthy so Eryx didn't push.

"Fair enough, no pressure," he said easily. "I appreciate you looking out for me either way."

"Really though, you doing alright handling it all?" Richard said softly.

Eryx considered his response. Ever since taking him under his wing, Richard had become a trusted mentor.

"Honestly? It's been a major adjustment," Eryx admitted. "I question sometimes if I made the right call joining up. The training is brutal and the missions…" He shook his head.

Richard nodded sympathetically. "Have you talked to Alex about your doubts at all?"

"Yeah, he's been great about it honestly," Eryx said. "Even offered me an out if I needed a break from the hero stuff."

"And what did you decide?" Richard asked gently.

Eryx sighed. "I'm sticking with it for now. Like you said, I've got these powers now. Feels wrong not using them to help people."

Richard drove in thoughtful silence for a moment. "Well if you want my honest take…I think you've got what it takes to be one hell of a hero. But it's gotta be your choice, because you believe in it. Anything else will just wear you down over time."

Eryx nodded slowly, letting Richard's wisdom sink in. He was right - the only way forward was embracing his purpose with his whole heart.

"Yeah, you might be right," Eryx mused. "This life chose me for a reason. It's where I'm meant to be." Saying it aloud bolstered his conviction.

Richard smiled. "There's the fire. You're gonna change the world, kid. Never doubt that."

Eryx smiled back gratefully. With Richard's guidance, he was ready to meet his future, in music and heroism alike.

Eryx gazed out the window as Richard drove them from his

apartment into the buzzing heart of the city. The lights of Times Square bathed the streets in a kaleidoscope of neon as they made their way to Eternity Records' flagship location.

Nestled between glittering billboards and packed theaters, the sleek high-rise stood out with its bronzed exterior and massive logo emblazoned across the top floors. Eryx still got a rush seeing their label prominently dominating the Midtown skyline.

Pulling up to the sleek modern building that now housed Eternity Records, Eryx felt a bittersweet pang remembering Sam's infectious passion for music. He couldn't help chuckling softly at the cheekily divine name he and Richard had chosen for the relaunched label. A little wink to their true lineages.

"What's got you smiling?" Richard asked.

"Just thinking Sam would get a kick out of what we've built here," Eryx said. "All of it's for him, in a way."

Richard nodded, eyes glinting with shared emotion. "Wherever he is, I know he's damn proud of you."

Eryx swallowed the lump in his throat. "Couldn't have done any of this without you either, you know. Stepping in when you did…it saved me."

"Hey, no getting sappy on me now," Richard chided gently. "We've got work to do and an empire to run."

Eryx laughed, the melancholy lifting. Richard was right - the past was honored in their present successes. And the future awaited them now inside Eternity's walls, where they continued molding new artists every day.

Squaring his shoulders, Eryx followed Richard out of the car and into the towering edifice, ready to meet what came next.

Eryx was relieved to find no paparazzi lurking around. He hoped his visit would go unnoticed by the vultures hungering for any glimpse into his private life.

Stepping into the sleek modern lobby with Richard, Eryx immediately felt at ease surrounded by familiar sights. Framed photos of Sam dotted the walls, interspersed with platinum records from the label's top artists. Sleek furniture and minimalist black and bronze decor gave the space an upscale yet edgy ambiance.

Eryx had provided input on the aesthetics, wanting to design an environment where artists felt safe, respected, and creative. Somewhere Sam would have been proud to bring his discoveries.

As they crossed the lobby, Richard checked his phone calendar. "Your potential new manager should be waiting in Meeting Room A. You ready for this?"

Eryx blew out a breath, nerves fluttering. "As I'll ever be. Let's do this."

But as they reached the meeting room door, Richard stopped him with a hand on his arm. "Actually, I should hang back out here while you two talk."

Eryx blinked in surprise. "What? Why aren't you coming in?"

"I don't want my presence influencing your impressions," Richard explained. "This needs to be your genuine reaction to see if you two click."

Though reluctant, Eryx understood Richard's point. This was about forging a new working relationship separate from his existing ones.

"Alright, flying solo it is," Eryx sighed. "Wish me luck." He hugged Richard briefly before steeling himself and entering the room.

Once inside meeting room A, Eryx found a man in a tailored suit gazing out the windows at the New York skyline. As he turned, Eryx sensed something powerful emanating from him - this was no ordinary mortal.

They shook hands as the man introduced himself in a friendly yet assured tone. "Eryx, good to meet you. I'm Brad Byrne."

Eryx's brows furrowed. "You're not just a human manager, are you?

I'm picking up something…more."

Brad let out an easy laugh. "Can't slip much by you, huh kid? You've got the sight, just like your patron." He gestured to a chair. "Have a seat, we've got a lot to discuss."

Warily, Eryx sat across from him. "So what exactly are you then?"

Brad waved a dismissive hand. "In due time. For now, let's just say I was curious to meet Apollo's newest vessel." His sharp green eyes glinted knowingly. "Needed to confirm the rumors myself."

Eryx tensed, hackles raising. "And what business is that of yours?"

"Peace, I mean no harm," Brad assured, reading Eryx's defensive posture. "Merely sought to connect with an old…associate from brighter days."

Eryx frowned, sensing there was more to Brad's cryptic words about connecting with an "old associate." But the manager smoothly redirected the conversation before Eryx could ask more questions.

"I know you must have questions, but first let's talk business," Brad said briskly, opening a sleek leather portfolio. "I want to share more about my experience and vision for your career."

Warily, Eryx allowed the subject change, making a mental note to press Brad for answers later. "Alright, let's hear your pitch then."

Over the next hour, Brad outlined his impressive history guiding superstar clients to global success. He highlighted innovative marketing strategies tailored specifically to Eryx's talents and fanbase demographics.

"I want to help you create a bold, unique sound that honors your past works while pushing your artistry forward," Brad said. "Experiment more with mixing genres, collaborations, visual components."

Despite his unease around Brad's evasiveness earlier, Eryx found himself intrigued by his ambitious ideas. The proposal reflected a deep understanding of Eryx's style and vision as an artist.

"You've clearly done your research on me," Eryx said, impressed in spite of himself. "Have to say, the ideas sound promising."

Brad smiled. "I aim to help my clients reach their full potential. And I know you've only begun scratching the surface of yours."

As the meeting delved into touring plans, Eryx hesitated, thinking of his responsibilities with the Shadowguards. Globe-trotting tours would be tricky to manage now.

Sensing his reluctance, Brad said, "Speak your mind, Eryx. I'm open to any thoughts or concerns you have."

Eryx shifted in his seat. "It's just…I have other commitments these days that make extensive touring difficult."

"Ah, your newfound purpose with a certain exceptional group," Brad said knowingly.

Eryx blinked in surprise until Brad added, "Relax, your secret's safe. I understand better than most about duty."

Reassured by Brad's discretion, Eryx explained further about wanting to limit time away while still promoting new albums.

Brad nodded thoughtfully. "There are always alternatives we can explore. Shorter tours, mixed virtual and live shows, flexibility with dates. We'll make it work."

Relieved, Eryx's anxiety over how to balance his two worlds eased slightly. Brad really seemed to grasp his needs and priorities on all fronts. With compromises, they could craft a new normal that allowed him to fulfill both his passions.

As their meeting wound down, Brad leaned forward, steepling his fingers. "Before we finalize this partnership, there's one more thing I'd like to explore with you."

Eryx raised an eyebrow. "We're not gonna have to fight or something, are we?" he joked.

Brad let out an easy chuckle. "No, nothing so dramatic. I simply want to see your musical skills firsthand. Shall we step into the studio?"

Before Eryx could respond, Brad snapped his fingers and a shimmering portal swirled open. Taken aback, Eryx glanced around what was clearly a professional recording studio, but with an old European flair.

"Where are we?" Eryx asked, eyes wide as he took in the high arched ceilings with exposed wooden beams and ornate iron sconces holding flickering candles. Thick velvet curtains blocked any natural light from leaking in through expansive windows.

The warm glow of the candles illuminated a Steinway grand piano on a Persian rug, flanked by various string instruments along the curved stone walls. Plush leather chairs and polished mahogany surfaces completed the dignified aesthetic.

"Did you just portal us somewhere beyond the veil?" Eryx questioned, the otherworldly atmosphere prickling his senses.

Brad simply winked. "A convenient little booth I maintain outside the bounds of Earth. Don't worry, nothing will harm you here." He lounged comfortably on the sofa and motioned for Eryx to make himself at home.

Eryx slowly approached the grand piano, trailing his fingers along the intricate carvings adorning its wood finish. "This place is incredible."

Brad leaned back casually, regarding Eryx with an appraising eye. "Let's just say I have certain talents for manipulating the fabric of reality. Bending time and space is but a trivial matter."

Eryx's curiosity only grew at the vague response. He approached a collection of antique instruments along the wall, reverently running his fingers over wood and strings while pressing for more information.

"Are you immortal then?" Eryx asked. "Or have some connection to the gods like me?" He plucked an ornate lyre, notes resonating brightly in the candlelit room.

Brad smiled mysteriously. "In a manner of speaking. My lineage is ancient, but has been forgotten by most." His sharp gaze turned distant. "I walk unnoticed through the ages, moving between mortal and divine realms."

Intrigued, Eryx set down the lyre and leaned against the grand piano. "So you use your abilities to find talented artists and guide their careers?" It seemed an eccentric passion for one with such power.

"Music and art transcend all boundaries," Brad said fervently. "I seek those with the gift to create it, and help them share their vision. The world needs beauty more than ever in these times."

Eryx nodded thoughtfully, struck by Brad's genuine zeal that matched his own. Perhaps they were kindred spirits of a sort after all. Two custodians of music's living legacy.

"Well, I'm eager to see what we might accomplish together then," Eryx said sincerely, trusting in his initial gut instinct about Brad.

The manager's grin held anticipation and promise. "Oh, we will create wonders. Of that I have no doubt…"

"Richard doesn't know about your abilities, I take it?" Eryx asked.

Brad grinned. "Let's just say Richard's talents lie elsewhere. Mine allow a more direct approach."

Though intrigued by Brad's power, Eryx still felt guarded. "Alright, well why bring me here? What are we doing exactly?"

"I want you to try channeling Apollo's essence into your music," Brad explained, eyes glinting eagerly. "Has he aided your talents in such a way yet?"

Eryx considered the novel suggestion. *What do you think, Apollo? Any merit to what he's proposing?*

The god stirred within him pensively. *This Brad seems oddly familiar, though I cannot place from where. But his theory has potential I had not fully pondered before.*

Bolstered by Apollo's openness, Eryx moved to pick up an acoustic guitar, taking a steadying breath. He closed his eyes, turning his focus inwards and reaching for the glowing essence of the god within.

Warmth bloomed in his chest as he tapped into the divine power. Strumming slowly at first, the notes rang out with increasing resonance, infused with rich, vibrant energy.

The guitar seemed to play itself as Eryx gave himself over to Apollo's spirit. The melody soared, complex and soul-stirring. Eryx swayed, lost in the current of sound pouring from his fingers.

When the final notes rang out, Eryx opened his eyes, feeling almost drugged by the intensity of the experience. The music had transported him, woven from its own living magic—a taste of true synergy between mortal and godly gifts.

Across the studio, Brad was grinning broadly. "Incredible! I could feel Apollo's presence awaken within the song. Your souls are meant to create as one."

Eryx blinked, steadying himself against a rush of dizziness. The power thrumming through him was intoxicating but overwhelming. He took a few deep breaths as the high faded.

"That was…amazing, but really intense," Eryx admitted. "I've never felt that kind of energy before."

Brad nodded. "It takes practice to hone celestial abilities. But you two have potential beyond imagining." His sharp green eyes were alight with excitement.

After their intense musical experiment, Brad conjured an intricate contract from his briefcase in a flourish.

"Look this over in full, consult your legal team," he advised Eryx. "No need to commit right away. Sleep on it."

Eryx nodded, grateful for the time to review the lengthy document in depth before signing his career over. But if he was honest, his gut was already leaning toward accepting Brad's offer. The man simply felt like the right fit going forward.

They shook hands firmly, and Brad left him with one last piece of advice: "Remember, true power comes only from embracing all of who you are. Don't silence any part of your nature."

Pondering the cryptic sentiment, Eryx exited the conference room to find Richard waiting expectantly.

"So, how'd it go in there?" Richard asked, eyes searching Eryx's face. "You were chatting for over an hour."

Eryx just smiled. "Really well, I think he could be a great match. But he wants me to think it over before committing."

Richard drew him into a relieved hug. "As long as you're happy, I'm happy. But I was worried when you took so long!"

Guilt twinged in Eryx over worrying Richard by being transported to the studio. But he simply squeezed Richard reassuringly without elaborating on Brad's talents. Some things were still best kept under wraps.

Richard couldn't drive Eryx home, so he borrowed the company car instead.

After saying goodbye to Richard, Eryx settled into the plush leather driver's seat of the luxury sedan. Fishing his phone out of his pocket, he winced seeing several missed calls and texts from Alex over the past hour.

Quickly he tapped Alex's number and held the phone to his ear. After a couple rings, his boyfriend's relieved voice came through.

"Eryx! There you are, I was getting worried when you didn't pick up earlier," Alex said.

"Babe, I'm so sorry I didn't get your calls during the meeting," Eryx apologized profusely. "My phone was on silent this whole time."

"It's alright, just glad nothing happened to you," Alex assured, the tension easing from his tone. "How'd the label meeting go?"

Eryx started the car, pulling out of the underground garage. "Really great actually. I think this manager could be a perfect fit."

"That's awesome!" Alex said sincerely. Eryx could hear his smile through the phone. "You'll have to tell me all about it later. Are you coming to the headquarters today?

"Absolutely, just need to pop home and change first," Eryx confirmed, already planning the rest of his day. "Is everything okay? You sound kind of serious."

Alex hesitated briefly before replying. "Nothing to worry about, we can talk here. I'll see you soon."

"Take care," Eryx responded, but he detected a subtle strain in Alex's voice that left him pondering as he ended the call. Clearly something had happened on the investigative front.

Arriving home, Eryx quickly shed his business attire and donned comfortable jeans and a graphic tee. He contemplated baking a treat to share with the team, recalling their delight when he'd first brought cookies. The domestic task would soothe his nerves over whatever news awaited at HQ.

After preheating the oven and laying out ingredients, Eryx lost himself in the familiar steps of mixing and scooping cookie dough onto trays. The aroma of chocolate chips and vanilla enveloped him, carrying nostalgic memories of baking with his mother as a child.

While the cookies baked, Eryx refilled the pets' food and water, chuckling as Cerebus inhaled his kibble. A few hearty scratches behind the ears for Mr. Whiskers, and both animals were content.

Pulling the baked goods from the oven, Eryx transferred the steaming cookies into a container, eager to get on the road. Alex's cryptic tone nagged at him—he needed to find out what new development had emerged.

The afternoon sun was high as Eryx arrived at Shadowguard headquarters, cookie container in hand. He exchanged cheerful greetings with the receptionist before entering the elevator that required fingerprint access to reach the upper operational floors.

Stepping out on the top level that housed the briefing room and offices, he steeled himself for whatever news awaited, hoping the treats might lift spirits for a moment. Time to discover what new clues Alex and the team had uncovered.

6

Raving Afterlife

Alex

Alex sighed as he flipped through the latest reports from the Shadowguard teams. As commander of the elite Ultra unit, it was his responsibility to oversee the operations of the other teams - Alpha, Beta, and Omega. Though they were all highly trained, Alex liked to keep a close eye on things.

He skimmed over the details of Alpha Team's latest reconnaissance mission in the Paris catacombs. Nothing too out of the ordinary. The Beta squad had tracked down a rogue banshee in Dublin without incident. All routine checks.

Alex leaned back in his desk chair, running a hand through his tousled hair. He was grateful for the moment of peace, but he could never fully relax. Not with the fate of the world often hanging in the balance. His shoulders bore the tension of his duty.

A familiar soul connection plucked at Alex's consciousness, instantly bringing a smile to his face. Eryx was back. He tried not to be too needy or possessive, but their souls were literally intertwined. Being apart was painful.

Alex's office door creaked open and the handsome blonde poked his head in, flashing a megawatt grin.

"Honey, I'm home," Eryx announced cheekily.

Alex chuckled, the sound rumbling from his muscular chest. "Welcome back, babe."

He crossed the room in quick strides and pulled Eryx into a searing kiss. As their lips met, sparks of warmth cascaded through their bond. Alex cradled Eryx's face, reacquainting himself with every plane and angle.

Too soon, Eryx pulled back, his crystal blue eyes dancing with mischief. "Down boy, I come bearing gifts." He held up a basket brimming with cookies.

"Are those for the team?" Alex asked hopefully. He knew firsthand that Eryx was a phenomenal baker, inheriting his skills from his past life as Apollo.

"Yep! Figured I owed them for dipping out today." Eryx set the basket on Alex's desk before wrapping his arms around his boyfriend's trim waist. "But I saved a special batch just for you, my dark and brooding king."

Alex chuckled again, the sound rumbling even lower in his chest this time. "You know all my weaknesses, don't you?"

"You betcha." Eryx leaned up on his toes to steal another quick kiss.

Alex set the cookie basket aside, he wrapped his arms around Eryx's waist. "So how was your day, babe? Before the big cookie baking extravaganza."

Eryx leaned into his embrace. "It was pretty good actually. I met with that new potential manager."

"That's right," Alex recalled. As Eryx's music career took off, they'd discussed getting him professional representation. "How'd it go?"

"Well…" Eryx hesitated, his exuberance dimming slightly.

Alex sensed his unease through their soulbond. He gently guided

Eryx over to the leather chair and pulled him down onto his lap. The intimate contact made Alex's heart race, but he tried to focus. "I sense a 'but' coming. What happened, my sun?"

Eryx absently played with Alex's fingers. "Nothing bad exactly. But I got a weird vibe from the guy. He knew a little too much about me. About us."

Alex's brow furrowed. "What do you mean?"

With a sigh, Eryx explained, "He mentioned things - about my past, my powers, our connection - stuff no normal human manager would know. It was like he could see right through me."

"Did he give you a name?" Alex asked. Being Apollo's vessel, Eryx's life was still in danger from those who wants his power. This manager could be one of them in disguise.

But Eryx shook his head. "He was very cryptic about his identity. But oddly, my instincts say I can trust him. Apollo agrees." He placed a hand over his heart where the god resided in his soul.

Alex considered this, then said, "If your gut is telling you to give him a chance, then do it. I trust your judgment." He squeezed Eryx reassuringly.

Eryx smiled, visibly relaxing. "Thanks, babe." He gave Alex a quick peck on the lips before asking, "So what happened on your end while I was gone? Any breaks in the case?"

Alex tensed slightly at the reminder. "I spoke with Alpha Hansen. He confirmed that none of his wolves were involved in our Jane Doe's murder. It was definitely staged to look like a shifter attack. The Alpha also mentioned that Moonblood has been popping up again in the area."

Eryx's eyes widened at the name of the dangerous sorcerous drug. "That can't be good."

"We'll figure it out," Alex said firmly. "One step at a time. For now, let's just be thankful for the quiet moments like this." He pulled Eryx closer and kissed his temple.

Eryx hugged Alex tight, reassuring warmth flowing between them. "You're right. We'll tackle the bad stuff when we have to. But right now, it's just you and me and these awesome cookies!"

His spark returned as he hopped up and grabbed the basket. "Come on, time for Operation Cookie Monster with the team!"

Cookie basket in hand, Eryx bounced into the Shadowguards' briefing room with Alex following behind.

Marcus leapt up, eyes zeroing in on the baked goods. "Are those what I think they are?" he asked, practically drooling. With his enhanced shifter speed, he could cross the room in the blink of an eye if he wanted.

Alex chuckled, placing a restraining hand on his shoulder before the sugar-crazed man could swipe the entire basket. "Down boy. There's enough to go around."

"But I want one nooow," Marcus whined. The others laughed at his antics.

"Patience, grasshopper," Eryx teased. He began passing out the cookies as Marcus vibrated in place.

Alex surveyed his team fondly as they enjoyed the treat. Lily closed her eyes in bliss at the first bite while Emma and Olivia immediately began comparing flavors. Lucas set his cookie beside his keyboard, not wanting crumbs in the tech. Gabe read something on his tablet, absently nibbling.

They all needed this moment of reprieve, Alex mused. The case had put them under mounting pressure. But seeing his friends banter and laugh lifted Alex's spirits. Eryx's light had that effect, coaxing joy out of even the darkest of days.

Once everyone had a cookie, Eryx asked, "Where's Finn? He's missing cookie time."

"Still working on that rogue sorcerer we brought in," Alex replied.

"Trying to get something useful out of him about the traffickers he works for."

Eryx shook his head sympathetically. "Poor guy is gonna work himself to death down there. Can you call him up?"

Alex nodded and tapped the communications screen on the wall. Finn's exhausted face popped up. Dark circles haunted his kind eyes and his hair stuck up at odd angles.

"Oh Finn, you look positively dreadful!" Eryx exclaimed.

Finn managed a wan smile. "Occupational hazard I'm afraid. The perils of being chief medic to you reckless heroes."

His voice was lighthearted but Alex sensed his bone-deep weariness. "Come on up and take a break," he urged. "Have Doctor Lacroix take over for now."

Finn hesitated but eventually relented under Eryx's pleading gaze. "Oh all right. I'll be up in a few." His image blinked out.

While they waited, the team launched into reminiscing about their past adventures. Laughter filled the room as they recalled funny mishaps and mistakes.

"Remember when Marcus got chased five blocks by that little old lady after he accidentally knocked over her fruit cart?" Olivia giggled.

"Hey! She was surprisingly spry for ninety-two," Marcus protested, rubbing his backside at the memory.

"We pulled the security footage and watched you get whacked by her purse over and over," Emma snickered.

Marcus groaned dramatically. "You all are the worst friends ever."

"Nah, we just bust your balls cause we love you," Lily teased, blowing him a kiss.

Their chuckles died down as Finn entered, drawn by the mouthwatering aroma. He practically moaned at his first bite.

"Oh sweet mercy, this cookie is transcendent!" he declared. "Eryx, dear boy, you've outdone yourself."

Eryx preened under the praise. "Chocolate chip and some mint chocolate. Nothing but the best for all of you." He leaned contentedly against Alex.

Looking around the room, Alex felt a swell of gratitude. Moments like this were fleeting, but they meant everything. A reminder of why they fought so hard and risked so much.

For each other. Their found family. Laughter in the dark.

The laughter died down as the last crumbs of Eryx's cookies disappeared. Alex treasured these too-brief moments of levity with his found family, but he knew it was time to get back to business.

He turned to Finn, who was savoring his last chocolatey bite. "Did you manage to get anything useful out of our magical mystery guest down in the medical bay?"

Finn shook his head regretfully after swallowing. "I'm afraid not. He's still deep in an arcane coma - seems to have put himself under some kind of failsafe spell. My guess is to prevent himself from revealing anything if captured."

"Any other leads on him then?" Alex asked.

"Take a look at this." Finn pulled up an image on the central holoscreen via his SHD bracelet.

The high-tech bracelet projected a set of medical charts with Finn's notes highlighted. He explained, "I detected an unusual neurotransmitter spike consistent with what we've seen in Moonblood users. I believe our sorcerer friend was under the influence when you brought him in."

"But Moonblood only works on shifters," Gabe pointed out. "It shouldn't affect a regular human mage."

Finn nodded. "True, but it seems the drug has been modified from its original form to work on other supes. I'll need an active sample to analyze the new chemical composition."

"There's also the issue of that summoning staff he used," Lily added.

"It's not the standard Staff of Umbra that the Order have. This one holds some serious dark power."

Eryx perked up at the mention of an enchanted weapon. "Haphaestus could probably shed some light on the staff's origins."

Alex smiled proudly at his insightful mate. "Good idea. If anyone knows magic weapons, it's him. I'll pay the old smithy a visit but for now let's focus on this issue." He turned back to the group with a determined gleam in his dark eyes. "It seems Moonblood is at the heart of this. We need to figure out who's distributing it and how. Cut it off at the source."

"I think I can help with that," Lucas spoke up in his quiet, unassuming way. Alex nodded for him to continue.

"I did some digging into the victim's last known whereabouts based on how she was dressed when found. Signs point to her being at an underground rave - there's only one club in the area that holds events like that: Afterlife."

Alex felt a swell of pride for his brilliant team. "Nice work. Looks like we'll be going clubbing tonight then."

After their long day, Alex and Eryx stumbled through the door of their apartment, barely making it two steps before Alex had Eryx pressed against the wall. Their lips crashed together fiercely, hands roaming.

"I've been wanting to do this all day," Alex growled against Eryx's mouth. His boyfriend let out a breathy laugh which quickly turned into a moan as Alex slipped his hands under his shirt.

They shed clothes rapidly on their way to the bedroom, leaving a haphazard trail across the floor. As soon as they collapsed onto the bed, naked limbs tangled, their lovemaking began in earnest.

Alex took Eryx with a passion that bordered on desperation, touching and kissing every inch of his sun-kissed skin. Eryx responded in kind, meeting Alex's fervor with his own until they lay spent and satisfied.

Unfortunately their afterglow was short-lived. The bed suddenly dipped under the weight of an exuberant ball of fluff and slobber. "Cerberus!" Alex scolded with a laugh as the overgrown pup showered them in enthusiastic kisses.

He ruffled the dog's fur affectionately. "I guess someone wants his walk." Alex regretfully extracted himself from Eryx's embrace and the tangle of sheets to get dressed. He dropped one last lingering kiss to Eryx's perfect lips. "Be back soon, babe."

Eryx waved him off with a contented smile, cuddling their Mr. Whiskers. Alex's heart swelled at the cozy domestic scene.

Out in the crisp night air, Cerberus strained eagerly at his leash as they made their way to the nearby dog park. Alex let the dog loose to play, settling on a bench beneath the stars.

Suddenly the air crackled with electricity - the harbinger of an arriving god. Alex was on his feet in an instant as Thanatos materialized before him, hidden from mortal eyes by a veil of Mist.

Cerberus bounded over to greet the god excitedly. Thanatos indulged the pup with a few ear scratches before facing Alex somberly. "I have news on Dolos."

Alex tensed. "Were you able to find him?"

"He's currently imprisoned in Tartarus," Thanatos revealed. "But he said he'll tell you what you want to know if you help break him out. Apparently Winston is responsible for his imprisonment."

Alex absorbed this with a frown. "I'll have to pay the old man a visit and get the full story." He clasped the death god's shoulder. "Thank you, my friend. Let me know if you learn anything more."

Thanatos nodded and vanished, taking the electrical charge in the air with him. Alex gathered Cerberus and hurried home, mind racing.

He found Eryx in the kitchen studying a document. Alex pressed a kiss to the nape of his neck in greeting. "What are you working on, babe?"

"Just reviewing the contract from my potential new manager," Eryx replied, leaning into Alex's embrace. "I want to have a lawyer look it over before I sign anything."

Alex perked up. "I can ask Themis to review it if you want a supernatural legal expert's opinion."

"That would be amazing! Thank you." Eryx turned and planted a grateful kiss on Alex's lips.

Alex glanced at the clock as he and Eryx broke from their kiss. "We should start getting ready if we want to make it to Afterlife on time."

Eryx set down the contract he'd been examining and took Alex's hand, leading him playfully toward the bathroom. "Shower first?" he asked, eyebrows waggling suggestively.

Alex laughed and allowed himself to be tugged along. They took their time washing up, exchanging gentle caresses and tender kisses under the warm spray. The stress of the day melted away, leaving only blissful closeness.

After their shower, they moved to the bedroom and began going through their wardrobes, trying to find the perfect club-worthy outfits. Alex held up a dark Henley shirt against his muscular frame as Eryx studied himself in slim black jeans and a shimmery button-down.

"Too flashy?" Eryx asked, testing out a couple dance moves and watching the shirt shimmer under the light.

Alex smiled indulgently. "You look perfect, as always."

Finally dressed - Alex in an all-black ensemble that complemented his tousled dark hair and brooding aura, while Eryx wore stylishly ripped jeans with a silvery shirt bringing out his golden glow - they deemed each other ready.

Alex checked the address Lucas had sent, then offered Eryx his hand. "Shall we?"

Eryx linked their fingers and they headed out into the night. The drive was quiet but charged with anticipation. As they turned onto Fifth Avenue where the club awaited, Alex brought Eryx's hand to his lips.

"Remember, we're here to have some fun too, not just work," he murmured. Eryx's answering smile lit up the car like sunshine.

Alex parked strategically - easy escape route if needed, but inconspicuous. Before exiting, he and Eryx tightened their psychic shields, masking their presence.

As Alex and Eryx made their way down fifth Avenue towards Afterlife , the sounds of the city surrounded them. Music and raucous laughter spilled out of bars and restaurants packed with weekend revelers. The sidewalks were crowded with groups dressed to the nines, waiting in lines behind velvet ropes or looking for their next destination.

Neon lights splashed colorfully across the bustling avenue, giving everything a surreal, carnival-like aura. Street performers played guitars on corners while artists sold paintings laid out on the sidewalk. The air was alive with energy and excitement.

Eryx walked closely beside Alex, their joined hands a point of warmth in the controlled chaos. Alex kept his senses on high alert, automatically scanning faces, sniffing the air, checking sightlines. But even he couldn't help being swept up in the electric ambiance.

As the pulsing lights of Afterlife came into view, he exchanged a charged look with Eryx.

They were stopped by a bouncer who waved them through and seemed friendly enough for a shifter.

Inside Afterlife, deep mahogany walls and leather furnishings gave an air of luxury mixed with edge. Accents of polished silver and amethyst glassware glinted in the moody purple lighting. The dance floor was packed with revelers moving rhythmically to the pulsing beat, lost in their own little worlds.

Over the din, snippets of laughter and conversation could be heard as patrons clustered around the gleaming black granite bar or lounged in sleek booths. The savory scents of street food from late-night vendors carried in each time the front door swung open. An undercurrent of pheromones and anticipation charged the atmosphere.

Alex surveyed it all warily from his vantage point, every sense heightened. But the energy was more exuberant than threatening as partygoers simply looked to have a good time in one of the city's hottest clubs. For now at least, the mission could wait - there was fun to be had.

Alex chose a table near the edges, with good sightlines to all exits. He and Eryx ordered drinks to blend in and settled in to wait for their team, hands loosely joined atop the table.

One by one, Alex spotted each of his teammates entering Afterlife in disguise. They arrived separately to avoid drawing suspicion, blending into the crowds.

Alex was impressed by their ingenuity. Lily had woven flowers into her hair and wore a bohemian-style dress, looking every inch the free-spirited clubgoer. Lucas sported some fake piercings and a punk rock tee, hiding his nerdy persona. Emma wouldn't have looked out of place on a runway in her shimmery minidress and strappy heels.

It was rare to see his team outside of their usual tactical uniforms. Alex realized he needed to organize more of these casual team outings. His found family meant the world to him, but it was easy to get caught up in the mission and forget to just enjoy each other's company.

Marcus slid into the seat beside Alex, subtly nodding in greeting. "Ready to get this party started, boss?" he said with a grin.

Undercover or not, Marcus was clearly excited at the prospect of letting loose on the dance floor later.

Alex shook his head in amusement. "All business first. We're here for intel, remember?" But he made a mental note to make sure they all took time for a little fun too. After all they'd endured, his team had earned it.

Soon the group was assembled and trading updates discreetly via coded phrases. Finn and Emma peeled off to start covertly scanning for traces of magic. Olivia headed to the bar to chat up the pretty Fae bartender. Gabe was already tapping away on his SHD, hacking into the club's security system. Lily sashayed onto the dance floor to get an empathic read on the crowd.

Alex sat back and observed his team, pride and affection welling up. However tonight went, this was already shaping up to be a mission to remember.

7

Troubles in the Afterlife

Eryx

Alex said he'd have whatever he was having, then gave him a quick kiss and a playful slap on the behind before heading off into the pulsing crowd.

Eryx smiled as he watched Alex disappear into the sea of dancing bodies. Things had been going well between them lately, ever since the whole fiasco with the a couple of months ago.

He was still getting used to having an actual boyfriend, let alone one who was the infamous Lord of the Underworld. But Alex's broody stoicism balanced him out nicely.

As Alex walked away, he called back over his shoulder teasingly, "Don't take too long at the bar, pretty boy. I'll be waiting for you on the dance floor."

Eryx laughed and waved him off. "Yeah yeah, give me a few minutes. Gotta make sure I get the good stuff."

He saw Alex shake his head in amusement before vanishing into the crowd. Eryx took a moment to appreciate how good his boyfriend looked tonight.

Eryx sighed contentedly. He really was a lucky guy. Handsome, heroic, and his. Well, time to get those drinks he promised. Can't keep the Lord of the Underworld waiting, after all.

As Eryx made his way to the bar, he wondered what Alex would be like on the dance floor later. His fighting style was all elegant, controlled power - he imagined that translated to some pretty slick dance moves too. Maybe Alex would even give him a private show in his room when they got home. The thought made Eryx grin in anticipation. Focus, he told himself. Drinks first, sexy times later.

"Hey, go easy on the poor guy," Eryx teased as he sidled up next to Olivia.

Olivia rolled her eyes dramatically. "Oh please, I'm not after him. I'm waiting for his colleague, the brunette witch. Saw her make the drink order for those warlocks in the VIP section earlier."

Eryx raised an eyebrow, surprised. "Didn't know you swung that way."

"I go both ways," Olivia replied casually as she sipped her neon cocktail. "Don't really make a big deal of it. The team doesn't even know."

"Well, thanks for telling me," Eryx said sincerely. He was touched that the normally aloof pyromancer trusted him enough to share something so personal.

Olivia gave a small smile then gestured at Eryx. "What about you? How's the music career going?"

Eryx exhaled heavily. "Oh, you know…it's going. The label's got me a new manager. And the paparazzi are relentless."

"Hey," Olivia gave his arm a supportive squeeze. "You'll get through it. After the crap we've faced, dealing with the media will be a cakewalk."

Eryx chuckled softly. "Yeah, you're probably right."

Just then, the bartender that Olivia was eyeing came over to take

Eryx's order, giving him a friendly smile.

"I'll take two gin and tonics, please. And uh-" Eryx discretely motioned the bartender closer. "Any chance you could give my friend your number? She's got her eye on you."

The bartender grinned and nodded conspiratorially. After mixing the drinks, she slyly slipped a folded napkin into Olivia's hand.

Olivia peered at Eryx curiously as he collected the drinks. "What did you tell her?"

"Oh, just that you think she's cute," Eryx said with faux nonchalance.

Olivia's eyes widened in surprise, then her face broke into a genuine smile. "Damn. Thank you."

"Don't mention it," Eryx laughed, heading back to find Alex. Moments like this reminded him why he fought so hard to protect the mortal realm. For all its chaos and darkness, there was still light, still hope. All you had to do was look.

Eryx found Alex standing in the shadows, observing the club patrons with an intense gaze. His fingers idly traced the faded scar on his forearm, a nervous habit from his days as Hades. Eryx often forgot that beneath Alex's youthful appearance lurked an ancient, unfathomable power.

"One gin and tonic, as requested," Eryx announced, breaking Alex's pensive stare.

Alex accepted the drink with a small smile. "Thanks. Any luck gathering intel?"

Eryx shook his head. "Nothing substantial yet. You?"

"Same," Alex sighed, sipping his drink. "This place has some serious warding magic protecting it. Finn and Emma are trying to dismantle it, but no guarantees."

Eryx nodded, casting his senses outward. Now that he focused, he could feel the thrum of arcane energy woven through the club's very walls. Cracking those wards would take time.

"We'll get what we came for," Eryx said resolutely. "Just have to be patient."

Alex gave him an appraising look. "You seem different lately."

"Oh? How so?"

"Calmer. More focused." Alex tilted his head. "The Eryx I first met was always charging forward, consequences be damned. But you've changed."

Eryx considered this, absently swirling his drink. "I guess nearly destroying the world makes you rethink things," he admitted ruefully. "I was reckless back then. But I know now that if I want to achieve real good, I need wisdom just as much as courage."

Alex smiled, grey eyes glinting with pride. "You're growing into a fine hero, you know that?"

Warmth rushed through Eryx at the unexpected praise. "Couldn't have done it without you."

They clinked their glasses together in a silent toast, shoulders pressed companionably together.

After a few moments, Eryx turned to Alex with a playful grin. "So, feel like dancing?"

Alex shook his head ruefully. "Oh no, you know I've got two left feet."

"Come on, it'll be fun!" Eryx cajoled, tugging at Alex's arm. "No one here knows who we are, so we don't have to worry about causing a scene."

"I'd rather not embarrass myself, thanks," Alex replied wryly.

But Eryx was having none of it. He swiftly drained both their glasses and set them on a nearby table. "Too bad, you're dancing with me, mister."

Ignoring Alex's protests, Eryx dragged him by the hand onto the crowded dance floor. The deep rhythmic bass pulsed through their bodies as strobe lights flickered hypnotically overhead. Eryx let the music move through him, years of performing kicking in as he rolled his hips and waved his arms fluidly.

Alex stood awkwardly at first, trying to mimic Eryx's smooth motions but looking more like a malfunctioning robot. Eryx stifled a laugh and moved behind Alex, guiding his hips with his hands.

"Relax, just feel the rhythm," he instructed. Gradually Alex loosened up, the tension easing from his muscles as he let Eryx lead him. Before long they were swaying in unison, pressed close in the darkness.

"See, not so bad right?" Eryx murmured in Alex's ear.

"Mm, I guess not," Alex conceded, the trace of a smile on his lips. His hands gripped Eryx's waist almost possessively as they moved together. Eryx had never seen this carefree, playful side of the normally stern Underworld lord. He found he quite liked it.

As they swayed to the pounding beat, Eryx leaned in close to Alex's ear. "Think of it this way, we won't be too obvious and I thought from the vantage point we can see more things happening."

Alex nodded, eyes scanning the crowd. "You're brilliant, just remember to keep your eyes peeled." He tapped his earpiece discreetly. "Gabe, Lily, anything suspicious?"

Gabe's voice came through the comms. "All quiet in the back alleys so far."

"I'm not sensing any hostile intent around the hall and bathrooms," Lily added. "But I'll stay alert."

"Copy that," Alex replied. "But try to have some fun too. We are at a club, after all."

He flashed a roguish grin at Eryx before pulling him tighter against his body and moving with surprising grace. Eryx's eyes widened in appreciation - he had no idea Alex could dance like this.

"Well well, look who's got moves," Eryx teased, matching Alex's footwork. "Been holding out on me, huh?"

Alex laughed, the sound warm and rumbling. "What can I say? Perks of having centuries to practice."

He spun Eryx in an elaborate twirl before drawing him back, their chests pressed flush. Alex's strong hands cradled Eryx's hips as they rocked together. The strobe lights painted hypnotic patterns across their entwined bodies.

Eryx was mesmerized by this unguarded version of Alex, his usual brooding façade replaced by relaxed confidence. In this sea of anonymity, the legendary Lord of the Underworld was simply a man dancing with his boyfriend.

As the music reached a crescendo, Alex dipped Eryx dramatically, supporting him with one muscular arm. Face to face, their noses almost touched, and Eryx saw his own exhilaration mirrored in Alex's gleaming eyes.

Righting them both, Alex pulled Eryx into a swift, heated kiss before releasing him with a roguish wink. "Not bad for two left feet, eh?"

Eryx could only shake his head in happy disbelief. "You continue to surprise me."

After a few songs, Eryx spotted a raised stage at the back where karaoke was just wrapping up. An idea formed. He tapped the hidden comm unit in his ear. "Gabe, can you hear me? I've got a plan."

"Loud and clear," came the reply. "Whatcha thinking?"

Eryx quickly explained his idea to use the stage to get an aerial view and record the club interior.

Gabe chuckled in approval. "I like it. Sending the spy-glasses your way now."

A minute later, Marcus appeared at Eryx's side clutching a pair of modified glasses and a baseball cap. "Here you go, man. This should let me see whatever you see up there. Maybe we'll spot something useful."

Eryx donned the disguise and gave Alex a reassuring peck on the lips. "Time for an impromptu concert. Don't worry, I'll be careful."

Alex looked wary but nodded. "Just watch your back. And try not to bring the whole place down with that voice of yours," he added wryly.

Grinning, Eryx made his way through the crowd as the MC announced auditions for the next singer. Other patrons eyed him curiously but didn't seem to recognize him. Eryx volunteered eagerly.

"Alright, let's give it up for our next brave soul!" the MC proclaimed as Eryx took the stage. The crowd whooped appreciatively.

Squinting through the glasses, Eryx scanned the dance floor until he spotted Alex leaning against the far wall, watching him intently. He threw a wink in his direction before launching into an upbeat pop song, carefully modulating his vocal power.

As he sang, Eryx panned his gaze across the club, looking for anything suspicious. The glasses transmitted a live feed to Gabe, providing multiple angles of the interior. But at first glance nothing seemed out of the ordinary, just revelers drinking and dancing the night away.

As Eryx belted out the chorus, putting his supernatural vocals on display, he let his gaze casually sweep the crowd. At first nothing seemed amiss - just the usual revelers drinking and dancing under the pulsing lights.

But then movement at the far edge of the dance floor caught Eryx's eye. Three shadowy figures huddled in a booth, heads bowed in furtive conversation. One of them slid a small package across the table, which another figure swiftly pocketed.

Eryx subtly angled his head so the spy glasses could focus in on the group. He saw Gabe's voice come through the earpiece.

"Got eyes on them, thanks Eryx. Definitely looks shady but I can't make out faces from this high angle. Think you can get lower without drawing suspicion?"

Careful not to miss a beat of the song, Eryx descended the stage steps while ad-libbing a vocal run. He gradually worked his way through the crowd, pretending to interact with the audience while steadily nearing the booth.

Once he had a direct sightline, Eryx launched into the final chorus, holding a sustained high note that had the crowd enraptured. As all eyes were on him, he quickly ducked down as if overcome by the emotion of the song, angling the glasses directly at the dealers. Gabe gave an approving affirmation in his ear at the clear footage being transmitted.

Knowing he couldn't hold the awkward pose for long, Eryx wound up the song and thanked the audience, who cheered enthusiastically, none the wiser. Eryx spotted Alex waiting near the edge of the dance floor and made a beeline for him.

"You were amazing up there," Alex said, planting a kiss on Eryx's lips. "Hopefully we got what we needed."

Before Eryx could reply, Lily's voice sounded over the team channel. "Everyone back to the table, I've got something."

Exchanging a look, Alex and Eryx hurried to regroup with the others. Finn and Leo had arrived in their absence, and greeted Eryx with quick hugs.

"Sorry we're late," Finn said sheepishly. "Someone was a bit insatiable before we left." He shot a teasing look at Leo, who just grinned unapologetically.

They all crowded around the table as Alex asked, "What've you found, Lily?"

Gabe spoke up first. "Thanks to Eryx's recon on stage, we got footage of what looks like a deal going down."

He projected the video feed from Eryx's glasses onto the table's surface. It showed the three figures exchanging a small bundled package.

Lily manipulated the image, zooming in on one figure's profile. "I did a search through our databases and found a match. Thomas Drake, low level vampire for the Eastside Coven." She pulled up a mugshot of a pale, tattooed man.

Alex's expression hardened as he studied the image. "Good work, team. We can't let Drake slip away tonight, he's our first solid Moonblood lead. Gabe, monitor all exits in case he tries to bolt. Everyone else, keep eyes on him from here and be ready to pursue if needed."

The team voiced their acknowledgement and refocused on their target. Eryx turned to Alex curiously. "So what's the deal with this Eastside Coven anyway? I'm still getting the hang of all the supernatural politics."

Alex nodded in understanding. "The Eastside Coven is one of the more notorious groups operating in the city. They've been causing chaos for decades - trafficking, violence, you name it."

"Man, this stuff is so complicated," Eryx sighed. "Going to take me forever to learn it all."

Alex smiled reassuringly. "You'll get there. Took me centuries to figure it out." He gently bumped Eryx's shoulder. "But you've got a great teacher."

Eryx laughed. "Can't argue with that!" He stood up a bit unsteadily. "Anyway, too many drinks - I'm gonna hit the bathroom."

Alex nodded, refocusing on Drake as Eryx made his way through the crowd. Inside the bathroom, he quickly used the facilities, swaying slightly from the alcohol buzz. As he washed his hands, a smooth voice spoke from behind him.

"Quite a set you put on out there. Big fan."

Eryx tensed, glancing up at the mirror to see Drake leaning casually against the wall, watching him intently. So much for keeping eyes on him.

"Oh uh, thanks," Eryx said neutrally, playing dumb as he dried his hands.

Drake prowled closer. "Don't be so modest. You've got real talent. And up close, even more tempting." His eyes trailed over Eryx's neck hungrily.

Warning signs blared in Eryx's mind - Drake had made him as more than human. He gripped the sink tightly as Drake approached. "Look man, I think you should step back."

Drake chuckled. "Or what? I don't scent any magic on you. A helpless little human like you can't stop me from taking what I want."

He lunged rapidly at Eryx, who reacted on instinct, letting his power surge out. A concussive wave of energy erupted from Eryx, slamming Drake backwards into the wall before he could lay a hand on him.

Drake peeled himself up slowly, staring at Eryx in shock. "What the hell are you?"

Eryx tapped his comm unit. "Alex, got a situation in the bathroom. Our friend Drake decided to pay me a visit." Then to Drake he said coldly, "Let's just say you really don't want to piss off my friends and I."

Horrified realization crossed Drake's face. "You're a fed?"

"Worse."

With a burst of vampire speed, Drake shot towards the door in panic.

Alex came in rushing, eyes blazing and immediately went to him.

"You okay?" Alex asked Eryx tersely.

As they hurried back into the club, Alex quickly tapped his comms. "Team, we've got a situation. Drake made Eryx and is on the run, headed toward the main floor. Marcus, get ready to intercept."

"Copy that, I'm already moving to cut him off," Marcus responded tersely.

"Emma, work crowd control," Alex directed. "Make sure no one panics when this goes down."

"On it," Emma replied. "Preparing a subtle compliance spell now."

They emerged from the hallway to see Marcus zooming past after a fleeing Drake, who roughly shoved clubgoers out of his path. Cries of surprise rang out, but the patrons remained docile and unfazed, thanks to Emma's magic.

"I've got all exits covered remotely," came Gabe's voice. "He's not getting out without us knowing."

Alex surveyed the scene quickly. "Lily, status?"

"Close by with Finn, moving your way," Lily responded. "I sensed the panic spike, what do you need?"

"Be ready to assist Marcus with capture," instructed Alex. "But keep collateral damage minimal."

Finn chimed in. "I've got medical supplies prepped in case things get hairy."

"Appreciate it, doc," said Alex. He tapped Eryx's shoulder. "With me, we're going after Drake."

As Alex coordinated the team, Olivia's voice came over comms: "I've got eyes on Drake from the mezzanine. I can slow him down with a fireball if needed."

"Hold off for now, let Marcus take point on capture," Alex responded. "But be ready."

"You got it, boss," said Olivia.

Lucas added, "Sir, I'm scrubbing security footage and planting false leads in case the police investigate. No direct trail back to us."

"Appreciate it Lucas," Alex said tersely, focused on getting Eryx medical attention. "Make sure Gabe backs up all the data first."

"Already on it," Lucas confirmed. "I'll have a bot flood social media with theories blaming rival gangs too. We were never here as far as the public knows."

"That vampire sure is fast." Alex said to Eryx.

"He's fast, but Marcus is faster," Eryx said as they followed the chaotic trail.

Sure enough, Marcus tackled Drake to the ground near the bar. But the vampire managed to flip Marcus off of him with preternatural strength. As Drake scrambled up, Eryx saw a gun appear in his hand, aimed shakily towards him.

"Look out!" Alex yelled, rushing forward. But it was too late - the gunshot echoed painfully loud. Eryx felt the bullet pierce his shoulder in a burst of hot pain before he collapsed.

Dimly he heard Alex roar in rage and the screams of nearby clubgoers. Eryx clutched his bleeding shoulder, watching through blurred vision as Alex seized Drake and slammed him viciously down, the vampire's head cracking against the floor.

8

Cursed Soul

Alex

As Eryx collapsed from the gunshot, Alex roared in anguish and rage. This couldn't be happening. Eryx had to be okay, he just had to be.

Alex tapped his comm unit urgently. "Marcus, get Eryx out of here and to Finn for emergency treatment. Now!"

Marcus was already lifting Eryx's limp form. "On it, meet you back at base." He sped away, weaving through the panicked crowd.

Drake was still scrambling through the chaos, trying to make an escape. Alex's vision tunneled - nothing else mattered but making this bastard pay. He charged forward with terrifying speed, grabbing Drake by the throat and slamming him viciously onto the hard floor.

"No one hurts him and lives," Alex growled, eyes glowing with green fire. He squeezed tighter, feeling Drake's panicked breaths rasping under his grip.

Drake clawed frantically at Alex's hand. "Let…me…go…" he choked out.

Alex pushed his face closer, baring his teeth. "Give me one good reason not to end you right here."

To his surprise, Drake managed a strangled laugh. "Oh I've…got plenty…of reasons…" He wrenched an arm free and fumbled urgently in his pockets.

Alex frowned in confusion, then his eyes widened in dismay as Drake produced a small vial. "Have fun with this!" Drake gasped out, smashing the vial on the floor.

Alex instantly recognized the swirling silver liquid that now coated the sprinkler system. "Moonblood," he growled. "Everyone, cover your noses!"

But it was too late - the fire sprinklers activated, raining the potent supernatural narcotic through the club. Alex was forced to release Drake as panicked patrons began violently transforming all around him, overcome by uncontrollable bloodlust and madness.

A roar sounded behind Alex as a hulking werewolf leapt at him, jaws slavering. He spun and blasted it back with a burst of hellfire. "What a nightmare," he muttered, tapping his comms. "Team, status update!"

"Trying to cloak us from the mortal authorities," came Emma's strained reply over sounds of destruction. "But it's pure chaos here!"

Gabe chimed in next. "Drake slipped away in the confusion. I think Leo went after him."

Alex swore as he continued fending off crazed vampires and werebeasts descending into a supernatural brawl. "Someone contain Drake! He cannot leave with that Moonblood sample."

"On it!" Leo replied fiercely through the comms. "The bastard's not getting away from me."

A snarling werewolf leapt at Alex, who blasted it back with a surge of hellfire. The club was plunging into utter chaos as the Moonblood took hold of the infected patrons, reducing them to mindless violence and bloodlust.

Alex grabbed a nearby chair and smashed it over an advancing vampire, splintering the wood. The crazed bloodsucker just laughed maniacally, fangs bared as it kept coming.

With a grunt of effort, Alex seized the vampire by the shoulders and hurled him bodily into a cluster of brawling werebeasts. But two more took the downed vampire's place, a feral glint in their reddened eyes.

"Down boy," Alex growled, unleashing twin streams of flickering green fire from his palms. The vampires screamed as the blessed hellfire scorched their undead flesh, buying Alex some breathing room.

Spinning around, Alex came face to snout with an enormous werewolf, its hot breath huffing down over him. Before Alex could react, the wolf swiped a massive clawed hand, shredding Alex's shirt and leaving deep furrows across his chest.

"Oh, it's like that, huh?" Alex spat. Eyes blazing with infernal light, he grabbed the werewolf by the muzzle, physically heaving the giant beast over his head and slamming it down onto a table with a savage roar. The table splintered under the massive impact.

Alex had no time to catch his breath before two more werewolves barrelled into him, sending him crashing through the ruined bar. Glass rained down as Alex wrestled with the hybrids, their teeth and claws shredding his clothes and skin.

With a burst of desperate strength, Alex conjured bindings of ghostly green flame, searing the wolves and forcing them to recoil. Alex leapt up, grabbing a broken liquor bottle and smashing it over one werewolf's head, then blasting the second point-blank range with hellfire.

Breathing hard, Alex tapped his comm unit. "Gabe, Emma - status? These beasts just keep coming!" He punctuated his words by hurling a fireball to deter a hissing cluster of vampires.

"Still trying to cloak us from the authorities!" Emma responded tersely over the sounds of destruction.

"Leo managed to grab Drake, I'm tracking them now," reported Gabe.

Alex gritted his teeth. They just had to contain this long enough for the tainted water to dissipate. A bone-rattling roar announced another werewolf joining the melee. With no other options, Alex summoned his dreaded sword in a swirl of green flame.

"Let's dance, fleabag," he declared as the wolf charged. He swung the sword in a wide arc, carving a deep gash across the werewolf's chest and narrowly avoiding its raking claws.

Snarling in fury, the lycan thundered forward again, only to be met by Alex's whirling sword separating its head cleanly from its shoulders. The creature collapsed in a heap, shifting back to human form.

Alex lost himself in the violent melee, relying on centuries of combat experience. He had to end this quickly before the whole place came down. Out of the corner of his eye, he saw a shock of blond hair making its way toward the sprinkler controls. Alex's heart leapt - Eryx was on his feet!

With a final blaze of golden light, Eryx destroyed the sprinkler system, stopping the spread of contaminated water. The remaining Moonblood-soaked figures soon collapsed unconscious as the narcotic rapidly wore off.

Alex rushed over to Eryx, who sagged against the wall looking pale and drawn. "You're okay! What are you doing up?" Alex asked worriedly, supporting him with an arm.

"Couldn't...let you have...all the fun," Eryx quipped weakly. But his face was tight with pain.

"Easy there, hero," said Alex gently. "We've got this covered now. Let's get you patched up."

Leo returned dragging an unconscious Drake. "He's contained," Leo reported with satisfaction.

Alex nodded. "Nice work, all of you. Let's get out of here before the authorities arrive."

Back at the secured Bearcat, Alex helped Eryx hobble inside, wincing at the growing bloodstain on his shirt.

Finn immediately eased Eryx down and began examining the gunshot wound. "Sorry I lost sight of you back there," he said regretfully as he cut away Eryx's shirt.

"Not your fault, doc," Eryx assured through gritted teeth. "Happened too fast."

Alex did a headcount of who was present. "Gabe, you good? The rest of the team make it to the other transport?"

Gabe nodded from the driver's seat. "Yup, already radioed ahead. We'll meet them back at base." He gunned the engine and the vehicle roared into motion.

Alex sank down next to Finn and Eryx, adrenaline still pumping through his veins. "How's he looking?"

Finn's brow was furrowed in focus as he cleaned and dressed the injury. "No major organs or arteries hit, so that's good. The healing spells are already kickstarting his recovery. I'd say bed rest for a day or two and he'll bounce back."

Relief washed over Alex. Eryx was going to be okay. The night could have ended so much worse.

Eryx gave Alex a weak smile. "See? I'm fine, babe. Don't get your leather pants in a twist."

Only Eryx could make jokes after nearly dying, Alex thought with a mix of exasperation and awe. His resilience never ceased to amaze.

The rest of the ride back to headquarters was quiet, the atmosphere still tense from the chaotic mission. Finn kept a watchful eye on Eryx's vitals while Alex held his hand, grounding himself in the comfort of Eryx's presence.

Back at Shadowguard headquarters, the team helped Eryx out of the

Bearcat and into the briefing room. The others were already gathered around the table, including Leo who normally only joined them from his position at the HIB.

Alex eyed Leo urgently as they got Eryx settled into a chair. "Drake secure in the holding cells downstairs?"

Leo nodded. "Yeah, me and Olivia locked him up tight. He's not going anywhere."

"What the hell happened tonight?" Lily asked without preamble as Alex sat beside Eryx and gripped his hand comfortingly. "Things clearly got out of control back there."

Alex recounted the chaotic events - pursuing Drake into the bathroom, him producing a vial of concentrated Moonblood, the raining sprinklers that sent the club into a frenzy.

"Were you able to retrieve any of the Moonblood sample?" Lily questioned once Alex finished.

He shook his head, shame welling up. "No, Drake smashed the vial on the floor deliberately. I failed to secure it."

Eryx and the others immediately voiced protests, defending Alex's actions. But self-recrimination still gnawed at Alex - he should have been better prepared.

"Actually…" Gabe spoke up tentatively. "I may have managed to grab a bit of the leftover Moonblood from one of the infected patrons before he fled the scene." He held up a small sealed container.

Alex straightened with interest. "Get that to Finn for analysis on the double. Any scrap could prove useful."

Finn took the vial eagerly. "I'll start tests right away, see if I can reverse engineer the compound."

"So where do we go from here?" Lily asked pointedly, always focused on the next strategic steps. "And what are we doing with Drake?"

"Interrogation," Alex said decisively. "We need to know how he got that concentrated sample, where the main production is happening.

If he talks, it could blow this whole operation open."

After deciding to interrogate Drake, Alex turned to Marcus. "Take Eryx home and stand guard there. He needs rest, and protection."

Eryx started to protest, but Alex fixed him with a no-nonsense look. "No arguments. You were just shot and dosed with Moonblood. I'm not risking you getting hurt again tonight."

With a reluctant sigh, Eryx allowed Marcus to help him up and hobble out, Lucas joining them as extra security.

Alex then addressed Finn and Leo. "You two should head out as well. Don't want questions if Leo gets spotted here."

Finn nodded. "Call if you need any medical assistance. I'll analyze the Moonblood sample at my clinic."

After they left, Alex gathered Olivia, Gabe, Emma and Lily. "Let's head to the interrogation room. Time to see what Drake knows."

In the observation chamber, they watched through the one-way glass as Gabe and Olivia dragged a struggling Drake in and forced him into a chair, chaining his arms and legs. Drake spat curses at them, but couldn't break free of his bonds.

Once they rejoined the group, Lily asked "So how are we playing this? Bad cop, worse cop?"

Alex considered for a moment. "Let's start soft. Lily, use your skills first to see if he'll open up willingly."

"Got it," Lily affirmed, then entered the interrogation room. They observed her make friendly conversation, get Drake a drink of water, ask gentle questions about his involvement. But Drake stayed stubbornly silent, glaring at her balefully.

After thirty fruitless minutes, Lily exited the observation room. "He's not talking. I think we need to turn up the heat."

Alex's expression darkened. "Then it's my turn."

He and Lily re-entered the interrogation room. Drake glowered as Alex took a seat across from him.

"This would go easier if you cooperated," Alex said calmly. "But if you refuse, we'll be forced to…take drastic measures."

Drake snarled. "Do your worst, Shadowguard scum. You can't break me."

Alex nodded to Lily, who placed a hand on Drake's forehead. Her eyes glowed white as she tapped into her psychic abilities. Drake's bravado melted into pants of terror as Lily pried open his mind.

After a minute, Lily released him, frowning. "There are powerful blocks in place. I can't get through."

"Let me try something," said Alex grimly. He closed his eyes, channeling the ancient power of the Underworld. When he opened them, Drake recoiled - Alex now radiated the terrifying aura of Hades.

"Will you talk now, vampire?" Alex thundered, voice echoing with infernal might. He seized Drake by the throat and hoisted him effortlessly aloft.

Drake choked in panic. "I can't! There's a spell stopping me!"

Alex tightened his grip. "Explain, quickly."

"The coven…they put a curse on us," Drake rasped. "No one in the network can reveal details or we die!"

Alex's mind raced, then he turned to Lily. "Be ready to contain him. I have an idea."

Drake looked between them fearfully. "W-What are you doing?"

Alex summoned a swirling orb of green hellfire into his palm. "Breaking your curse."

Before Drake could react, Alex plunged the fiery hand into his chest. Drake screamed in agony as infernal flame seared his undead flesh. Alex focused, gripping the tainted strands of Drake's soul essence. With a savage wrench, he ripped the darkened soul right out of Drake's body.

Drake's lifeless form slumped forward, vacant eyes staring ahead. In Alex's palm, the vampire's corrupted soul essence writhed and pulsated like a living thing - the culmination of Drake's centuries of evil and malice given form.

As a fallen god of the Underworld, Alex could perceive souls in a way mortals could not. What he held was no ethereal abstraction, but a twisted mass of smoky shadows, flickering with sickly violet light from Drake's supernatural corruption. The soul's surface boiled with faces and memories trapped in eternal torment.

Alex recoiled instinctively from its foul energy. Few beings could touch a soul directly without being utterly overwhelmed. But Alex channeled his infernal power, barely managing to contain the soul's writhing malevolence. This was incredibly risky magic - most would be instantly driven mad by contact with such concentrated evil.

But Alex knew he had precious few options. With gritted teeth, he focused on modulating the soul's esoteric energies, trying to extract Drake's essence from the clinging darkness. If he could cleanse it just enough, they had a chance to bypass the curse and finally get some real answers.

Alex regretted the necessity, but nothing mattered more than stopping the Moonblood threat. Sometimes salvation came at a steep price. Alex just prayed the others could purify Drake's soul before its innate vileness overcame them all. This was their last desperate gambit, fueled by hope of prevailing against encroaching darkness.

"Lily, see if you can cleanse this enough for me to question it," Alex said urgently. "We only have minutes before it degrades."

Lily nodded and held her hands over the soul, channeling her purifying earth magic into it. Alex tapped his comms. "Gabe, seal this room in case this goes south."

"On it!" Gabe responded quickly. Arcane sigils glowed to life on the walls as he locked down the space.

Alex could see Lily straining as she fought back against the soul's engrained evil. "Hurry, I can't contain this for long," she warned through gritted teeth.

Nodding, Alex turned to Emma who had entered behind them. "Emma, use your enchantment skills to compel him to answer honestly once I reconstitute this."

Taking a steadying breath, Alex forced the unstable soul back into Drake's body with an infernal incantation. Drake jerked upright with a gasp, eyes crazed. Before he could speak, Emma grasped his head, weaving a quick honesty spell.

"What is your operation's end goal?" Alex demanded. "Why the Moonblood trafficking?"

Drake struggled against the magic compelling him, but choked out, "We don't know the full plan! We're just distributing as instructed!"

"Where are you making the drug?" Alex pressed. "How widespread is this?"

"The main production facility is underneath the city," Drake revealed through gritted teeth. "It's a massive underground labyrinth only the inner circle can access! I don't know more than that!"

Sensing the compulsions weakening, Alex turned to Lily urgently. "Contain him again, quick!"

With visible effort, Lily halted the soul's degradation once more. But sweat beaded her brow with the strain. "I can't hold this much longer," she warned.

Alex swore under his breath. This confirmed a city-wide Moonblood conspiracy, but too many details still eluded them. For now, though, Drake had given them their first solid lead.

"Let it go," Alex directed Lily reluctantly. "We got enough for now."

Lily released her power, and Drake collapsed forward, soul unstable but restored enough to animate his undead form. Alex and Lily stepped out to reconvene with Gabe, Emma and Olivia.

"Get him on ice in the cells for now," Alex instructed wearily. "We need to research any underground facilities that could hide a major drug lab."

"On it, boss," Gabe affirmed, already typing away on a tablet. "I'll start collating all known cave systems, abandoned subway lines, anything big enough to hold production."

Alex nodded, finally allowing himself to feel a spark of hope. The night's disasters had yielded a pivotal clue thanks to his team's quick thinking and skill. Now they had a direction at last.

"Nice work in there," Alex praised Lily and Emma. "That took real finesse to pull off on short notice."

The two women smiled tiredly, the night clearly having drained their magical reserves.

"Go rest up, all of you," Alex directed gently. "We'll continue the hunt tomorrow."

Alex took one of the team's discreet vehicles back home after the interrogation. Inside the apartment, he found Eryx, Marcus, and Lucas lounging on the couch watching TV, with Cerberus and Mr. Whiskers dozing at their feet.

Alex couldn't help but smile seeing them laughing together so casually. After high-risk missions like tonight, he was glad his team knew how to unwind and enjoy lighter moments between the darkness. It spoke to the bonds of trust they had forged.

"Honey, I'm home," Alex announced jokingly as he entered.

The three men looked over in surprise. Marcus gave a casual salute from where he was sprawled on the recliner. "Yo bossman. How'd it go after we cleared out?"

Alex sighed, running a hand through his hair. "Dead end unfortunately. But drake had given us some useful information as to where they are storing Moonblood."

Eryx's face fell in disappointment. Alex knew how much his boyfriend hated seeing him take on his more frightening Hades aspects.

Alex leaned down to give Eryx a reassuring kiss. "Don't worry about me, I'm fine. All part of the job, even if I don't like it either."

Marcus and Lucas seemed to sense the couple wanted privacy, and bid their goodbyes for the night. After they left, Eryx asked Alex to recount the full events back at base.

Alex recapped the failed interrogation and soul magic ritual as best he could. Eryx listened solemnly, clearly troubled but trying not to show it.

"I'm sorry you had to resort to those extremes," Eryx said quietly when Alex had finished. "I know how much you hate revealing that side of yourself."

Alex gave Eryx's hand a grateful squeeze. His boyfriend knew him so well. "I'll do whatever's necessary to stop this threat, even embrace the darkness if I must. But having your light to guide me makes any struggle bearable."

Eryx gifted him with a radiant smile that never failed to lift Alex's spirits. "Then I'll just have to stick close and keep shining it for you."

Alex chuckled. "Much appreciated, my own personal superstar." He leaned in for a lingering kiss, the stress of the night easing. As long as he had Eryx's support, he could weather any storm.

"Come on, let's head to bed," Alex suggested gently. "You still need rest, doctor's orders."

Eryx laughed. "Only if the fur babies can join us. I think they got used to snuggling tonight."

The hellhound and cat perked up at their names. Scooping them up, Alex and Eryx retired to the bedroom. Safe in each other's arms, the horrors of the day seemed distant. Moments like this made everything worth fighting for. Alex knew as long as they stood united, the light would endure, no matter how fiercely the shadows raged.

9

Rescue

Eryx

"Are you sure this is the place?" Alex asked skeptically as the team stood at the entrance to a shadowy tunnel underneath New York City.

They were following up on the lead from Drake about the hidden Moonblood production facility. Gabe had spent days deciphering old city plans and utility maps to pinpoint this abandoned service tunnel that supposedly led to a vast underground warehouse.

Eryx eyed the dark, crumbling passageway uneasily. "So what exactly are we looking for down here?"

Alex turned to him, the glow of his conjured hellfire casting ominous shadows across his face. "Drake mentioned a massive underground labyrinth only the inner circle could access. If that's true, this tunnel should take us right to their main Moonblood production hub."

Kneeling down, Alex wrenched open the rusted manhole cover sealing the tunnel entrance. "Let's move quickly and quietly. Be ready for anything."

One by one, they descended the ladder into the oppressive gloom.

Eryx suppressed a shudder as his feet hit the wet stone floor, his enhanced senses overwhelmed. The fetid air was thick with the scent of decay and the incessant dripping of water echoed eerily off the walls. This place radiated wrongness - a creeping, visceral unease that raised his hackles.

As the group moved forward with Gabe navigating and Alex close behind him, Emma bumped Eryx's shoulder lightly. "So, why's tall, dark, and broody extra brooding today?" she asked teasingly.

Eryx chuckled, keeping his voice low. "Oh, Cerberus and Mr. Whiskers woke him up early by playing tug-of-war with the bedsheets. And we forgot to buy coffee."

"A grumpy Alex is a scary Alex," Olivia remarked from up ahead.

Marcus shuddered dramatically. "Remember that time we used the last of the French Roast? I thought he was gonna banish us all to the Fields of Punishment."

"I can hear you all back there," Alex said flatly, which only made the group stifle more laughter.

They continued down the crumbling tunnel, the oppressive atmosphere seeming to press down on them from all sides. Eryx tried not to show it, but he was starting to feel seriously claustrophobic. Their heavy tactical gear, weapons, and equipment didn't make moving any easier in the confined space either.

Still, Eryx didn't voice any complaint. He needed to appear strong and capable on this mission, both for the sake of the team and Alex. This is what he had signed up for, after all. A little discomfort was nothing compared to their goal of stopping the Moonblood conspiracy.

After what felt like hours of walking, Gabe held up a hand signaling them to stop.

"This should be it," he announced grimly. But as they shone their lights around, there was nothing except more tunnel.

Gabe paced the area, brow furrowed in concentration. "The warehouse is here, but it's warded. I can feel the magic." He began weaving a counter-spell, but quickly looked frustrated.

"What's wrong?" Alex asked tersely.

"These wards are too powerful," Gabe admitted. "Crafted using dark blood magic, if I had to guess. My countermeasures can't penetrate them."

Eryx spoke up hesitantly. "Is there another way we could break through?" All eyes turned to him, and he had to resist shrinking under the scrutiny.

Gabe pondered a moment, then nodded. "Your soulbound magic could theoretically overpower these wards. If you can channel the full divine force of Apollo's essence."

Eryx glanced at Alex, who gave him an encouraging look and took Eryx's weapons for him. Steeling himself, Eryx stepped forward and closed his eyes, trying to focus inward and harness his magic as Apollo had taught him.

He could feel energy humming through his veins, growing hotter as he tapped into his supernatural reserves. His hands began glowing with vibrant golden light, wisps of solar power curling around his fingers. The very air seemed to shimmer with building heat.

Opening his eyes, Eryx asked Gabe, "Point me to where the ward starts." Gabe indicated a section of blank tunnel wall. Nodding, Eryx placed both incandescent palms against the stones. Instantly the rock face began glowing as Eryx's purifying magic met the dark enchantments woven through it.

Beads of sweat formed on Eryx's brow from the exertion as he fought to overload the wards. The light around his hands intensified into miniature suns, pouring pure energy into the barrier.

Just when Eryx thought he couldn't channel any more power, the ward spell suddenly shattered with a resounding crack. Blinding illumination erupted through the tunnel as the concealment magic was destroyed. Eryx shielded his eyes as the walls seemed to vaporize, revealing a vast warehouse interior sprawling before them at last.

Panting, Eryx lowered his steaming hands, head spinning from tapping so deeply into his capabilities. He started as Alex gripped his shoulder supportively.

"You did it," Alex said, pride in his voice. "I knew you had this strength in you."

Eryx managed a tired smile. "All in a day's work for your friendly neighborhood magical Apollo vessel."

After breaching the concealed entrance, Alex turned to the team, expression hard. "Weapons ready. Move in quiet and careful - no telling what we'll find inside."

Guns raised, they infiltrated the mysterious warehouse slowly. Despite mentally bracing himself, Eryx was unprepared for the sight that awaited them. Endless rows of crates and boxes stretched into the gloomy distance, all branded with the now-familiar moon emblem of the drug ring.

"My gods," Olivia whispered. "There's enough Moonblood here to dose the whole city for years."

They moved cautiously between the stacks, hypervigilant for threats. The space seemed deserted, but loaded forklifts and scattered tools suggested recent activity. Up ahead, Eryx noticed figures shuffling listlessly as if in a stupor, paying them no mind.

"What's wrong with them?" Olivia questioned sharply, weapon trained on the oblivious workers.

Emma's eyes narrowed in focus. "They seem to be under some heavy-duty enchantment. I'm betting it keeps them docile and compliant."

Alex turned to her urgently. "Any way you can break them out of it?"

"I can try a counter-spell," Emma replied, already weaving delicate sigils in the air toward the entranced group.

"Watch her back," Alex told Marcus and Lucas tersely. "Eryx, you're with me. We need to see how far this stockpile goes."

Leaving Emma under their guard, Alex and Eryx continued exploring the endless shelves filled with the dangerous contraband. After several minutes, Lily's voice crackled over comms.

"Alex, something down here is blocking my remote access to the facility's systems. I can't get eyes or schematics on the full layout." Her frustration was evident.

"Keep trying," Alex responded. "Let us know if you break through."

Eryx kept one eye on their twisting path, wary of being caught off guard. Coming upon an unmarked steel door, he carefully tried the handle. It swung open freely, revealing pitch darkness beyond.

Switching on the light affixed to his rifle, Eryx edged inside what appeared to be a small prison block. He gagged at the overpowering stench of bodily waste and coppery blood. Makeshift cells lined the walls…and it was clear this was no ordinary jail.

Eryx's stomach turned imagining what sick 'experiments' had happened here under the cover of darkness. Panning the light, he saw most cells were empty…until his breath caught spotting a huddled figure in the back corner.

Approaching cautiously, Eryx saw it was a teen boy dressed only in tattered underwear, curled up and trembling. "Alex - I've got someone locked up back here," Eryx relayed through comms urgently.

Holstering his weapon, Eryx crouched outside the cell door. "Hey, it's okay," he soothed. "I'm here to help."

The boy flinched back at his approach, eyes wide and luminous with tears…or possibly blood. Eryx's heart ached seeing the trauma and fear in one so young. What horrors had he endured at his captor's hands?

"My name's Eryx," he continued gently. "I'm getting you out of this place."

The teen lifted his head warily. "Z-Zac," he whispered hesitantly. "But…they're coming…"

Before Eryx could respond, icy fingers grabbed his shoulder and flung him savagely against the far wall. Dazed, Eryx looked up to see a hulking vampire looming over him, fangs bared in a feral snarl.

"Shouldn't have come here, hero," the vampire growled. "Now you die."

Eryx grabbed his gun and opened fire at the attacking vampire. But strangely, the tranq bullets had no effect on the snarling bloodsucker. Something unusual was going on here.

With bullets ineffective, Eryx stowed his weapon and launched himself at the vampire bare-handed. Maybe old-fashioned brute force could take this freak down.

The vampire easily sidestepped Eryx's punch with preternatural speed, chuckling darkly. "Is that really the best you can do, hero? I'm just getting warmed up."

Eryx gritted his teeth, circling the vampire cautiously. He knew he could blast this thing away with his magic…but he was trying to avoid relying solely on his supernatural gifts. After all, sometimes a good solid punch worked wonders.

Putting his combat training to work, Eryx feinted left then swept low, trying to off-balance the vampire. But his opponent saw through the maneuver, countering with a vicious backhand that sent Eryx crashing into a shelf, scattering boxes of Moonblood.

Wiping blood from his mouth, Eryx struggled upright. The vampire was impossibly strong and fast - it was like his abilities were chemically enhanced somehow. Eryx wished Alex would show up…he could really use the backup right about now.

In a blur, the vampire closed in and seized Eryx by the throat, lifting him effortlessly. "Is this the best the you can muster? Pathetic," he sneered.

Just as Eryx's vision started to tunnel from lack of air, the vampire suddenly released him with an agonized scream. Eryx sagged to the floor gasping as his attacker collapsed convulsing, blood leaking from his eyes and ears.

Looking up, Eryx saw Zac standing unsteadily outside his cell, one trembling hand outstretched. The boy's eyes rolled back as he passed out from the strain.

Eryx lunged forward and caught Zac's limp body before he could hit the ground. Cradling the unconscious boy, Eryx staggered out of the room - right into a frantic Alex rushing in.

"What the hell happened?" Alex demanded, eyes quickly scanning Eryx for injuries.

"I'll explain later, but we need to get this kid out of here," Eryx urged.

Alex's gaze softened seeing the traumatized Zac in Eryx's arms. "Right. Let's move." He helped support the boy's weight as they hurried back the way they'd come.

Alex and Eryx hurried back toward the others, Zac's limp form supported between them. As they went, Alex tapped his comms. "Gabe, Olivia - report. Did you find anything useful?"

Olivia responded tersely, sounds of rummaging in the background. "Looks like some kind of lab area. Grabbing samples and research notes to analyze back at base."

"Good. Meet us at the tunnel entrance ASAP," Alex instructed.

They soon reached Emma, Lucas and Marcus just as Emma slumped back, sweat beading her brow as she tried unsuccessfully to break the workers from their enchantment.

Alex gripped her shoulder. "Enough, you're exhausting yourself. Whatever magic did this is too powerful." Emma nodded reluctantly, clearly frustrated at her failure.

Eryx's gaze swept the warehouse floor. His eyes widened as he spotted a shadowy figure watching them from atop a stack of crates, casually twirling a cane. Before Eryx could react, the mystery man vanished.

"We need to move, now," Eryx urged Alex tersely. "I think whoever's behind this knows we're here."

No sooner had he spoken than the entranced workers' heads snapped toward them in unison, their expressions morphing into unnatural rage. Eryx's gut twisted. Their escape just got a lot more complicated.

"Marcus, get the kid out of here!" Alex barked. Marcus scooped up Zac and sprinted for the exit.

Weapons raised, the rest tried to hold off the oncoming horde, but quickly found themselves overwhelmed. Eryx fired round after useless round while Alex slashed through vampires with hellfire blades. But there were too many.

Olivia and Gabe arrived from their scouting to find the chaotic scene. Taking in things quickly, Olivia began hurling fiery bolts to thin the enraged crowd.

Eryx found himself tossed painfully to the floor yet again. Looking up, he spotted the mystery man from earlier sauntering casually through the battlefield toward him.

"You have something I want," the man purred, foul magic crackling at his fingers. "Hand over the boy your friend took, and I'll consider letting you leave alive."

Eryx conjured a glowing lance, leveling it shakily. "Over my dead body."

The man sighed in annoyance, then vanished as Eryx's lightbeam speared the spot where he'd stood. They were out of time - Eryx turned to Alex desperately. "We need to burn this place to contain them!"

Alex's expression hardened, but he gave a terse nod. Olivia unleashed a torrent of fiery magic, igniting the Moonblood saturating the warehouse. Gabe quickly shielded their escape route as they sprinted for the tunnels.

They finally spilled out onto the street, singed and exhausted. Alex gripped Eryx's shoulder, face lined with worry. "Are you hurt? Who was that man?"

Eryx shook his head grimly. "No injuries. But that seemed to be whoever's behind this whole operation. We clearly just threw a wrench in their plans if they showed up personally." He met Alex's eyes. "We have a lot to figure out."

Back at headquarters, Eryx hurried to find Marcus in the briefing room with Lily. "How's the kid? Is Zac alright?" he asked urgently.

Marcus nodded. "Finn's got him isolated in the infirmary. Running tests and trying to flush the Moonblood from his system."

Eryx sagged in relief. After all Zac suffered, at least he was safely out of enemy hands now. Alex wrapped an arm around Eryx in wordless support, grounding him.

Once assembled, Alex addressed the team seriously. "We need to analyze everything we learned on this mission. Lily, what've you got?"

"I managed to hack into their systems briefly while you were inside," Lily reported. "Found plans referencing several other hidden facilities we can target next."

Alex turned to Lucas. "Work with Lily to pinpoint locations. We need to hit them hard and fast before word spreads about what happened today." Lucas agreed readily.

"Gabe, Olivia - what did you grab from their lab area?" Alex asked next.

Gabe gestured to a case they'd brought back. "Chemical samples, research data, hard drives. If there's a formula for Moonblood or the process used to engineer it, we'll find it."

Alex nodded approvingly, then prompted Eryx. "And you mentioned something about enhanced vampires?"

Eryx quickly recounted the strange attack, the vampire's immunity to tranqs and abnormal speed and strength. "You're right, they seem to be experimenting with some sort of super-soldier formula. But there was something different about Zac..."

He explained how Zac single-handedly took down the vampire. "I think there's a reason they kept Zac prisoner. Something special about him they were exploiting."

Alex frowned deeply. "This is worse than we realized then. Weaponized, chemically-enhanced vampires could make the chaos Moonblood's already causing seem tame." His expression hardened with resolve. "But now we know who we're up against. And we'll be ready for them."

After the debrief, Eryx turned to Lucas urgently. "Can you dig up anything on Zac? Relatives, where he's from?."

Lucas's fingers flew across the keyboard. "On it. I'll see what I can find."

Alex drew Eryx aside with a concerned look. "How are you holding up? Really?"

Eryx started to shrug it off, then slumped a bit. "Honestly? What I saw down there is gonna haunt me. The cells, the experiments…it was bad, Alex."

Alex gripped his shoulders supportively. "I know this is eating you up. But thanks to you, Zac's safe now. We have to trust Finn to take care of him. And we'll make sure whoever did this pays."

Eryx managed a small grateful smile. No matter how bleak things got, Alex always reassured him.

Lucas called them back over. "Okay, found his records. Zac Felton, seventeen. Been in the foster system since he was a baby, moved around a lot. Reported missing a couple months back."

Eryx's heart clenched, imagining how alone Zac must feel. "We should stay with him when he wakes up. Kid's got no one right now."

Alex nodded understandingly. Through their soulbond, Eryx could feel his fierce protectiveness toward Zac stirring already.

In the medical wing, they looked through the observation window at Zac's unconscious form hooked up to various machines. Finn soon emerged, looking weary.

"How is he, doc?" Eryx asked worriedly.

"I managed to purge the drugs from his system, but there's extensive damage," Finn reported. "He's stable for now, but it's a waiting game until he regains consciousness."

Alex frowned contemplatively. "Any idea why the Moonblood didn't drive him into a frenzy like the others when he was captive?"

Finn sighed. "There's something in his blood chemistry resisting the effects. Could be his latent magic at work, though the nature of it remains unclear."

Eryx tensed anxiously. "He's just a kid. What could they have wanted with him?"

"We'll get answers when he wakes, don't worry," Finn assured gently.

After requesting to stay by Zac's side when he wakened, Eryx and Alex headed off. Alex turned his focus back to the mission.

"Did you find anything useful from the Moonblood sample Gabe retrieved previously?" he asked.

Finn nodded slowly. "Traces of dark energy woven through it - which would explain its potency and dangerous qualities. But I am still trying to see if there's more at work."

"We found more samples from the facility," Alex told him. "Get what you can from analyzing those as well. Anything could be a breakthrough."

Finn agreed, then sighed grimly. "On another note, the sorcerer's body continues deteriorating. Chances of revival for questioning are slim now."

Alex's jaw tightened, clearly frustrated by the setback. "Keep me updated regardless. We need answers."

After finalizing details with Finn, Alex turned to Eryx. "Let's head home and regroup. It's been a long day."

Eryx was more than ready to leave the stresses of the mission behind for the evening. But as they approached their apartment door, his senses prickled - something was off. Unlocking it cautiously, they found the interior untouched, but a figure was lounging on their couch petting a content Cerberus and Mr. Whiskers.

Eryx tensed until the man looked over at them casually, his regal features and immaculate suit instantly recognizable.

"Winston," Alex growled. "To what do we owe the intrusion?"

Zeus, currently going by Winston Thorne, smiled genially. "Can't I see how my son and my brother are faring? And we need to talk."

10

Godly Visit

Alex

Alex tensed as Winston turned to Eryx. "Hello, son."

In an instant, Alex felt a seismic shift through his soulbond with Eryx. His partner's eyes flashed crystalline blue, his posture changing subtly. Alex realized with a start that Winston's 'son' was now Apollo.

"*Father*," Eryx replied calmly. *"It's been some time."*

Alex was taken aback by the gentle smile Winston gave his divine child. It was an expression of such sincerity that the often harsh deity rarely showed.

"Too long, unfortunately," Winston agreed wistfully. "But I'm here with a warning - you are running out of time." His gaze darkened. "There are larger forces at work than you realize."

Alex stepped forward angrily. "You have the audacity to come here and tell us that we are running out of time when you're the one asking for our help."

He felt his infernal aura flicker dangerously. But Eryx placed a steadying hand on his arm, soothing his ire through their bond.

"Peace, both of you," he mediated gently. *"Shouting and blame will solve nothing now. Let's talk civilly so we might understand Father's purpose here."*

Winston gave Eryx an appraising look. "You've matured, son. Your human has been a good influence it seems."

Alex bristled at the term but remained silent as Winston continued. "But prolonging possession will drain your host. Best let him regain control."

"Of course, Father," Eryx acquiesced. His eyes flashed back to blue as Eryx returned. He sagged a bit, disoriented.

Alex was there instantly, supporting Eryx and guiding him into a chair. Their hands entwined, Alex focused intently on Winston.

"Enough vagueness. What do you know about this Absalom's body being missing from the fifth hell? And why keep us in the dark until now when time's allegedly running out?" Anger simmered beneath Alex's words.

Winston's perpetual smile faded. "We thought it mere rumor at first, dismissed by the one who brought it to my attention."

Alex's eyes narrowed, suspicion dawning. "Let me guess…Dolos told you about this, didn't he?"

At Winston's solemn nod, Eryx looked between them confusedly. "I'm sorry, who's Dolos?"

"An infuriating trickster god with a penchant for causing chaos," Alex explained derisively.

Winston sighed. "And who now languishes in Tartarus for threatening Ganymede as collateral in exchange for information." His eyes flashed warningly. "No one endangers him without consequence."

Alex was well aware of Winston's extreme protectiveness toward the beautiful mortal youth Ganymede. But he couldn't resist poking a bit.

"Out of curiosity, how's your wife dealing with you fawning over your male cupbearer so much lately?" Alex questioned, raising an eyebrow. "Can't imagine she's thrilled at how much attention you give your young lover."

A flicker of irritation crossed Winston's features at the mention of his notoriously jealous spouse. "My relationship with Ganymede is none of Hera's business. I won't tolerate her taking out her frustration on him."

His fist tightened briefly on his cane. "Ganymede simply serves as my cupbearer. Any rumors of something more are nonsense." But there was a defensive edge to Winston's tone that suggested otherwise.

Things clicked into place for Alex. "So that's why you imprisoned him. But Dolos clearly knew more than you realized if this Absalom threat proves real." He met Winston's gaze unflinchingly. "Thanatos told me that Dolos wants out of Tartarus in exchange for what he knows"

Winston didn't deny it. "Troublesome as he is, the trickster has his uses. But I cannot act directly to free him.

Alex felt his anger rising. "Bullshit. You're the one who tossed him in Tartarus in the first place. So why the hell can't you bust him out yourself?"

Winston turned, expression grave. "Because that would violate Olympian laws, laws I am bound by even as King."

"Oh cut the crap," Alex snapped. "You made those damn laws and break them whenever you damn well please. What's the real reason you can't free Dolos yourself?"

Winston stepped toward the window, gazing broodingly at the sprawling cityscape. "While Morvain had me imprisoned during the war, he syphoned a portion of my cosmic essence to release Kronos from his eternal jail."

Winston held up a hand, faint sparks dancing across his fingers. "My divine power has not fully regenerated since. I cannot descend to Tartarus now without revealing that vulnerability." His tone held thinly-veiled frustration.

Eryx looked puzzled by this revelation. "Wait, so is Kronos still free somewhere then? I thought all the myths said he was locked away."

Alex met his boyfriend's curious gaze. "We never got full clarity on what happened to Kronos or Morvain after the war ended. Their current whereabouts are a mystery."

He turned back to Winston. "But now at least we know why you refuse to get directly involved here. You're still weakened, and your pride won't allow that to become common knowledge."

Winston inclined his head in acknowledgement. "Indeed. So you see the necessity of discreetly retrieving Dolos in my stead." His penetrating eyes bored into them. "By any means necessary."

Alex crossed his arms. "Then you better tell us exactly what we're walking into down there. No more half-truths if you want our help."

If Winston wouldn't confront this threat personally, then Alex would drag the details out of him piece by bloody piece.

A question from Eryx interrupted his brooding. "Don't you rule over Tartarus though? Being King of the Underworld and all?"

Alex sighed. "I govern parts of the realm, yes. But Tartarus has never fallen under my domain. He's more than a prison - Tartarus is an ancient primordial deity, like Kronos."

Alex met Eryx's gaze. "Entering his domain won't be a simple stroll. It's exceptionally dangerous."

Eryx's jaw set stubbornly. "Then I'm definitely going with you. My abilities could help."

"Absolutely not," Alex refuted heatedly. "I won't allow you anywhere near that place."

"You can't just bench me, Alex!" Eryx argued, frustration bleeding through their bond. "We talked about you trying to sideline me like some damsel in distress."

Alex struggled to rein in his temper. "This isn't about your ego. Tartarus could obliterate your soul without even trying! Just because Apollo's hitched a ride doesn't make you invincible."

"I never claimed that," Eryx shot back. "But I won't sit helpless on the sidelines either when I can lend my powers to this fight."

Before Alex could unleash the tirade on the tip of his tongue, Winston stepped in. "The boy is right, Alex. You'll need his light to safely traverse Tartarus." Winston gave Eryx an appraising look. "He may surprise you."

Alex ground his teeth, warring irritation and anxiety battling it out. "I'll consider it," he bit out reluctantly. "But first, tell us what we'll face down there, assuming I agree to this madness."

Winston nodded. "It will be difficult, certainly. But remember - only united do we stand a chance against the rising darkness." His gaze was heavy with meaning. "Allies can be found even in the unlikeliest places, if you know where to look."

Alex exhaled irritably. "Fine, enough mystical crap. Just tell us plainly - what do we need to get Dolos out of Tartarus?"

Winston turned solemn. "You'll require a key fashioned by Hephaestus, capable of opening any lock or barrier between realms. But crafting it necessitates...potent components."

Eryx looked uneasy. "What kind of components are we talking about here?"

Alex continued brooding, anxiety gnawing at him over Eryx insisting on this suicidal quest. But they needed results, regardless of the risk.

"To forge the key, you will need my blood..." Winston materialized a glowing vial, "...and the Stormcaller's Essence." He placed the vial carefully in Eryx's hand.

Eryx examined the divine fluid curiously. "So why's a bit of your blood so important exactly?"

Alex shook his head. "You can't fathom the immense power contained in a deity's life-force. Our blood doesn't work the same as mortals' - it's near-sentient cosmic energy."

He met Eryx's eyes intently. "Guard that vial with your life. In the wrong hands, even a drop of Winston's blood could yield catastrophic power."

Eryx nodded, tucking the vial away securely. "Got it. And what's this storm essence we need?"

Winston answered solemnly, "A substance drawn from the heart of a celestial tempest - holding the raw might of the heavens within it. Our brother Poseidon alone can summon such storms."

Alex dragged a hand down his face. "Fat chance of Poseidon gifting us a bit of his precious storm magic. He's notoriously possessive of his 'toys'."

But Winston looked undeterred. "Then you must convince him, by any means necessary. The fate of this city depends on it."

Alex stood abruptly. "Assuming I even agree to take Eryx on this lunatic quest, we've clearly got our work cut out for us." He started pacing, mind racing.

"Hey, take a breath," Eryx said gently, stopping Alex's frenetic movements with a touch. "We'll figure this out together. We can do anything - you've said so yourself."

Looking into Eryx's earnest eyes, Alex felt his anxiety dial down slightly. As daunting as their task appeared, Eryx's faith never wavered. And Alex knew that kind of light could illuminate even the blackest pits of hell.

Winston fixed them both with a stern look as he prepared to depart. "I have granted what aid I can by providing my blood. But I must caution you - the trickster god Dolos is not to be trusted. He sows chaos wherever he treads."

His eyes flashed dangerously. "If you insist on pursuing this path, be on your guard. Dolos will seek to manipulate you for his own designs."

"We're well aware of his reputation," Alex replied. "But if he truly knows anything about this Absalom threat, we have to try."

Winston shook his head resignedly. "So be it. Just know I cannot intervene should things go awry. This quest ventures beyond my sight." He leveled a heavy gaze at Alex. "Keep each other safe. You will need all your combined strength."

Alex met Winston's stare unflinchingly. "We can handle ourselves. Wouldn't be the first time we stared down danger."

Still, unease stirred within him. They knew well the tricks and cunning Dolos was capable of. Outfoxing the fox would be no easy feat.

With a final solemn nod, Winston stepped back and was consumed by a crackling portal. The scent of ozone lingered even after the magical gateway vanished.

Alex sighed wearily once the king of gods had departed. "Well, that was suitably ominous. At least we have a direction now, vague as it might be."

He met Eryx's eyes. "Whatever comes next, we do this together. Promise me that much at least?"

Eryx smiled and pulled Alex close. "Always."

They shared a quick kiss, drawing strength from each other for the challenges ahead. Then Eryx's stomach rumbled loudly, breaking the heavy mood.

Once he was gone, Eryx tossed Alex the precious vial of godly blood. "Here, better keep this somewhere safe." He stretched casually. "So, pizza sound good? I'm starving."

Alex just looked at Eryx for a beat, then huffed a laugh. Trust his boyfriend to effortlessly puncture tense moods. It was one of the countless things Alex adored about him.

"You read my mind," Alex said, tucking away the vial securely. "Half pepperoni, half pineapple right? Even if fruit on pizza offends me deeply."

Eryx grinned unrepentantly. "Hey, don't knock it til you try it! The sweet and savory combo is amazing."

Alex just shook his head, smiling. While waiting for the delivery, they took Cereberus out for a quick walk. The fresh air helped clear Alex's buzzing thoughts.

As they strolled hand in hand, Eryx gave him a sidelong look. "So… have you decided if you'll let me go with you on this quest yet?"

Alex tensed slightly. "I'm still not convinced it's a good idea. Tartarus is perilous even for me."

"You keep saying how powerful our bond makes us together though," Eryx countered. "Shouldn't we face challenges as a team?"

"This isn't just some challenge, it's a bloody deathtrap!" Alex snapped. Seeing Eryx's hurt expression, he reined in his temper. "I can't lose you," he said quietly.

Eryx's gaze softened. He twined their fingers together. "You won't. Have a little faith in me…in us."

Looking into Eryx's hopeful eyes, Alex felt his reservations wavering. His instinct was to protect, but he knew Eryx needed to find his own strength.

"I'll consider it," Alex conceded reluctantly. "Just promise me you'll be careful down there if I agree."

Eryx smiled brightly. "Always am. We've got this!"

Alex wished he shared Eryx's confidence. But his boyfriend's luminous optimism had pulled him through darker times before. Together, he knew they could weather any storm.

Back home, they dug into the pizza while watching TV, Eryx eventually dozing off on Alex's shoulder.

Alex gently lifted Eryx in his arms, carrying him towards their bedroom. Eryx's body felt warm against his chest, and Alex couldn't help but admire his boyfriend's beauty. As he laid Eryx on the bed, his eyes traced the contours of Eryx's body, appreciating every curve and muscle.

With a mischievous smile, Alex began to undress Eryx, slowly removing each piece of clothing with a teasing touch. As each layer fell away, revealing more of Eryx's naked form, Alex's anticipation grew. There was a raw hunger in his eyes, a primal desire to connect with his lover on a deeper level.

As they moved together, their bodies entwined, Alex let himself get lost in the sensations. It began with a gentle tenderness, their lips softly exploring each other's skin, their hands caressing and teasing every sensitive spot. The air in the room grew heavy with desire, their moans and whispers filling the space

Alex could feel the intensity of their desire building, the heat between them rising with each passing moment. Their bodies moved with an urgency, a hunger that consumed them both. The room was filled with the sounds of their moans and the rhythmic creaking of the bed beneath them, a symphony of their carnal desires.

With a mischievous glint in his eyes, Alex's hand reached for the drawer beside the bed, revealing an array of toys and restraints. Eryx's eyes widened with a mix of excitement and trust, his body trembling in anticipation. The air crackled with electricity as they both knew they were about to venture into uncharted territory.

"I've got something special in mind for you tonight," Alex purred, his voice dripping with desire. "Are you ready to be my willing plaything?"

Eryx's breath hitched, his voice filled with a mix of anticipation and submission. "Yes, Alex. I trust you completely. Show me what you've got."

A wicked grin spread across Alex's face as he selected a silky blindfold from the drawer. He gently secured it over Eryx's eyes, plunging him into a world of heightened sensations and anticipation.

Eryx's heartbeat quickened, his body trembling with a delicious mixture of excitement and vulnerability.

"Feel my touch, Eryx," Alex whispered, his voice a sultry caress. "Every stroke, every kiss, will be intensified by the absence of sight. You'll surrender completely to the pleasure I give you."

As the blindfold heightened Eryx's senses, Alex's hands began to explore every inch of his lover's body. Fingers trailed along heated skin, leaving trails of goosebumps in their wake. Lips followed, leaving a trail of searing kisses and nibbles, igniting Eryx's desire even further.

Eryx's moans filled the room, his voice a symphony of pleasure and need. "Fuck, Alex! More, please. I need more of you."

With a wicked smirk, Alex reached for a set of restraints, securing Eryx's wrists to the bedposts. The sensation of being bound heightened Eryx's arousal, a mixture of vulnerability and trust coursing through his veins.

"Now you're completely at my mercy," Alex growled, his voice a delicious promise. "I'm going to take you to the edge, Eryx. I'm going to make you beg for release."

Eryx's body arched, straining against the restraints as Alex's mouth descended on his most sensitive areas. The combination of pleasure and helplessness sent shockwaves of ecstasy through his body, his cries of pleasure mingling with the sound of the bed protesting beneath them.

The intensity of their connection grew with each passing moment, a fiery bond formed through their shared exploration. Every touch, every whispered command, brought them closer to the edge of oblivion. They were lost in a world of pleasure, their inhibitions discarded as they surrendered to their primal desires.

As they reached the peak of ecstasy, their cries of pleasure filled the room, a symphony of raw passion. The release washed over them, leaving them breathless and sated, their bodies trembling with the aftermath of their shared bliss.

Alex gently removed the blindfold, revealing Eryx's dazed, blissful expression. Their eyes met, a spark of satisfaction passing between them.

"You're incredible, Eryx," Alex murmured, his voice filled with awe. "Thank you for trusting me, for allowing me to explore these depths of pleasure with you."

Eryx's lips curled into a satisfied smile. "I trust you completely, Alex. You always push us to new heights, and I'm forever grateful for that."

With their bodies intertwined, they held each other close, basking in the afterglow of their passionate encounter.

Alex gazed down at Eryx's sleeping face, feeling emotions no words could fully capture swelling in his chest. Moments like this together in blissful afterglow were treasures beyond price to him.

Brushing back a lock of Eryx's hair, Alex marveled that this brilliant firebrand of a man could unravel his ancient spirit so completely. For eons he believed himself fated to eternal loneliness on his accursed throne.

Yet this defiant mortal had slipped past every barrier like they weren't even there, awakening feelings inside Alex he'd forgotten he was capable of. Because Eryx saw him as more than the grim Lord of the Underworld - he saw the man still inside.

Here in their haven away from ever-present dangers, Alex drank in the gift of Eryx's presence. His light that filled Alex's days with joy and purpose again. His golden flame that made Alex feel human instead of a relic out of time.

Alex pressed a soft kiss to Eryx's brow and whispered ancient oaths - vows to brave any darkness and fight any foe to keep Eryx's precious light safe. Because it wasn't just Eryx, but also the soul of Apollo residing within him, that Alex swore to protect.

Their path ahead was shrouded in uncertainty, but Alex didn't fear what lay in store. Through any storm, fire or war, they would walk it together. No sinister force could extinguish a spark as bright and enduring as the dawn.

Eyes growing heavy, Alex curled around Eryx, sharing breath and heartbeat. And though sleep still eluded his immortal spirit, just having his beloved near lulled Alex's mind into blessed tranquility.

11

Taking in Strays

Eryx

Eryx fidgeted in the minimalist waiting area, anticipation and unease warring within him. He wasn't sure what to expect from the formidable Themis.

Alex's words from that morning echoed through his mind.

"Don't let her sharp tongue or piercing stare shake you. Themis takes some getting used to, but there's no one better at spotting contractual tricks and trapdoors." Alex said before he left that morning.

Eryx snorted. "Gee, that's reassuring. Should I bring a shield and helmet too?"

Alex had given him a crooked smile. "Nah, she won't actually smite you. But don't fold either. Stand your ground respectfully. Impress that upon her and you'll be fine."

The office door opened taking him out of his thoughts and a slender man in an impeccable suit gestured for Eryx to enter. "Ms. Themis will see you now."

Eryx followed him into the office, his eyes widening. The space was lavish bordering on gaudy, with white and gold furnishings that seemed at odds with the sleek hall. Seated regally behind a massive golden desk was Themis. Eryx's breath caught at her beauty - smooth dark skin contrasted strikingly with her pale suit and the bright surroundings.

She gazed at him neutrally and he had to suppress a sudden urge to squirm under that penetrating stare. "Please have a seat Mr. Ross."

Eryx sat slowly, thrown by her pleasant tone. He had expected to be raked over the coals, not greeted cordially.

Themis graced him with a hint of a smile. "It's lovely to finally meet Apollo's newest vessel. You've caused quite the stir."

Eryx felt himself flush, the designation still feeling utterly bizarre to him. "Uh, thanks. But really it's still just me - Eryx."

Themis inclined her head. "My apologies. What brings you to my office today?"

Eryx retrieved the contract from his bag. "I was hoping you could review this employment contract? Alex thought it would be wise but didn't specify any concerns."

Themis accepted the document. As she scanned it Eryx added awkwardly, "Alex also mentioned you can be rather…intimidating."

Themis glanced up, eyes glinting with humor. "Let me guess, he warned you to be wary of me?"

Eryx rubbed his neck self-consciously. "Essentially, yes."

Themis chuckled. "Alex means well but he does have a penchant for dramatic pronouncements."

She focused on the contract while Eryx studied her office. Despite the almost aggressive opulence, he detected notes of Themis' personality. The view of the city skyline, the discreet picture of three young women - her daughters perhaps? It lent warmth to the space.

"Well," Themis finally announced. "This contract contains some concerning ambiguities but nothing legally alarming. I would still advise reviewing it carefully and negotiating clearer terms around compensation and intellectual property rights."

She slid the document back to Eryx along with a sheet covered in red pen scribbles.

Eryx blinked at the copious notes. "That was fast. And thorough - thank you."

"Of course. I'm happy to help anytime." Themis templed her fingers. "So, how are you adjusting to hosting Apollo?"

Eryx exhaled heavily, leaning back. "Honestly? It's weird. I'm slowly getting a handle on these new abilities but having another consciousness lurking in my mind? Beyond bizarre."

"I'd imagine so." Sympathy flickered across Themis' face. "The gods can be rather…capricious. But for what it's worth, Apollo chose well in you."

Eryx flushed again. "I wish I had your confidence. Alex is endlessly patient but I still feel like the clumsiest, most clueless vessel ever."

"Give it time," Themis advised gently. "Gods have always expected mortals to adapt swiftly to their immense power. Unreasonable if you ask me. Be kind to yourself - this great destiny was thrust upon you and mistakes are inevitable. Focus on learning one step at a time."

"I know, I know," Eryx sighed, running a hand through his hair in frustration. "It's just…I feel like I'm drowning trying to harness these insane cosmic powers inside me. One moment I'll nail some intricate light weaving spell and the next I accidentally set something on fire because I got distracted."

He let out a hollow laugh. "Hell, yesterday I fried my toaster when I was just trying to make breakfast. My poor neighbors probably think I'm a hazard to society at this point."

Themis made a sympathetic noise. "It certainly sounds over-whelming. But you must remember - no mortal is born inherently understanding the intricacies of wielding divine magic."

She leaned forward, capturing his gaze with her dark, soulful eyes.

"I have witnessed many a vessel struggle in your shoes. Some never manage to fully control their volatile new abilities. Others are driven mad by the forces they harbored."

Eryx paled at that, panic constricting his chest. Themis reached over and grasped his hand firmly.

"Peace, Eryx. What I am saying is that what you describe - the chaotic outbursts, the wild fluctuations in skill - it is all perfectly normal at your stage. With time and teaching, you will gain competence and confidence."

Her stern expression softened. "Most importantly, remember that you need not walk this path alone. Mysteries and magic can be trying teachers - let your mortal allies support you through the difficult lessons."

Eryx nodded slowly, gratitude and relief swirling within him. Perhaps he had been too quick to pigeonhole Themis as an intimidating force to be wary of. Her razor wit was balanced by genuine wisdom and empathy.

"I really appreciate you taking the time, Themis," he said earnestly. "You've given me a lot to think about...and helped ease my worries. I guess I better work on being kinder to myself."

Themis graced him with a brilliant smile. "Excellent. And do come to me anytime you need counsel or simply a sympathetic ear." She leaned back, regarding him fondly. "I must say, after speaking with you myself, I can see why Apollo would choose you even if his methods leave something to be desired."

"About that..." Eryx rubbed the back of his neck awkwardly. "I don't want to give the impression that Apollo is forcing me into things against my will. Everything I've done - agreeing to be his vessel, joining Alex to investigate magical threats - those were all my choices."

He met Themis' thoughtful gaze. "I'd be lying if I said this power isn't scary sometimes. Or that having a god in my head doesn't freak me out on occasion." Eryx gave a wry half-smile. "But despite his flair for the dramatic, Apollo has let me retain free will. The decisions are still mine…for better or worse."

Something almost like pride flickered in Themis' ageless eyes. "I am pleased to hear that. Still, I imagine it is no easy path Apollo has set you on by awakening such formidable magic within you." Her tone gentled. "My central point remains - be patient with yourself. And do not be afraid to seek aid when the mysteries become too heavy a burden to bear alone."

Eryx left her office feeling lighter than he had in weeks, her sagacious words still ringing in his thoughts. Perhaps Alex had been right after all.

After the meeting with Themis, Eryx slid on his shades and cap on the way to his car, hoping to avoid recognition. Ever since publicly resurfacing as Apollo's vessel he'd been hounded relentlessly by paparazzi and tabloids. He grimaced remembering Alex's logical but annoying argument about needing his own wheels to escape the media vultures. Eryx still preferred the subway, but he had to admit having a quick getaway option was nice.

When he pulled up outside Eternity Records he sighed, spotting the cluster of photographers loitering near the entrance. "Damn bloodsuckers," he muttered. No way was he running that stalker gauntlet.

He called the front desk for a workaround. "Hey Carrie, bit of a situation out front - any magic employee entrances to slip me in unseen?"

"Rear parking lot has a basement entrance," came the cheerful reply. "I'll buzz you into the underground garage."

Eryx thanked her and maneuvered towards the back, gratified when the metal gate lifted automatically. He took the elevator up and soon found himself outside Brad's new corner office. After a perfunctory knock Eryx stepped inside to find his new manager shuffling paperwork.

Eryx entered to find Brad seated behind an imposing mahogany desk, impeccably dressed in a sharp suit as he reviewed documents. Brad set his pen down and folded his hands, regarding Eryx coolly. "Mr. Ross, so good of you to stop by. Please have a seat."

As Eryx settled into the leather chair, Brad continued in polished, businesslike tones, "I trust you come bearing the signed contract?"

Eryx flashed a lopsided smile, retrieving the annotated documents from his messenger bag. "Freshly reviewed by a very thorough consultant who gave her legal blessings."

Brad nodded. "Excellent. My legal team will verify everything is in order."

"What's the plan moving forward though? PR-wise I mean."

His gaze sharpened. "Now, going forward it is imperative we handle your public exposure delicately but decisively to mitigate further media harassment. I am scheduling a brief, lowkey press conference to announce your partnership with Eternity Records. You'll give a short statement and answer a handful of questions."

Eryx exhaled slowly. "Yeah I get it. Rip the bandaid, give the vultures some fresh meat so I can actually focus on making music." He smiled wryly. "I don't love it but no pain no gain right? Just don't throw me naked on that PR altar huh?"

Seeing Eryx's grimace, Brad raised a conciliatory hand. "Believe me, I understand such spectacle grates on artistic temperament. However, this morsel will divert the wretched vultures as you focus on your creative endeavors." He permitted himself a tight smile. "Do you find these terms acceptable?"

Eryx inclined his head. "Very prudent strategy. I appreciate you limiting the media melee so I can concentrate on my music unimpeded."

"Excellent. My assistant will forward the conference specifics shortly so mark your calendar." Brad stood, extending his hand. "A pleasure finalizing our partnership, Mr. Ross. I look forward to an auspicious collaboration."

Eryx slid into his car, the leather seats still holding the day's warmth as he fired up the engine. He synced his phone and dialed Alex, the call connecting to his earpiece as he pulled onto the street.

"How'd it go with hurricane Themis and the label?" Alex asked wryly by way of greeting.

Eryx huffed a laugh as he drove. "Really well actually. Themis wasn't nearly as intense as you made out. She seemed almost..." He grasped for the right word. "Nurturing? Gave me some really solid advice about going easy on myself with all these new abilities."

He heard Alex make a vaguely disgruntled sound. "What, no verbal evisceration or icy glare of doom?"

"Dude, she was super thoughtful and understanding - you made her sound like some strict mother figure but reality was the total opposite."

Alex grunted. "Well aren't you teacher's pet. Glad she went easy on you at least."

Eryx just chuckled, coasting up to a red light. As he idled he caught a figure in the side mirror snapping photos of his car. "Ah hell, paparazzo at six o'clock," he bit out angrily. Of course the vultures had tracked him. "Gotta shake this leech, talk soon."

"Watch your six," Alex returned sharply before disconnecting.

The purr of the motorcycle grated on Eryx's nerves as the paparazzo tailed him relentlessly through winding backstreets. His frustration mounting, he decided it was time to lose his unwelcome shadow.

As they coasted toward an intersection, Eryx summoned a glimmering orb of light, imbuing it with a scattering spell. With a flick of his fingers he sent the shimmering bubble gliding into the path of the oncoming bike. It burst in a blinding flash and the photographer swerved with a cry, distracted.

Seizing the opening, Eryx raised a sound barrier across the road behind him and accelerated away, tires squealing. Weaving between vehicles, he tuned out the dopplering wail of his pursuer's engine with a thought, muffling it to silence.

At the next turn he spun suddenly to face the wrong way, his car now invisible. With vicious satisfaction he watched the disoriented bloodsucker roar past, unable to track his vanished quarry.

He watched in the mirror with vindictive satisfaction as the photographer circled in confusion before roaring away. "Let's see you chase a ghost, jackass," Eryx muttered.

The stunt had brought him near the Shadowguard's concealed headquarters. He slipped into an alley, dismissing the glamour before pulling into their underground lot. As an extra precaution he extended his senses, but his unseen pursuer seemed to have abandoned the hunt.

Eryx's stomach rumbled loudly as he locked up. Spotting the time, he realized he'd missed lunch during the eventful day. Dion's diner Crave was only a few blocks over - surely the team was hungry too. He shot Dion a quick text as he walked. He got a response back saying the he was not in today and just give it to his assistant.

As Eryx approached the counter, his phone lit up with Alex's number. "Hey there," he greeted. "I'm just getting food, figured you all could use fuel…"

"Appreciate the thought but need you back here now," Alex interrupted, tone oddly gentle. "Zac's awake."

Eryx nearly dropped the phone. Heart suddenly hammering, he managed to confirm he was on his way before scribbling the lunch order absently. Zac was conscious. After days of worrying, not knowing if he would pull through.

Eryx strode quickly into the Shadowguard's lobby, the smell of takeout burgers and fries in hand. Marcus seemed to materialize, relieving him of the food before he could speak.

"Alex is with the doc in the med wing," Marcus supplied, anticipating Eryx's question. "They're prepping Zac as we speak." He flashed a daring grin. "I'll get these set up in the bullpen for when you guys wrap. But no promises I won't sneak a few fries in the meantime."

Eryx clapped his shoulder with mock sternness. "Guard that grub with your life. Our young pal probably hasn't had a decent meal in ages." A cloud passed over his face as he considered how Zac must be feeling. Shaking it off, he headed for the elevators.

Stepping out into the sterile hall of the med bay ratcheted Eryx's nerves tighter. He realized his hands were shaking faintly as he approached Zac's room. Pausing outside the door, he drew in a slow breath, bracing himself before pushing inside.

Alex and Dr Sloan stood conversing over the bed where Zac was propped against pillows. Hearing the door, Zac glanced over, his wan face brightening in recognition. "It's you," he said warmly.

Eryx moved closer, relieved by the clarity and life in those eyes, so different from their previous glassy sheen. "Told you I'd help. How ya holding up Zac?"

The kid shrugged his bony shoulders. "Still foggy I guess. But way better without all those wicked shadows messing with my head."

Alex wrapped an arm around Eryx, regarding Zac solemnly. "We can't express how glad we are you pulled through. It was touch and go for awhile according to the good doctor here."

"Oh absolutely, quite dire when you first arrived," Dr Sloan added seriously. "But your resilience is truly extraordinary young man."

Zac looked down, abashed. "I really can't thank you all enough for, y'know, saving my life. Didn't expect anyone to give a crap honestly…" He trailed off, wringing the bedsheet nervously. When he glanced back up, his eyes glistened. "Seriously though, how can I repay you?"

Eryx's heart clenched at the lost, lonely look on Zac's face. He flashed what he hoped was a reassuring smile. "No repayment needed, just focus on recovering your strength." He hesitated briefly before adding gently, "You're welcome to crash with us awhile if you want."

"Oh I couldn't..." Zac began but Alex cut him off.

"We insist. Once Doc gives the all clear, mi casa es su casa."

Doc Sloan nodded. "His vitals check out remarkably well given the ordeal. All traces of Moonblood are gone too but I'm still puzzling out what gifts he harbors." He gave Zac an encouraging wink. "No rush unlocking those secrets though."

Eryx squeezed Zac's shoulder. "What happened is still fuzzy for you I bet. We're happy to listen when you're ready."

Zac nodded slowly. "Yeah maybe, someday. It's all too much right now. But thank you, truly. I'd love to not be alone."

His shy, grateful smile made Eryx's throat tighten. No one so young should feel so isolated. He and Alex shared a resolute look - they would make damn sure this extraordinary kid felt safe and supported from here on out.

The rest of the day passed uneventfully - no new intel or rumblings on the Order's movements to be found. After debriefing with the team, Eryx felt frustration gnawing at his gut. Whatever the fanatics were scheming, the lack of chatter put him on edge.

When Dr. Sloan cleared Zac for release from the medical ward, it was a welcome distraction. They found him some spare clothes and shoes in the storeroom before heading home.

As they entered the apartment, the patter of paws heralded Cerberus and Mr. Whiskers arrival. Both pets immediately flocked to Zac, tails wagging eagerly at the newcomer. Zac's wan face lit up as he crouched, laughing softly while stroking their fur.

Eryx and Alex exchanged a pleased smile at the tender scene - animals were excellent judges of character after all. This shy, gentle kid was undoubtedly worth protecting.

After giving Zac a brief tour, they showed him the cozy guest room. "Home sweet home, at least for now," Alex said lightly. "Holler if you need anything, 'kay?"

Zac hovered uncertainly in the doorway. "I really can't thank you guys enough for all this. Feels too good to be true if I'm honest." He scraped a hand through his shaggy hair, not quite meeting their eyes. "I'll try not to be a hassle."

Eryx's chest clenched hearing Zac automatically put himself down. He placed a hand on his shoulder. "You're no hassle man, just focus on getting your feet back under you." He hesitated then asked gently, "Does it feel good to be somewhere secure?"

Zac's hesitant nod and whispered "yeah" told Eryx volumes about how seldom he'd had stability. With a final squeeze, they left him to rest.

Padding quietly into the living room, Eryx scrubbed both hands down his face before glancing sidelong at Alex. "This mystery gets more concerning. What the hell did they put him through that leaving him terrified to accept kindness?"

Alex exhaled heavily. "Whatever it was, clearly traumatic enough to make him feel undeserving of care." His eyes darkened, a spark of hellfire in their depths. "Mark my words though, the who hurt him will regret harming that innocent soul."

Eryx grimaced, images of Zac's scars and tattoos swimming behind his eyes. "No question. Thing is why him specifically? What made Zac their target?" He met Alex's troubled gaze. "You think it involves the strange magic in his blood?"

"Seems likely." Alex crossed his arms. "Could be they hoped to replicate it or exploit his power somehow. Either way..." His expression grew thunderous. "They'll never lay another damned finger on him."

Eryx nodded firmly. After surviving hell itself, Zac deserved better than to fear his gift being twisted against his will. They would shelter him until he healed enough to decide his own path.

12

Confusing Evidence

Alex

Alex's eyes fluttered open, the morning sunlight casting a warm glow across the room. As he slowly regained consciousness, he became aware of Eryx's lips wrapped around his hardened length, his mouth moving with practiced skill. Waves of pleasure washed over Alex, his body responding eagerly to the intimate attention.

A low groan of pleasure escaped Alex's lips as he ran his fingers through Eryx's hair, gently guiding him, urging him to take more. The sensation of Eryx's warm mouth and skilled tongue working their magic elicited a pleasurable ache deep within him. It was a delicious way to wake up, a carnal invitation to indulge in the pleasures of the flesh.

Eryx's lips moved with an expert's touch, his tongue swirling around the sensitive head, drawing forth moans of pleasure from Alex's lips. The intensity of their connection was palpable, a testament to the trust and desire they shared.

"Oh, fuck," Alex gasped, his voice laced with desire. "Don't stop,

Eryx. Just like that."

Eryx's mouth continued its ministrations, his movements becoming more urgent as he sought to bring Alex to the brink of ecstasy. The sound of their mingled moans filled the room, their shared desire echoing off the walls.

Alex's hips instinctively bucked into Eryx's mouth, seeking more of that incredible pleasure. The tension in his body coiled tighter with each passing moment, his release building like a tidal wave ready to crash over him.

As Eryx skillfully worked him towards the edge, Alex's grip on the sheets tightened, his body trembling with need. Pleasure surged through him, radiating from the point where Eryx's mouth enveloped him, spreading throughout his entire being.

With a final, desperate thrust, Alex succumbed to the overwhelming pleasure, his body convulsing as he spilled his release into Eryx's waiting mouth. A guttural moan tore itself from his throat, a primal expression of his satisfaction and release.

As the waves of pleasure subsided, Alex's body relaxed, his breathing slowly returning to normal. Eryx gently released him, a satisfied smile playing on his lips as he crawled back up the bed to lie beside Alex.

"You are incredible," Alex whispered, his voice filled with a mixture of awe and gratitude. "Thank you for starting our day with such intense pleasure."

Eryx's eyes sparkled with affection as he snuggled closer, pressing a soft kiss to Alex's lips. "I live to please you, Alex."

Alex wrapped his arms around Eryx, pulling him into a loving embrace. The warmth of their bodies mingled, their connection deepening with each passing moment.

Alex told Eryx they needed to shower after their fun. He playfully tickled Eryx as he carried him into the bathroom. The warm water cascaded over them as they washed each other clean.

Once they finished showering and started drying off in their bedroom, Eryx turned to Alex, concern creasing his handsome face.

"So what's the plan for today?" he asked.

Alex sighed, running a hand through his damp, dark hair. "It's time for us to visit Poseidon. We need to get that last part to forge the celestial key."

Eryx's blue eyes widened in surprise. He finger-combed his golden blonde hair nervously. "The celestial key…you really think we're ready for that?"

"We have to be," Alex said grimly. "It's the only way to break Dolos out of Tartarus."

"You know we're going to have to tell the team about this eventually, right?" Eryx said.

Alex's jaw tightened. As much as he hated to admit it, Eryx was right. But the thought of putting the people he cared about in harm's way…it made Alex's gut twist with anxiety.

"I don't want to put them at risk," he said finally. "This is our burden to bear."

Eryx stepped closer, his hand coming up to cup Alex's stubbled cheek. "Like it or not, they're already at risk just by being associated with us. They deserve to know the truth."

Alex leaned into the touch, craving the comfort of his lover's warmth. He knew Eryx spoke wisely, but the protective instinct raging inside him recoiled at the notion.

"What about Zac?" Eryx asked gently. "He's just a kid. We can't involve him in this."

At the mention of their young psychic ward, Alex's eyes clouded with pain. The kid had been to hell and back already. Alex would die before letting him get hurt again.

"No," he said vehemently. "Zac's been through enough. I don't want him involved, at least not yet."

Eryx nodded, empathy shining in his eyes. He understood Alex's need to shield the innocent. "I'll call Ari and Dion, see if they can look after Zac while we're gone."

Alex let out a shaky breath, relief washing over him. At least Zac would be safe. He drew Eryx into a fierce embrace, holding him close. Eryx nuzzled Alex's neck, placing a gentle kiss on his skin.

"It's going to be ok," he murmured. "We'll figure this out together."

Alex clung to him like a lifeline, wishing he could freeze this moment forever. No matter what darkness lay ahead, with Eryx by his side, he could face anything.

After a long moment, he pulled back reluctantly. "Come on," he said gruffly. "Let's grab some breakfast first. We've got a long journey ahead."

Alex and Eryx headed to the kitchen to grab some breakfast before their journey. As Eryx cooked up eggs and bacon, Alex set the table and poured food for their pets.

The sound of a door opening made Alex turn. Down the stairs came Zac, still bleary-eyed from sleep. Mr. Whiskers and Cerberus rushed over, nearly tackling Alex in their eagerness to greet him. Alex laughed and gave them both affectionate scratches.

Zac hovered in the doorway uncertainly. Alex's heart went out to the kid. He'd been through hell at that illegal testing facility before they rescued him. Now more than ever, Zac needed the security of family. Alex was determined to give him that sense of belonging here.

"Morning Zac," Eryx called warmly. "Hungry?"

Zac nodded, shuffling over to help set the table. Alex and Eryx exchanged a proud parental look as the boy took initiative. In the short time he'd been with them, it was clear Zac yearned for guidance and purpose.

Once the food was ready, they sat down to eat. As they dug in, Eryx said gently, "Zac, we need to head out for work today. But don't worry, you'll have company - people here to get you anything you need."

Zac's eyes clouded with anxiety. "You're…leaving me?"

Alex's heart clenched. "Just for the day," he reassured. "And we'll be back before you know it."

"Why can't I come?" Zac asked plaintively.

Eryx shared a knowing look with Alex. They couldn't involve Zac in the dangers ahead. The kid had endured enough hardship already. But they needed a reason that would provide comfort.

"You're part of this family now," Eryx said warmly. "That means having a proper home and space of your own. We want to make sure you get settled in and feel at home here while we take care of some…business matters."

Zac ducked his head, a small smile tugging at his lips. Alex could tell the idea of belonging resonated deeply.

They had just finished eating when the doorbell rang. "That'll be your companions for today," Eryx said.

Zac followed them eagerly to the door. Eryx opened it to reveal Ari and Dion, who had agreed to watch over Zac.

"Where's the kid at?" Dion grinned, ruffling Zac's hair.

Zac wrinkled his nose. "I'm not a kid, I'm an adult." But there was no malice in his protest.

"How was your trip, Ari?" Eryx asked as she stepped inside.

"Tons of fun, but it's nice to be back." She smiled warmly at Zac. "Ready for a day of relaxation?"

Zac nodded, visibly relaxing in her calm presence. Alex felt a rush of gratitude - he could tell Zac would be in good hands.

"Call us if you need anything," Alex said as they prepared to leave. "And feel free to use the credit card to get Zac any supplies or things to make his space more comfortable."

Ari and Dion promised they would take good care of him. As Alex and Eryx headed out, he felt a pang leaving Zac behind. But this was for the best. The boy had endured enough hardship for one lifetime. Right now, more than anything, he deserved the simple joy of building a home. Alex would make sure he got that chance.

Alex and Eryx arrived at Shadowguard headquarters to find the team already gathered in the briefing room. As they took their seats, Alex's gaze swept over the familiar faces - Gabe, Lily, Lucas, Emma, Olivia. His trusted inner circle. But they couldn't know the full truth, not yet.

"Let's get started," Alex said. "Gabe, any updates on the Jane Doe case?"

Gabe leaned forward, expression grim. "I got a call from Leo. He found something in the body he wants us to look at ASAP."

Alex frowned. That didn't sound good. If the medical examiner was asking them to come examine a corpse in-person, it had to be significant.

"What about the Moonblood investigation?" he asked, turning to Lucas and Lily. "Any progress accessing the distribution network?"

Lily shook her head, frustration in her green eyes. "Their systems are heavily encrypted. We're close to cracking them but need more time."

"Keep at it," Alex said. "We need to cut off supply and destroy existing stock before this gets any worse."

Deadly addictive and unpredictable, Moonblood was wreaking havoc on the streets. Addicts were turning violent, even feral. If they couldn't stop the spread soon, the city would descend into chaos.

Alex looked to Olivia and Emma next. "Reach out to Elder Lucius, see if the vampires know anything useful. Discreetly."

They nodded. Vampire politics were complex - one wrong step could turn the reclusive covens against them. But they might know something about who was distributing this new menace. It was worth the risk of inquiries.

"I want you to take lead on operations today, Lily," Alex said finally.

Gabe frowned in surprise. "Why? Is something wrong?"

"Just have some personal business to deal with after we visit the morgue." Alex avoided his probing stare. "I'll fill you in soon, I promise."

Beside him, he felt Eryx shift restlessly. They couldn't keep deceiving their team much longer. But if Alex told them the truth it would only put them all at risk. Alex refused to let that happen.

Lily was watching him closely, eyes narrowed. Alex suppressed a wince. Yeah, he was definitely getting an earful from her later. Aside from Eryx, Lily was the only one who knew about Absalom's body. She wouldn't buy his excuses forever.

But for now, the team simply nodded, respecting Alex's judgement even if they didn't understand his motives. He was thankful for their trust, but hated misleading them, however necessary it might be.

Soon this would all be over, he told himself.

"Alright, let's get to work," Alex said gruffly, standing up. "We don't have any time to waste. Lives are depending on us."

As the rest of the team filed out to attend to their tasks, Eryx caught Alex's arm, concern in his blue eyes.

In truth, he was wound tight as a bowstring. The secrecy, the perilous quest ahead...it was taking its toll. But he refused to burden Eryx with his doubts. They had enough to worry about.

Once they were out of earshot, Lily grabbed Alex's arm, her piercing green eyes demanding answers.

"Alright, what's really going on?" she asked bluntly. "Don't make me force it out of you."

Alex sighed, knowing resistance was futile. "We're planning to meet with Poseidon. There's something we need from him."

Lily's eyes widened in alarm. "Poseidon? Why?"

"It's...complicated." Alex hesitated, but the determined glint in

Lily's eyes left no room for omission. Resigned, he quickly explained about Dolos' demands to Thanatos in exchange for information on Absalom's body.

As he spoke, fury boiled in Lily's gaze. "Let me get this straight - you made a deal to break someone out of Tartarus? Are you out of your mind?"

"We didn't have a choice," Eryx interjected gently. "Absalom poses too great a threat. We have to find his body before someone resurrects him."

"Even so, going to Tartarus is suicide!" Lily retorted. She grasped Alex's shoulders, fear cracking her voice. "You can't do this. I won't let you."

Alex met her fiery gaze steadily. "I have to. You know there's no other way."

Lily's hands slipped from his shoulders, resignation weighing down her frame. She knew better than anyone how duty compelled him down perilous paths. "Just...promise me you'll be careful. And call if you need backup." Her eyes shimmered with emotion. "We're family, Alex. We stand together, always."

Alex pulled her into a crushing embrace. However dark the road ahead, with his family beside him, he could face the shadows without fear.

"I promise," he rasped.

As they pulled back, Alex turned to more practical matters. "Any idea where we can find Poseidon?"

Lily considered a moment. "I'll have Marcus ask Hermes. As messenger of the gods, he'll likely know Poseidon's location."

Alex nodded. That was a good plan. Divine domains were often shifting, ephemeral things. Hermes kept track of who dwelled where.

"We'll meet him at the morgue," Alex decided. Neutral ground, and they needed to examine those strange markings again anyway.

"Stay safe," Lily implored, pulling them both into one last fierce embrace. "Watch each other's backs. And call me the instant you return."

Alex smiled gently. However ominous their quest, with Eryx guarding his back, he had nothing to fear.

"We'll be back before you know it," Eryx promised. His steady faith never failed to ground Alex against gathering storms.

In the car on the way to the morgue, Eryx glanced over at Alex, his brow furrowed with concern. "Hey, you doing okay?"

Alex gave him a tired smile. "Yeah, I'm alright. Just feel bad about keeping secrets from the team."

Eryx nodded sympathetically. The secrecy weighed on him too, he could feel it on their soulbond but it was necessary to protect everyone.

When they arrived, Leo greeted them cheerfully in the lobby. As Alex gave the medical examiner a warm hug, he was grateful for Leo's friendship. Ever since Leo started dating their medic Finn, he'd become like a brother.

"What did you need us to see?" Alex asked as they followed Leo deeper into the morgue.

"You'll understand when I show you the body," Leo said cryptically.

As they walked, Eryx asked, "So how are things going with Finn?"

Leo's face lit up at the mention of his boyfriend. "Really great. We're finally moving in together next week."

"That's awesome, congrats," Alex said, smiling. He was happy for them. Finn and Leo both deserved that joy.

They arrived at the cold chamber holding the supernatural corpses. Leo led them to the Jane Doe's body. As he prepped the exam table, he said, "Put on some protective gear before we get started."

Once they were all suited up, Leo slowly unzipped the black body bag, the sound harsh and jarring in the cold, sterile room. As the plastic folded back, the pale, lifeless face of the Jane Doe was revealed. Leo's latex-gloved hands moved with practiced precision as he examined the corpse lying prone before them.

Alex's gaze zeroed in on the ugly gashes torn across the front of her shirt. Despite the dark stains, the ragged edges were clearly visible. Claw marks. But from what sort of creature, he couldn't begin to guess.

Leo carefully shifted the tattered fabric, exposing the wounds underneath. "The cause of death was exsanguination, like I noted before." His voice was grim. "But here's the weird part…"

He held up a small glass vial, a Q-tip stained red inside. "This blood on her shirt didn't come from her body." Leo's brown eyes were clouded with frustration. "I already ran it through the database. No DNA matches found. This wasn't a shifter that attacked her."

Alex shared an uneasy look with Eryx. The lack of clues only deepened the mystery surrounding this victim. And mysteries had a way of turning deadly in their experience.

Leo moved down the body, indicating the deep, ragged furrows carved into the flesh just below her sternum. "No idea what could have left these marks," he said. "No traces of saliva, skin cells, or viable DNA recovered." He shook his head, lips pressed thin. "And magically, this body is clean. No traces of residual energy, forensic artifacts, nothing."

Alex could sense Leo's acute frustration. The lack of concrete evidence left them with no real leads. He squeezed the M.E.'s shoulder reassuringly. "You did good work," he said firmly. "get the swab sample to Gabe ASAP, see if he can match the blood."

But inwardly, Alex felt the same simmering unease. A dangerous supernatural was stalking the city, untraceable and unknown. They needed to identify the killer before the body count grew.

Having a rogue supernatural with unknown abilities running loose in their city was alarming, but at least it was a lead.

They said goodbye to Leo, who promised to call if anything else strange turned up. Back in the car, Alex gripped the vial tightly, his jaw set with determination.

"We need to crack this case soon," he said grimly. "I have a bad feeling things are escalating dangerous quickly."

"We will," Eryx assured him. "The team will analyze that blood sample and hopefully ID the killer. In the meantime, we focus on finding Absalom. One crisis at a time."

Alex nodded, trying to ignore his churning unease.

13

The Sea God

Alex

As Alex and Eryx stepped outside, they found Hermes casually leaning against their car, looking ready for a night out clubbing. Alex suppressed a smile - trust Hermes and his flashy fashion choices.

Hermes grinned widely when he saw them. "Hey guys!" He swept Eryx up in an enthusiastic hug.

"Good to see you, Hermes," Eryx chuckled.

Hermes turned to Alex next, quirking one dark eyebrow. "So, you wanted to see me?"

"I'm sure Zeus filled you in," Alex said wryly. Gods loved to gossip, after all. "We need you to take us to Poseidon right away."

At that, Hermes' playful demeanor vanished. He nodded solemnly. "Got it. Let's go then."

With a casual wave of his hand, Hermes opened a shimmering portal into the supernatural veil. As Alex stepped through, all his senses were instantly assaulted. The air felt thinner here, crackling with raw volatile magic that raised the hairs on his arms. The sky roiled

144

with unnatural streaks of color - sickly greens and purples bleeding together like a fresh bruise.

Alex peered downward and had to stifle a curse. Instead of stable earth, the ground writhed with inky tendrils of shadow, oozing between flashes of jagged rock. He quickly pulled his foot back as a smoky tendril reached for his boot.

"Careful where you step here," Hermes noted behind him. "Things are a bit less solid on this side of the veil."

Alex shot him a grim look. "I noticed."

He felt Eryx close the distance between them, posture tense and alert. Alex was grateful for his steady presence at his back. This was Eryx's first venture past the veil, and Alex could only imagine how unsettling the twisted landscape must seem to him.

Cautiously, they continued forward, avoiding the grasping wisps of darkness. Strange sounds echoed around them - distant shrieks and howls, the occasional bone-chilling scream. Alex forced down a shudder, gripping his celestial bronze dagger tighter.

As they moved through the volatile environment, Alex's senses strained for any sign of threats. His ears picked up the faint skittering of claws on stone, the heavy tread of footsteps just out of sight. Glowing eyes peered from the gloom before vanishing swiftly. The shadows here teemed with monsters, he realized, and kept his power simmering close beneath his skin, ready to unleash it.

"The veil is weaker," Alex observed with a frown. "What's causing it?"

Hermes' expression turned grim, his usual lightheartedness vanishing. "Ever since the war with Kronos, the boundaries have been wearing thin. Zeus and Nyx are trying to prevent a total collapse."

Alex's frown deepened at this news. As the former ruler of the underworld, the stability of cosmic barriers had been his responsibility. Why was he only just learning of the deterioration now?

Seeing his scowl, Hermes added reluctantly, "After you left the underworld, they assumed your...duties were finished."

Anger simmered in Alex's gut. And yet the gods still presumed to call on him for aid when they desired it. "How convenient for them," he muttered bitterly.

Eryx touched his arm, ocean-blue eyes gentle with sympathy. Alex knew his lover chafed at the callous machinations of the gods as much as he did.

"What does the veil normally look like?" Eryx asked Hermes curiously. "Before all this trouble started?"

Hermes gazed into the distance, his expression wistful. "It was the most breathtakingly beautiful thing I've ever seen. Shimmering there like a translucent curtain of light - every color you can imagine flowing and blending together."

Hermes' cadence took on a lyrical quality as he described it. " Gleaming strands of magic weaving in and out. Smooth and strong, but rippling like water in a gentle breeze." His eyes clouded with sorrow. "Now it's just tatters and mist, slowly unraveling at the seams."

"Can it be repaired?" Eryx's voice was low but urgent. If the veil failed, untold horrors would be unleashed into their world.

Hermes spread his hands helplessly. "I don't know. This has never happened before."

Alex squeezed Eryx's hand, attempting to project confidence. "We'll find a way," he promised roughly. As long as they stuck together, even this couldn't stop them.

Eryx gave him a small smile in return, but anxiety still lurked in his eyes. They both knew the terrible stakes now facing them all. Failure was not an option. The veil had to be repaired, no matter the cost.

Hermes clapped them both on the back. "We should get moving. Poseidon doesn't like to be kept waiting." His usual humor remained muted, the levity gone from his features.

Eryx shot him a sympathetic look. "Gods and family politics - so dysfunctional."

"You can say that again," Hermes sighed.

They continued on in pensive silence. Soon Hermes halted and waved open another shimmering portal. As they stepped through, the warm ocean air hit their faces. Alex scanned their surroundings - a small deserted island surrounded by endless blue waters.

"Where are we?" Eryx asked, squinting against the bright sun.

"Middle of the Atlantic," Hermes supplied. "This is the doorway to Poseidon's current domain."

"What took you guys so long? Lucas is about to combust from the heat," said a familiar voice behind them.

Alex whirled around in surprise to see his entire team standing there, with Lily at the forefront. How had they gotten here without him sensing it?

Lucas theatrically waved a hand in front of his face. "Why's it so bloody hot in here?"

Olivia smacked him upside the head. "We're in the middle of the Atlantic, idiot. Of course it's hot."

Bewildered, Alex turned questioningly to Hermes.

The god sighed. "I brought them here. They were very…persistent." He shot an amused glance at Marcus. "Couldn't say no."

Alex struggled to wrap his mind around this new development. He turned back to his team, shock and frustration seeping into his tone.

"What are you all doing here?"

Gabe stepped forward, muscular arms crossed over his chest. His stare bored into Alex's. "Lily told us everything. About the missing god, why you're really looking for Poseidon." His voice hardened. "Were you ever planning on letting us in on it?"

"I didn't want any of you getting hurt over a mess we gods created millennia ago," he said gruffly.

Emma moved to Gabe's side, compassion shining in her hazel eyes. She had always been the peacemaker among them. "Alex, you don't have to shelter us. Whatever the danger, we can face it together."

Alex looked away, emotions churning. He had lost too many people over his long existence to easily accept putting those he cared for in harm's way. But Emma's quiet words resonated deeply.

Marcus spoke up next, irreverent as always. "Come on boss, you really think we can't handle a little godly drama? We've been through worse crap than this."

Despite himself, Alex huffed a weak laugh. Marcus did have a talent for diffusing tension. The speedster's enthusiasm could be infectious.

Seeing his resolve wavering, Lily added gently, "We're a team, Alex. Nothing can break the bonds of trust between us. Not anymore." She clasped his shoulder, green eyes earnest. "Let us help fix this, together."

Alex's protests died on his lips. Gazing around at his friends - his family - united around him, he knew Lily spoke the truth. They had fought and bled beside each other. He could no more abandon them now than cut out his own heart.

"You're right," he admitted wearily. "We face this as one." Relief broke across their faces. Whatever came next, they would meet it together.

Alex turned to Eryx, who gave him a subtle nod of encouragement. Wise as ever, his lover had known Alex's barriers would crumble before their unwavering loyalty. Shored up by their support, he finally felt ready to confront Poseidon.

Hermes clapped a hand on Alex's shoulder. "Your faith in them is well placed," he said with a smile. "Together, nothing can stand against you."

Lily shot him a knowing look. "I had to tell them. Like it or not, they're a part of this."

Alex exhaled slowly. She was right. He met each of their earnest gazes in turn. "I'm sorry for keeping you in the shadows. I thought this wasn't your burden to bear."

Hermes clapped a hand on his shoulder. "Your intentions were good. But you can't fight what's coming alone." His ageless eyes were grave. "We stand together…or fall divided."

The truth of his words resonated through Alex. United with his found family, he could face any darkness.

Lucas broke the pensive silence. "Right, now that we're all on the same page - are we meeting a god or what?"

Alex huffed a laugh, trust and warmth filling his chest. However great the challenges ahead, with his team - his family - beside him, they would conquer it all.

He met Eryx's ocean blue gaze and saw his own resolve reflected there. Wordlessly they turned together, striding as one toward the cave entrance where Poseidon awaited. The trials to come would push them all to their limits. But the bonds between them were unbreakable now. Together, they could achieve anything.

Alex turned around to see a man rise from the sea, gripping a gleaming bronze spear.

"Lord Poseidon awaits you in his palace," the guard intoned gravely.

Alex exchanged a wary glance with Eryx, then nodded to the guard. "Very well. Take us to him."

He knew Poseidon resided in Atlantis, the mythical city he'd built centuries ago, now lost beneath the waves. Its location shifted constantly to avoid detection. Alex hadn't returned since Apollo's downfall, but with Eryx at his side, it seemed fitting to visit the hidden metropolis once more.

The guard thrust his spear down and the sea itself split open, waves peeling back to reveal a winding staircase of coral descending into blue depths.

"Subtle," Eryx muttered wryly.

Hermes chuckled. "Subtlety was never Poseidon's strong suit. He does love theatrics."

Alex had to agree. Among the gods, only Zeus surpassed Poseidon's flair for drama. With a shared look of amusement, they followed their guide down into the heart of the ocean.

As they emerged from the rocky tunnel, the sight before them made Alex's whole team gasp in awe - all except Lily, who had seen Atlantis before.

The fabled city sprawled out before them in a vast expanse, enclosed in shimmering domes of magical energy that held back the crushing pressure of the ocean above. Sleek towers carved from luminous coral and abalone shell rose up on all sides, glinting iridescent in the ambient light.

The lines of the buildings and streets were elegant but alien, following the sweeping curves of shells and nautilus chambers. Everywhere, azure glows and bioluminescent coral cast a soft aqua luminescence across the metropolis.

Looking up, Alex could glimpse sea life swimming far above them, mundane fish and even the occasional whale drifting through Poseidon's aqueous domain. The domes allowed visibility in and out of the sunken city.

As they walked deeper into the streets, the strange beauty and advanced technology of the place continued to astonish Alex's companions. Streets paved in mother-of-pearl were trafficked by silent vehicles that rode on frictionless bubbles of air.

Holograms flickered around architectural ornaments, translating from Atlantean into modern tongues for any visitors. Merfolk and other aquatically-adapted supernaturals went about their business, eyeing the group with distant curiosity.

"This place is incredible," Emma breathed, turning in a slow circle to take it all in.

Even jaded Lucas looked impressed, whistling under his breath. "Gotta say, Poseidon has some nice real estate here."

Their guide led them onward through marvels of cyclopean architecture and teeming undersea life. Alex drank it all in, memories of ages long past stirring. How long had it been since he walked this city as Hades, brother in arms with Poseidon? Ages upon ages…

At last they arrived at an opulent domed structure their guide identified as Poseidon's palace. Bioluminescent jellyfish and schools of angelfish drifted lazily around the ever-shifting exterior walls.

As the doors slid open, Alex steeled himself. Poseidon could be temperamental, with a penchant for drama and games. This visit likely wouldn't be easy, especially with Alex needing something from him.

But one look at Eryx's steady blue eyes, and Lily's calm strength beside him, bolstered his nerve. With his found family at his side, he could brave anything, even the sea god's legendary wrath.

As Alex's team entered the throne room, their footsteps echoed across gleaming marble floors, the stone swirled with pearlescent seashell patterns. Soaring arched ceilings towered overhead, adorned with elaborate mosaics depicting scenes of Poseidon's power - raging storms, clashing sea battles, fantastical aquatic creatures.

The hall was lit by azure glows pulsing from bioluminescent algae contained in intricate sconces along the walls. The light rippled across their faces, casting everything in an otherworldly aqua hue.

At the far end rose a magnificent conch shell made of lustrous abalone, towering at least twenty feet high. Its inner whorls had been sculpted into a seat, with steps leading up to the opulent shell-throne.

There, draped across the throne in studied nonchalance, lounged the sea god himself. Poseidon cut an imposing figure, bare-chested with a sculpted physique, a neatly-trimmed beard, and flowing dark hair decorated with strands of pearls.

His alert sea-green eyes tracked their approach, though he feigned boredom. The power coiled in his frame belied his relaxed pose. Alex could see the deceptive danger lurking beneath the surface, like a tiger shark waiting to strike.

As they drew near, Poseidon shifted, sitting upright. Power flowed off him in palpable waves as he took on the mien of an ancient god and mighty ruler. The theatrics were unnecessary but very much Poseidon's style.

Flanking his throne stood two hulking guards with fish-like features and webbed hands that clutched wickedly barbed spears. Their bulbous eyes watched the group warily, gills on their necks pulsing.

The throne room's opulence sought to impress visitors with grandeur and intimidate with implicit menace. But Alex wasn't swayed by such pageantry. He'd sparred with Poseidon before, knew both his pride and his unpredictability.

This negotiation required absolute focus. One misstep could turn the capricious sea god from ally to enemy in a heartbeat. Alex steeled himself, gesturing for his team to hang back. Only he could navigate these treacherous waters.

Lily and Eryx moved to flank him in silent support. Together, they approached the throne and the mercurial god awaiting them. Alex met Poseidon's assessing gaze evenly, refusing to be cowed.

Alex instructed the others to hang back - this negotiation was delicate, and he knew Poseidon of old. Only he, Eryx, and Lily would speak.

They approached the throne, and Poseidon's voice boomed out in greeting. "Brother! It's been too long since we met face to face." His smile was sharp as a shark's. "When Zeus told me of your visit, I was most intrigued."

Alex remained unruffled by the dramatics. "Then Zeus has informed you of the situation with Absalom's missing body."

Poseidon rose, closing the distance between them. "Indeed, most concerning news. I assume you've come seeking my aid in finding it?"

"Not exactly." Alex measured his words carefully. "There are details Zeus chose not to share with you."

One of Poseidon's eyebrows rose. "Oh? Do tell."

"We need access to the Leviathan's Stormcaller essence," Alex revealed bluntly. "Zeus claimed you alone know its location."

Poseidon looked thoughtful. "The Stormcaller's essence, you say… and did my dear brother happen to mention why you require such a thing?"

Alex resisted the urge to pinch his nose in exasperation. Trust Zeus to withhold vital context from his own brother. "We need it to forge the celestial key. In exchange for that key, Dolos will reveal the location of Absalom's corpse."

Comprehension dawned on Poseidon's face. "I see. Quite the tangled web my brother has woven. So like him to portray himself as hero against the coming darkness." His mouth twisted wryly.

Alex huffed in agreement. Zeus did love grandstanding at others' expense.

Poseidon turned his sea-green gaze on Lily next. "Persephone, still as lovely as ever in this life. Your new look suits you." Then his attention shifted to Eryx. "And you must be Alex's fated lover, former host of my nephew Apollo. An honor."

Alex bristled at the appraising look Poseidon gave Eryx, pulling his lover possessively close. After waiting so long to reunite with Eryx, he wasn't about to tolerate any covetous gods eyeing what was his.

"Can we focus on the task at hand?" Alex bit out tersely.

Poseidon held up his hands in a conciliatory gesture, though his eyes still danced with amusement. "Peace, brother. I mean no ill intent toward your mate." His expression turned serious once more. "Now, you seek the Stormcaller essence. Why should I grant you such a boon?"

Alex stood tall, holding the sea god's inscrutable gaze. "Without it, Absalom's resurrection is all but inevitable. You know as well as I the devastation he would unleash upon this world." He willed Poseidon to understand the urgency. "This is our one chance to stop him."

For long moments, Poseidon merely studied him and nodded. "The Leviathan protects the Stormcaller essence. You must prove yourselves worthy of wielding such might."

He slammed the butt of the trident on the marble floor. The sound reverberated through the hall like rolling thunder. "Pass the Leviathan's trials, and the essence shall be yours. Fail, and perish."

Alex silently cursed. Trust Poseidon to make this as difficult as possible. But they had no choice.

He met Lily's determined emerald gaze, then Eryx's stalwart blue one. Together, they would not fail, no matter the risks. The world depended on it.

"We accept your challenge," Alex proclaimed.

Poseidon's smile was fierce and wild. "Excellent." He crossed back to his throne. "My son Triton will escort you to the sacred caves. Prepare yourselves - the Leviathan shows no mercy to the unworthy."

With that ominous warning, he waved them away imperiously. Alex and his companions turned to follow Triton, who had entered silently, his expression grave.

The trials ahead would push them to their limits. But united, Alex knew they would prevail. The Stormcaller would be theirs, no matter the cost.

Too much depended on their success.

14

Leviathan

Eryx

Triton led them to the outskirts of Atlantis, then instructed everyone to pair up. With a wave of his hand, bubbles of shimmering air enveloped each pair, allowing them to breathe and move freely underwater.

Eryx took Alex's hand as they floated up, encased in the sphere. It felt solid around them, though slightly yielding to touch. Eryx peered at the glossy surface, mesmerized.

"You sure these bubbles are safe?" Lucas asked nervously as he rose inside his own alongside Olivia.

Triton flashed a roguish grin. "Completely safe. I make them all the time to impress sea nymphs." He waggled his eyebrows playfully.

Olivia made a disgusted sound. "Ugh, typical boastful male." But there was amusement in her tone rather than true annoyance.

"Hey, it works. The ladies find me irresistible," Triton said, puffing out his chest in mock bravado.

Emma laughed, the sound muffled inside her bubble with Gabe. "Considering you're half god, I'll bet they do."

Triton preened comically before turning serious once more. "Right, enough chatter. Let's dive."

He plunged into the ocean depths ahead of them, swimming with preternatural speed. Their bubbles trailed in his wake, propelled by some invisible force.

Eryx tightened his hold on Alex's hand as the ocean yawned below them. The bubble's glossy membrane flowed smoothly over his skin, allowing sensation but keeping the freezing water at bay. Magic thrummed through its every atom.

"Incredible," he marveled. "I can see why sea nymphs would find this romantic."

Alex chuckled. "Gods do know how to show off when courting." His thumb stroked Eryx's reassuringly. "But I'd take a nice dinner over this any day."

Eryx smiled. "Agreed. Candlelight and wine beat freezing ocean depths."

Eryx gasped as alien ocean scapes unfurled around them on all sides. Triton led them through forests of kelp swaying hypnotically in the currents, past spiraling manta rays and schools of neon fish. The ocean's beauty was breathtaking.

After what felt like hours of diving deeper, a rocky outcrop emerged from the gloom. Triton angled toward a cave entrance in the submerged cliffside. Hovering at its mouth, Eryx could make out huge stone doors etched with swirling glyphs that seemed to shift in the watery light.

"That's a big damn door," Lucas remarked. The rest of the team murmured in awed agreement.

Triton held out his hand, summoning his trident in a flash of blue light. The prongs glowed as he traced patterns in the water, mirroring the runes on the stone. In response, the massive doors trembled, then slowly swung open.

One by one they slipped inside, clicking on waterproof flashlights to pierce the darkness. Past the entrance, the cave opened up into a vast subterranean space. Triton led them upward through a tunnel until they emerged onto an island of rock surrounded by still black water.

As their bubbles popped, Eryx took a grateful breath of fresh air. "What is this place?" he asked Triton, peering around in wonder.

"The Abyssal Maw," Triton intoned grimly. "Where the souls of the damned come to be judged."

Eryx felt a chill race down his spine. For set being a place of judgment, it carried a palpable aura of malice.

"So who's doing the judging down here?" Marcus piped up.

Triton's smile was ominous. "The Leviathan itself. This way."

He set off down a jagged passageway, the shadows seeming to cling to him as he passed. Sharing an uneasy look with Alex, Eryx followed warily, their companions close behind.

The claustrophobic tunnel opened into a vast cavern, shrouded in gloom. Shapeless things skittered at its edges beyond the reach of their lights. The oppressive atmosphere magnified tenfold here - this place was ancient, and steeped in pain.

Then Eryx glimpsed it rising from the subterranean lake - a gigantic, undulating form, faintly glowing. Scales shifted across its hulking body as massive fins propelled it silently through the water. Two baleful eyes reflected their lights back like molten gold.

"The Leviathan," Triton pronounced grimly.

Eryx's mouth went dry as the monstrous creature rose from the black water. Every primal instinct screamed at him to flee. But they had come too far - the Stormcaller essence must be theirs.

The Leviathan's voice reverberated painfully inside his mind. "Who dares enter my domain?"

Triton stepped forward casually. "Oh, drop the dramatics, old man."

The Leviathan blinked in surprise, then chuckled. "Triton, my boy! What brings you here?" His demeanor transformed in an instant, no longer ominous but positively jovial.

Eryx shared a stunned look with the others. This was the terrifying monster meant to administer their deadly trials?

Triton jerked a thumb at them. "Brought some mortals seeking the Stormcaller essence. Dad sent them your way to prove themselves."

The Leviathan peered at them curiously. "Is that so?" He sank below the water, only to burst up right before them. Eryx jumped at the tremendous splash, gaping at the massive yet majestic creature.

"He's...beautiful," Eryx blurted without thinking.

The others looked at him askance, but the Leviathan let out a delighted laugh. "I like this one! Refreshing change from the usual cowering."

Hermes grinned and said fondly, "He's always been a big softie at heart. Scary when riled though."

The Leviathan shot Hermes a toothy smile. "Hermes! Been too long, my friend."

Before they could get further distracted, Alex stepped forward decisively. "Leviathan, please explain your trials so we may begin."

The creature focused once more on Alex, recognition dawning in his glowing eyes. "Hades. Very well." His voice took on a somber tone. "There will be three trials. Only three of you may participate - one per test."

His gaze shifted to Eryx, thoughtful. "However, I sense this young man may succeed where others would falter. He must face the final trial."

Alex immediately protested, but Eryx squeezed his hand reassuringly. "I can do this," he insisted. "Trust me."

Though reluctant, Alex nodded. Turning back to the Leviathan, he volunteered to take the first trial, and Lily the second. Eryx would face the last.

The Leviathan sank into the water, satisfied. "So it shall be. Prepare yourselves."

As Alex moved to the first starting point, Eryx pulled him into a fierce embrace. "Be careful," he implored.

Eryx watched as Alex stepped forward, squaring his shoulders. "I will face the first trial," he declared to the Leviathan.

The cavern rumbled, stones tearing free from the ground to form a ring. Alex moved into the makeshift arena as the Leviathan explained the rules.

"This trial will test the strength of your soul. Defeat my champion, and pass the first gate."

At his words, a hulking creature emerged opposite Alex, it's body rough stone given life. Jagged obsidian claws flexed eagerly as molten eyes fixed on Alex.

Eryx's chest tightened. He knew Alex could hold his own in combat, but this foe seemed formidable. All he could do was offer silent encouragement as the battle commenced.

Alex opened with a barrage of hellfire, but the blistering flames only seemed to anger the creature. It barreled forward, stone claws seeking Alex's vulnerable flesh. He barely managed to evade its grasp, tucking into a roll and coming up to drive his dagger at its flank.

But the blade merely chipped against the stony exterior. The thing was built like a tank. As it whirled with frightening speed, Alex only just avoided being disemboweled by those glassy claws.

Eryx could see him tiring - this battle was one of attrition, and Alex had already expended tremendous effort. As the creature pressed its advantage, horror clawed at Eryx's gut.

"Alex, you can do this!" he yelled desperately. But his lover was being forced back under the creature's merciless assault.

In that moment of despair, realization struck Eryx - this was a test of Alex's soul. An idea sparked. Closing his eyes, Eryx delved inward, using his soul bond to connect with Alex's essence. Warmth suffused him, along with steely strength.

Drawing on his power as Apollo's vessel, Eryx funneled a surge of energy along their link. "Use my strength," he called out to Alex. "We'll win this together!"

Across the arena, Alex's eyes suddenly blazed with golden fire. With a roar, he went on the offensive, celestial power exploding from his fists. The creature tried to recoil, but Alex pressed his advantage mercilessly.

With one last staggering blow, the stone behemoth crashed to the ground in pieces. The cavern shook with its defeat. As the dust settled, Alex stood tall amidst the rubble, chest heaving with exertion but unharmed.

Eryx let out a whoop of delight, pride and relief surging through him. Together, their souls were unstoppable. This was only the first trial, but Eryx now had faith they would conquer all of them.

The Leviathan nodded in approval as Alex rejoined Eryx. "Well done, Hades. You have passed the first trial."

Alex pulled Eryx into a fierce kiss. "I couldn't have done it without you," he said warmly when they parted. "On to the next trial."

Bolstered by Alex's success, Eryx turned to watch Lily stride forward for the second trial. Her green eyes were hard with determination as she stepped into the arena.

The Leviathan intoned, "This trial will test your fortitude and strength of will. You may not employ magic - only your mortal skills and spirit."

Lily handed her weapons to Gabe for safekeeping. "What must I do?"

"Defeat all of my champions, and you shall pass the gate." Ominous shapes began emerging from the shadows.

The trial commenced in a flurry of violence. Lily spun and struck like a viper, felling opponents with ruthless efficiency. Watching her, Eryx was reminded how deadly Persephone could be when roused.

But as the fight dragged on, the endless wave of foes began to take its toll. Eryx could see Lily tiring, her strikes coming slower, blocks more sluggish. It seemed the champions were draining her, siphoning away her vitality by proximity.

Eryx ached to intervene, but resisted. This was Lily's trial to pass or fail. So he cheered her on, willing his strength to bolster her flagging reserves.

Finally, only one opponent remained. Lily swayed on her feet, pushed to the brink of collapse. The demonic creature stalked toward her, anticipating an easy kill.

When it lunged, Eryx cried out, certain she was done for. But at the last second, Lily exploded into motion. With a primal scream, she unloaded every ounce of her remaining energy into a devastating series of blows.

The beast collapsed and lay still, its neck wrenched at an unnatural angle. Breathing hard, Lily shoved its carcass with her boot for good measure before turning to face the Leviathan.

Eryx whooped joyously, pride and awe swelling in his chest. Against all odds, Lily had triumphed through sheer force of will.

The Leviathan dipped his massive head in acknowledgment. "Well done. You have passed the second gate."

Gabe rushed to support Lily as she limped from the arena, clearly exhausted but radiant in her hard-won victory.

Now only Eryx's trial remained. As he stepped forward, Alex pulled him into a fierce embrace. "You've got this," he murmured. "I believe in you."

Filled with courage, Eryx turned to face his own test. With Alex's faith empowering him, he knew he would not falter, no matter what he faced. Side by side, they were unstoppable.

And he refused to fail when so much depended on their success.

The Leviathan's voice boomed out. "To pass the final gate, you must face me in combat. This will test your courage, young vessel."

Eryx tensed as the Leviathan issued his challenge. Beside him, Alex stepped forward angrily.

"That's absurd!" Alex protested. "Eryx is still mastering his power. How can you expect him to defeat a primordial deity?"

The Leviathan remained impassive. "What say you, vessel? Will you forfeit the trial and fail in your quest?"

Before Alex could argue further, Eryx placed a hand on his chest. "Alex, stop. I accept the challenge."

Alex gripped his shoulders urgently. "Eryx, think about this. You don't have to do it - we can find another way to get the essence."

Eryx met Alex's worried gaze calmly. "We both knew trials awaited us here. This is mine to face."

"But he's too strong, you could get hurt!" Alex insisted.

Eryx took Alex's hands in his own. "I know you want to protect me. But we're partners now - you need to trust me to handle things like this."

Alex looked tormented. Eryx could see the war within him - the desire to shield Eryx warring with respect for his autonomy.

"Please, Alex," Eryx implored. "Have faith in me. In us."

Alex closed his eyes, jaw clenched with tension. Eryx could sense him waging an internal battle between fear and trust. Finally Alex exhaled and met his gaze.

"I don't like it," he admitted. "But you're right. We're in this together now - I can't act like I need to shield you from everything."

He drew Eryx into a fierce embrace. "It goes against every instinct, but I do trust you. Just...be careful in there. Promise me."

Eryx hugged him back tightly, pride welling within him. Alex had come so far from the overprotective guardian deity he once was.

"I promise," Eryx murmured. "We'll get through this trial together."

Alex cupped his face and kissed him deeply. As they parted, Eryx saw faith and encouragement shining in Alex's eyes, bolstering his courage.

"I believe in you," Alex said. "Now go show that overgrown eel what you're made of."

Steeling himself, Eryx strode into the stone arena carved from the cavern floor. The cold dampness of the subterranean chamber seeped through his clothes, raising goosebumps on his skin. Across from him, the Leviathan slid smoothly over the rocks to enter the makeshift battleground.

Despite his bravado, Eryx's mouth went dry as the monstrous creature coiled before him. Every primal instinct screamed at him to flee from this apex predator. Its serpentine body was as thick around as an ancient oak, scaled hide shimmering in the ghostly light. Twin lambent eyes fixed on Eryx with predatory focus, reflecting his own nervous face back at him.

"To make this an even fight, I will not use my true form," the Leviathan rumbled. "But call on all your power, vessel - you will need it all to survive me."

Eryx steeled himself as the Leviathan began to shift, its body undulating sinuously. Ripples spread across its vast scaled hide as the creature started to shrink and change shape. Eryx glimpsed human features taking shape beneath the reptilian exterior.

The creature's giant serpentine head was the last to transform, jawline narrowing and eyes migrating to the front of its face. Flowing dark hair sprouted from its scalp, framing sharply defined features. With a final ripple across its body, the Leviathan settled into the shape of a towering man garbed in a simple kilt, hair spilling past broad shoulders.

Despite the human guise, power still crackled ominously around the deity. Eryx could feel it bearing down on him, pressing like an invisible weight. This was no mortal man he faced, but a divine being who had lived for eons uncounted.

The Leviathan flexed his arms, testing his borrowed human muscles. "Come, vessel," he commanded, beckoning Eryx forward. "Prove your might against me…if you dare."

Swallowing hard, Eryx sank into a fighting stance. Though his opponent now wore a human face, the primal aura of ancient malice remained unchanged. Those depthless eyes pinned Eryx in place, stripping away all pretense to expose the frightened human within.

This battle would push Eryx to his limits. But he refused to surrender or flee. Too much was at stake - he had to prevail, no matter the cost.

Closing his eyes, Eryx reached deep within, communing with the soul sharing his form. *Apollo, lend me your strength for this fight.*

The answering voice echoed from his depths, resonant and commanding. *I've been waiting for a chance to fight again. Let'go*

Eryx hurled twin orbs of golden fire at the Leviathan, then leapt forward, empowered fists wreathed in flames. But the deity easily batted aside the fireballs and evaded Eryx's reckless strikes, keeping his hands casually behind his back.

With a negligent swipe, the Leviathan backhanded Eryx across the arena. He hit the cavern wall hard enough to drive the breath from his lungs.

"Foolish boy," the Leviathan rumbled. "Rage and desperation will only lead to defeat." His fathomless eyes pinned Eryx in place. "You must focus. Channel Apollo's power - let your souls connect."

Eryx coughed, regaining his feet unsteadily. The Leviathan was right - he needed to fight smart. Impulsive attacks would never breach his opponent's defenses.

Closing his eyes, Eryx drew deep of Apollo's essence, feeling their spirits align. *Are you ready?*

The answering voice rang with conviction. *Let's show him what we're made of.*

Eryx's eyes snapped open, blazing with golden light. He raised his hands, harnessing the symphony of vibrations resonating through air, earth, and water. With a shout, he redirected them at the Leviathan in a visible ripple of force.

The blow landed squarely, and for the first time, surprise flashed across the Leviathan's face. He slid back several feet before bracing himself.

"Well struck!" He bared his teeth in a fierce grin. "But do not relent!"

The Leviathan summoned the power of the sea, walls of water crashing toward Eryx from all sides. Instinctively, Eryx wove a shield of vibrating air molecules, diverting the deadly waves around himself.

They clashed again and again, the chamber trembling with the force of their blows. Eryx struck with fists and blades of shimmering sound. The Leviathan answered with devastating tidal waves and spears of ice.

To Eryx's companions, it was a spectacle unlike any they had witnessed - two divine beings unleashing primordial forces fueled by courage and desperation. Blinding light warred with engulfing darkness, the arena fracturing under the punishing impacts.

Though tossed about like a rag doll, Eryx refused to yield. He channeled every ounce of Apollo's majesty, countering the Leviathan's wrath with razor-focused power.

At last, as Eryx deflected a lightning bolt aside, their eyes met in a brief moment of stillness. The Leviathan inclined his head in acknowledgement - this battle was a draw.

As both lowered their hands, the churning elemental power ebbed away. Eryx sank to his knees, utterly spent but elated. Together, they had fought a deity to a standstill.

The Leviathan studied Eryx with newfound respect. "Well done, vessel of Apollo. You have passed the final trial."

As the Leviathan pronounced them victorious, Eryx asked between labored breaths, "Was that…really necessary?"

The deity approached and grasped his hand in a powerful grip. "I wanted to see for myself if Apollo chose well. You have more than proven your worth, young vessel."

Alex rushed over and embraced Eryx fiercely. "I never doubted you for a second," he murmured, then kissed him hard.

Eryx laughed weakly. "Sure you didn't, old man." But he happily returned the embrace, pride and relief coursing through him.

He turned back to the Leviathan. "So what now? We passed your trials."

The deity inclined his head. "Behind me lies the final gate, and beyond it, the Tree of Essence. Take what you have earned."

The massive doors ground open. Inside lay a glowing tree, its branches heavy with shimmering fruit. Eryx's jaw dropped at the sight.

Reverently, Alex approached and plucked a single fruit, placing it in a pouch. "One essence - no more," he said gravely. Taking more could kill the tree.

"Well that was anticlimactic," Emma noted wryly. Eryx laughed, the tension breaking.

They made their way back through the twisting tunnels, the Leviathan and Triton escorting them. At the shoreline, Alex grasped Triton's arm. "Thank your father for us. And tell him he's welcome to visit New York soon."

Triton grinned. "I'll let him know. Safe travels, friends." With a final wave, he dove below the waves, heading home.

Alex turned to the group. "You all head back. Eryx and I have one last stop - we need the key forged."

Eryx took a deep, satisfied breath. "Hard to believe it's only been a day. Feels like we've been gone a week."

Alex smiled and laced their fingers together. "Time always gets distorted when gods and magic are involved." He gazed out at the fiery golden reflections on the calm water. "It is getting late though. We should keep moving if we want to make it to Hephaestus before nightfall."

Eryx nodded. "Right. Let's not waste any time." He turned to glance back at the closing portal, expression growing serious once more. "The hardest part is still ahead of us."

Alex squeezed his hand. "We knew going into this it wouldn't be easy. But we've faced the trials and won." Alex met his eyes, resolve shining in his own. "Together, we can handle anything they throw at us next. We'll free Dolos and get the answers we need."

15

Celestial Key

Alex

Back in New York, Alex and Eryx headed to their house to check on Zac. Entering quietly, they found Ari, Dion, Zac, and the pets all asleep on the couches.

Alex shut the door firmly, the sound jarring after the muffled silence of the empty house. He watched as the group stirred from their naps, blinking sleepily. A warm feeling rose in his chest at the domestic sight. After the chaos of the day's trials, coming home to this simple peace meant everything.

Ari and Dion yawned, peering at Alex and Eryx in puzzlement. "Hey, you're back! How'd it go?" Ari asked, her voice still raspy with sleep.

Eryx smiled, his handsome face softening. "We can catch up over some tea before heading out again. I'll explain everything." His ocean-blue eyes were bright with triumph, and Alex felt a surge of pride. Together, they had conquered every obstacle so far.

"Where are you going now? Can I come?" Zac asked eagerly.

Alex ruffled Zac's damp hair, marveling at how quickly he had come to care for this orphaned teen. "We're visiting an old friend," he explained. "You're welcome to join us if you'd like."

Zac's whole face lit up at the invitation, and Alex felt his heart swell. After all Zac's hardships, seeing him so openly enthusiastic and engaged was profoundly gratifying.

As Zac rushed off to get ready, Alex followed Eryx into the cozy kitchen, the scent of brewing tea leaves enveloping him. He leaned back against the smooth marble counter, letting the familiar environment ground him. After the chaos and danger of the day's trials, simply being home felt soothing.

Dion tilted his head, studying Alex and Eryx with sharp eyes. "So where exactly did you two disappear to earlier?"

Eryx hesitated, uncertainty furrowing his brow. "I didn't know if we should share the details..."

Alex waved a hand reassuringly. "It's fine, I'll catch them up." Taking a deep breath, he quickly explained everything - Absalom's missing body, the ominous meeting with Dolos, and the harrowing trials they'd faced in Atlantis. Saying it all aloud made their quest feel even more dire and monumental.

Ari let out a low whistle, her eyes wide. "You guys don't do anything by halves, huh?" She shook her head ruefully. "So much happening while I was away!"

"What can we do to help?" Dion asked earnestly, ever stalwart and loyal. Alex felt a rush of gratitude for his steadfast friend.

"For now, just helping us with Zac is enough," Alex answered after considering a moment. "The kid needs stability and safety. This is the first real home he's had."

Ari smiled fondly. "He's such a sweet boy, if a bit shy still." Her voice held a distinctly maternal warmth. "We're happy to help give him that stability here."

Dion added more grimly, "The kid's got impressive latent power too, though I can't pinpoint the type yet."

Alex and Eryx shared an uneasy look. If Zac had untapped magical potential, there was no telling what those wretched scientists had intended to use him for. The thought made Alex see red.

"No matter what abilities he has, we won't let anyone take Zac back there," Alex declared vehemently. The rest of the group nodded in solemn agreement. They would protect their young ward at all costs.

Zac's light footsteps bounding down the stairs broke the pensive silence. Alex took a deep, steadying breath, forcing his rage down. Right now, what mattered most was keeping the boy happy and safe. With his found family around him, he knew Zac would have the life he deserved.

Alex couldn't help smiling as Zac bounded down the stairs. The oversized clothes he was swimming in made him look even younger. We're going to have to start feeding this kid more, Alex thought.

Glancing out the window, Ari grimaced. "Uh oh, looks like the press found you guys again."

Eryx sighed apologetically. "Sorry about that, we must've forgotten to lose our trail on the way back."

Alex waved a hand unconcernedly. After everything they'd been through, nosy reporters barely registered. "We had a lot on our minds, don't worry about it."

"Dion and I will head out the back way and draw them off for you," Ari offered.

Zac peered out the window curiously. "Why are all those people here?"

Ari ruffled his hair playfully. "Our Eryx here is a big music star. They all want to catch a glimpse of him."

Eryx rolled his eyes in embarrassment. "Very funny. It's really not that dramatic."

Dion chuckled at their antics. Turning serious, he said, "You call us if you need anything, okay? The kid's got our numbers." He tousled

Zac's hair fondly.

Ari added, "We picked you up some clothes and a phone, since it looks like you're swimming in those."

Alex smiled gratefully. "Thanks again for all your help." Dion and Ari had become like family. He was lucky to have them.

After they left, Zac turned to Alex eagerly. "So where are we going?"

"To visit an old family friend at my old house upstate," Alex explained carefully. No need to overwhelm the kid by mentioning gods and celestial weapons just yet.

Exiting the building, Alex was relieved to see the media circus had dispersed. Their constant hounding was the last thing they needed right now. This mission required utter secrecy.

As they drove to Alex's old warehouse, now Hephaestus' residence, he felt a pang of nostalgia. He missed that restored building sometimes, full of memories from his early days back on the mortal realm. But with Eryx's celebrity status, they'd needed more privacy eventually. At least the place had gone to someone who would care for it properly.

Beside him in the passenger seat, Eryx glanced back fondly at Zac stretched across the backseat. The teen had quickly dozed off after they got on the highway, worn out from the eventful day.

As Alex stole glimpses in the rear view mirror at Zac's sleeping face, looking younger and unguarded, his chest swelled with protectiveness. After enduring so much hardship alone, the orphaned boy had found a real home and family with them. A sense of peace Alex wanted to preserve.

Zac's long legs were folded awkwardly to fit his tall frame across the seat. Alex made a mental note to start looking at larger vehicles. They'd make sure their newest addition got everything he needed, including comfortable transportation.

This scrappy kid had been through hell, but Alex would move heaven and earth to help him flourish now. With Eryx's steady strength beside him, together they could give Zac the happy, loving home he deserved. The family they all deserved.

"Did you have any relatives growing up?" Alex asked softly once the kid stirred awake. "Anyone looking for you now?"

Zac shook his head, eyes downcast. "No, I've been in foster care since I can remember. The families always said I brought them bad luck, so I got bounced around a lot."

Rage ignited in Alex's gut at the thought of anyone calling this child 'bad luck.' Gently, Eryx reached back to squeeze Zac's hand. "You're not going anywhere now. You'll stay with us from here on out."

Alex met his eyes firmly in the rearview mirror. "That's a promise. You're part of this family."

Zac ducked his head, but Alex glimpsed his small, grateful smile. They would give him the home he deserved, no matter what.

When they pulled up to the house, Hephaestus was already outside waiting, accompanied by…a dog? Alex blinked in surprise as the energetic pit bull yanked a grinning Hephaestus over to greet them. Who knew the gruff old god was a dog person? Though he had to admit, they looked good together.

"Welcome!" Hephaestus bellowed warmly. "And who's this young fella?"

Alex gently nudged Zac forward. "This is Zac, our newest addition. Zac, meet Hephaestus." At the name, Zac's eyebrows rose, but he wisely remained silent.

Zac asked carefully. "As in…Hephaestus?"

Alex winced. So much for breaking the supernatural news gently.

Thankfully, Hephaestus just laughed, unfazed. "That's my official godly name, yeah. But I go by Harry around here - less conspicuous." He waved them toward the house. "Let's take this inside."

Alex herded a bemused Zac and Eryx into the living room. He really hadn't meant to spring the whole immortals and magic thing on the kid so abruptly. Parenting was a learning curve, it seemed.

Once they were settled, Hephaestus - Harry - released his exuberant pitbull to explore. Turning to Zac, he said kindly, "I imagine you've got a lot of questions now, son."

Zac nodded slowly. "Yeah, you could say that." He looked between Alex and Eryx. "So if he's the Greek god Hephaestus…are you gods too?"

"It's complicated," Eryx hedged. "Alex here is Hades, former Lord of the Underworld. But I'm just a mortal who got…mixed up in divine affairs."

Alex cleared his throat. No use hiding it now. "It's true. Though most of us live as ordinary people these days. Our era of rule has passed."

Zac took that revelation in stride. "Huh. I thought Hades would be more ominous." He cocked his head. "The myths definitely got that wrong."

Alex huffed a surprised laugh. "Never judge a book by its cover. But yes, the legends tend to exaggerate." It was refreshing to speak freely with someone new.

Harry clapped Alex on the back. "He seems mean, but he's a big softie inside. But try not to piss him off." He gave Zac a playful wink.

Alex just rolled his eyes indulgently. It was nice seeing Harry in good spirits again after all he endured. Captivity in the Abyss had taken a toll, but his friend seemed happy now.

"Right, now that introductions are done, let's see this project of yours," Harry said, leading the way to his forge.

Alex raised an eyebrow at his friend. "You built your own forge here?"

Harry let out a hearty laugh. "I'm a god, aren't I? I can make myself at home." He beckoned eagerly for them to follow. "Wait until you see it!"

Alex couldn't help grinning as he trailed after the enthusiastic inventor. It was wonderful seeing Harry in such high spirits again after his captivity in the Abyss. That harrowing ordeal had clearly taken a toll. But now Hephaestus seemed revived, his passion for creation rekindled.

As they descended the basement steps, Alex felt a rush of anticipation. The last time he'd seen Harry's forge was millennia ago on Mount Olympus. He could only imagine what ingenious marvels his friend's brilliant mind had conjured here.

Stepping into the basement, Alex's jaw dropped. Harry had crafted a forge that blended old world artistry with sleek modern technologies and magical enhancements. Ancient tools lined weathered stone walls, while robotic arms assisted at high-tech workbenches. The centered giant kiln glowed with runic symbols of power.

Seeing Alex's look of awe, Harry grinned. "With a little help from Hermes' boy Marcus and his tech-savvy buddy Lucas, I've got all the latest gadgets down here now too."

"This is incredible!" Alex said sincerely. Beside him, Eryx and Zac voiced similar sounds of amazement.

Harry practically preened at their praise. "I'm rather proud of it myself. Almost better than my old Olympian forge, though don't tell Zeus I said that." He laughed heartily before turning serious. "So what's this project you need help with?"

Alex quickly explained their quest for the celestial key and need to enter Tartarus. Harry's stormy eyes darkened at the implications. "Releasing a prisoner from the Pit won't be easy. But you know I'll help however I can."

Before Alex could reply, they heard a small gasp behind them. He turned to see Zac staring wide-eyed into the distance. "Zac? You alright?" Eryx asked gently.

Zac seemed to shake himself out of some reverie. "I…I heard that name. Absalom." He met Alex's gaze anxiously. "The people holding me mentioned him several times."

Alex's breath caught. He knelt before Zac urgently. "Who were these people? Can you remember anything else?" This could be the break in the case they desperately needed.

Zac bit his lip, clearly trying to recall hazy memories. "I don't know who they were. But I heard Absalom's name a few times. They said he was a powerful vampire." His face scrunched with concentration, then relaxed apologetically. "I'm sorry, that's all I can remember."

"Hey, you have nothing to apologize for," Alex said seriously. "This is really helpful. It means the cases are connected." He squeezed Zac's shoulder, pride swelling. "You did good, kid."

Zac gave a small, relieved smile. they were one step closer to the truth now thanks to him.

Alex turned back to Harry urgently. "We need you to forge the celestial key for us. I know going to Tartarus is risky, but we're out of options."

Harry regarded them solemnly. "I figured this was no simple request. But if you're set on this madness, I'll help as I'm able." He held out a broad hand. "Let's have these ingredients then."

Alex handed over the vial of Zeus' blood and the pouch containing the Stormcaller's essence. "Will this be enough for you to work with?"

Harry examined the items critically before nodding. "Aye, I can make it work." He waved them toward the stairs. "Now off with you lot. Creating celestial weapons is delicate business. I'll call you back when it's ready."

They didn't argue, quickly vacating the forge. Upstairs in the cozy kitchen, Alex took comfort in the familiar setting. This had been his home once. He still missed it sometimes.

Noticing his pensive look, Eryx wrapped an arm around his waist. "Do you regret moving?"

Alex smiled softly, leaning into his touch. "No. You're my home now, wherever we are." He brushed a tender kiss to Eryx's lips, gratitude swelling in his chest. As long as they were together, he was home.

Across from them, Zac fidgeted curiously. "So, if you're really Hades, doesn't that make Eryx your husband instead of Persephone?"

Eryx smirked, clearly enjoying Alex's discomfort. "I'll let you field that one, old man."

Alex just sighed in exaggerated annoyance. "The legends got a lot wrong, kid. The gods' relationships were always more…complex than people realized."

As Zac continued peppering them with curious questions, frantic shouting suddenly erupted from outside.

Alex and Eryx shared an alarmed look. "Something's wrong out there," Alex said grimly.

More panicked screams echoed through the walls, along with snarls and roars that raised the hairs on the back of Alex's neck.

He turned urgently to Zac. "Stay here, lock the doors, and don't come out until we say it's safe."

Zac's eyes were wide. "But what's happening?"

"We'll handle it," Eryx said in a gentle but firm tone. "Just please, stay inside where it's secure."

The teen still looked anxious, but he nodded. Alex ruffled his hair quickly before drawing his sword. "We'll be back soon. You'll be safe here."

Another terrified shriek spurred Alex into motion. "Let's move," he told Eryx tersely. Together they raced outside, dreading what new chaos awaited them now.

The scene was utter pandemonium. People were screaming and fleeing down the street in a panic. Massive wolf-like creatures stalked through the suburban neighborhood, attacking anyone in their path.

Alex's blood ran cold - the beasts seemed to be drinking the blood of their victims.

"What the hell?" Eryx exclaimed beside him. "Are you seeing this? They're like vampire wolfmen!"

Clenching his jaw, Alex wreathed his fists with hellfire. "We need to draw them away from the civilians. Get these people to safety!"

They quickly formed a plan - Eryx would help escort bystanders away and erect barriers, while Alex confronted the blood-crazed monsters head on to distract them.

Alex charged straight toward the nearest lycanthrope, his sword alight with blazing flames. But when he struck, the creature deflected his blow with unnatural speed and force, staggering him back. Alex realized this was no normal monster. Cunning intelligence gleamed in its glowing eyes.

"Give him back to us," it growled gutturally, "or everyone here will suffer!"

Alex tensed. 'Him' could only mean Zac. They had come for the boy. Like hell that was happening.

"Not a chance!" Alex snarled back defiantly. In response, the beast let loose an ear-splitting howl. More converged from the shadows, surrounding Alex with snapping jaws dripping viscous red.

Alex and the creatures clashed violently, but blows that could shatter stone barely slowed the beasts. Alex barely managed to twist away from the fangs aimed at his vulnerable throat.

"Alex! Behind you!" Eryx shouted in warning. Alex spun, raising his flaming blade just in time to deflect the wolf lunging for his unprotected back.

Together they fought desperately against the endless tide, but their attacks seemed useless against the monsters' preternatural power. Eryx threw up a golden barrier to shield against the slavering assault. "What are these damn things?" he panted.

"No clue, but they hit harder than any shifter I've seen," Alex gritted out. They were badly outmatched by the creatures' ferocity.

Just as the pack moved in to kill, they suddenly froze in unison, letting out garbled yelps before collapsing limply. Alex stared around in shock and confusion. What had happened?

A faint noise drew his gaze upward to see Zac standing rigidly on the porch, one hand extended. To Alex's abject horror, blood was streaming down the boy's face from his nose and ears. Before Alex could react, viscous red began rapidly pooling around Zac's feet.

"Zac!" Alex shouted, heart seizing in fear. But the teen's eyes had already rolled back as he crumpled bonelessly to the concrete.

Alex and Eryx raced desperately to reach Zac, but dread already filled Alex's gut. Zac had done this somehow - saved them by using a terrifying power that had clearly caused him grievous harm.

As Eryx gently lifted Zac's limp body, Alex barked urgent orders to his team over the phone. "Get Dr. Sloan here immediately! Zac is badly hurt."

16

Hole of Glory

Eryx

Eryx watched as Alex gently laid Zac onto the bed. The boy looked pale and weak, but he was breathing steadily.

"He saved the day again," Eryx said, giving Alex a small smile. After being attacked by those vicious vampire-wolf hybrids, if not for Zac and his strange blood magic, they all might be dead.

Alex nodded, his expression grim. "They want him for a reason. I think it's because of the power that courses through his blood. His magic."

Eryx was about to agree when the air suddenly felt charged, like before a thunderstorm. The smell of burning ozone became prominent. He tensed, knowing this was not a good sign - it meant someone from the veil was approaching.

A portal shimmered into existence in the middle of the room. Out stepped Thanatos, his tailored suit still looked immaculate as ever. Eryx had always found the god of death rather intimidating.

"You're right, Alex," Thanatos said, his voice like gravel. "They want the boy as a vessel due to his magic. Zac is not just an ordinary blood mage. He is a hemomancer - the last living one."

Eryx's eyes went wide. "What do you mean he's the only one left? Surely there are more?"

Alex pinched the bridge of his nose, looking exasperated. "That's why he was able to defeat those hybrids. Hemomancers were killed off due to their potent blood magic. At higher levels, it allows the user to control a person forcibly, even rip blood out of them to form constructs. It's extremely powerful, one of the most effective types of magic in combat."

Eryx swallowed hard as he digested this information. No wonder Zac was being hunted. But they would protect him. "We'll just have to keep him safe then, and help him learn to control his powers."

Alex glanced at Thanatos sharply. "Why are you here?

Thanatos waved a hand dismissively. "You're running out of time - Ares is on the move to execute Dolos before he can talk."

Alex glanced at him sharply. "We don't have the Celestial Key yet. Can you run interference with Ares?"

Thanatos gave a solemn nod. "Harry is nearly finished forging the key, so hurry. I will do what I can to stall Ares." With that, he opened another portal and vanished.

Eryx shook his head in irritation. "As cryptic and mysterious as ever."

"More like a pain in my ass," Alex grumbled.

A knock sounded at the door. Alex opened it to reveal Gabe. "Dr. Sloan is here," Gabe said.

"Let him in to check on Zac," Alex replied, stepping back.

Dr. Sloan entered, his kind face creased in concern. As the medic for Alex's team, the Shadowguards, Finn was skilled in both human medicine and healing magic. He immediately went to Zac and began examining him gently.

"Do you know what's wrong with him, Finn?" Eryx asked worriedly.

Finn nodded, his expression serious. "Using his blood magic put a massive strain on his body. I need to get fluids and a blood transfusion started right away."

The doctor worked quickly, starting an IV line and hanging a bag of blood. As the vital fluids began flowing into Zac, a bit of color returned to his wan face. After a few minutes, the boy's eyelids fluttered open weakly.

"Wha...what happened?" he croaked.

Alex stepped forward, relief washing over his rugged features. "You saved us, but it took a lot out of you. How do you feel?"

"Really tired...and weak," Zac murmured. His dark eyes were full of confusion and fear.

Eryx gave him a reassuring smile. "Just rest. Finn's taking good care of you - you'll be back on your feet in no time." At least, he hoped that would be the case.

Alex drew Finn aside and they spoke in hushed tones. Eryx stroked Zac's hair soothingly until the boy drifted back to sleep. Poor kid - he had been through so much, and now this. But they would find a way to help him master his rare gifts.

After a few minutes, Finn finished conferring with Alex and came back over. He gently checked the IV lines and monitors. "The fluids and blood are helping. His vitals are stabilizing. But he'll need plenty of rest and time to recover - using that much hemomancy power at his age is incredibly dangerous."

Alex nodded. "We'll make sure he takes it easy. Can you ward this room to mask his presence? If those hybrid creatures could sense him before, they may return."

"Of course. I brought some artifacts that will make this space undetectable." Finn opened his bag and removed some carved stones and vials of liquid, quickly setting up protective wards around Zac's bed.

As the doctor worked, Eryx noticed Alex slip quietly from the room, his jaw set. Eryx had a good idea of where he was going - to check with Hephaestus if the Celestial Key was ready yet. They were in a race against time now.

Once Finn finished the wards, he came over to Eryx. "The best thing for Zac now is rest. I'll come check on him regularly and continue transfusions. Call me if anything changes."

"We will. Thank you, Finn." Eryx clasped the doctor's shoulder gratefully.

Alex then told Finn, "Wait for us in the living room so we can update each other on what's going on."

After the doctor left, Eryx looked at Zac's sleeping form worriedly. "I'm coming with you to Tartarus, whether you like it or not," he told Alex stubbornly.

Alex grasped his shoulder, a faint smile touching his lips. "I know there's no stopping you."

Eryx turned to him with determination. "We can't let them have Zac."

"I know. We'll do everything possible to prevent that," Alex assured him. He caressed Eryx's face gently and kissed him. "Now come on, let's go talk to the others."

They found the team gathered in the living room. Eryx sat down beside Marcus and Olivia, who both gave him reassuring pats.

Alex debriefed everyone, recounting the attack by the vampire-wolf hybrids.

Emma's eyes widened. "How is that possible? We've never encountered anything like them before."

Gabe nodded grimly. "The experiments. That's what they must have been doing at the Moonblood site."

"You're right," Alex confirmed. "Assuming our deductions are correct, the Jane Doe case is connected to Moonblood and the missing vampire god."

Eryx could feel the tension in the room rising. This was big - and dangerous.

"So what now?" Marcus asked, breaking the heavy silence.

Alex's expression was grave. "Once Hephaestus finishes the Key, Eryx and I will be going to Tartarus. In the meantime, I need all of you ready for action in the morning. Gabe, dig deeper into the blood sample Leo sent - see if you can find a DNA match. Lucas and Lily, keep hacking systems for any clues. Emma and Olivia, stay here with Zac."

Everyone nodded, faces set with determination. Eryx felt a swell of pride for this loyal team.

Finn spoke up. "I'll monitor Zac's condition closely. His recovery is priority one."

"Good. We'll reconvene soon," Alex said. "Get some rest, all of you. We've got a long fight ahead."

The others dispersed to their rooms. Eryx lingered, lost in worried thought about Zac.

Alex touched his shoulder. "Hey. He's safe for now, thanks to you and Finn. We're going to get him through this."

Eryx managed a faint smile. "I know. I just hate feeling powerless. That poor kid's been through enough."

"We all have," Alex said quietly. "But we stick together, like always. That's how we'll win."

Eryx nodded, drawing strength from Alex's calm confidence. They had never backed down from a fight yet.

Alex studied him with knowing eyes. "You should get some sleep. Tartarus won't be easy, even with the Key."

"I'll try." Eryx sighed, feeling the weight of exhaustion. He started to turn away, then paused. "Alex? What if…what if I can't handle it down there? I don't have your resilience."

Alex grasped his shoulders firmly. "You can do this. You're the strongest person I know, Eryx." He pulled him close. "Whatever comes at us, we'll face it together."

Reassured, Eryx finally went to bed, Alex's words echoing in his mind.

Eryx slept fitfully in the makeshift bed next to where Zac was recovering. He woke early, unable to find Alex anywhere. After checking on Zac, Eryx went looking for Alex, figuring he must be down in Hephaestus's forge.

As Eryx approached the basement door, he heard voices - Alex and Hephaestus speaking intensely.

"Are you sure about this, Alex?" Hephaestus was saying, sounding concerned.

Eryx entered the forge. "Sure about what? You're not planning on going to Tartarus alone, are you?" he demanded, looking between them anxiously.

Alex waved him over. "No, just strategizing for Tartarus. My powers will be weaker there, so weapons from Harry seemed prudent."

Eryx still caught the tail end of an uneasy glance between them. "What aren't you telling me?"

Harry sighed heavily. "Alex wants to draw the guards away using dangerous magic. I tried dissuading him, but he insists the risk is worthwhile."

A cold fist seemed to close around Eryx's heart. "Absolutely not! We swore to face this together." Desperation rose in him at the thought of Alex in harm's way.

Taking Eryx's hands, Alex held his gaze intently. "You're right, I'm sorry. It was just an option, but I won't pursue it." Sincerity shone in his eyes. "No more talk of me being bait. I promise."

Relief coursed through Eryx. He knew Alex just wanted to protect him, but some prices were too steep. They would find another way.

Hephaestus looked mollified. "In that case, let me show you the weapons I prepared." He led them to a heavy vault door and entered a code. The thick metal door swung open with a groan, revealing a dim interior.

"Come, see what I have forged for your quest," rumbled the smith god.

Eryx followed Alex inside, eyes widening at the sight of so many ornate, gleaming weapons lining the walls and displays. This was a legendary arsenal.

Harry gestured them over to a specific rack holding a bow and spear. "These should aid you if your powers fail in Tartarus."

He lifted down the elegant bow reverently. "This was Apollo's finest weapon - the bow he wielded in the Great War. I forged it myself, imbuing the gold with his essence so it would never break."

Hephaestus offered it to Eryx, who accepted it with awe. The moment his hands closed around the grip, he felt his magic resonating within the mystical weapon, like reuniting with an old friend.

"Use it well, vessel of Apollo," Harry said solemnly.

Eryx nodded, temporarily speechless. He traced a fingertip over elaborate runes etched into the golden limbs. Apollo had touched this, fought with this. Now it was his.

Alex hefted an ornate silver spear that seemed to radiate shadowy power. "What magic does this one possess?"

"Like you don't remember. You once used that spear to cut down a legion of rebellious demons," Harry recounted. "It will still answer your call in times of need."

Gripping the legendary weapons, Eryx and Alex exchanged a wordless look. The tide had turned. They were no longer walking unarmed into the Pit.

Harry regarded them seriously. "Remember the key is your priority. Get in, get out." His craggy features radiated paternal concern. "And return alive."

Alex clasped the burly smith god's shoulder. "We will. And we'll have your arsenal to thank."

As they turned to go, Hephaestus called Eryx back for a moment. "Apollo's bow has additional gifted properties. Channel an infusion of your power thusly…"

Taking the proffered bow, Eryx focused, letting his magic flow into the weapon. Before his eyes, it transformed into a gleaming gold ring on a chain.

"Amazing," he breathed. He repeated the process and the bow reformed. "I can summon it at will!"

Harry nodded approvingly. "Yes, a safeguard for when it is not needed. You master it quickly." His tone held affection.

Deeply touched by the smith's faith and gift, Eryx embraced the sturdy god. "Thank you, for everything."

Hephaestus patted his shoulder with a gnarled hand. "Go. Be the light that guides you both from the darkness."

After gearing up with the armor and weapons Hephaestus provided, it was time. Alex conjured a fiery portal into the Underworld, but Harry stopped them before they could step through.

"Take this," the smith god said gruffly, pressing the Celestial Key into Alex's hand. "Guard it with your life. It will only work once."

Eryx met Harry's intense gaze. "Watch over Zac for us while we're gone. Tell him we'll be back soon."

Harry clasped Eryx's shoulder with a heavy hand. "You have my word. Now go - time runs short."

With a final nod, they turned together and passed through the portal, leaving the mortal world behind.

Eryx blinked as his eyes adjusted to the strange, muted light. They stood in a vast desert valley, empty and still. Sparse dunes stretched to the hazy horizon. Despite the bleak landscape, he felt they were not alone here.

"The Valley of Lost Souls," Alex confirmed grimly, scanning their surroundings. "We must move quickly."

Eryx shivered though he felt no temperature, only a profound absence of life. "What happens if we linger too long?"

Alex's face was etched with tension. "Our souls begin to unravel, like the ghosts trapped here for eternity."

Suppressing another shudder, Eryx stuck close as they traversed the dead valley. The faint sound of anguished whispers threaded the air but no beings could be seen. He focused on the reality of Alex beside him.

After some time, Alex halted abruptly. "This is it - the Pit lies below." Dark power flowed around his fists as he slammed them down. The desert floor ruptured, revealing a deep, spiraling cavity.

Peering over the crumbling edge, Eryx glimpsed only fathomless blackness. He looked to Alex, who gave a terse nod.

Peering over the crumbling edge, Eryx glimpsed only fathomless blackness. He looked to Alex, who gave a terse nod.

"Ready for this?" Alex asked.

Eryx swallowed hard. "As ready as I'll ever be."

"Hold on tight." Alex pulled him close and leapt into the void.

Eryx's stomach lurched as they plunged into endless shadow. He gripped Alex tighter, unable to tear his eyes from the terrifying view. Strange wisps and echoes surrounded them as they fell for what seemed an eternity.

Finally, the ground rushed up to meet them. Eryx landed in a crouch, knees protesting. Beside him, Alex was already scanning their bleak surroundings, spear at the ready.

They were in a gloomy, cavernous pit surrounded by sheer bronze walls. Beyond lay ever-deepening layers of impenetrable night. This was the Prison of Tartarus itself. Ancient, terrible power throbbed in the very bedrock beneath them.

Alex pressed something into Eryx's palm - the Celestial Key. "Take this. Use it when you reach Dolos's cell. And run if I tell you to."

Eryx started to argue but the look in Alex's eyes silenced him. This was Alex's personal hell - Eryx had to trust his instincts. With a tight nod, he slipped the Key into his pocket.

They moved cautiously through the maze of stone tunnels. Senses strained, Eryx constantly expected an attack. Suddenly the hair on his neck prickled. A split-second later, Alex threw up a shield of dark energy around them.

A rumbling bellow revealed their attacker - a hulking cyclops. It pounded furiously on Alex's shield as he yelled, "Go, quickly! I can't hold this for long."

Eryx took off down the left-hand tunnel. Behind him came sounds of titanic battle - the cyclops roaring, Alex's shouted curses. Guilt flared in him at leaving Alex to fight alone, but he had no choice. Gritting his teeth, he focused on his goal.

Grotesque shapes stalked him from side passages, but Eryx dispatched them with arrows before they got close, Apollo's golden bow singing in his hands. The further he went, the stronger the evil presence grew, sapping his energy.

Rounding the corner, Eryx skidded to an abrupt halt with a hissed oath. A monstrous nine-headed hydra blocked his path, all heads hissing in anticipation. Acrid venom dripped from gleaming fangs as it slithered toward him.

Cursing under his breath, Eryx rolled aside as the hydra struck, poison splattering the stone where he'd stood. He fired arrows at the darting heads while dodging savage bites, but they barely pierced the armored hide.

The heart, came Apollo's voice in his mind. *Aim for the heart!*

"Easier said than done!" Eryx grunted, barely avoiding the drizzling venom. "This thing has nine heads trying to eat me!"

He fired relentlessly to distract the writhing heads, seeking an opening. A sweeping tail knocked him off balance and talons raked his shoulder. Crying out in pain, Eryx scrambled away from the gaping maws.

Use my light to blind it, Apollo guided. *Then strike while it is confused.*

Wincing, Eryx called on Apollo's power, gathering golden light in his left hand. As the hydra loomed over him, he hurled the blazing orb into its central head's eyes.

The hydra reared back, blinded. Seizing his chance, Eryx took aim at the exposed chest cavity and let an arrow fly. It burst into flames, piercing deep. The hydra thrashed in agony, claws gouging the rocks.

Not waiting to see if the beast was dead, Eryx clutched his bleeding shoulder and raced onward. He had to find the prison cells. Alex needed him.

Dizzy from pain and effort, Eryx leaned against the wall. "I can't keep going like this," he panted.

Let me heal you, Apollo's soothing voice filled his mind. *You must be at full strength.*

Eryx nodded wearily and relinquished control. Warm golden light enveloped him, sealing his wound and restoring his energy. Power thrummed through his veins.

My abilities are unaffected by Tartarus, Apollo explained. *Use my gifts to aid you.*

"Thank you," Eryx said fervently. With the sun god's blessing bolstering him, he felt ready to face anything.

Panting, Eryx didn't hesitate before racing onward. He had to find the prison cells. Alex was counting on him.

17

Jailbreak

Eryx

This hellish place was endless. Doubt crept into his mind - had coming here with Alex been a mistake? But it was too late for regrets now. All he could do was keep moving.

Rounding a corner, Eryx stumbled upon a trail of dark blood splattering the stone. Crouching to inspect it, he determined it was fresh. Warning prickling his neck, Eryx followed the gruesome trail, bow drawn and ready.

The sound of fighting grew louder as he stalked down the tunnel. Peering around a pillar, Eryx saw Thanatos battling a tall, armored figure. With a shout, Thanatos was flung hard against the cavern wall.

Eryx rushed over and grasped Thanatos's arm, helping the injured death god to his feet. Blood dripped from a cut on Thanatos's forehead and he seemed to favor his left leg.

"Are you alright?" Eryx asked with concern.

Thanatos scowled and wiped the blood from his mouth with the back of his hand. "What took you so long?" he growled, though his voice lacked its usual venom.

Eryx noticed Thanatos's golden eyes were slightly unfocused with pain. Whoever he had been fighting was clearly formidable. Unease trickled down Eryx's spine - what fresh threat awaited them now?

A chillingly familiar laugh echoed around the cavern walls. Eryx's gut twisted with dread as he turned to face the tall figure emerging from the shadows. Even in the dim light, the god of war's cruel beauty and arrogant smirk were unmistakable.

"Welcome, Apollo's vessel," Ares drawled, looking irritatingly immaculate in his tailored black suit. "Come here to die?"

Eryx clenched his fists, magic and rage surging through his veins. His palms itched to grasp his bow and wipe the smug look off Ares's too-handsome face.

"I made you bleed once before, Ares," he bit out. "Don't tempt me to do it again." The memory of their vicious duel months ago was fresh in his mind.

Ares' smile only widened, turning vicious. "Last time was a fluke," he purred. "This occasion, I came prepared." He waved a gauntleted hand lazily.

The sound of eerie wails and hisses filled the cavern as a horde of shadowy specters flooded out of the darkness. Their smoky forms swirled toward Eryx and Thanatos, red eyes glowing with malicious hunger.

Cursing under his breath, Eryx glanced back at Thanatos. "Can you still fight?"

The death god hefted his massive obsidian sword in both hands, eyes blazing with rage beneath his pale brows. "These shades barely scratched me, child. Let us end this serpent."

Despite the bravado in his words, Eryx noticed Thanatos's hands shaking slightly on the sword hilt. He was clearly weakened from his previous battle. They would have to fight smart to survive this.

Gripping his bow, Eryx turned to face the wraiths' advance. Their claws reached for him hungrily. He channeled Apollo's golden light into his arrows.

"On my mark!" he yelled over the shrieks. Eryx loosed a volley of blazing arrows to clear some space. The purified arrows vaporized the dark beings on contact.

"Now!" Eryx shouted. He and Thanatos surged forward to engage the shades in close combat. Eryx wielded his bow like a staff, kicking and slamming the wraiths back. Thanatos sliced through them with powerful swings of his massive sword. But for each one cut down, two more appeared from the darkness.

Surrounded by ravenous specters, Eryx's mind raced for a solution. Ares watched safely from above, laughing as he summoned more wraiths. They couldn't keep fighting like this - eventually he and Thanatos would tire and be overwhelmed.

Use my light, came Apollo's voice within his mind. *It will banish these shadows.*

Eryx closed his eyes briefly, channeling the sun god's radiance into his being. *I'll try. Lend me your strength.*

Drawing on that divine power, he infused his arrows with blazing purity.

He fired at the swarming specters, clearing a space around them. The light arrows burned away the dark beings on contact. But the reprieve was brief as Ares kept summoning reinforcements.

Spying an opening, Eryx called to Thanatos over his shoulder. "Watch my back! I'm going for Ares." Before the death god could respond, Eryx charged forward, loosing more light arrows to carve a path upward.

Ares's smile turned mocking as Eryx leapt up to his perch. "You seem to have a death wish, little hero?" he taunted, casually summoning his accursed spear, Doru.

Jaw clenched, Eryx fired an arrow but Ares swatted it away lazily.

The war god moved with liquid speed, striking like a viper. Eryx barely evaded the gleaming spear tip, feeling it slice through his tunic.

You must Predict his moves, Apollo advised. *Outthink him.*

Gritting his teeth, Eryx tried to follow Apollo's guidance, but Ares seemed to anticipate his every attack. The war god was stronger than their last battle, his strikes suffused with shadowy power. A vicious kick to the chest sent Eryx skidding back, the wind knocked from his lungs.

"Getting tired yet, boy?" Ares smirked, not even winded.

Wiping blood from his mouth, Eryx silently pleaded with Apollo. *What do I do? He's too strong.*

Have faith, came the soothing reply. *Darkness cannot withstand the light when fully unleashed.*

Staggering up, Eryx barely raised his bow in time to deflect Ares's next strike. The force of the blow snapped his bow in half, sending him crashing to the unforgiving rocks. Agony blazed through him.

Towering above him, Ares pointed his spear at Eryx's heart. "Surrender the Celestial Key and perhaps I'll let you live to see daylight again."

Defiantly, Eryx spat blood at the war god's boots. "Why…are you trying…to revive Absalom?" he ground out.

Ares smiled coldly. "Isn't it obvious? With his power, we will reshape this world. You and Alex have been thorns in my side for too long." His eyes narrowed. "And you stole his vessel."

Eryx bared his teeth in a bloody grin. "You'll never take Zac. Not while I live and breathe."

Ares shrugged. "That can be remedied." He raised Doru for the killing blow. "Any last words?"

Eryx closed his eyes, bracing himself. A sense of failure crushed his heart. He had let Alex down, let everyone down. A tear slipped down his cheek.

Suddenly, a roar of fury split the air. Eryx's eyes flew open to see Alex materialize between him and Ares, black flames wreathing his body. The spear clanged uselessly off Alex's shield.

"Get away from him," Alex snarled, his eyes burning with hellfire. He blasted Ares back with a column of flame.

Thanatos gripped Eryx's arm, hauling him upright. "Can you stand? We must finish this snake."

Nodding shakily, Eryx retrieved his broken bow. Together, they joined Alex advancing on Ares. Side by side, their combined powers forced the war god into retreat.

With a final cry of rage, Ares vanished in a swirl of shadows. "This isn't over!" his disembodied voice rang out. "You cannot stop us from ruling."

Eryx sagged against Alex in relief as the last traces of Ares' presence faded. The contact helped ground him after the harrowing battle. Alex's hands were infinitely gentle as they inspected Eryx's injuries, sending warmth through his battered body.

"I'm sorry I didn't reach you sooner," Alex murmured, regret heavy in his voice.

Eryx managed a pained smile, touched by Alex's protectiveness. "You got here just in time. That's all that matters."

Glancing down at the shattered remnants of Apollo's bow, Eryx grimaced. "Harry's gonna kill me for breaking this."

Thanatos scoffed, sheathing his massive sword across his back. "It's a divine weapon, fool. It cannot be permanently broken. Simply resummon it."

"Oh, right." Feeling foolish, Eryx channeled his power into reforming the bow. It coalesced good as new in his hands. Handy magic item perks.

With the immediate threats gone, he took stock of their situation. "What now? Any idea where they're keeping Dolos?"

Thanatos gestured toward a tower of glassy black rock atop a nearby rise. "There. The highest security tower for imprisoning gods." His mouth twisted in distaste. "Getting inside will be…challenging."

Alex's jaw was set with determination. "We have to hurry. The longer we linger here, the more our energy will drain." He turned to Eryx. "Can Apollo shield you from that somehow?"

Eryx considered, then nodded. "He says Tartarus doesn't affect him like it does full gods. I think his power will keep me going." Having the sun god's backing was proving incredibly useful.

"Good. We may need you at full strength again soon." Alex's tone was grim. This rescue mission was far from over.

They set out toward the forbidding prison tower, cutting down any monsters in their path. Eryx's thoughts turned to their mission. "So what's Dolos's story anyway? Why do you dislike him so?"

Alex's lip curled in a sneer. "He's a trickster god. Like Loki, but far weaker. Always bargains and deceit with that one." His fists clenched. "Not someone I'd trust."

Thanatos added darkly, "He also tried seducing Zagreus multiple times. I cannot forgive that."

Alex raised an eyebrow at the death god. "You and my son, hmm? Why am I just learning about this now?"

Thanatos cleared his throat awkwardly. "Oh look, we're here."

Eryx bit back a smile. Even in the bleakness of Tartarus, some light could be found. He only hoped they could succeed and return home safely.

At the tower's base, Thanatos held up a hand. "This place is riddled with traps and wards. Take one wrong step, and you're dead." His golden gaze was grave. "Even gods are not immune."

Alex cracked his knuckles, undeterred. "Just means we'll have to be careful. I can disable some of the magic traps - my powers are uniquely suited for it. Eryx, your light will reveal concealed snares."

Eryx nodded, impressed by Alex's quick strategic thinking. Together, their combined gifts would help navigate this.

Passing through a dark fissure in the rock, they entered the tower's shadowy confines. Instantly Eryx felt an oppressive aura weighing down on him, even as Apollo's essence fought against it. Strange glyphs and wards glowed ominously along the walls and floor. This place was designed to sap even a god's strength.

Alex took the lead, muttering spells to disarm potentially deadly runes. Eryx followed closely, sending out pulses of light to unveil hidden triggers and traps. They progressed slowly through the maze of precarious halls and stairwells.

After what seemed like hours, they reached a massive door barring their path. More wards and chains bound it closed. Eryx could sense Dolos's presence just on the other side.

Alex held out a hand. "Give me the Key - it's time to free our tricky friend."

Eryx pulled the Celestial Key from his pocket and passed it over, feeling its power thrumming through the metal. He hoped Dolos's aid would be worth all they'd endured obtaining it.

Taking the Key, Alex stared grimly at the towering door. "This better pay off," he muttered. Stepping forward, he slid the Key into the locking mechanism. It flared with blinding light as the door dissolved to mist before them.

Peering inside, they beheld Dolos, slumped pale and emaciated against the far wall. Guilt twinged in Eryx's chest. Trickster or not, the god's condition was pitiable.

Stepping over the threshold, Eryx aimed and fired, shattering Dolos's chains with golden arrows. Alex was instantly at the weak god's side, supporting him.

"You came after all," Dolos rasped, managing a faint version of his usual fox-like grin. "I'm touched."

Frowning, Alex looked to Thanatos. "What happened to him? He looks drained near to death."

Shame crossed Thanatos's angular features. "Ares got here first. He brought the Mimic to feast on Dolos's essence."

Eryx shuddered. Sven's insatiable thirst was a formidable weapon. Anger and resolve hardened within him - they had to stop Ares's plans.

"Can you walk?" Alex asked Dolos gently. "We have a long journey back."

Dolos waved a frail hand. "I have some strength left." But his legs buckled with his first steps. Wordlessly, Alex lifted the god onto his back. Dolos didn't argue or make any clever quips. Eryx's worry deepened - just how weak was he?

They had nearly reached the exit when approaching footsteps rang out. Cursing under his breath, Alex hefted his spear in his free hand. Eryx and Thanatos also readied their weapons as the first wave of guards rounded the corner.

The room was soon filled with the cacophony of battle. Alex fought fiercely despite carrying Dolos, his spear cutting down all who neared. Eryx provided cover fire with his bow while Thanatos sliced through enemies with wide sweeps of his massive sword. But they were badly outnumbered in the confined space.

"We must get above ground to escape!" Thanatos shouted over the din. "Portals cannot be opened here!"

Jaw clenched, Eryx continued firing even as his arms ached. They just had to last long enough to fight their way out. But weariness dragged at his limbs. Even with Apollo's gifts, he was flagging.

Abruptly, the tower ceiling exploded in a rain of rubble. Eryx ducked, shielding his head as debris rained down. Through the dust cloud a figure dropped down, hefting a massive fiery greatsword. It struck the ground with earth-shaking force, knocking everyone off their feet.

Blinking dust from his eyes, Eryx gaped as the newcomer rose to his full height - it was Zagreus!

Alex broke into a broad grin, relief washing over his rugged features. "Son! Your timing is impeccable."

With a roguish wink at Thanatos, Zagreus flashed his crooked grin. "You can thank dear Thanatos here for betraying your location. Figured you all could use some help."

Alex glanced between Zagreus and Thanatos with a knowing look. Thanatos suddenly became very interested in a spot on the ceiling.

Shaking his head in amusement, Alex turned back to Zagreus. "Where are your sisters? Are they safe?"

"Macaria's fighting the hydra, trying to keep it occupied. Melinoe awaits us topside," Zagreus explained. "We need to move quickly - these beasts won't stop until we're dinner."

Alex nodded, hefting his spear. "Then let's carve a path out of this pit." He turned to Eryx and Thanatos. "You heard the man, time's wasting!"

Together the four of them fought as one, slowly battling through the endless tide of guards and monsters. Zagreus and Thanatos took the front line, their combined skills a deadly force. Eryx provided cover fire from behind alongside Alex, who still carried the weakened Dolos on his back.

Bit by bit they neared the exit, leaving a trail of golden dust and bodies behind them. But the creatures kept coming relentlessly. Eryx's arms burned from the endless draw and release of his bow. Sweat stung his eyes. He wasn't sure how much longer he could keep this up.

Sensing his fatigue, Alex shot him a worried look even as he skewered two guards on his spear. "Stay with me, Sunshine. We're almost there."

Eryx gritted his teeth and pushed past the trembling in his limbs. He would not fail Alex and the others. Not when freedom was in sight. With a roar, he drew on Apollo's essence and channeled blazing Sunfire from his bow, incinerating a whole wave of creatures instantly.

Squinting toward the battling hydra, Eryx could make out a slender, dark-haired female figure darting around it. As she rolled to evade a snapping head, the light caught her face. Eryx realized this must be Macaria, Zagreus's sister.

Like her brother, Macaria had one green eye and one blue one. A spiked leather collar adorned her throat above her black leather armor. She wielded a staff expertly as she battled the writhing hydra.

"Zagreus, a little help here!" Macaria called out in frustration. "This damned thing keeps regrowing heads when I cut them off!"

Zagreus sighed. "It is a hydra, sister dear. Patience." He strode forward, raising one hand. As he sliced his palm with a dagger, dark blood magic began swirling around him. Slamming his bloodied hand to the ground, Zagreus yelled an incantation.

The hydra let out an unearthly shriek as it began burning from the inside out, its flesh melting away to leave behind only a charred skeleton. Zagreus straightened with a satisfied nod, the glowing runes on his arms fading.

"Blood and rebirth magic," Alex explained to Eryx matter-of-factly. "Handy skills of the chthonic gods."

Eryx studied Zagreus pensively. Perhaps he could teach Zac more control over his own blood powers…

"We must keep moving," Thanatos urged gravely. "The hydra will regenerate soon."

Macaria fell into step beside them, greeting her father briefly before turning curious eyes on Eryx. "So you're the famous vessel Apollo chose," she remarked. "I don't believe we've met. I am Macaria."

Up close, her mix of delicate and sharp features was striking. Eryx gave a polite nod. "Eryx. Well met."

Macaria's gaze turned wry. "You're good for father dear, I think. He needs some light in his life."

Alex made a grumbling noise but Eryx sensed his secret pleasure at his daughter's approval. It seemed even Tartarus' gloom could not dampen Alex's contentment right now.

They trekked on, following Thanatos toward the distant portal. Eryx felt his steps growing heavier, but Alex's strong presence at his side kept him going.

At the bottom of the steep passage leading up, Melinoe awaited them impatiently. Tall and skeletally thin, her appearance lived up to her title as goddess of ghosts.

"Took you fools long enough," she greeted them irritably. "Let's get out of this pit."

With her power, she lifted them all from the depths. Eryx gulped down sweet, clean air as they rose into the mortal realm. Below them the hole sealed itself, blocking Tartarus from view.

Alex carefully lowered Dolos down, keeping one supportive hand under the trickster's elbow. "Can you stand?"

Dolos stretched gingerly. "I believe so. A bit wobbly still, but intact." His sharp eyes fixed on Alex. "I suppose now you'll be collecting on my promise."

Alex crossed his arms, his expression stern. "You supposed correctly. But first, you'll return with us and rest properly to recover your strength." His tone brooked no arguments.

Dolos tilted his head, regarding Alex curiously for a moment before acquiescing with a graceful dip of his chin. "As you wish. The mortal realm may be safest for me at present, until I am restored."

Eryx hid a smile. Even diminished as a mortal, Alex's innate authority prevailed.

Turning to the siblings, Alex grasped each of their shoulders warmly. "Thank you for coming to our aid. We owe you all."

Zagreus shrugged carelessly. "You'd have managed without us

eventually." But pleasure lit his mismatched eyes at his father's praise.

"Stay safe, both of you," Macaria said seriously. With farewell embraces, the two retreated back to the Underworld.

Alone again with Alex, Eryx finally allowed himself to relax fully. They had conquered Tartarus and survived. Together, he was beginning to believe nothing could stop them for long.

Alex drew him close, relief etching his rugged features. "Let's go home," he murmured.

Satisfied, Alex turned to open a portal back to the human world. Eryx kept a steadying hand on Dolos as they stepped through into Harry's living room once more.

The trickster god glanced around with interest at their surroundings. "Quaint," he remarked.

Alex guided Dolos to sit on the couch. "I'll have our healer examine you shortly. For now, make yourself comfortable and don't try anything reckless." His dark gaze remained wary and watchful.

Dolos held up his hands innocently. "I promise to be on my best behavior. You have my gratitude for the rescue, after all." His tone was earnest, though Eryx still sensed they would have to stay alert around the crafty god.

For now though, Dolos was their guest. Eryx fetched him a blanket and glass of water, which Dolos accepted with surprise and thanks. Soon the trickster's eyes drifted shut in much needed rest.

18

Art of the Deal

Alex

"Are you sure we can trust him?" Eryx asked Alex.

"We don't have much choice but to trust him for now," Alex sighed. "Dolos is bound by an unbreakable curse courtesy of Nyx - he cannot speak an outright lie without forfeiting his life. It's the one assurance we have of his cooperation."

Alex vividly recalled Nyx confronting the trickster after one deception too many. The primordial goddess of night had been ruthless in binding Dolos's powers, ensuring he could never again spin falsehoods with impunity. It was a cold comfort now.

Pushing aside his misgivings, Alex turned his mind back to their return from Tartarus. He and Eryx had stumbled bloodied and exhausted from the portal into Harry's living room, Dolos's frail body supported between them.

As Alex and Eryx stumbled through the portal back to Harry's house, they were greeted by the sounds of Zac and Harry bickering at the kitchen table.

"Qat is totally a word!" Zac insisted, pointing at the Scrabble board between them. "It's an evergreen shrub, see, it's right here in the dictionary."

Harry shook his shaggy head dismissively. "Rubbish! You made that up, there's no way that's real."

"I did not! Just look it up if you don't believe me," Zac shot back.

Alex cleared his throat loudly to interrupt them. Both Harry and Zac's heads swiveled toward the new arrivals.

"Alex! Eryx! You're back!" Harry exclaimed, hastily rising from his chair. Concern creased his craggy features as he took in their disheveled state. "

"Is that the trickster god?" The teen peered curiously at Dolos's slumped form.

"Yes, but he's badly weakened," Eryx answered gently before Alex could admonish Zac not to get too close. "Tartarus took a heavy toll."

Harry's bushy brows drew together in concern as he helped ease Dolos into a chair. Alex quickly outlined what they'd faced below and the dire state they'd found Dolos in.

"Hmph, serves the sneaky bastard right," Harry grunted, though his hands were careful as he examined Dolos. "But you did right bringing him here to recover."

"We need to get him to a room to recover," Alex had said wearily.

"Use the one Zac's been staying in," Harry offered gruffly. Between them, he and Eryx had borne Dolos upstairs and settled him into the cozy guest room. Alex's every nerve tingled with caution, but Dolos had made no resistance, slipping immediately into restorative sleep.

Going back to the present, Alex studied Eryx's pinched, thoughtful expression. He knew his partner still harbored doubts about freeing Dolos, but what choice had there been?

"Zac seems happy enough at the diner with Dion for now," Alex remarked, hoping to distract Eryx from fruitless worry.

A faint smile crossed Eryx's face at the memory of how eager Zac had been to work a shift at the lively diner. "He loves it there. We'll pick him up after dealing with our new guest."

Alex repressed a grimace at the reminder of dealing with their new guest. Dolos may have vital information, but Alex did not relish being indebted to the sly trickster god. Hopefully Dolos would uphold his bargain quickly so they could be rid of him.

Arriving at Harry's house, Alex found the burly forge god already sipping his morning coffee. Harry waved them over to the table, pushing the pot toward them.

"Figured you boys could use the fuel after the night you had."

Alex shot him a grateful look as he poured himself and Eryx each a strong cup. The hot, bracing liquid helped ground him after their harrowing ordeal.

As they drank, Eryx inquired politely about Dolos's condition. Harry's craggy features took on a contemplative cast.

"He's resting alright for now. Hard to gauge anything beyond the physical yet - gods heal in their own time, especially after trauma." Harry's tone held a grudging note of sympathy.

Alex nodded silently. Whatever Dolos's flaws, Alex understood the lingering effects of torment. He would not wish such darkness upon anyone, even a soul as crafty as the trickster god.

Eryx set down his mug and moved toward the pantry. "I'll whip up something nourishing for when he wakes. No doubt the poor fellow could use a decent meal."

Despite his ingrained wariness, Alex couldn't help a surge of warmth toward his partner. Eryx's inherent compassion never ceased to soften his own jaded edges.

Harry refilled their mugs, glancing shrewdly at Alex. "So what's the plan when old sly boots is back on his feet? We're venturing into deep waters here, dealing with the likes of him."

"We need whatever information he promised on the forces gathering strength." Alex's voice was grim. "Something dire is building, and Dolos claimed to have knowledge of it. Once he fulfills his word, we part ways."

Harry grunted ambiguously, taking a long draught of coffee. Alex could feel his old friend's skepticism toward trusting Dolos's words. In truth, Alex shared many of the same doubts. But he had vowed to free the trickster, and so they must see this bargain through. Even gods of old must stand by their oaths, as burdensome as they became.

A thought struck Alex then, stirring an old worry. "What of the staff we seized, the one mimicking your Umbra? Any insights on who could craft such a false divine weapon?" If their hidden enemies had harnessed even a fraction of that power…

Harry's brows crashed down like a thundercloud. "It should not be possible, not without my forge…or…" His eyes widened. "The Mimic. When he took my essence in the Abyss. Could he have gained the means to replicate my gifts?"

Eryx's breath hissed between his teeth as the realization struck. "An act of godlike power. But Sven is no true deity, so any staff he forged would be diminished."

Alex's fingers drummed on the table as he processed this disturbing potential lead. "Could someone finish the work? Empower the fake staff fully?"

Harry shook his head firmly. "They would first need the blood of Hecate, its original owner. Her essence binds and controls the primal magic within." He held Alex's gaze intently. "Without it, any copy will remain unstable, inferior."

Alex allowed himself a small measure of relief. At least that avenue seemed barred for now. But it was one more piece of this shadowy puzzle they must unravel before their enemy completed it.

Alex braced himself before entering the trickster's room. Time to start collecting answers.

They found Dolos reclining comfortably against a pile of pillows, looking far more vibrant than the wisp they'd pulled from Tartarus. Sharp eyes regarded Alex with curiosity as he lowered himself into a chair across from the bed.

"I trust you have sufficiently recovered for us to have a discussion?" Alex kept his tone neutral.

Dolos inclined his head gracefully. "Indeed. Ask, and I shall answer what I can." His hands fidgeted subtly with the bedsheets, the only outward sign of nerves.

Alex studied Dolos closely as the trickster god affirmed he was ready to answer their questions. Despite his casual tone, Dolos's hands fidgeted subtly with the bedsheets - the only outward sign of nerves Alex could detect. Strange, considering Dolos's usual unflappable demeanor.

"Very well. Let's start with why Ares wants you dead. What do you know that provokes his wrath so?" Alex kept his gaze fixed on Dolos's face, watching intently for microexpressions.

Dolos leaned back against the pillows with a sigh. "Because I know the truth of who pulls his strings. Ares is but a pawn of Morvain, used to sow chaos."

Alex tensed, shooting a sharp glance at Eryx. They had suspected the Order was involved, but to have it confirmed… This went beyond a single rogue god.

Jaw tight, Alex bit out, "And what is Morvain's purpose? What does reviving Absalom accomplish for them?"

"Absalom is to join their ranks, adding might to their numbers," Dolos answered, spreading his hands. "Morvain seeks to shatter the veil between realms, to unleash Kronos himself upon humanity."

Alex felt cold dread seep into his bones. Kronos the Titan, father of Zeus and his siblings, was an ancient force of immeasurable destruction. If he was freed from Tartarus… It did not bear thinking about.

"Who aids them here on earth? How do they mean to revive Absalom?" Alex demanded urgently.

"The Eastside coven - their elder vampire has a pact with Ares," Dolos revealed. "The chaos wrought by the hybrid monsters fuels the ritual to restore Absalom. But they lack his vessel..." Understanding sparked in the trickster's eyes.

Eryx leaned forward intently. "Zac. They intended him as the vessel, didn't they?"

Dolos nodded gravely. "His blood matches Absalom's essence. Without the proper vessel, the ritual cannot be completed."

Alex rose and paced, raking a hand through his hair. "That's why they hunt Zac. But why not simply use Absalom's original body for his spirit?"

Sadness flickered over Dolos's face. "Once destroyed fully, not even divine flesh may be remade. I know not why, only that it is so."

Silence fell as Alex absorbed this. If Dolos spoke true, they at least still had a chance to stop Absalom's resurrection by protecting Zac. The boy was safe for the moment, but clearly in grave danger.

Turning back to Dolos, Alex kept his voice low and commanding. "Tell us then, trickster - how do we stop them? Where does their power originate?"

Dolos met his gaze unflinchingly. "I have relayed all I know of use regarding Morvain's plans. You have the tools you need." He hesitated. "I only wish I could offer more, but my reach is not what it was."

Satisfied that Dolos had upheld his end, Alex finally broached the subject of payment. "You've given us valuable insights, now we must discuss your terms. What is it you ask in return for this knowledge?"

Alex tensed, waiting for demands of power or leverage over them. But Dolos merely smiled, the expression making him seem almost boyish.

"All I wish is to live freely in this world, without fear or stigma," the trickster god replied simply. "I believe it is time for me to relinquish the mantle I have worn so long. A fresh start, turning over a new leaf as mortals say."

Alex studied Dolos closely, suspicion rising. Such an innocuous request seemed out of character somehow. "What's your true angle here? You expect me to think you seek nothing more?"

Dolos raised his hands placatingly. "You are owed the truth. After so long mistrusted and confined, I wish only a peaceful existence where I might rediscover myself." His eyes were earnest.

Alex sensed no deception in the words or Dolos's open expression. Could the trickster god truly be turning over a new leaf? Alex almost dared believe it, but stayed wary. "Then consider your request granted, provided it brings no further harm."

Dolos bowed his head in acquiescence. "You are kind to take me at my word. I swear you shall not…" He broke off with a choked gasp, face contorting in a pained rictus.

Alarmed, Alex flung aside the bedcovers and recoiled at the jagged shard of celestial steel buried deep in Dolos's side. How could they have missed such a grave wound? Pain and shock must have masked it from their healer's inspection.

"Eryx, help me!" Alex barked urgently. "We need to remove the shard for him to heal."

At Alex's terse explanation, Eryx moved swiftly into action. His hands glowed with warm healing light as he hovered over the injury. "On my mark, draw it out quickly!"

Jaw clenched, Alex gripped the slick end of the fragment. At Eryx's signal he pulled hard, eliciting an agonized shriek from Dolos. But it came free, allowing Eryx to fully knit the ragged flesh.

Panting, Dolos looked up at them with glazed eyes. "You have my deepest thanks," he rasped weakly.

Alex clapped his shoulder. "Just rest easy now. We'll speak more soon." Relief coursed through him that they'd found the obstacle in time.

After Dolos drifted to sleep, Alex pulled Eryx into his arms. "You did well. Your gifts have grown strong." Pride swelled within him at his partner's progress.

Eryx flushed, pleased. "I try every day for you and the others." He kissed Alex softly.

Gazing at his brave, compassionate mate, Alex felt his resolve harden. For those he cared for, he would fight with his last breath to protect their future.

Leaving Dolos to his rest, Alex swiftly enacted a ward upon the room that would alert him immediately if anyone hostile got near. He hoped the trickster god could truly start anew, but caution seemed wise.

Descending to the living room, Alex found Harry just returning from walking his dog. The smith god's shaggy brows rose in inquiry.

Alex quickly outlined all they had learned from Dolos about Kronos, Morvain's plans, and the Eastside Coven's involvement. Harry listened intently, his weathered face creasing further with concern as the details emerged.

When Alex finished, Harry let out a low whistle. "Kronos released would mean doom for all humanity. We must take any action to prevent this."

Alex's jaw tightened with resolve. "I agree. We'll pursue every avenue to obstruct Morvain's ritual and protect the mortal realm." After so recently regaining hope, he refused to lose this fragile world they'd built.

Harry idly stroked his dog's head. "And what's to be done with our slippery guest upstairs? Can Dolos be trusted wandering freely?" Wariness etched the forge god's tone.

"I've allowed him sanctuary here, for now at least," Alex sighed. "If you could aid his recovery and adjust to mortality, I would consider it a personal favor."

Harry harrumphed but nodded. "I make no promises how hospitable a host I'll be, but the blighter can stay until he's healed."

Alex clapped his shoulder gratefully. "That's all I ask. Thank you, old friend." Harry's protection would help smooth Dolos's transition.

Just then, Alex's communication device began beeping insistently from his pocket. Checking it, Alex saw an urgent summons from Gabe flashing across the screen. Finally they had a solid lead.

"Harry, we have to go, but call if any issues arise with our guest," Alex said briskly. At Harry's assurance, he turned on his heel, Eryx following closely.

Arriving at Shadowguard HQ, they headed straight for the lab where Gabe and Lily were studying a large monitor intently. They both looked up, relief washing across their faces.

"Boss, Eryx, finally! We've been trying to reach you for ages," Gabe said excitedly. "We got a match on the blood sample from our Jane Doe."

Alex's pulse spiked with anticipation. "Explain, now."

Alex immediately asked who the blood sample matched to.

Gabe replied, "One Rick Schulz, lives over on Fifth Avenue - same area we found our Jane Doe victim."

Alex's thoughts raced. Fifth Avenue bordered the Eastside Coven's territory. "Does he have known ties to the coven? Criminal affiliations?"

Lily pulled up a photo of Rick on the screen. "Records show he's been busted selling vampire blood before. And suspected of dealing for the Eastside crew."

"So either a vampire or hybrid out of control," Eryx mused. "Regardless, he's our prime suspect now."

Gabe nodded firmly. "The evidence trail points decisively to him. I'll start surveillance, find the optimal time to bring him in."

Pride swelled in Alex's chest at his team's competency and drive. "Excellent work. Get everyone prepped for a briefing."

As Gabe and Lily rushed to gather the others, Alex turned to Eryx. "I need to check in with Dr. Sloan about our captives. Meet you shortly?"

At Eryx's acquiescence, they parted ways. Arriving in the medical ward, Alex found Dr. Sloan studying charts with a grave expression. "What's the status, Doc?" Alex asked without preamble.

Dr. Sloan sighed heavily. "I'm afraid the corruption from the dark magic was too severe in both subjects. They've passed." His aged features were creased with dismay.

Alex's shoulders slumped slightly upon hearing the captives hadn't survived. He had hoped to somehow redeem them, misguided as they were. It was a faint but persistent hope he'd carried since his days as Hades, Lord of the Underworld.

Back then, so many lost souls came under his domain, judged and sentenced to their fates. Though necessary, it had weighed on him over the eons. He saw the shades of who they'd been in life, before despair or vengeance twisted them.

Now, he preferred saving lives over condemning them. But sometimes healing came too late, the damage beyond even magic's power to mend.

"Then we shall give them proper burials," he told Dr. Sloan heavily. "They were still people led astray by forces beyond their control." He owed them that much dignity at least.

It was all one could do - mourn the potential lost, while honoring the spirits they had been. Not every soul could be saved, but laying them respectfully to rest was a duty Alex bore seriously, both then and now.

Some things left their mark, even on gods reborn mortal. Alex glimpsed the man he'd been, and hoped the man he was now did that grave mantle justice, however he could.

Dr. Sloan gave him a sympathetic look. "Of course. I'll make the arrangements." He hesitated. "If I may also check on your new guest, to assist his recovery?"

Gratitude washed over Alex. Dr. Sloan's dedication to healing was a light against the surrounding darkness. "Please do, you have my thanks. Harry will explain the situation."

Just then, Olivia's voice patched through on his comm. "Sir, you and Eryx have visitors waiting in the briefing room." Her tone held barely suppressed mirth.

Frowning, Alex hurried to meet this unexpected guest. He froze upon seeing Zac grinning at him, Dion hovering apologetically behind. Before Alex could react, Zac bounded over to engulf Eryx in an enthusiastic hug.

"Isn't this place so cool?" Zac exclaimed, head swiveling to take in all the advanced equipment. "I wanted to see your secret lair up close!"

Despite himself, Alex felt an answering smile touch his lips at the boy's infectious excitement. He raised an eyebrow at Dion in inquiry.

The wine god held up both hands. "Hey, don't look at me. The kid's persistent, wouldn't take no for an answer." But his eyes were fond as he watched Zac chatter eagerly at Eryx about his day.

19

Too late

Eryx

Eryx glanced over at Alex and could see the tension in his jaw as he stared at the photo. He didn't need any magical powers to know what Alex was thinking. After the mess with Dolos, the last damn thing they needed was more trouble from the Order.

"Hey," Eryx said, touching his arm. "We'll figure this out. We always do."

Alex gave him a small smile that didn't reach his eyes. "I know. I just wish we'd had more time to recover from the last disaster before diving into a new one."

"Welcome to life with the gods," Eryx said wryly. A never ending cycle of one crisis after another.

Zac bounced on the balls of his feet, craning his neck to see the photo. "Ooh, let me see!"

Alex angled it away with a frown. "Absolutely not. You're not getting involved in this."

"But I want to help!" Zac wheedled. He turned his pleading eyes to Eryx. "Eryx, tell him to let me see it. If it's one of the guys from the lab, I'll totally recognize him."

Eryx wavered, seeing his logic even as uncertainty gnawed at his gut. Zac was like a little brother to him. Letting him tag along to hunt down dangerous blood mages didn't sit well.

But Alex was already shaking his head. "Doesn't matter if you can ID him. It's too risky."

Zac's face fell. Before Eryx could say anything, he blurted out, "I can handle myself! I've got powers now too, remember?"

"Untrained powers," Alex said bluntly. "These are experienced killers we're dealing with, not schoolyard bullies."

Zac flushed. Eryx winced inwardly at Alex's poor choice of words, knowing how desperate Zac was to prove himself. Uh oh. An argument was the last thing they needed. Time for damage control.

Eryx stepped between them, holding up a hand. "Easy, both of you," he said gently. He glanced at Alex pointedly. "There's no need for insults. Zac knows the risks." He looked back at Zac. "But Alex is right about your lack of training. Things could get dangerous."

Zac's scowl deepened. "You just want me out of the way too," he accused. Behind Eryx, Alex made an exasperated noise.

"No," Eryx said patiently. "But we care about your safety. There are better ways for you to help right now. We just need to figure this out first."

He watched Zac wrestle with his desire to prove himself versus his knowledge that Alex and Eryx were far more experienced at this supernatural combat thing. The guy had abandonment issues a mile wide thanks to his jerk parents; Eryx understood his desperation to feel valued. But taking him vampire hunting wouldn't help.

Finally Zac's shoulders slumped. "Fine," he muttered. "Guess I'll just hang back here."

Eryx squeezed his shoulder. "We do need your help. Just not in the field yet." He paused. "Here, take a look at the photo. You recognize him?"

Alex made a sound of protest but Eryx ignored him. Zac's face lit up as he took the picture, scrutinizing it eagerly.

"Yeah I know him! He was there when they tried to experiment on me." His mouth twisted. "He took a lot of my blood. Jerk."

Eryx squeezed Zac's shoulder again. "I'm sorry about what you went through. But you recognizing Schulz helps - now we can track him down."

He glanced over at Alex meaningfully. If they found the scientist, they'd likely uncover more clues about the missing vampire legend's resurrection.

Understanding sparked in Alex's midnight eyes and he gave a curt nod. Message received.

Zac bounced eagerly on the balls of his feet again. "So can I come with you guys to grab Schulz? I'll stay in the car and just point him out, I swear!"

Alex opened his mouth, clearly about to issue another refusal. Before he could, Eryx jumped in.

"That could work," he said slowly. Alex cut him a look of disbelief but Eryx barrelled on. "With Zac's ID, we'd spot Schulz faster instead of going in blind."

"Please please please!" Zac begged, clasping his hands together dramatically. "I just want to be useful for once. And I already know all about crazy vamp science thanks to those freaks experimenting on me." His expression darkened for a moment.

Alex hesitated, his resolve weakening. Eryx could practically see the indecision warring in his stormy eyes. Time for one final push.

Eryx put a hand on Alex's arm, meeting his gaze. "We can keep him out of direct danger but use his knowledge," he said quietly. "The kid just wants to help, that's all."

Alex looked away, jaw tightening. Then his shoulders slumped in defeat. "…Alright," he muttered. "But you stay in the vehicle no matter what!" He glared at Zac warningly. "I mean it!"

Zac's face lit up. "Yess! Don't worry boss-man, I'll be good." He made an exaggerated scout's salute. Alex just rolled his eyes with a grumble. But Eryx could tell he was struggling not to smile.

The others chuckled in amusement at Zac's antics. Olivia grabbed his arm, steering him from the room. "I'll help prep the puppy for his first op," she said with wink over her shoulder.

"Hey I'm not a…okay yeah I'm totally the adorable team mascot," Zac laughed. Their voices faded down the hall.

Eryx turned back to Alex who had his arms crossed, scowling. Uh oh. Eryx tapped into his diplomatic skills honed from millennia dealing with grumpy Underworld gods and spirits. Time for some sweet talking.

"I know you've got issues with putting civilians at risk," he began gently. "But Zac already knows too much to stay on the sidelines. At least this way we can keep him controlled in the Bearcat. He'll be warded up and out of the way."

Alex just grunted, staring at the far wall stonily.

Eryx tried a different angle. "Look at it this way - the kid clearly needs to feel involved with the group. To have a purpose after the trauma he endured." He lowered his voice persuasively. "If we deprive him of that, it will just drive Zac into riskier behavior trying to prove himself behind our backs."

At that, Alex's eyes slid back to lock with his, resignation lurking in their depths. Eryx suppressed a grin. Hook, line and sinker. As an immortal who had guided countless souls, he understood psychology. Now to gently reel Alex in.

Eryx wrapped his arms loosely around Alex's waist. "We've been where Zac is, desperately needing guidance and yearning to understand who we are. What we can do." He raised a meaningful eyebrow.

Alex flinched almost imperceptibly. Bullseye. For all his flaws, Hades had a soft spot for outcasts like himself and Zac. His lover sighed, deflating with reluctant acceptance.

"Fine," Alex grumbled. "Zac can ride along. But only to ID Schulz! Then he's heading right back here."

Eryx smiled. "Deal." He leaned in to brush a light kiss to Alex's cheek in thanks. "Now let's go catch ourselves a suspect."

Thirty minutes later, they were piled into Alex's beloved Bearcat, enroute to Schulz' last known location. Zac fidgeted in the backseat, practically bouncing with excitement between Olivia and Gabe. His enthusiasm reminded Eryx of an overeager puppy on its first trip.

He glanced over to see Alex's hands gripping the steering wheel tightly, tension visible in his frame. Reaching over, Eryx laid a hand comfortingly on his thigh. Alex shot him a grateful look, some of the strain easing from his body.

The Bearcat rumbled through the streets as Alex followed the GPS to Schulz' last known address. When the cultured voice announced their arrival, Alex pulled to the curb with a frown.

"That can't be right," he muttered.

Eryx took in the dilapidated brick building, weathered by time and the elements. The whole block looked outdated and worn, clashing with the sleek highrises nearby.

"Maybe the records are outdated?" Eryx suggested uncertainly. Why would a scientist live here?

Alex's eyes narrowed. "Maybe. Or it's a trap."

He drummed his fingers on the steering wheel before glancing back at Marcus. "You're with us. The rest of you stay alert just in case this goes sideways."

The others voiced their agreement. Zac started to unbuckle his seatbelt to climb out.

"Oh no, dear," Olivia said, grabbing Zac by the arm gently. "You're staying put." Ignoring his loud protests, she strapped him back in securely.

Alex's mouth quirked but he hid it quickly, exiting the Bearcat with Eryx and Marcus on his heels. Together they approached the front stoop cautiously. The building appeared deserted, most of the windows boarded up or broken. Marcus blurred in a circuit around the perimeter before rejoining them.

"Nothing obvious nearby. No traps or tripwires either." He reported.

Alex nodded. "Right. Let's see who's home then." He mounted the steps and pounded loudly on the door. "Schulz! Open up, we just want to talk." Silence greeted them. Alex glanced at Eryx. "Well, I tried to be polite."

He stepped back and slammed his boot near the handle, shattering the lock. The door swung inward with a prolonged creak. The three men stepped warily inside.

Compared to the crumbling exterior, the interior gleamed under the fluorescent lights, the space dominated by bulky equipment and machinery. Eryx's eyebrows rose in surprise. Some kind of lab then?

Alex prowled deeper inside, alert for any nasty surprises. Finding none, he relaxed minutely. "Fan out. Look for anything related to the Order's plans with Absalom."

They split up to search. Eryx trailed his fingers along one machine with complex tubes and vials. Next to it sat an examination table with thick leather straps. Unease trickled down his spine. This set up seemed designed for live subjects. Images of Zac being tormented here rose unbidden in his mind. Anger burned within him.

Rifling through folders and papers on a desk yielded no clues. He moved towards the back rooms to continue his search. Rounding a partition, he saw a heavy steel door ajar. Cautiously pushing it wider, he stepped through into near darkness. The space was smaller, filled with hulking, strange shapes. Along the far wall were rows of...

"Alex!" Eryx yelled, pulse racing. His breath fogged in the chilly air. What was this place?

Footsteps pounded towards him. Alex burst into the room, flames coiling down his arms to illuminate the macabre scene. He froze at Eryx's side, eyes widening.

Along each wall were rows of vertical glass chambers like elongated coffins. Within floated humanoid shapes suspended in glowing blue liquid, various tubes and wires attached. Eryx drifted closer to peer inside one capsule. His stomach clenched.

The being inside appeared human. But it was clearly dead, pallid flesh gaunt and eyes sunken. Dark fanged teeth protruded past its blue-tinged lips. A vampire.

"There must be dozens of them," Marcus said in hushed dismay behind them.

Rage kindled in Alex's eyes, smoke pouring from his clenched fists. He turned on his heel and stalked from the grisly room, tension in every line of his powerful frame. Alarmed, Eryx hurried after him. That murderous wrath could only mean one thing, Alex was unleashing his hellfire.

Sure enough they emerged to find the lab wreathed in dark flames, hungry and hot. Marcus stepped back from the intense heat but Eryx rushed forward, uncaring of the fire's bite. He had to stop Alex before he lost control and burned down the whole block!

"Alex, stop!" Eryx grabbed his rigid shoulders. Alex tried to shake him off, wide-eyed gaze fixed on the ravenous flames as they devoured file cabinets like tinder. Eryx tightened his grip desperately.

"Alex, look at me!" he shouted. "You have to stop this now before it spreads!"

With painful slowness, Alex finally dragged his eyes to meet Eryx's. Sanity was gradually returning to their blue-flame depths but his breath still came in ragged pants.

Eryx cradled Alex's face between his hands, guiding him back from the brink as the dark fire died down. But inwardly, dread curled tighter in his gut. This was only the beginning. Much worse likely awaited them. And if Alex lost control again…Eryx feared the carnage he might unleash. They had to find a way to stop it before his powers consumed him.

As Eryx picked through the rubble, movement caught his eye. He froze, breath catching as he spotted a pale hand protruding from beneath a fallen beam. Fingers curled limply like a macabre mannequin.

Heart racing, he hurried over and with Alex's help shifted the heavy chunk of ceiling off the still form. Eryx reeled back with a choked gasp, bile rising in his throat.

There lay the savaged corpse of Rick Schulz, shredded by the unexpected blast. Blackened flesh and gaping wounds seeped crimson blood across the floor. Unseeing eyes stared upwards in permanent shock at his abrupt, violent demise.

"No chance he survived this," Alex bit out grimly. "The coward got caught in his own trap."

Eryx just numbly nodded, unable to tear his eyes away from the gruesome proof of their situation worsening. "Or they got to him first." Their one solid lead, dead. And soon they'd be facing an resurrected legendary vampire if they couldn't stop the Order in time.

Footsteps pounded up and Lucas careened around the partition, eyes wild. "Guys, we gotta move! There's a bomb about to blow this whole place!"

Alex jerked upright. "What?! How long do we have?"

Lucas shook his head. "sixty seconds if we're lucky!"

Fear clutched Eryx's chest but Alex was already barking orders. "Marcus, get Zac clear!" The speedster blurring from sight was their only response. Alex turned to Gabe. "Contain the blast if you can!"

Gabe frowned, even as azure spell-power flowed from his hands. "I'll try but bomb magic needs specific wards. I can maybe shield us somewhat." The dome of energy enveloped them with a hum as the bomb ticked down.

Eryx focused inward on that golden well of power, attuning himself to ambient vibrations. If he could manipulate the sound waves when it blew to siphon off energy...

"I can attempt dampening the effects," he said tersely. Alex's eyes snapped to his and he gave a brisk nod. Do what it takes was the clear message.

"Brace yourselves!" Gabe yelled.

The tremendous explosion sent a massive fireball rolling towards them like a juggernaut. Searing orange flames and clouds of choking dust expanded rapidly outwards, consuming everything in their path.

Eryx's heart froze in his chest for one terrifying instant. If Gabe's shield or his sound manipulation wavered for even a moment, they would be engulfed and incinerated instantly. Their lives now balanced on a razor's edge of disaster.

He saw Gabe brace himself, fingers contorted like claws, face straining from the effort of pouring more power into the protective bubble. Azure light flared and stretched around them.

At the same moment, Eryx locked every fiber of his being on tightening the invisible forcefield woven from manipulated soundwaves and vibration. As the leading edge of flames collided violently, he felt the concussive shockwave impact their shield like a physical blow, seeking weaknesses.

The very air felt energized, pressing inward like a smothering blanket as smoke and debris battered their tenuous barrier. Eryx tasted blood from biting the inside of his cheek as he reached deeper inside himself. He siphoned more of Apollo's essence, channeling it desperately into maintaining the quivering wall of disrupted sound frequencies. Just a few more seconds!

Beads of sweat rolled down his face, muscles burning. The shield groaned warningly under the onslaught but neither man yielded any ground. They had people relying on them and Eryx would be damned if he failed them now!

At last, aching slowness, the churning flames lost momentum. Howling destruction died down to an ominous crackle amidst swirling ashes. Gabe and Eryx collapsed together gasping raggedly for oxygen, utterly spent. But they had held the line. The shield diffused, winking out as pulsing magic faded from Gabe's fingers.

Lucas let out a shaky laugh, wiping soot from the lenses of his glasses with trembling fingers. "Holy hell…we're still alive somehow."

Marcus straightened from where he had instinctively crouched in anticipation, having zoomed back from getting Zac clear, and clapped them weakly on the shoulders. "Hell of a job, both of you."

Eryx managed a weary nod before turning anxiously, seeking Alex in the wreckage. He spotted him several feet away surveying the smoldering ruins, wrath etched into his face at the gruesome sight of Schulz's corpse. Alex's thoughts and emotions were surely raging unchecked.

As if sensing his concern, Alex visibly gathered the tattered remnants of his composure. He strode over to squeeze Eryx's shoulder, stormy eyes conveying silent gratitude. They had endured. For now.

Alex ordered curtly, "Search for anything useful then we're gone. I want every scrap related to their plans."

The others scrambled to comply, sifting debris with gloves and bags. After long minutes, Alex nodded. "That'll have to do. Let's move before more trouble finds us."

They headed for the crumbling exterior wall when Emma held up a hand. "Hold up. We've got incoming vultures." She pointed meaningfully at the swarm of news vans pulling up outside, reporters already swarming forth like ants.

Eryx cursed under his breath, shoulders tensing. He couldn't risk being spotted by press now. Too many awkward questions he couldn't answer. "I can't be seen here," he bit out tersely. "It'd invite disaster."

Lily nodded in understanding, grabbing Emma's arm. "We'll run interference with the media. You guys slip out the back quickly." Over her shoulder, she added, "Stall them as long as you can!"

The two women headed out to confront the press mob. Eryx hoped their skillful excuses and distractions would keep attention diverted. He turned to Alex, features set grimly. "Let's move before this gets more complicated."

Alex jerked his chin in silent agreement. Together, they slipped away through a crumbling hole smashed in the building's rear just as cameras started flashing out front. They piled into the idling Bearcat where Zac was bouncing excitedly in the backseat despite his ordeal.

Eryx barely had the door shut before the teen was blurting out questions about the explosion. "Holy crap, was that nuts or what?! Are you guys okay? Did you find Schulz?"

Alex tersely rebuffed the barrage as he guided the vehicle smoothly from the chaotic scene. Eryx gave Zac's shoulder a brief squeeze, relief washing through him that their young friend was safe. "We made it out, barely. As for Schulz..." He hesitated, loathe to describe the gruesome death.

Sensing his discomfort, Alex spoke up gruffly. "You were brave today, Zac. Kept your head and didn't panic when things got hairy. We owe you for the solid intel." It was likely as close to praise as Zac could expect from the brusque man.

But it was enough. Zac practically glowed at the words. "Really? Awesome!" He bounced excitedly again. "Man, sign me up to help kick more bad guy ass!"

Eryx snorted wryly at his enthusiasm. "Whoa there, killer. Let's get you properly trained and school first before any more field work, yeah?" He raised an eyebrow. "Speaking of, you get your license yet or should I drive us back?"

"No license yet but I totally got this!" Zac made a grab for the wheel, eliciting curses and swats from Alex. Eryx leaned against the door, chuckling as they batted each other away. The playful respite lifted some weight from his shoulders momentarily. He wished it could last.

20

An Offer to Refuse

Eryx

Eryx stood by the floor-to-ceiling windows of the penthouse, peering down at the media vans and reporters clustered on the sidewalk far below.

"Can I pelt them with stones?" Zac asked eagerly, popping up beside Eryx and pressing his nose to the glass. "Just a few little ones?"

Eryx laughed, the sound echoing in the open concept living space. "As tempting as that sounds, I don't think Alex would approve."

"You're no fun," Zac grumbled. He scratched at the fresh scab on his arm from yesterday's battle. The wound hadn't fully healed yet, even with Eryx and Finn's efforts. Hemomancer blood was tricky.

Alex strode into the sunlit living room, shaking his head. "No assaulting the press. We need them on our side."

Zac rolled his eyes dramatically. "But they're so annoying!"

"Part of the job," Alex said dryly. He glanced at Eryx. "Any changes down there?"

Eryx peered through the floor-to-ceiling windows again. The reporters seemed subdued today, lacking yesterday's feverish energy.

Only a few diehard journalists lingered on the sidewalk after the big reveal at Schulz's mansion had yielded no results.

"No, just the usual vultures. I think the excitement has worn off for now."

Alex nodded, the lines on his forehead easing slightly. Eryx knew the media circus troubled him. Alex liked to operate in the shadows, unseen and unnoticed. Having his business splashed across the headlines went against all his instincts.

"We'll give them a few more days to lose interest," Alex decided. He checked his phone with a frown. "Anything from Lucas and Lily?"

Eryx shook his head. "Not yet. But they'll call as soon as they crack the encryption on Schulz's files."

"Let's hope so." Alex's jaw tightened. "We're running out of time. The Order could be putting their plans in motion as we speak."

Eryx stepped closer, resting a hand on Alex's tense shoulder. He sent a subtle pulse of healing energy into the knotted muscles. "We knew this wouldn't be easy or quick. But we've made progress."

Alex covered Eryx's hand with his own, the simple touch easing some of the worry in his eyes. "I know. I just wish we could have found more. We wasted precious hours searching that place."

Schulz had covered his tracks perfectly. Almost too perfectly.

Eryx's phone buzzed, jolting him from his thoughts. He glanced at the screen and winced. It was Brad, his manager. Again.

Guilt gnawed at Eryx. He'd been neglecting his music career lately, too caught up in supernatural disasters. But Brad and the record label had been patient with him, giving him space to figure things out. He owed it to them to at least talk.

Eryx swiped to accept the call. "Hey Brad, what's up?"

"Eryx, my man! How's it going?" Brad's effusive voice filled the penthouse. "Haven't heard from you in a while. Started to think you'd gone off the grid."

Eryx rubbed the back of his neck. "Yeah, sorry about that. Things have been…crazy around here." That was an understatement.

"No problem, Any chance you can stop by the studio this afternoon?"

Eryx hesitated, glancing at Alex. As much as he wanted to focus on his music again, the timing wasn't ideal.

Alex nodded firmly. "Go. We've got things covered here for now." His expression softened. "Don't put your life on hold forever."

Warmth bloomed in Eryx's chest. Alex always had his back, making sure he didn't lose himself in supernatural chaos.

"Alright, I'll be there," Eryx told Brad. They quickly hammered out the meeting details.

As Eryx ended the call, Alex turned to Zac. "Go with him. We're not taking chances, even for quick trips."

Zac bounced in place eagerly. "Yes! This'll be awesome." His enthusiasm dimmed. "But, um, are you sure you want me along? I won't, like, mess things up?"

Eryx smiled reassuringly. The kid had come a long way in just a few weeks. He was still struggling to find his place in the world, but his courage and good heart shone through. With time, guidance, and proper schooling, Zac could gain the confidence he lacked.

"You'll do great," Eryx said warmly. "Could be fun to give you a mini music lesson while we're there, if you want."

Zac's eyes lit up. "Seriously? That would be epic!"

Alex handed Eryx a set of keys. "Take one of the discreet cars. Avoid attention."

Eryx nodded. Dealing with the mob of reporters downstairs sounded exhausting right now. He was tired of the media circus constantly hounding him for gossip and drama about his new life. Maybe someday he'd give them just enough to satisfy their curiosity. But not today.

Eryx and Zac managed to sneak through the underground parking garage unseen. As they drove, Zac fiddled with the radio, flipping through stations. Eryx gripped the wheel, mind wandering.

"Do you ever wonder what happened to his parents?" Zac asked abruptly.

Eryx blinked, caught off guard by the question. "Whose parents?"

"Schulz," Zac clarified. "I mean, they must've noticed he was evil, right?" He shrugged. "Just makes me curious."

Eryx's chest tightened, thinking of his own dysfunctional parents. "I don't know Schulz's family history. But Alex and I will make sure you have the support you need from now on."

Zac ducked his head, cheeks reddening slightly. "Thanks. That really means a lot."

Eryx patted his shoulder. "Anytime, kiddo."

They rode in comfortable silence the rest of the way. Despite everything, Eryx felt hopeful.

Eryx and Zac thankfully arrived at Eternity Records without being followed by the media. Eryx pulled into the basement parking garage and found an empty spot.

"Home sweet home," Eryx murmured as he killed the engine. The familiar sight of the garage eased some of the tension that had been knotting his shoulders lately. He hadn't realized how much he missed this place.

They took the elevator up to the main lobby. Eryx blinked in surprise when the doors opened to reveal Richard waiting on the other side.

"Well hello stranger!" Richard greeted cheerfully. "Been a while since we've seen you around here."

Warm affection rushed through Eryx at the sight of his friend. He stepped out and pulled Richard into a quick hug. "I know, I'm sorry. Things have been insane."

Richard waved it off. "Don't worry about it. But you should come out with the band sometime. We miss you!"

Eryx rubbed his neck sheepishly. He really had been neglecting his friends lately, too caught up in supernatural disasters. "Definitely. I promise we'll plan a night out."

It was then Richard seemed to notice Zac lingering behind Eryx. "Oh hey, who's this?"

Eryx gestured the teen forward. "Richard, meet Zac. He's a friend who's been staying with me and Alex." Technically true, though the full story was far more complicated. "Zac, this is my buddy Richard. We work together sometimes."

"Cool guitar, man!" Zac said, nodding at the case Richard had slung over his shoulder.

Richard grinned. "Thanks! So Zac, do you like music as well?"

Zac shrugged modestly. "I like music, but I'm not very good yet."

"Well hey, anytime you want tips, let me know," Richard offered kindly. "Could even give you some lessons if you're interested."

Zac's eyes went wide. "Seriously? That would be awesome!"

Eryx smiled, glad to see Zac coming out of his shell a bit. Making more friends would be good for the kid.

"So what are you doing here?" Richard asked Eryx. "Meeting with Brad?"

"Yeah, Brad wanted to discuss things," Eryx explained.

Richard nodded knowingly. "Well, I was just heading to meet Landon for a session. How about I keep an eye on Zac till you're done? Give him the VIP tour and stuff."

Eryx raised an eyebrow. Richard's cheeks pinked slightly at the mention of Landon. Oh ho, what was this now?

"That cool with you, Zac?" Eryx asked.

"Hell yeah! Can we raid the snack room too?" Zac pleaded.

Richard laughed. "I think that can be arranged."

Eryx clapped Zac on the shoulder. "Alright kiddo, mind your manners with Richard. I'll come get you when I'm done."

"No problem. Go make some hits!" Zac said with an enthusiastic fist pump.

Chuckling, Eryx made his way down the familiar halls toward Brad's office. The sights and sounds of the studio instantly put him at ease - the low thrum of bass from a practice room, the smell of coffee wafting from the lounge. It felt good to be back.

As he approached Brad's door, raised voices echoed from within. Eryx slowed, catching a hint of Brad's irritated tone.

"For the last time, we don't know where he was taken, but we're not authorizing any rescue missions!" Brad was saying angrily. "I don't care how powerful you think you are, Thor. Smashing into that facility will only make things worse."

There was a pause as the person on the other end of the phone responded loudly.

Brad scoffed. "Then tell Loki to use his magic to find a more subtle way in. I want to help, but you know I have my own thing going on."

Eryx's eyes widened. Thor and Loki? As in the actual Norse gods? Did other pantheons exist in the modern world too?

He heard the audible smack of Brad's phone being slammed down forcefully onto the desk. Brad must be really on edge dealing with angry gods.

Taking a steadying breath, Eryx knocked briskly and let himself into the office. "Hey Brad, everything okay in here?"

"Eryx!" Brad plastered a smile on his face, though tension radiated from him. "Sorry about that. Just some pushy clients."

Eryx slid into the chair across from the desk, acting casual while his mind raced. Brad's weak excuse didn't fool him - something major was clearly going on with the Norse gods. He made a mental note to ask Alex about it later. But for now, he played along.

"Sounded pretty heated," Eryx remarked. "What was that about?"

Brad waved a hand dismissively. "Oh nothing, just an unreasonable request. I shut it down quickly."

"So…" Eryx changed the subject. "You wanted to talk?"

"How are you doing, really? With all the changes lately, I wanna make sure you're in a good headspace before we dive into new music." Brad asked softly.

Eryx hesitated, considering his words carefully.

"I'm doing okay," Eryx said finally. "The past few months have been a rollercoaster, no doubt. And juggling everything hasn't been easy."

Brad nodded sympathetically. "I can only imagine. Your life changed overnight." He leaned forward, expression serious. "If it's too much, no one would blame you for wanting to step back from the spotlight for a while. You could take a break, figure things out."

Eryx tensed slightly. Was Brad telling him to choose - music or the supernatural world?

"What are you saying?" Eryx asked cautiously.

Brad held up his hands. "Hey, no pressure either way. But if you wanted to focus on your new…extracurricular stuff instead, we'd understand. I know the Shadowguard keeps you busy."

"Nothing gets by you, huh?" Eryx said ruefully.

Brad chuckled. "I keep my ear to the ground. Gotta look out for my favorite client." His expression turned serious again. "So what'll it be? The music biz will still be here if you ever want back in. But I know you've got important work to do with Alex and the others."

Eryx chewed his lip, conflicted emotions swirling. He missed the simple joys of performing and creating. Music was his first love, woven into his soul. Could he really walk away, leave that part of himself behind?

Yet the fight against the Order was so dire. Lives hung in the balance - mortal and supernatural alike. Eryx had these gifts, these connections. Didn't he have a duty to use them for good?

As if summoned by Eryx's turmoil, Alex's face flashed in his mind.

His steadfast belief that Eryx could master both worlds, not have to sacrifice one life for another. Alex had never asked him to choose… only to follow his heart.

"I don't want to stop making music," Eryx said slowly. "It's too much a part of me. But I can't abandon Alex and the others either." He met Brad's eyes. "I want to find a way to balance both, with your support."

Brad broke into a wide smile. "I was hoping you'd say that. We've got your back, Eryx. However we can help you pull double duty, just say the word." He extended his hand. "So whaddya say we start prepping the next big hit?"

Relief crashing over him, Eryx clasped Brad's hand firmly. Together, they could make this work. He didn't have to give up any part of himself.

"Let's do this."

After deciding to pursue both music and the supernatural mission, Eryx felt like a weight had lifted from his shoulders. With Brad's support, he could have the best of both worlds.

Brad shuffled some papers on his desk and glanced up. "So now that that's settled, there is one other thing we should discuss…"

Eryx tensed slightly. Brad's hesitant tone reminded him too much of doctors bracing to share bad news. "What's up?"

"Well…" Brad dragged a hand through his artfully tousled hair. "The media circus lately has been intense. We want to get ahead of it, control the narrative before rumors get out of hand."

Eryx grimaced. He knew exactly where this was headed. "You want me to do an interview?"

"A press conference, actually." At Eryx's apprehensive look, Brad held up a placating hand. "Nothing too invasive. Just confirm you're doing well, share some album details, that kind of thing."

When Eryx still looked uncertain, Brad softened his voice. "This is your chance to tell your story, Eryx. Don't let the vultures put their own spin on it."

Eryx worried his lip. He hated media spectacle and BS drama. But Brad had a point - refusing interviews only fueled more prying speculation. Better to confront it directly.

"Alright," Eryx conceded. "But I don't have to answer anything too personal, right?"

"Of course, you steer the ship," Brad promised. "My team will help craft some safe, friendly questions. Anyone gets out of line, we shut it down."

Eryx nodded, feeling a bit better. With preparation, he could handle one press conference. Hopefully that would get the media buzzards off his back for a while.

"We'll set it up in two days," Brad continued. "Gives you time to prep. And we'll have you announce the new album title - Phoenix. A powerful rebirth metaphor."

"I like it." The name felt right, symbolizing his emergence from recent trials and trauma like a phoenix from ashes.

"As for what's next…" Brad's eyes glinted eagerly. "Your comeback album is going to be epic. We're pulling out all the stops - music videos, tour, the works."

Eryx blinked. "Whoa, hold up. I can't just take off touring for months right now. My…other obligations make that impossible." Protecting the mortal realm came first, after all.

Brad held up a hand. "Don't worry, we've got flexible options. We'll do promotional appearances and pop-up shows in between your missions." His voice dropped to a conspiratorial whisper. "We can even work the supernatural elements subtly into the live performances if you want. Give the fans a taste of your new magic."

Eryx laughed. "Let's not get carried away. Baby steps." But the idea of incorporating music and magic, his two great passions, had appeal. Together they could create something extraordinary.

The press conference made him nervous, but sharing his new sound with fans again would be electrifying. And he trusted Brad to handle the business side smoothly.

Now he just had to fill Alex in on the plan. Something told him Alex wouldn't love the increased public exposure. But it was time to step back into the spotlight on his own terms.

Eryx left Brad's office feeling lighter than he had in weeks. With his manager's blessing, he could finally unite his music and his supernatural mission. Whistling, he pulled out his phone to call Richard and check on Zac.

"Hey man, how'd it go with Brad?" Richard asked.

"Really well," Eryx said as he headed for the parking garage elevator. "We're gonna start prepping the new album soon. Where are you guys at?"

"Coffee shop down the block. Zac's on a donut sugar high," Richard chuckled.

Eryx laughed. "I'm on my way now—"

He froze as the elevator doors slid open, revealing a tall figure leaning casually against the side of his car. Eryx's breath caught. Even in the shadows, that stark bone-white face was unmistakable.

"Eryx? You there?" Richard's voice echoed tinnily through his phone.

"I'll call you back," Eryx said tightly, hanging up. He steeled himself as the mimic Sven pushed off the car and prowled toward him. This confrontation had been inevitable, but Eryx had hoped for more time.

"Well hello, little godling," Sven purred, coal-black eyes boring into him. "Fancy running into you here."

Eryx stood his ground as Sven circled him slowly. "What do you want, Sven?"

Sven tutted. "Now now, is that any way to greet an old friend? I merely came to talk."

"We're not friends," Eryx said sharply. "Now get to the point before I remove you." He summoned a warning spark of golden light to his palms, though he knew it was likely futile against the mimic's absorbed magic.

Sven clicked his tongue. "Still so quick to turn to violence. Have you learned nothing traveling with the great Alexander?"

He leaned in, voice dropping to a sibilant whisper. "But you do not need to follow his doomed crusade. Join us, Eryx, and we shall rule these pathetic mortals together."

Revulsion churned in Eryx's gut. "I'll never help you enslave innocent people. Now leave before I make you."

Sven sighed, an exaggerated look of pity twisting his cadaverous face. "Once so much potential, now nothing but a vessel for a faded myth. Apollo has made you disappointingly weak." He shook his head sadly. "No matter. We shall free you from his influence in time."

Fear trickled down Eryx's spine but he forced himself to meet Sven's fathomless gaze steadily. "Stay away from me and my friends. This is your last warning."

Sven smiled, displaying a mouthful of teeth. "Oh, I am not here for you today. We have...other interests."

Dread congealed in Eryx's stomach. "If you touch Zac—"

"The boy?" Sven laughed, a horrible rasping sound. "Morvain has great plans for him. His blood magic ancestry makes him quite special." Sven leaned in close, pale breath grazing Eryx's cheek. "Give him to us freely, and we shall permit you and Alex to live. Refuse, and we will take him by force along with your lives."

Rage erupted in Eryx, hot and visceral. With a snarled curse, he hurled a bolt of sound at the mimic. But Sven merely canted his head, blinking lazily as the energy blast passed harmlessly through him.

Jaw clenched, Eryx tried to summon his bow, but only wisps of light appeared. Sven's morbid chuckle echoed through the garage.

Of course—the stolen magic that allowed him to nullify magic.

"Did you think your paltry tricks would work on me twice?" He was suddenly inches from Eryx, cold fingers grasping his chin in an iron grip. Eryx struggled vainly as Sven forced him to meet his inhuman gaze.

"I grow weary of these games," Sven purred. "Bring us the boy, or we will peel the flesh from your bones and take him ourselves." He pulled Eryx close, fetid breath hot in his ear. "This is your final chance."

Then he struck, fist slamming into Eryx's chest with the force of a freight train. Agony exploded through him as he was flung back, skidding across the hard concrete.

Through the ringing in his ears, Eryx heard rather than saw Sven vanish. He struggled to rise, only for his limbs to give out again. Darkness encroached on his vision. Hot liquid pooled under his cheek—blood.

As he drifted in and out of consciousness, panicked voices filtered through the haze. Richard and Zac swam into view, faces tight with fear. Zac's hands trembled as they applied pressure to Eryx's wounds.

"Eryx, hey, stay with us!" Richard was saying urgently. "We've got to get you to Alex, he'll know what to do."

Eryx tried to respond but only managed a faint groan. Alex…they had to warn him. Sven wasn't done with his twisted games.

As Richard and Zac carefully loaded him into the car, Eryx sent up a silent prayer. Please, just a little more time. They needed to protect Zac and stop Morvain's plans, whatever the cost.

Darkness pulled him under again. Through it all, Eryx clung desperately to one thought. Keep Zac safe. He had sworn to protect the boy, and he would not fail again. They would get through this, together. They had to.

•

<h1 style="text-align:center">21</h1>

Blood Is Currency

Alex

Alex strode through the dim halls of Elder Lucius's vampire coven, senses on high alert. After centuries spent in crypts and decrepit buildings, the Elders' current hideout was an old warehouse on the neglected outskirts of Manhattan.

Peeling paint, crumbling brick, and boarded up windows marked the exterior. Inside was little better - just barren concrete floors and rusted pipes. A far cry from the opulent havens Lucius used to prefer.

But after Sven's attack last month where he'd effortlessly infiltrated their weak defenses, kidnapping an fledgeling in the process, Lucius had decided they needed more advanced security. Hence this meeting to discuss plans for a new high-tech facility worthy of the corporate elite, with defenses to rival the Pentagon's.

At the end of the hall loomed a pair of ornate mahogany doors guarded by two hulking vampire sentries. Their cold eyes tracked Alex as he approached.

"Alexander Knight to see Elder Lucius," Alex informed them brusquely. "He's expecting me."

One of the guards nodded and opened the door, ushering Alex inside. He stepped into a lavish study, every surface gleaming with dark wood and brass. Floor-to-ceiling windows offered a breathtaking view of the New York skyline.

Seated at a massive desk was Lucius himself, blonde hair pulled back neatly, an indolent smile curling his lips. "Alex, welcome. Please have a seat."

Alex sank into the proffered leather chair, back ramrod straight. "Lucius. Thank you for agreeing to meet."

Lucius inclined his head graciously. "Of course. We have much to discuss." He steepled his fingers. "Now, how can I help the great Alexander today?"

Alex didn't bother with pleasantries. Lives were at stake. "What do you know about recent activity from the Eastside Coven? We have evidence they're involved in trafficking dangerous supernatural materials."

Lucius pursed his lips. "Ah yes, Eastside. Reckless upstarts with no sense of discretion." He gave an elegant shrug. "Alas, I know little of their current operations. Once they split from my leadership, we became rather…estranged."

Alex studied the Elder vampire, searching for any hint of deception. But Lucius's ageless face remained impassive.

"Is that so?" Alex kept his tone neutral. "Perhaps you know who leads them now? Or where they're located?"

Lucius hesitated, steepling his fingers. "While I do not know the location, I have heard rumors of who rules the Eastside coven now." He leaned forward. "They call him Nero, and claim he possesses powers beyond any vampire they've encountered. Though I've yet to meet him myself."

Alex's eyes narrowed, thoughts racing. Nero…the name was unfamiliar. A new player who had swiftly seized control by eliminating rivals.

"Interesting," Alex said evenly, not letting on how valuable that fragment was. "Well, if you do discover anything actionable about Nero or Eastside's operations, do let me know."

Lucius spread his hands. "Of course. Rogue elements like them threaten us all. I wish I could be of more assistance in your investigation." He arched a pale brow. "I don't suppose you've uncovered their base in your searches?"

"Our leads are still developing," Alex replied vaguely. Let Lucius make of that what he would. He decided to shift gears.

"While we're on the topic, have you noticed an uptick in Moonblood circulation lately?" Alex watched the vampire closely. "We have reason to believe a significant quantity has entered the market."

Something like hunger flickered in Lucius's eyes, there and gone in an instant. "Truly? How worrisome." He made a thoughtful noise. "I confess, some young upstarts have seemed rather…invigorated of late. Perhaps a new variant of the drug explains this."

An elegant crystal decanter of burgundy liquid on Lucius's desk caught Alex's eye. The vampire followed his gaze and smiled languidly.

"Can I offer you a drink?" Lucius lifted the decanter in invitation. "My own private reserve. Its bouquet is exquisite."

Alex tensed. "No thank you. I should be going." He needed to update the team on these new revelations.

But as Alex stood, Lucius held up a hand. "Please, one moment more. I believe we can help each other, Alex." He templed his fingers. "Together, we could finally eliminate threats like Eastside for good."

Alex crossed his arms. "Go on." He doubted he would like Lucius's proposal, but curiosity won out.

"It's quite simple." Lucius spread his hands. "Align with my coven. Our combined resources would allow us to crush lesser factions and unite all vampire kind under my banner." A ruthless grin flashed across his face. "Then New York's vampires would bow to my coven alone."

Alex stared at him coldly. "So that's your play? Monopolize power for yourself?" He let out a harsh laugh. "I don't think so."

Lucius remained unruffled. "Come now, do not dismiss the notion outright. Strength comes through unity, as you know well. The old ways of petty rivalries must end."

"Unity under you, you mean," Alex retorted. "I don't deal with tyrants, Lucius. Find some other lackey."

"Alexander. You cannot win this war alone. When the time comes, you will see the wisdom in my proposal."

Alex turned back to face the Elder vampire. "Perhaps. But for now, I have another question."

Lucius arched an elegant brow. "Oh? Do tell."

"What can you tell me about the vampire god Absalom?" Alex asked bluntly. "Does he still have loyal followers?"

Something like unease flickered in Lucius's ancient eyes. "Ah, the legend of mighty Absalom still persists in some factions. But my coven does not give credence to such tales."

Alex crossed his arms. "But others do? Enough to pose a threat if someone was attempting to resurrect him?"

Lucius steepled his fingers. "There are always those clinging to old myths and prophecies. Absalom's promise of godhood and power for vampires holds…appeal for some."

He sighed. "I confess, I have heard whispers in recent nights that a secretive cult devoted to him has arisen. Located somewhere in New York, or so the rumors claim."

Alex's pulse quickened. Concrete intel at last. "This cult - do you know anything about its members or leaders?"

Lucius spread his hands apologetically. "Sadly, no. It operates in great secrecy, though I have made discreet inquiries." He lowered his voice conspiratorially. "But between us, the East Coast coven may have ties."

Alex committed the name to memory. "I appreciate you being forthcoming. Any insight helps."

He made to depart, but Lucius called out. "One moment, Alex. I have something further that may assist your quest."

He opened an ornate drawer and withdrew an old photograph, handing it to Alex. It showed a powerfully built man with long dark hair and mesmerizing eyes. Danger and command radiated from him even in the faded picture.

"Alavar, one of the East Coast Elders," Lucius explained. "Also quite obsessed with Absalom's legend, from what I hear."

Alex stared down at the photo. Having a face and name to pursue was a massive breakthrough. "Thank you, Lucius. This could be just what we need."

Lucius inclined his head. "I wish you luck in unraveling this mystery. Absalom's power in the wrong hands could bring ruin." He lowered his voice gravely. "If you require resources, my coven's wealth and influence are at your disposal."

Before Alex could respond, his phone vibrated with an incoming call. It was Lily. He held up a hand. "My apologies, Lucius, but I need to take this."

He answered the call. "Lily, what have you found?"

"We got a location on another probable storage facility," Lily reported urgently. "An underground club in Brooklyn. Sending you coordinates now."

"Excellent work." Adrenaline flooded Alex's veins. "Assemble the team and get into position nearby. I'll join you shortly." This could be the breakthrough they desperately needed.

He ended the call and glanced at Lucius. "Duty calls. We will speak again soon." He tucked away the photo of Alavar. "You've given me much to consider."

Lucius smiled thinly. "Indeed. Remember, Alexander - alone we are vulnerable. But together, nothing can stand against us." He gazed at Alex meaningfully. "The choice is yours."

"We shall see." Alex inclined his head. "Farewell for now, Lucius."

As he departed the tower, anticipation hummed through Alex. The strands of the mystery were finally weaving together - Nero, Alavar, this hidden cult. All connected by devotion to a dangerous legend.

Alex pulled up a block from the coordinates Lily had sent, his black SUV gliding seamlessly into a space between two others. His team was already assembled on the sidewalk, armed to the teeth and thrumming with adrenaline. Time to find out what secrets this unassuming club hid.

Alex stepped out and nodded to Marcus and Emma who were prepping spell grenades. Lucas typed rapidly on a tablet while Gabe scanned the building, face scrunched in concentration.

"Lily's still scouting the wards and weak points," Gabe reported. "We're going in hard and fast once she gives the signal."

Alex checked his glocks, holstering them smoothly. "Remember, secure any evidence and prisoners if possible. But lethal force is authorized against hostiles." After the carnage at the last facility, they couldn't afford mercy.

At Alex's directive, Olivia hefted her massive Barrett sniper rifle. "Don't worry boss, we'll get answers one way or another." Her grin was pure predator.

They approached silently, slipping through shadows between street-lights. A faint pulsing aura marked the periphery of the wards ahead. Alex tasted the crackle of magic on his tongue, dark and caustic.

Marcus shuddered. "Ugh, feels like brimstone and stale blood. What kind of freak show are they running down there?"

"Nothing good," Alex murmured. A black void where the club

entrance should be made his hackles rise. Heavy illusion magic shrouded this place, concealing terrors within.

His phone buzzed twice - the entry signal from Lily. "Alright, we're up. Take your positions."

At Alex's command, his team surged forward in perfect synchronicity. Emma hurled two glowing orbs that adhered to the wards and started hissing. Lucas tapped on his tablet, muttering an incantation. The air rippled as he neutralized external defenses.

Gabe and Marcus flanked the void entrance, wielding spell-etched battleaxes. At Alex's go signal, they smashed the axes into the inky darkness. It shattered like glass, revealing a set of metal doors warped by intense heat.

Alex felt a surge of pride. In mere seconds, his people had broken sorcery few could penetrate. He and Olivia took point, blasting the doors off their hinges.

The team flooded inside, fanning through the neon-lit corridors with weapons ready. The throbbing beat of club music echoed strangely, but no guards responded to the alarm. The entire place seemed deserted.

Unease prickled Alex's spine. Where was everyone? This made no sense for a highly sensitive facility.

They cleared room after room, finding no signs of life. Equipment lay abandoned, half-full glasses still sitting on tables. It was a Marie Celeste scenario - as if everyone had simply vanished. Or been taken...

At the end of a hall, they encountered a heavy steel door emanating the unmistakable energy signature of moonblood. Jackpot. But before they could blast it open, a bloodcurdling scream echoed from within.

Alex's stomach dropped. "Take it down, now!"

Marcus, Emma, and Gabe combined their strength to force the massive door. Inside was a scene from hell itself.

Bodies littered the floor, vampires and shifters alike savagely slaughtered. In the center, a hulking horned beast with elongated jaws like a Moroi vampire fed on a writhing woman.

At the intrusion, it released its prey and twisted to face them with an inhuman snarl. Behind it, three more hybrid monsters stirred, blood dripping from their fangs. Moonblood perversions -violent, primal killers.

With guttural roars, the beasts charged. Chaos erupted as Alex's team met them head-on. Lucas and Emma hurled offensive spells from the rear alongside Olivia's sniper fire.

Alex emptied clip after clip into the frenzied hybrids while also barking orders. Every instinct screamed this was a trap - they needed to end this quickly.

The beasts fought with rabid fury, shrugging off shotgun blasts and magic strikes. But under the Shadowguards' relentless assault, one by one the abominations fell.

As Alex plunged a blade into the final hybrid's throat, a slow clap echoed from the doorway. He whirled to see a tall, dark-haired male observing them with an amused smile. Power and arrogance oozed from his deceptively relaxed posture.

"Bravo, Shadowguards," the stranger purred in a deep baritone. "An impressive display." His cold gaze fixed unerringly on Alex. "I was hoping we might chat."

Fury boiled Alex's blood at the violation here. "Who the hell are you?" he bit out harshly.

The man's smile turned vicious, showing the barest hint of fangs. "Come now Alexander, surely my reputation precedes me?" At Alex's silence, he gave an elegant shrug.

"No matter. Since we'll be seeing a great deal of each other, allow me to introduce myself." He executed a mock bow. "Nero D'Angelo, at your service."

Alex froze. Nero. This was the Eastside leader Lucius had warned about.

Rage exploded through Alex. "You did this," he growled. "Made these abominations with stolen blood."

Nero sighed. "Sadly, waste is inevitable in scientific progress. But their sacrifice brought such valuable data." His eyes gleamed with dark anticipation. "Imagine an army born of moonblood, unrelenting and invincible. Soon reality."

"Over my dead body," Alex spat. He charged Nero heedless of the danger, blood roaring in his ears.

Nero braced for the impact, feet sinking into a wide stance. At the last second before their collision, he twisted with viper-quick speed to avoid Alex's blow.

But Alex anticipated the dodge. He spun into a low sweep kick that connected solidly with Nero's legs, sending the vampire stumbling. Alex pressed the advantage, raining heavy fists down on his opponent.

Nero staggered under the brutal strikes, unable to mount a defense. Alex's knuckles split from the force of the impacts, but he ignored the pain, focused only on inflicting maximum damage.

Just when it seemed Alex had gained the upper hand, Nero started to laugh - a grating, scornful sound.

"Not bad, not bad," he chuckled mockingly, spitting blood. "Seems I underestimated your ferocity."

With blinding speed, his hand shot out to grip Alex's throat in an iron vise. Razor-sharp claws extended from his fingertips, piercing Alex's skin. Alex choked, claws scraping at the unbreakable stranglehold.

"But you have much to learn about true power, mortal," Nero purred. He hurled Alex across the room to crash into a bank of computers. Alex lay stunned amidst the wreckage as Nero stalked toward him.

"Get away from him!" Olivia shouted, raising her sniper rifle. Before she could fire, Nero made a sharp gesture, sending her weapon flying from her grasp.

"No interference," Nero commanded. He flicked his wrist and an invisible force slammed Olivia brutally against the far wall. "This lesson is for Alexander alone."

Nero was a blur of lethal motion, sword cleaving the very air. Alex struggled to evade the blinding strikes, unable to match his opponent's preternatural speed.

Alex cried out as Nero's blade carved a burning gash across his shoulder. Hot blood soaked his shirt as he stumbled back. Laughter rang in his ears.

"Is this the extent of your power?" Nero taunted. "You are unworthy of your lineage."

Rage boiled in Alex's veins. He would not be bested here, not with so much at stake. This monster would not prevail.

Reaching deep within, Alex tapped into his divine heritage, long-slumbering magic awakening. Power roared through him, ancient and intoxicating.

The shadows in the room deepened, writhing toward Alex in response to his rising aura. Ghostly flames sprang up around the perimeter, casting an infernal glow.

Nero hesitated, wary surprise flashing across his face at this display. Sensing his advantage, Alex pressed the attack.

With a feral cry, he summoned hellfire, wreathing his fists in white-hot flames. The temperature spiked as he landed blow after scorching blow on Nero, driving the vampire back.

Nero conjured his sword to block the strikes, but the black blade began to warp and melt under the intense heat.

"Impossible," he hissed. "No mere mortal commands such fire!"

"I am no mortal," Alex thundered. He blasted Nero with a column of flames that sent the vampire crashing through a divider wall.

Before Nero could rise, Alex grasped the seething shadows with Underworld magic. He wove the darkness into smoky chains, binding

Nero's limbs and throat.

Nero strained against the bonds, face contorting in disbelief and rage. Crimson light flared in his eyes.

"You cannot defeat me!" he spat, fangs bared. "I am eternal!"

"Brave words." Alex tightened his grasp, causing the shadowy restraints to constrict like snakes. Nero fell to his knees, visibly weakening. Alex stalked forward, hellfire coalescing in his palm. "But every reign ends."

He hurled the fiery projectile toward Nero. Just before impact, Nero threw back his head and unleashed an ear-splitting roar.

A shockwave of telekinetic force exploded outward, shattering Alex's bonds. Nero surged upright, cloak billowing around him.

"Enough games," he hissed, eyes burning with cold fury. "When next we meet, only one walks away."

Alex readied another strike, but smoke obscured his view. When it cleared, Nero was gone.

Alex surveyed the damage, chest heaving. They had survived the battle, but the toll was grave. And Nero had escaped to fight another day.

This war was far from over. But Alex had finally tapped into his divine arsenal. Next time, the advantage would be his.

Alex extended a hand, calling his fallen sword back to his grasp. The familiar weight steeled his resolve.

As the smoke cleared and Nero vanished, Alex became aware of a deep ache in his soul - his bond with Eryx crying out in distress. Fear pierced him, sharp and cold.

Something was wrong. Eryx was hurt.

Alex pressed a hand to his chest, reaching out along the soul-tether. He sensed Eryx's presence flickering weakly, felt his pain echoed in Alex's own body.

"Boss, you good?" Gabe gripped his shoulder, scanning him

worriedly. The others gathered around, battered but standing.

"It's Eryx," Alex gritted out. "Something's happened, he's in bad shape." Alex was already moving, pain forgotten. "Get back to base now! I'm going ahead."

He tore open a portal, shadow magic propelling him through space in an instant. The dark foyer of their building materialized around him.

Lily greeted him, face drawn. "Alex! Eryx is in the med bay with Dr. Sloan."

Alex burst into the med bay to see Eryx sitting on an exam table while Dr. Sloan tended his injuries.

Richard was slumped in a chair nearby, looking battered but alert. At Alex's entrance, he shot to his feet.

"Alex, thank god you're here," Richard said urgently. "

Alex gripped Richard's shoulder, conveying silent gratitude that he'd gotten Eryx to safety. He turned as Zac hovered up from where he'd been curled miserably in the corner.

"Alex, I'm so sorry," Zac choked out. "This is all my fault. Eryx got hurt protecting me." His eyes shimmered with tears.

Alex's heart wrenched at the boy's distress. He gently clasped Zac's neck. "The only one at fault is the on who did this. You did well getting Eryx help."

Zac managed a shaky nod, scrubbing the tears away. "I tried to stop the bleeding with my magic."

"You did good, kid," Eryx said warmly from the exam table. "We'll all heal up and be back at it in no time."

In three long strides Alex was at his side, hands cupping Eryx's face urgently, searching for further injury. "What happened? Are you alright?"

Eryx covered Alex's trembling hands with his own. "I'll be okay. Just had a run-in with our least favorite mimic." His expression darkened.

"Sven paid me a visit."

Fury roared through Alex, his gut twisting. "Did he do this to you?" Eryx's wounds told a story of vicious brute force.

At Eryx's hesitant nod, Alex had to resist the urge to put his fist through a wall. Sven would pay dearly for this act.

Dr. Sloan interrupted gently. "Several fractured ribs and some internal bleeding, but nothing too worrisome now that I've got him stabilized and his healing has already started."

Alex managed a terse nod of thanks. He kept his hands on Eryx, as though sheer will could shield him from further harm.

"What did Sven want?" Alex asked tightly. "What was his message?"

Eryx's eyes darkened with remembered fear. "He wanted Zac. Threatened to take him by force if we didn't hand the kid over." His voice dropped. "And he cancelled out my magic. I couldn't fight back."

Rage and guilt churned within Alex. He should have been there, should have protected what was most precious. This was his fault.

Eryx gripped Alex's wrist, expression fierce. "Hey, don't go there. We knew they would come for Zac eventually. But we stopped them this time."

Alex slowly regained control, compartmentalizing his fury for later. Eryx was right - Zac was safe, and that was what mattered most. They would be ready for Sven's next move.

Alex gently traced the bruise on Eryx's jaw. "I'm just glad you weren't more gravely hurt. When I felt your pain through the bond…" He swallowed hard. "I've never been more scared."

Eryx leaned into his touch. "I'll be alright. Sven caught me off guard, but he won't again." His voice dropped to a fervent whisper. "I knew you would come."

Overwhelmed with relief and tenderness, Alex rested his forehead against Eryx's. No further words were needed. They took comfort simply from each other's presence, the soul bond thrumming between them.

After a moment, Dr. Sloan discreetly finished applying bandages. "The worst is over. Just take it easy for a few days." He offered Eryx a kind smile. "I'll give you two some space now."

Alone, Alex helped Eryx gingerly to his feet. Though still in pain, Eryx straightened defiantly. Alex had never admired anyone more.

"Sven will regret the day he crossed us," Eryx declared vehemently. "We end this threat once and for all."

Pride swelled in Alex's chest. Together, they would be unstoppable. Sven would fall, and Zac would remain safely with them.

Alex clasped Eryx's shoulder, meeting his determined gaze. "No one harms what is mine."

The promise resonated between them, sealing their united front. Alex had defied death itself for this man. He would destroy any who tried to take Eryx from him again.

But that battle was for another day. Right now, he simply needed Eryx close, safe in the circle of his arms.

Alex drew him in, heedless of injuries. Eryx buried his face against Alex's neck with a faint sigh. For now, the coming storm did not matter. They had each other. And that was enough.

After Dr. Sloan gave his final instructions, Richard approached looking weary but resolute.

"I should head out, let you guys rest up," he said, clasping Eryx's uninjured shoulder lightly. "Call me if you need anything, yeah?"

Eryx smiled tiredly. "Thanks Ric, I appreciate you having my back today."

Richard turned to pull Zac into a quick hug. "Stay tough, kiddo." He ruffled Zac's hair, eliciting a faint grin from the still-shaken teen.

Alex walked Richard out, conveying his sincere gratitude with a look. Richard had proven his loyalty once again.

With the med bay now empty, Alex helped Eryx slowly to his feet.

He was grateful for Eryx's new godly essence accelerating his healing, but knew it would still take time to recover fully.

"Let's get you home to rest," Alex murmured, keeping a supportive arm around Eryx as they made their way downstairs.

In the car, Zac promptly fell asleep in the back seat, the day's trauma finally catching up with him. Alex watched the teen's face smooth out, innocence briefly restored. No child should have to endure what Zac had.

"I'm sorry I wasn't there when Sven came for you," Alex said quietly. "But I swear he won't touch Zac or you again."

Eryx shook his head. "You have nothing to apologize for. We both had missions today. I'm just glad you're safe as well." His jaw clenched.

Alex gripped Eryx's hand, conviction steeling his spine. Together they would shield those in their care.

Upon arriving home, Alex carried a sleeping Zac to his room. Cereberus and Mr. Whiskers immediately curled up on either side of the boy, standing guard. Alex's heart swelled at the sight.

He stopped in the doorway, drinking in this moment of peace. The quiet didn't last long in their world, so he cherished it when he could.

Alex eventually retreated to his own bedroom, unsurprised to find Eryx waiting there. Without a word, he went to his mate, hands gentle as he examined Eryx's bandaged wounds.

"Hey, babe," he said softly, his voice laced with tenderness. "I'm here. I won't leave your side."

Eryx's eyes flickered open, and a weak smile graced his lips. "Alex," he whispered, his voice filled with relief. "I... I need you."

Alex's heart clenched at the vulnerability in Eryx's voice. He knew exactly what his mate needed, both physically and emotionally. Without hesitation, he climbed onto the bed, positioning himself next to Eryx, their bodies pressed close. "I'm here. I'll take care of you."

Leaning down, Alex pressed a gentle kiss to Eryx's forehead, his lips lingering there for a moment. He wanted to convey the depth of his love, the reassurance that everything would be alright. "Tell me what you need," he whispered against Eryx's skin.

Eryx's eyes locked with Alex's, filled with a raw desire and trust. "I need you, Alex," he breathed, his voice laced with need. "I need to feel your touch, your warmth. I need to lose myself in you."

A surge of desire shot through Alex, igniting a fire within him. He wanted to give Eryx everything, to be the source of his pleasure and comfort. With a gentle hand, he caressed Eryx's cheek, his thumb tracing soothing circles. "You'll feel nothing but me, love. I'll take away the pain and replace it with ecstasy."

Eryx's breath hitched, his body responding to Alex's touch. "Please," he pleaded, his voice low and desperate. "Take me, Alex. Make me forget everything but you."

Alex's heart swelled with a mix of love and lust. He wanted to give Eryx the release he craved, to bring him to the edge of pleasure and push him over. With a slow, deliberate movement, he trailed his fingers down Eryx's chest, feeling the rapid rise and fall of his lover's breath.

Their eyes locked in an intense gaze, Alex leaned in, capturing Eryx's lips in a searing kiss. The taste of Eryx, the feel of their tongues dancing together, sent a jolt of electricity coursing through his veins. He deepened the kiss, pouring every ounce of his love and desire into it.

As they parted, their breaths mingling, Alex's voice was filled with a mix of passion and devotion. "I'll give you everything, Eryx. I'll make you forget the pain and drown you in pleasure. You're mine, and I'll take care of you."

Eryx's eyes sparkled with anticipation, his voice a whisper of need. "Take me, Alex," he moaned, his hips arching towards his lover. "Fill me with everything you've got. Make me yours."

With a hunger that matched Eryx's, Alex moved with purpose, his hands roaming Eryx's body with a possessive touch. Their bodies melded together in a symphony of desire, each touch and caress igniting a new wave of pleasure.

As their passion intensified, the room filled with their moans and gasps, the sound of their bodies colliding and their love intertwining. They moved together, a dance of need and surrender, lost in a world where nothing else mattered but their connection.

In that moment, as they gave themselves to each other, Alex knew that their love transcended the pain and the challenges they faced. They were connected in a way that nothing could break, their bodies and souls entwined in a love that burned brighter than any flame.

And as they soared to the heights of pleasure, their cries of ecstasy filling the room, Alex held onto Eryx tightly, vowing to always be there for him, to be his refuge in a world that often felt chaotic.

22

Setting Up the Stage

Eryx

Eryx blocked Alex's strike, bracing against the impact that sent vibrations up his arms. He responded with a low kick that Alex deftly avoided. They broke apart, circling each other on the training mat.

"You're still favoring your left side," Alex noted. "Don't try to hide your injuries. I can tell when you're hurting."

Eryx grimaced, adjusting his stance. Alex was right - his healing ribs were aching after an hour of intense sparring. But the physical pain helped distract from the sting of recent failures.

"I'm good to keep going," Eryx said stubbornly. Ever since Sven had ambushed him, Eryx was determined to hone his skills. He would never be caught defenseless again.

Alex's eyes softened with understanding. But he held up a hand. "That's enough for today. Pushing yourself too hard will only slow the healing."

Frustration simmered in Eryx's gut, but he respected Alex's judgment. With a sigh, he limped to the bench along the wall and grabbed a towel to wipe the sweat from his eyes.

Alex sat beside him, shoulder pressing against Eryx's in silent support. "Talk to me. What's really going on?"

Eryx stared down at his hands, anger welling up again. "I should have been able to stop Sven. But without my magic, I was useless. Helpless." He jerked his head up. "I can't let that happen again."

"Hey…" Alex gripped his shoulder. "You kept Zac safe against a powerful enemy. No one could have asked for more."

Logically Eryx knew Alex was right. But the humiliation of being toyed with and soundly defeated still burned.

"I need to be stronger," Eryx said vehemently. "Both physically and with my magic."

Understanding flashed in Alex's dark eyes. He was no stranger to pushing himself relentlessly in pursuit of impossible standards. It was how he had survived the Underworld.

"Alright," Alex said after a moment. "If extra training helps ease your mind, we'll make time for it. You know I'm always here to support you."

Gratitude rushed through Eryx. Alex never dismissed or judged his fears. He simply gave Eryx what he needed, whether assurance or a push. It was a precious gift.

Eryx let his head drop onto Alex's shoulder. "Thank you. I just…I need to be someone Zac and the others can rely on. Not a liability."

Alex's arm encircled him, radiating strength and warmth. "You could never be one. You're the heart that holds us together, Eryx."

Emotion clogged Eryx's throat. He didn't fully believe that after so many past failures, but Alex's faith lifted some of the weight from his spirit.

They sat in comfortable silence until the twinge of broken ribs forced Eryx upright. Alex helped him carefully to his feet.

"Up for another round?" Alex asked.

"You're on." Eryx said confidently.

Eryx pushed through the pain, determined to continue training. He needed to be prepared for the next attack.

He faced off against Alex on the combat mat, sunlight gleaming off his drawn bow. Alex held his Stygian iron spear at the ready, eyes calculating.

"Remember, don't rely only on sight," Alex instructed. "Use all your senses to anticipate your opponent's actions."

Eryx nodded, reaching inward for that extra perception Apollo's essence granted him. The ambient sounds of the gym sharpened - squeaking shoes, pattering heartbeats, the whistling spear as Alex lunged…

Sensing the attack, Eryx rolled left, firing off an arrow mid-dodge. But Alex spun his spear to deflect the shot, not breaking momentum.

They exchanged more blows at blurring speed, Eryx using both bow and fists. But Alex's spear always intercepted his attacks before they could land.

Frustration mounting, Eryx tried to sweep Alex's legs. But Alex vaulted the strike and dove on him, pinning Eryx to the mat with the spear leveled at his throat.

"You're still not listening," Alex chided gently. "Relying on just your eyes makes you vulnerable."

He rose and extended a hand to help Eryx up. Eryx gritted his teeth against the flare of pain in his ribs.

"Again," he bit out. "And this time, don't hold back."

Alex arched an eyebrow but backed up and raised his spear. Eryx closed his eyes, tuning out visual distractions. He channeled his focus into his other senses.

The whistle of Alex's spear cutting the air warned him a blink before it would have struck. Eryx tilted his head, feeling the wind of its passage across his cheek.

Using the sound cues, he could track Alex's movement and attacks. Eryx continued avoiding strikes with eyes still closed, trusting his hearing alone.

But staying purely on the defensive wasn't the answer either. Eryx needed to press his sudden advantage.

When Alex lunged again, Eryx pinpointed the attack vector based on the spear's sound. In the split second before impact, he drew his bow and loosed an arrow.

Eyes flying open, he saw Alex frozen in place, spear halted inches from Eryx's chest. The arrow had sliced cleanly through the spear's head, rendering it useless.

A grin of exhilaration broke across Eryx's face. "I did it!"

Alex smiled, pride glowing in his gaze. "Well done. I knew you had it in you." He squeezed Eryx's shoulder. "With practice, you can master this sensory skill. It will give you an edge in battle."

Eryx's chest swelled at the praise. He had turned a weakness into a strength. Each little victory brought him closer to being the guardian Zac needed.

They spent the rest of the session honing Eryx's new ability. By the end, even Alex's supernatural speed couldn't land a hit on him. Eryx's confidence grew with each successful counter.

As Eryx ducked a kick and swept Alex's planted leg out from under him, he felt a rush of gratitude. Alex always knew exactly how to bring out his best.

After another intense round of sparring, Eryx's aching muscles forced him to take a break. He sank down beside Alex on the edge of the training mats, gratefully accepting the offered water bottle.

As he gulped down the cool liquid, Eryx gazed out the floor-to-ceiling windows at the NYC skyline stretched before them. Dusk was falling, painting the sky in hues of orange and pink. From up here, the city almost looked peaceful.

But darkness lurked in its veins, threats old and new gathering force. Eryx lowered his eyes with a tired sigh.

"You okay?" Alex asked gently. "We can call it a day if you need to rest."

"I'm alright." Eryx rotated his stiff shoulder with a wince. "Just getting lost in my head."

Alex was silent, sensing Eryx's inner turmoil. He simply waited for Eryx to gather his thoughts. One thing Eryx loved most was that Alex never pushed or judged.

"Do you think I'll be ready?" Eryx asked finally, voicing his deepest fear. "Strong enough to face Sven when he returns?"

Alex turned to face him. "You've made incredible progress mastering your skills and power."

Eryx shook his head. "It's not enough though. Sven is ancient, ruthless. And I'm still just...me." He dropped his gaze. "Untested. Unworthy of Apollo's gift."

"Eryx." Alex gently tilted his chin up. "You are one of the most extraordinary people I have ever known. With or without Apollo's essence." His dark eyes bored into Eryx's. "You shine brighter than any myth or legend. I have no doubt you will eclipse even the gods one day."

Emotion clogged Eryx's throat. He saw only sincerity in Alex's face. Somehow this man believed in him more than Eryx believed in himself.

"I won't let you down," Eryx managed hoarsely. "I'll keep training until I'm strong enough to protect Zac and stand at your side."

Alex clasped his shoulder. "You already make me stronger, never doubt that." He smiled crookedly. "We're building something here the pantheon has never seen - a true union of different worlds."

Eryx's heart swelled. Alex was right. Together they were carving a new path. And united, no power could withstand them.

Eryx would nurture the fledgling divinity within him, just as Alex had honed his Underworld gifts. And with work, one day they would be unstoppable.

But today, Eryx was content to simply sit here as the sun set over their city, head coming to rest on Alex's sturdy shoulder.

Resting against Alex after training, Eryx's thoughts turned to Zac. The teen had wanted to join them again today, but Eryx thought more ordinary activities would be good for him right now.

"How do you think Zac's doing with Zagreus?" Eryx asked. "I hope he's not too disappointed we didn't let him come along."

Alex chuckled. "Zag will keep him occupied, don't worry. He was excited to 'hang out with the little dude' today."

Despite his son's rough exterior, Zagreus had a big heart, much like his father. Eryx was glad the boisterous god had agreed to mentor Zac. They both could use more positive male guidance.

"Do you think Zac is ready for combat training though?" Eryx chewed his lip uncertainly. "I don't want to rush him into danger."

Alex squeezed his shoulder. "You're right to be cautious. But remember, he won't always have the luxury of staying on the sidelines. Best he learns to defend himself while we can still protect him."

Eryx nodded slowly. As much as he wanted to shelter Zac from their violent world, Alex had a point. When threats came calling again, Zac needed to be prepared.

"Yeah, you're probably right," Eryx conceded. "I just worry with his trauma, throwing him into fighting could do more harm than good."

"That's why we'll take it slow, gauge his reactions." Alex's expression softened with understanding. "I know you only want what's best for the boy. We both do."

Warmth bloomed in Eryx's chest. However uncertain he felt, Alex's steadfast strength never wavered. Together they would find the right path.

Eryx thought back to that morning.

"Can I come train with you guys again today?" Zac had asked eagerly over breakfast. When Eryx and Alex exchanged an uncertain glance, his face fell. "Oh. Right. Guess I'm not ready yet."

"Soon, kiddo," Eryx assured him. "But my friend Zagreus offered to hang out with you today instead. I think you'll really like him."

Zac perked up. "Is he another god?" At Eryx's amused nod, he pumped his fist. "Sweet! Way more fun than getting my butt kicked."

They'd left Zac happily chattering about which games he wanted to try. Zagreus would look after the boy; Eryx needed to trust that.

Back in the present, Alex nudged Eryx gently. "You still with me? Don't spiral into worst case scenarios."

Eryx huffed a laugh. "Busted. I can't help worrying though."

"I know. But Zac has all of us watching out for him now." Alex smiled crookedly. "He's resilient, like his dads."

Joy sparked through Eryx at being called that. Zac wasn't theirs by blood, but it felt right nonetheless.

"Yeah, he is pretty tough," Eryx agreed proudly. With time and care, Zac would flourish here.

After a much needed rest, Eryx and Alex were heading back down to the training floor when Gabe called urgently.

"We've got visitors up in the briefing room," he informed them. "Sounded important so we told them to wait."

Eryx and Alex exchanged bemused glances. Gabe's tone implied unfamiliar guests. They quickly cleaned up before taking the elevator upstairs.

The team was already assembled around the table when Eryx and Alex entered. At their questioning looks, Lily crossed her arms.

"Our 'visitors' got antsy waiting," she said dryly. "Wanted to talk right away."

Eryx turned to see two figures lounging by the window - Dolos and

Harry. Though still pale and moving gingerly, Dolos wore his usual sly grin. Harry hovered close, as though afraid the injured god might collapse any second.

Alex arched an eyebrow. "Dolos. Shouldn't you still be recovering?"

Dolos waved a hand airily. "I'm quite well enough for a short excursion. Had some intriguing news I couldn't wait to share."

Harry shot Dolos an exasperated look. "I told you we should've let them come to us. But try arguing with him lately…"

Interesting. The dynamic between them seemed to have shifted since Harry helped free Dolos from Tartarus. Almost like…equals? Eryx filed that away to ponder later.

"Alright, you have our attention." Alex crossed his arms. "What was so urgent?"

Dolos's playful look vanished. "I've received word from my eyes and ears outside Tartarus. The Order is preparing to make their move - and soon."

Cold dread washed through Eryx. On instinct, he moved closer to Alex. "The ritual? To raise Absalom?"

Dolos nodded grimly. "The last pieces are in motion. If they succeed…"

"It would unleash hell on earth," Alex finished darkly. Jaw tightening, he met Dolos's gaze. "Do you know where and when they plan to perform the ritual?"

Dolos sighed regretfully. "Alas, my weakened power cannot pierce the veil sufficiently to pinpoint those details. But you have little time left to stop them."

The mood in the room turned grim. Marcus cracked his knuckles menacingly while Emma whispered to Olivia about ammunition stocks. They had all known this reckoning was coming, but the reality sinking in was chilling.

Alex gripped Eryx's shoulder briefly before focusing on Dolos.

"We're grateful for the warning. This gives us a chance to prepare our next move." His eyes narrowed slightly. "But what do you want in return for this information?"

Dolos blinked in surprise, then laughed. "My dear Alex, not everything is transactional. Consider this a gesture of good faith." He spread his hands. "My only goal is stopping the Order from abusing powers they do not understand."

Eryx studied the former god of deception closely, probing for duplicity. But for once, Dolos appeared sincere. His time imprisoned seemed to have changed him.

Alex too looked thrown off guard by the lack of demands. "Regardless, you have our thanks," he said finally. "This insight may help turn the tide."

Dolos inclined his head. "I hope so. But now I really must be getting back before my keeper has a fit." He flashed a cheeky grin at Harry, who simply rolled his eyes with familiar exasperation.

They said brief goodbyes, then the two gods departed. The team looked to Alex expectantly amid the heavy silence.

"Thoughts?" Lily prompted.

Alex rubbed his jaw, gaze distant. "If Dolos is right, we're nearly out of time. We need to shore up our defenses here while redoubling efforts to locate the ritual site."

He focused on Eryx and the others. "Finn and Lily, coordinate with everyone and the other allies we can trust. Make sure their strongholds are also prepared."

Finn and Lily nodded sharply and started making notes.

"Gabe, you and Emma keep working contacts, street intelligence," Alex continued. "Anything that gets us closer."

The two gave quick assurances, already heads bent strategizing.

Alex turned to Eryx. "You're with me." Then turned to Lucas and Marcus. "Help each other and look for the Absalom temple that Elder

Lucius mentioned."

"On it," Eryx promised. Anything to protect their makeshift family.

Alex surveyed them all, eyes blazing. "We end this threat for good. Whatever it takes."

Around the table, grim but resolute faces stared back. They would triumph or perish united.

The meeting concluded soon after, tasks assigned. But as the others filed out, Eryx lingered, needing a private moment.

Sensing his unease, Alex drew him into a sheltered corner. "Talk to me. What's going on in that head of yours?"

Eryx leaned into Alex's steadying presence. "After all this time, it's finally coming to a head. What if we can't stop them?" He hesitated. "I don't want to lose this. Us."

Alex tilted Eryx's chin up, expression fierce. "You won't. whatever happens, we'll face it together." His thumb grazed Eryx's cheek tenderly. "Don't give up hope. It's your light that will guide us through the darkness ahead."

After the briefing, Eryx and Alex headed to meet Zac and Zagreus at Dion's diner. Eryx could use the comfort of family after the ominous news.

When they arrived, Zac immediately barrelled into them, wrapping them in an enthusiastic hug. Eryx's heart swelled. In such a short time, this boy had become precious to them both.

"There are my favorite old dudes!" Zac said brightly, dragging them toward a booth.

Dion and Zagreus occupied one side, looking relaxed after a day of magic lessons and gaming. Eryx slid in across from them while Alex embraced his son in a warm, back-slapping hug.

"How was training, kiddo?" Eryx asked, ruffling Zac's hair. "Zag didn't beat you up too badly, I hope?"

Zagreus laughed heartily. "Nah, the little man's got talent! Almost took me down a few times." He grinned at Zac. "You'll be ruling the arena in no time."

Zac's cheeks flushed at the praise. "It was awesome! Zag showed me how to use my blood magic to make weapons and barriers and stuff." His face scrunched adorably. "Didn't love getting tossed on my butt though."

"That's how you learn," Dion assured him with a kind smile. "Sounds like you two had quite the adventure today."

Alex clasped his son's shoulder. "Thank you again for looking after him, Zagreus. I know your guidance will help him greatly."

"Anytime, Pops. Kid's a riot to hang with." Zagreus nudged Zac playfully. "Plus I need a worthy rival in multiplayer games. These old fogies can't keep up."

Laughter filled the table. Zac's eyes shone with joy at having found friends who understood him. Eryx treasured seeing the teen so carefree and at ease.

After they'd ordered heaping plates of comfort food, Dion fixed Eryx and Alex with a piercing look. "So, what's the latest with your investigation? Any developments?"

Eryx's gut tightened remembering Dolos's warning. He and Alex took turns recapping the day's troubling revelations.

Zac's face fell guiltily. "This is all because of me, isn't it? If I wasn't-"

"No." Eryx cut him off firmly. "The Order would've pursued their insane plans with or without you, kiddo. None of this is your fault."

Alex nodded in agreement. "If anything, you gave us the key to uncovering their plot. We'll stop them, thanks to you."

Zagreus cracked his knuckles menacingly. "Too right. Anyone who tries hurting our boy here answers to me now."

Zac ducked his head, cheeks pinking. But his small smile radiated shy pleasure at having these fierce protectors in his corner.

Before Eryx could respond, the air warped as a portal sliced open, depositing a tall figure garbed in a tailored suit. Thanatos.

"Evening, gentlemen," the reaper intoned. "Apologies for the intrusion, but I come bearing an urgent message."

Alex was instantly on alert. "What is it?"

Thanatos' expression was grim. "The Fates bid me warn you - the Order has found a way to accelerate their ritual. It will reach completion by tomorrow's moonrise."

Shock rooted Eryx in place. Tomorrow?! They'd assumed they had weeks, even days before the ritual commenced. But if the Fates decreed it imminent…

Alex was already rising, expression thunderous. "We need to gather the others immediately." He gripped Thanatos' shoulder. "Thank you, my friend. Please keep watch for any further signs."

Thanatos dipped his head. "I shall. May fortune favor you all in the coming battle." With that, he vanished as abruptly as he'd arrived.

The rest of the meal passed in a tense blur. Eryx's gut churned with dread, but one glance at Zac's frightened face fortified his resolve. He would let nothing threaten their boy or their city.

Tomorrow, the war to decide humanity's fate began. And Eryx would face it with his family and allies at his side, come what may. They would win, or die trying.

23

Taken

Eryx

"Are you sure I can't make them bleed a little, just for fun?" Zac asked eagerly as Eryx navigated downtown traffic toward the press conference venue.

Eryx chuckled and shot the teen a look. "Absolutely not. We're trying to win them over, not traumatize them."

Zac slumped in his seat. "You never let me have any fun." But there was no real heat behind his grumbling.

That morning, Zac bounded eagerly into the kitchen, catching Eryx and Alex finishing breakfast.

"Is it time to go yet?" he asked, practically vibrating with excitement. "I wanna see the cool stage setup!"

Eryx chuckled at the teen's enthusiasm, but Alex frowned, leaning back in his chair.

"About that…" Alex began slowly. "I'm still not sure you should be attending the press conference, given the risks."

Zac's face fell. "What? But you said I could go for sure this time!"

"I know." Alex sighed, looking genuinely regretful to disappoint him. "But with the ritual looming, security is too uncertain."

"You did promise he could come," Eryx gently reminded Alex. He understood Alex's protectiveness, but didn't want Zac feeling excluded. "We'll keep him safe."

Zac turned pleading puppy-dog eyes on Alex. "Please? I'll stick close to Eryx the whole time, I swear!"

Alex wavered, then glanced at Eryx. "You're certain Dion and Ari will also be there? For extra protection?"

Eryx nodded. "They're meeting us at the venue. Between all of us, nothing will get near Zac."

Alex rubbed his jaw, then finally relented. "Alright. But at the first sign of trouble, get him out of there fast, understand?"

"Yes sir," Eryx said, winking at a grinning Zac. "We'll be cautious."

They finished preparing to leave, Eryx double-checking his outfit and notecards with talking points while Alex reviewed security plans with Marcus and Emma.

"Next light's green," Zac piped up, jolting Eryx from his musing. He eased the car forward, soon spotting the sleek high-rise venue Brad had chosen. Leave it to his manager to secure prime Rockefeller Center real estate.

As they pulled into the underground garage, Zac let out a low whistle. "Swanky. You really are famous, huh?"

Warmth rushed through Eryx at the note of pride in the teen's voice. "We'll see if I still have what it takes," he demurred, but Zac's faith bolstered his confidence.

Brad intercepted them in the lobby, grinning widely. "There are my stars! Ready to wow some reporters?"

Before Eryx could respond, Brad was steering him toward the backstage area, keeping up an eager stream of last minute instructions.

"Remember, no need to answer anything too personal," Brad said over his shoulder. "I'll be moderating and can shut down any out of line questions."

Eryx nodded along absently. He appreciated Brad's guidance, but his own thoughts were turned inward, preparing.

Backstage was controlled chaos - harried assistants checking mics, reviewing notecards, shouting occasional confirmation into headsets. Eryx's nose twitched at the now-familiar smell of fresh sawdust from construction of the set pieces.

Brad guided Eryx to a cordoned off green room. "Your glam team will be here shortly for final touch-ups," he explained. "In the meantime, make yourself comfortable!"

Eryx's gaze landed on two familiar figures relaxed on the plush couches - Dion and Ari. Relief coursed through him.

"You made it!" Eryx greeted them with quick hugs. "Thanks again for coming. It means a lot."

Dion waved him off with an easy smile. "Of course, we wouldn't miss it." He gestured to a mini fridge stocked with fruit boxes and bottled teas. "Help yourself to any snacks or drinks."

Eryx grabbed a bottle of honey lemon tea to soothe his parched throat while Dion and Ari caught him up on their latest misadventures trying online dating. Their playful banter helped settle his nerves.

Soon there was a brisk knock at the door before it burst open to reveal Richard standing there, guitar case slung over one shoulder.

"Surprise!" he announced, holding his arms out wide. "Brad thought you could use the moral support."

Eryx laughed and pulled him into a quick one-armed hug. "You have no idea. Really glad you'll be behind that curtain with me."

Just having his closest friends surrounding him backstage fueled Eryx's confidence. This was exactly where he was meant to be.

Too soon, the stage manager poked his head in. "Five minutes, folks!"

Brad appeared to usher Eryx toward makeup and wardrobe. "Looking good, superstar! Knock 'em dead out there."

On his way out, Eryx paused to pull Zac into a quick half-hug. "Stick close to Dion and Ari, okay kiddo? And be good - no tackling reporters."

Zac snorted. "Yeah, yeah, I'll be on my best behavior." His expression turned solemn. "Good luck. You got this!"

Heart swelling with affection, Eryx ruffled his hair. With his family at his side, he could conquer anything.

Soon Eryx stood just offstage, energy thrumming through every nerve as he listened to the buzzing crowd. This was his element.

Squaring his shoulders, he strode out to applause and camera flashes. Seeking out familiar faces bolstered his confidence - Ari, Dion, Zac, and Richard cheering him on from the front row.

Eryx took his seat beside Richard and Brad to field questions. The reporters initially lobbed easy ones about his upcoming album and creative process.

But as the conference stretched on, Eryx noticed one journalist watching him intently. Something about the man set his instincts on high alert, magic prickling. He shook it off, focusing on answering innocuously about tour plans.

Still, his gaze kept snagging on the silently observant man. Something sinister lurked behind that mild facade.

When it was finally the man's turn, he leaned forward, eyes boring into Eryx's. "How would you feel about dying today, Eryx Ross?" he asked softly.

Eryx froze, alarms blaring in his mind. That voice - he knew it from the carnage at the warehouse battle. This was one of Nero's creatures.

In a flash, the man's features contorted, bones cracking as he shifted into a hulking wolf-vampire hybrid form. The monster roared, sending the crowd screaming and scrambling away.

Eryx vaulted onto the stage, magic already gathering in his palms. "Run!" he yelled to his friends. This was about to get ugly.

The hybrid leapt at Eryx, swiping viciously with its elongated claws. Eryx rolled under the attack and came up firing arrows of golden light. But the creature shrugged them off with a guttural laugh.

"Eryx, down!" Richard tackled him from the side just as the beast spewed a viscous stream of acid where he'd been standing. The carpet sizzled, melting under the toxic spray.

"We've got to lure it away from the civilians!" Eryx shouted over the pandemonium and screams. The stage lights had gone dark, flashy effects adding to the chaos.

Richard nodded grimly, helping Eryx to his feet. Together they sprinted for the emergency exit doors, the hybrid hot on their heels. Suddenly Zac was beside them, face set with determination.

Eryx frantically activated his comms. "Alex, there are hybrids loose backstage!" he shouted over the screams. "We need help now!"

"Three minutes out," Alex confirmed tersely. "Stay alive!"

Eryx whirled, desperately searching for Zac and the others in the panicked crowd. Before he could spot them, the wolf-vampire hybrid lunged with a feral roar.

Suddenly Richard was there, iron staff whirling as he struck the creature back. "Go find the others!" Richard yelled. "I've got fangs here!"

Eryx nodded his thanks and took off just as more mutated beasts converged on Richard. His friend could handle himself. Eryx had to find their family.

He blasted through the stampeding civilians, magic allowing him to sense life forces nearby. There! A cluster of supernaturals - Dion, Ari, and Zac. But surrounding them, cruel intent emanated from a pack of hybrids.

With a burst of superhuman speed, Eryx raced toward their location, golden bow singing as he fired arrows into the pack. The beasts shrieked and scattered as his shots seared their flesh.

Eryx placed himself protectively between the hybrids and his friends. "Get the mortals out! I'll hold them off."

Dion gripped his shoulder briefly in thanks, then he and Ari began urgently herding people toward exits. Zac hesitated, blood already coiling down his wrists.

"Go with them!" Eryx ordered. "It's not safe for you here."

Jaw clenching, Zac finally obeyed, staying close to Dion's side. Eryx refocused on the regrouping hybrids, drawing on every ounce of Apollo's power thrumming within.

The beasts pressed their attack. Claws raked across Eryx's back before he twisted away, retaliating with bursts of golden flame and lightning. But more hybrids kept coming.

Then Eryx heard it - the ominous beeping of a planted explosive. Frantically he reached out with his magic, sensing the bomb's location nearby. They had minutes at most before it detonated.

"Bomb!" Eryx yelled to Richard across the chaotic room. "We have to contain the blast!"

Richard's face paled, but he nodded. Together, they began spinning a protective dome of magic around the device while also fending off slavering hybrids.

Eryx's focus split between maintaining the shield and scanning for his friends. Had Zac and the others gotten clear? If anything happened to Zac.

The bomb's beeping accelerated. They were almost out of time. Eryx poured everything he had into fortifying the magical barrier.

"Brace yourself!" Richard shouted.

The world seemed to erupt. The shockwave of the explosion slammed Eryx to his knees even inside the buffering shield. Debris and dust swirled outside it.

Panting, Eryx lowered the cracked but intact barrier. The blast radius had been contained, but the backstage area was ravaged. This was meant to be his triumphant return, not more chaos and ruin.

As Eryx surveyed the damage despairingly, a raspy voice spoke from the shadows.

"Take the boy. Leave the rest."

Ice flooded Eryx's veins. Before he could react, a hulking figure dashed forward with inhuman speed, snatching a struggling Zac into its arms.

"No!" Eryx screamed. He drew his bow, loosing a volley of light arrows at the kidnapper. But it dodged them easily, barreling for the exit with Zac trapped in its iron grip.

Fury and terror crashing through him, Eryx gave chase. He couldn't lose Zac, not after vowing to protect him. They'd promised Alex…

Bursting outside, Eryx frantically cast his senses outward, searching for Zac's unique energy signature. There! Already blocks away, moving fast.

Eryx summoned his godly speed, the world blurring around him as he raced over rooftops, desperate to catch up. But the kidnapper had too great a head start.

Heart in his throat, Eryx helplessly watched the rapidly shrinking form disappear into a doorway several blocks over. Zac was gone.

Eryx smashed his fist into the rooftop. They'd failed the boy when it mattered most. Rage and guilt churned uselessly within him.

Heavy footsteps pounded up behind him. Eryx didn't need to turn to recognize Alex's imposing presence. For a long moment, only the sound of their ragged breathing filled the space between them.

"What happened?" Alex finally ground out. "Where is Zac?"

Eryx slowly faced him, dreading seeing accusation in that gaze. "They took him. I'm sorry, I tried to stop them…" His voice cracked shamefully.

But Alex's expression held only fear and grief, not blame. He gripped Eryx's shoulder almost painfully tight. "We'll get him back," he vowed fiercely. "Whatever it takes."

Jaw clenched, Eryx could only nod and hope it was true. The Order had stolen someone that was theirs. Failure was not an option now.

Together, they turned to gaze out over the city, united in determination. The real battle was only beginning. They would save Zac or die trying.

Eryx focused on that single thought, using it to steady his frayed nerves. With Alex at his side, he could conquer the dark road ahead. For Zac's sake, for their family, he had to believe it possible.

24

Blood Soul

Zac

Zac had no idea where he was being taken. He struggled against the iron grip of the creature that had grabbed him, but it was useless. His blood magic wasn't working for some reason, and panic rose in his throat at the thought that this might be the last time he'd see his newfound family.

The creature leapt into a shimmering portal, dragging Zac along with it. He was dumped unceremoniously onto the stone floor of what looked like some kind of temple. Zac's eyes darted around, taking in the unfamiliar surroundings. Wherever he was, it gave him the creeps.

A voice spoke from the shadows. "I told you I'd get the boy, Father."

Another voice answered, this one colder and more commanding. "Make sure you make this clean and fast, Sven. You've already failed me once."

Zac watched a shadowy figure disappear into another portal before a tall, broad-shouldered man with jet black hair approached him. Sven, apparently. He knelt down in front of Zac, taking his chin in a vice-like grip. Zac tried to jerk away, but Sven held firm, examining his face closely.

"You were a real pain in the ass to track down, kid," Sven said with a sly grin. "But we've got you now."

Zac's mind raced, adrenaline pumping through his veins. He had to figure out what these lunatics wanted from him. "What do you want with me?" he demanded, trying to keep the shake out of his voice.

From the corner of his eye, Zac saw one of the other creatures in the temple stir restlessly. "Enough playing around, Sven," it rasped. "We need to start the ritual."

Sven shot the creature a deadly look, releasing his hold on Zac. "He was useful after all," Sven said as he strode toward the creature. Before Zac could react, Sven had plunged his hand into its chest, ripping out its heart in a spray of black blood. Zac flinched, bile rising in his throat. Sven lifted the heart to his mouth and took a huge, bloody bite.

"Anyone else tries to rush me, you get the same," Sven declared to the other creatures. Zac noticed them shrink back submissively. He could feel the anxiety and fear rolling off them in waves.

Sven turned back to Zac, an unsettling grin on his face. "Now, let's get down to business, shall we?"

Sven snapped his fingers, and two of the hulking creatures lumbered forward. Before Zac could react, they had grabbed him roughly by the arms, dragging him to the center of a strange symbol carved into the stone floor. Zac struggled against their viselike grip, but it was useless. Again.

They dumped him unceremoniously in the middle of the circle, right next to another body. Zac's breath caught as he realized it was a corpse - pale and lifeless. This must be the vampire god.

Revulsion twisted Zac's gut. Thoughts of Alex and Eryx rose unbidden to his mind. Zac could picture Alex's fury, the way his jaw would clench and his eyes would flash red with barely contained rage. And Eryx - he'd be frantic, desperate to find him and make sure he was alright.

Zac wished more than anything they would burst through the door right now, Eryx's fists blazing with golden light, Alex wielding hellfire. But the temple remained still and silent around him except for Sven's ominous footsteps echoing on the stone.

Sven pulled a wickedly curved dagger from inside his suit jacket, turning it over in his hands almost lovingly. The obsidian blade seemed to drink in the dim light, hungry for blood. Sven trailed the edge lightly down Zac's cheek in a twisted caress.

"Such potential in this blood of yours," Sven murmured. Before Zac could flinch away, Sven drew the dagger swiftly across his palm, opening up a deep gash.

Zac cried out at the sudden, stinging pain, instinctively trying to clutch his wounded hand to his chest. But Sven grabbed his wrist in an unbreakable hold, bringing Zac's bleeding palm up to examine it with an unsettling fascination.

When Zac continued struggling, Sven's hand snapped out, punching him viciously in the gut. Zac doubled over with a pained gasp, the breath driven from his lungs.

"Quiet now," Sven admonished. "Or the next one will really hurt." He lifted the dagger to his mouth, blood smeared across the sharp edge. Maintaining eye contact with Zac, he slowly licked the flat of the blade.

"Mm, potent," he chuckled darkly. "You're powerful, kid. But not as powerful as me."

He turned and slammed the dagger down into a groove carved into the edge of the circle. Zac's vision was starting to blur from the pain, but he thought he saw the symbols carved around him begin to glow. An intense pressure built in the air, making his ears pop.

Sven's voice seemed to come from far away as he began to chant in a guttural language Zac didn't recognize. The other creatures quickly took up the chant, the strange words overlapping in a cacophony that pounded against Zac's eardrums.

Power surged around him, invading his senses until he could taste it, crackling over his skin. The symbols below him blazed crimson, the bloody light filling his vision. This was it - whatever terrifying ritual Sven had planned, it was happening now. Zac could only pray that somehow, Alex and Eryx would make it in time.

The pressure built to an unbearable crescendo and Zac squeezed his eyes shut against the blinding red glow. There was a feeling like his body was being turned inside out, and suddenly the sensations stopped. The chanting voices cut off abruptly.

Zac cautiously opened his eyes. He was no longer in the stone temple. Instead, he found himself standing in a moonlit field of blood-red roses that stretched as far as he could see under a night sky. Zac turned in a slow circle, utterly confused. Where was he? Some kind of vision?

"Welcome, Zac."

The voice behind him was deep and mellifluous. Zac whipped around to see a tall, striking figure with long crimson hair standing amid the roses. He wore an elegant black robe that blended into the shadows. Though he appeared relaxed, power rolled off him in almost palpable waves.

Zac tensed warily. This had to be Absalom, the ancient vampire god they had been trying to prevent the Order from resurrecting. Which meant Zac was in deep, deep trouble. He instinctively tried to call on his blood magic, but still nothing happened.

Absalom chuckled, as if reading his thoughts. "Don't bother. Your powers won't work here."

Zac's mouth went dry, but he forced himself to meet those ageless dark eyes steadily. "Am I about to die then?" he asked with more bravado than he felt.

Absalom tilted his head curiously. "Die? Now why would you think that?"

Zac shrugged, trying to appear casual even as his palms sweated. "Isn't that what this whole creepy ritual is about? To turn me into your vessel or something?"

Absalom beckoned him closer with a pale, elegant hand. "Come. Walk with me."

Wary but curious, Zac approached until they were side by side, strolling through the endless, gently swaying roses. He snuck sidelong glances at the vampire. Up close, Absalom's skin seemed to glow in the moonlight, flawless and pale as marble. His fine-boned features were beautiful but cold. Still, Zac felt no malice or danger from him.

They walked in silence for a time before Absalom spoke again. "You are correct that there are those who wish to see me resurrected fully. But they act against my will."

Zac's head jerked toward him in surprise. "Wait, you don't want to come back?"

Absalom gave a small, sad smile. "No. I do not wish to return to a world filled with chaos and death. Once perhaps…" He trailed off, gazing up at the luminous moon. "I only did what I must to survive back then. But no more."

Zac listened in fascination as Absalom explained how he had taken steps before his imprisonment to prevent any possible resurrection. How weary he had grown of the struggles and politics of the supernatural world. Zac found himself sympathizing with this ancient, lonely god.

"What will happen to me if I do become your vessel?" Zac finally ventured.

Absalom turned to him, expression open. "Our souls would merge. We would be connected, and my powers would become available to you. You would be immortal."

Zac's eyebrows shot up. "Would I become a vampire too?"

Absalom chuckled. "No. Your hemomancer abilities will sustain my vampiric essence. If you accept this gift, you will remain yourself."

Zac chewed his lip thoughtfully. Immortality, ancient magic - it was tempting, but also frightening. And he didn't fully trust Absalom yet.

"How will I know you won't join up with the Order once we merge?" he asked point blank.

Absalom's expression darkened. "I despise what many of my once-followers have become. Deceit and cruelty are not what I envisioned for them. If we unite, I pledge to aid you and yours in stopping Morvain from perverting my lineage further."

Zac searched those fathomless eyes, but could detect nothing but sincerity in their depths.

Mind made up, Zac met Absalom's gaze steadily. "I'll do it. Our souls can merge."

Absalom studied him a moment before nodding solemnly. "A wise choice, I believe. Our union will bring balance and order back to the realms." He clasped Zac's shoulder.

Zac's thoughts raced. "Will merging with you help boost my powers? I'll need to be stronger to take on the Order."

"Yes, you will have access to all my abilities and knowledge." Absalom waved a hand and a ghostly image appeared hovering in the air - the ritual circle and cultists, frozen mid-chant. "When you return, the ritual will still be underway. You must disrupt it before they realize the spell has failed."

Zac studied the image, brow furrowed. "My blood magic wasn't working before when they grabbed me. Any idea why?"

Absalom frowned. "They must be using some kind of dampening spell on the temple itself. But our combined abilities should overcome it."

Zac smiled and said "Let's make a plan then…"

25

Blood Vessel

Alex

Alex paced the briefing room, tension coiled through every muscle. On the table, Dr. Sloan was finishing up treating the gash on Eryx's arm, a grim look on the doctor's normally cheerful face.

Eryx's expression was haunted, his shoulders slumped in a way Alex hadn't seen since those early days. It tore at Alex's heart to see his mate like this.

Kneeling in front of Eryx, Alex took his hands gently. "We're going to find Zac. I swear to you, we will bring our boy home."

Eryx gripped his hands tightly, meeting Alex's eyes for the first time since they'd escaped the aftermath of the disastrous press conference. Alex could read the roiling emotions there - bone-deep fear for Zac warring with useless anger at being unable to protect him. An echo of Alex's own feelings.

"We're running out of time," Eryx said hoarsely. "It's nearly moonrise. We both heard Thanatos' warning about what that means."

Alex's jaw tightened. The moon. Of course this insidious ritual would require the full moon to resurrect a creature like Absalom. They were on a ticking clock to get Zac back before the Order could complete whatever sinister ceremony they had planned.

Alex stood abruptly. "Gabe, get Elder Lucius on the line. Now."

Gabe nodded and tapped rapidly at his tablet. A few moments later, the vampire Elder's visage appeared hovering above the central holotable. For once, Alex was almost glad to see the smug bastard's face.

Lucius sat at an ornate desk, sipping what was likely blood from a crystal glass. Probably vintage virgin blood from the nunnery down the street, Alex thought sourly. Lucius arched one elegant brow at Alex's stormy expression.

"Have you given more thought to my generous offer of an alliance, old friend?" he inquired smoothly.

Alex bit back an acidic retort. As much as he despised asking vampires for aid, he was out of options and time.

"I don't have time for games right now, Lucius," Alex ground out. "Someone under my protection has been taken by the Order. They plan to use him in some ritual to resurrect Absalom."

For once, the annoying smirk faded from Lucius's face. "Well I guess you've already ran out of time."

"I don't think so," Alex said grimly. "My sources say they're planning a ritual requiring the full moon and we still have hours and that's enough."

Understanding dawned on Lucius, followed swiftly by calculation. "The temple ruins near the Woodlands. My spies reported suspicious activity there recently…" He tented his fingers. "I may have information on its location. For the right price."

Alex suppressed a growl of frustration. He should have known the leech would try to leverage this. But one look at Eryx's strained face had Alex swallowing his pride.

"Name it," he bit out.

A slow, satisfied smile curved Lucius's mouth, showing just a hint of fang. "Like I told you before this. Control of Eastside interests in the city would be a start. The Eastside coven has become…problematic of late."

Alex's hands tightened into fists. Dealing with the fallout of vampire power struggles was so far from his priorities right now. But if it led them to Zac…

"Fine," Alex ground out. "We have a deal. Send me everything your spies have on the temple location."

Lucius inclined his head, looking cats who got the cream. "Of course. I'll dispatch my own warriors to aid you in this…rescue mission." His smile turned cruel. "Oh, and one more thing - I have learned Alavar has met his end. It seems Nero got tired of the Elder."

The call ended abruptly, leaving Alex seething. He should have known better than to trust Lucius to trade fairly. But it couldn't be helped now - he'd just have to find a way to minimize vampire interference when this was over.

Right on cue, Gabe's tablet pinged with an incoming data packet. "Location coordinates for the temple just came through from Lucius. It's somewhere deep in the protected parts of the Woodlands."

Alex's lips flattened in frustration as the map display zoomed in on the temple ruins buried deep in the Woodlands. Finding this place without Lucius's insider knowledge would have been nearly impossible. The ancient forest's concealing magic barred most forms of scrying and tracking.

But knowing he now owed the sly vampire a debt of favor left a bitter taste in Alex's mouth. Lucius excelled at turning any situation to his own advantage. Alex could only hope he wouldn't come to regret this bargain.

Lily turned to him, eyebrows raised. "What was all that about an offer and alliance? Have you and Lucius been making backroom deals?" Though her tone was light, Alex could tell the question bothered her. Lily valued openness and hated vampire politics.

With a heavy sigh, Alex quickly summarized the "mutually beneficial partnership" Lucius had proposed, glossing over some of the more unsavory details. Eryx and Gabe already knew of it, but Alex had been putting off telling the rest of the team until after this crisis was resolved. He should have known Lily would pick up on the implications.

As expected, Lily looked troubled, opening her mouth to object. But Alex lifted a hand to forestall her.

"I know it's not ideal," he said wearily, "but we're out of options and nearly out of time. Zac's life hangs in the balance - we can't afford to be choosy about allies right now."

Lily subsided reluctantly. Alex knew they'd be revisiting this issue later, but for now she accepted the need for expedience.

Eryx stepped up, expression somber but determined. "You're right, saving Zac is what matters. We can figure the rest out after." Having Eryx at his back settled something in Alex. Together, they would find a way.

Alex turned to his mate, inspecting him critically. The bleeding had stopped thanks to Dr. Sloan's ministrations, but Eryx was still far too pale and drawn. "Are you sure you're up for this fight?"

Eryx waved off his concern. "I'll manage. The doc's healing mojo is already kicking in." He touched the ring around his neck. "Plus I've got a few tricks left."

Dr. Sloan nodded confirmation. "His vitals have stabilized and his healing is underway. He should be alright in a support capacity." It wasn't ideal, but they needed every able fighter they could get.

Alex looked around at his team, resolve hardening into steel. "Marcus, take Lucas and gear up. We're moving out as soon as the portal is ready." Both men immediately headed for the armory without question.

Alex turned to Lily next. "Contact the HIB, give them a sitrep and our coordinates once we have them. We may need backup or evac assistance." Lily pulled out her phone, already dialing.

That just left Gabe monitoring the portal calibration, Dr. Sloan prepping medical supplies, Emma and Olivia suiting up with Marcus and Lucas, and Eryx doing some breathing exercises to center himself.

As the team gathered round, he met each of their eyes in turn.

"I know you're all worried about Zac. So am I. But this is what we train for - saving innocents from forces that seek to harm them. Whatever the Order is planning ends tonight!"

Around him, Alex sensed backs straightening, jaws firming with resolve. Time to wrap it up.

"We don't know what we're walking into, but we do know one thing for certain - we're getting Zac back, no matter what it takes. We don't leave family behind. Are you with me?"

A chorus of determined agreement answered him. Alex nodded, a fierce swell of pride in his chest. "Then let's do this."

The portal flashed open, casting an eerie blue glow across their faces. Go time. Alex and Eryx took point, boarding one of the armored bearcat vehicles along with Marcus at the wheel. The others piled into the second with Lucas driving.

Tires spun and engines revved as they plunged into the swirling portal gateway. They emerged on a narrow forest trail, the trees crowding close on either side. Alex kept a sharp eye out, but detected no signs of ambush yet.

According to the map, the ruins were a fair distance in. The trees here were ancient, their energy pulsing across Alex's senses. Anything could be lurking in a forest this old and wild.

They hadn't gone more than three miles when several pale figures emerged from the shadows ahead, blocking the trail. Alex signaled

Marcus to halt. As the lead vampire stalked closer, Alex recognized him as one of Lucius's enforcers. Wonderful.

"We will proceed on foot from here," the vampire announced. "The ruins are warded against vehicles."

Alex bit back a snarl of frustration. Of course Lucius had left out that little detail. Forcing them to walk right into potential traps set by the temple's defenders. The bastard was counting on the Order weakening Alex's team first.

But they didn't have time to argue logistics. The sun was already kissing the horizon, the moon's rise close. Alex turned to Eryx and Marcus. "We hoof it from here. Stay sharp."

They left the bearcat in the vampires' care, plunging into the trackless forest. Alex felt Eryx draw subtly on his magic to heal himself, the branches and roots underfoot shifting to make an easier path.

Allowing vampires at their backs made Alex's skin crawl. He itched to ignite hellfire just to remind them of their vulnerable state here in his domain. But he restrained himself - Saving Zac came first.

The sun slipped below the trees, dusk falling under the canopy. Alex tilted his head back, assessing the moon's position. Too close to full for comfort; its influence already thrummed in his blood. Had to be affecting Zac even more as a blood mage.

Alex pushed them to move faster. The trees were thinning, ruins close. Almost there...

A bloodcurdling scream tore through the eerie twilight stillness - a scream in a voice that seized Alex's heart with icy fear.

Zac.

Zac's scream knifed through Alex like shards of ice. Without thinking, he broke into a run toward the sound, the others close behind. Branches whipped at his face and roots tore at his boots, but Alex pushed his body faster.

Had they already started the ritual? Were they torturing Zac? Alex's pulse pounded in his ears. If they'd hurt one hair on his head, there would be hell to pay. Literally.

Bursting past a wall of bushes, the temple ruins came into view, lit by the rising moon. Alex skidded to a stop, throwing up a shield of hellfire just as the ancient stones exploded outward with a boom that shook the earth.

Fiery projectiles rained down around them. Alex gritted his teeth, straining to hold the protective barrier against the onslaught. Out of the corner of his eye, he saw Eryx directing his own shield, the golden glow mixing with Alex's sapphire flames.

Working in tandem, they withstood the blast, though Alex could feel Eryx tiring. As the smoke cleared, Alex got his first clear look at the ruined temple—and felt his soul drop in dismay.

Zac stood amidst the rubble, eyes burning crimson, clothed in shadows that twisted around him. At his side was Sven, grinning like a fiend, the Staff of Umbra clenched in his fist. An honor guard of hybrid monsters flanked them.

"Zac!" Alex shouted desperately. "Get away from him!" But the boy didn't even react, his gaze frighteningly blank. Sven's grin widened, stroking the Staff as if it were a beloved pet.

"Too late for that I'm afraid, oh fallen one," Sven mocked. "The ritual is complete. Absalom walks the mortal plane again!" His grating laughter sent chills down Alex's spine.

Beside him, Eryx made a wounded noise. Alex's own heart shattered. They had failed. Despite all their efforts, Absalom now had possession of Zac's body and powers. Alex's hands curled into fists, hellfire coiling around them in agitation.

"Letting others do your dirty work for you, like the coward you are," Alex spat at Sven, grasping for anything to offset this nightmare. "I'll make sure you pay dearly for this!"

Sven's smug look vanished, replaced by cold rage. "We shall see who pays the price this night, hellspawn." He raised the Staff, the carved obsidian seeming to writhe. "Destroy them!"

At Sven's command, the hybrid monsters charged, their howls of bloodlust piercing the air. With a flick of the Staff, Sven tore open a portal, unleashing a swarm of shadowy wraiths that poured forth like a tide of living darkness.

But worst of all was the sight of Zac - no, not Zac, but Absalom wearing his stolen face - raising his hands as blood-red lightning crackled and coalesced around him, casting an eerie crimson glow across the battlefield.

Alex had no choice. With a snarl of defiance, he drew his sword and leapt to meet the oncoming threats, determined to carve a path to Zac no matter the cost. The first hybrid that reached him fell gurgling and headless before it even realized the danger, but Alex barely spared it a glance. These creatures were nothing, mere obstacles to be cut down. His only goal was to get to Zac.

He slashed and hacked his way closer, hellfire trailing from his blade in blazing arcs. Out of the corner of his eye, he could see Eryx throwing golden light darts with deadly accuracy, each one finding its mark in the hearts of their foes as he fought to clear a way to Zac.

But Zac - or rather, the dark god puppeting his body - was far from idle. With a cruel twist of his lips, he hurled spheres of crackling crimson energy into the melee, each one exploding with devastating force that sent friend and foe alike flying. The power he wielded was staggering, fueled by Zac's innate hemomancer abilities and amplified a hundredfold by Absalom's ancient might.

Alex barely managed to deflect a blast meant for him, throwing up a shield of hellfire at the last second. But even so, the force of it drove him back a step, his boots skidding across the blood-slicked ground. Absalom grinned at the sight, a vicious, hungry thing that held no trace of Zac's usual warmth.

Slowly, almost lazily, he began to gather even more blood magic between his hands, the air around him thrumming with barely contained power as he prepared a larger, more devastating attack.

Gritting his teeth, Alex charged forward with a shout, trusting his team to guard his back as he focused solely on disrupting the spell before it could wipe them all out. But Absalom seemed to anticipate his every move, twisting aside with preternatural grace before lashing out with a backhanded blow that sent Alex tumbling to the ground, his head ringing from the force of it.

Before he could even attempt to regain his feet, Absalom had pinned him in place with bands of solidified blood, the dark magic constricting around him like iron chains. Immobilized, helpless, Alex could only watch as those alien, crimson-lit eyes in Zac's youthful face glowed with malevolent anticipation.

"Now, pretender god, time to die," Absalom purred, a blood spear forming above Alex's heart, its point honed to a wicked edge. This was it, then. The end of the line. At least he would die fighting, a warrior to the last. Drawing in a final, shuddering breath, Alex let his eyes fall closed, bracing for the killing blow…

But instead of piercing agony, he felt the crushing bonds abruptly vanish, dissipating into wisps of fading magic. Eyes flying open in confusion, Alex saw Zac looming over him, his expression strangely conflicted – a far cry from the merciless cruelty of moments before.

Then, to Alex's utter shock, Zac leaned in close and whispered urgently, "Pretend and play along! I'll explain later!"

Alex stared up at him, hardly daring to believe his ears. Before he could even begin to formulate a response, Zac had straightened up, his face smoothing back into hard, pitiless lines.

"On your knees, hellspawn!" he snarled, his voice ringing with command. *"Your life is now mine."*

For a split second, Alex hesitated, torn between disbelief and desperate hope. Then, placing his trust in the boy he loved like a son, he allowed Zac to haul him roughly to his feet and shove him down to his knees, as if in supplication.

Out of the corner of his eye, he saw Eryx falter, lowering his weapons in bewilderment as he watched the scene unfolding before him.

Sven stalked over, a smug, triumphant grin stretching across his face. "Enough playing with your prey!" he snapped impatiently. "Finish them! The dawn of our new era is at hand!"

But Zac paid him no heed, his attention focused solely on Alex as he raised his hands, wreathed in writhing tendrils of blood magic. Alex tensed, his heart pounding wildly in his chest as he tried to read Zac's intentions.

Could it be? Was the boy somehow fighting back against Absalom's control, clawing his way back to the surface through sheer force of will? Hardly daring to breathe, Alex clung to that fragile sliver of hope like a lifeline.

"You will never use me for anything," Zac declared, his voice ringing out like a clarion call. And in that moment, Alex saw the truth in his eyes – not Absalom's malevolent red, but Zac's own warm eyes, alight with fierce determination and unwavering resolve.

Too late, Sven's smug expression morphed into one of dawning horror as he realized he'd been played. But before he could even think to react, Zac whirled on him, hands outstretched as he unleashed a veritable tsunami of hemomantic power directly at Sven.

It slammed into Sven like a runaway freight train, hurling him back against a broken stone pillar with enough force to crack the ancient masonry. Pinned there, helpless and writhing, Sven could only cry out in impotent rage and alarm as Zac bore down on him, snarling with the fury of the righteous.

Though Alex could see the toll it was taking on him, the strain of wielding such immense power etched in every line of his youthful face, Zac never wavered. Eyes blazing, he pressed the attack, pouring everything he had into keeping Sven contained.

"Find another god to prey upon," Zac spat, his words dripping with contempt. *"I will never serve monsters like you!"*

And with a final, tremendous effort, he ripped open a swirling vortex of shadow – a dark portal leading who knew where. Gritting his teeth, Zac flung Sven and the remaining wraiths into its gaping maw with a burst of blood magic, banishing them to some far-flung corner of the void.

Then, with a shuddering gasp, he let the gateway collapse in on itself, sealing the rift with a blinding flash of crimson light.

As the dark power faded from his eyes, Zac swayed on his feet, his strength utterly spent. But before he could crumple to the ground, Alex was there, catching him gently against his chest and lowering him down with infinite care.

Looking down into the boy's exhausted face, Alex felt a fierce swell of pride and love. Zac had done it. Against all odds, he had broken free of an ancient god's control and turned the tables on their enemies, all through his own cleverness and unbreakable spirit.

In that moment, Alex knew beyond a shadow of a doubt that Zac was a true hero – not because of any prophecy or divine birthright, but because of the strength of his own heart and the sharpness of his mind.

And as he cradled the boy close, murmuring words of reassurance and praise, Alex silently vowed that he would do everything in his power to nurture and protect this incredible young man he was proud to call his own.

"You're safe now, I've got you," he murmured. Zac gave him a faint but genuine smile before going limp in Alex's arms, exhausted from fighting Absalom's possession.

Alex scooped Zac up fully, cradling the precious burden close.

Around them, the hybrid monsters were regrouping, but Alex's people had the upper hand now. Time to finish this.

Alex turned to the lurking vampires with cold authority. "The hybrids are yours. But if any harm comes to my people, there will be hell to pay." One look at his granite expression had them bowing in acquiescence.

Satisfied they'd behaved for now, Alex gave the order to pull out. The team assembled around him, keeping wary eyes on the vampires now rounding up hybrid captives. Eryx came to Alex's side, relief and concern warring on his face as he looked at Zac's limp form.

"Is he…?" Eryx trailed off uncertainly.

Alex's hold on Zac tightened protectively. "He's just exhausted. But he's back in control." The realization still amazed him. Somehow, Zac had managed to fight off possession by an ancient god, if only temporarily. "We still don't know what's going on. Let's head back for now."

The team hurried from the ruins, anxious to leave the vampires and their creepy hybrid captives behind. Alex carried Zac the whole way, keeping up easily even with the extra burden. Having the boy safely back in his arms eased something in his chest.

Once they reached the bearcats, Alex passed Zac gently to Eryx so he could drive. But his eyes kept straying back to check on those two beloved faces. Zac was curled against Eryx's chest, sound asleep. Eryx just held him close, looking as relieved as Alex felt.

They were battered and bruised, but they were going home. And miraculously, they were bringing Zac back with them. The fight wasn't over, but they had defied the odds.

26

Light Redeemed

Eryx

Eryx stared down at the half-finished lyrics scrawled across the page, but his mind kept straying. It had been two days now since they'd rescued Zac from the Order's clutches. Two days of waiting and worrying as the boy remained unconscious, recovering from the ordeal.

Alex had urged Eryx to get out of the house for a while, so here he was trying to write music at a coffee shop. But focusing was hard when his thoughts kept drifting back to Zac's pale face on his bed.

According to Dr. Sloan, Zac's vitals were stable and his magic aura was untainted. He just needed time for his mind to heal after what he had been through. But not knowing when Zac would wake was eating away at Eryx.

With a sigh, he set down his pen and rubbed his eyes. It wasn't just Zac's condition preoccupying him lately. So much had happened in such a short span.

They'd handed the details of their Jane Doe case over to the HIB, providing edited details to avoid awkward questions. Lucius now dominated the Eastside after finding Nero's murdered body at the temple site.

All the hybrid captives were in a contained facility with Dr. Sloan researching treatments. Alex had incinerated every last drop of the Moonblood toxin as well. By all accounts, the threat was neutralized. For now.

But Eryx knew better than to think it was truly over. There were still many unanswered questions. And he hated waiting helplessly.

With a frustrated huff, Eryx tidied up his work space and headed out. Some fresh air would clear his head, and he could pick up some soup for when Zac woke. Eryx refused to consider any alternative. The boy would pull through - he had to.

The afternoon sun was bright after the coffee shop's cozy dimness. Eryx slipped on his shades and picked a direction at random. Once, wandering the city alone might have bothered him, but he felt at ease here now.

He found himself smiling slightly, remembering how adrift he'd felt those first months in New York. So much had changed since crossing paths with Alex. Not just gaining a family and purpose, but finding himself. He went where he wanted now, not directed by elder gods or prophecies. Eryx was finally shaping his own fate.

The upbeat ringtone of his manager cut into Eryx's musings. Fishing out his phone, he saw it was Brad and answered.

"Hey Brad, what's up?"

"Eryx! Thank god you're alright, man. I've been trying to reach you for days!" Brad's normally unflappable voice sounded relieved. "Are you okay?"

Guilt twinged in Eryx's gut. In the chaos after Zac's abduction, he'd forgotten to check in with his manager. "I'm fine, Brad, sorry for worrying you. Got caught up handling everything after..." He hesitated, unsure how much to reveal over the phone.

"Believe me, I get it," Brad said. "Just glad you and Richard made it out in one piece."

Eryx debated a moment before going with, "It's still under investigation. Hopefully they'll turn something up soon." No need to mention his own off-the-books methods.

"Well, take however long you need," Brad assured him. "Your health is what's important. We can reschedule any upcoming events."

Gratitude swelled in Eryx's chest. He really owed Brad for being so understanding. "Thanks, man. I'll keep you posted."

They said their goodbyes and Eryx tucked the phone away, thoughtful. Normal gigs and celebrity drama seemed almost trivial after contending with ancient resurrection cults. Maybe it was time to reconsider his priorities. But first, he had a kid to check on.

He was almost back to the annex when his phone buzzed again. Seeing it was Alex, Eryx quickly answered, nerves tingling.

"Everything okay?"

Alex's voice was warm with relief. "Better than. Our boy's awake, and asking for you."

Eryx came to an abrupt stop right there on the sidewalk, causing a businessman to swerve around him with an irritated huff. But Eryx didn't even notice, emotions surging.

"I'll be right there," he told Alex fervently, already hurrying toward where he'd parked the convertible.

Traffic laws were more suggestion than rule in Eryx's haste to get back home. He burned rubber the whole way, heart feeling lighter than it had in days. Zac was awake. Everything else could wait - Eryx needed to see his kid.

Tires screeched as he pulled into the underground garage. Cerebus' excited barking greeted him as the elevator opened directly into the annex. The enthusiastic hellhound nearly bowled Eryx over, but he just laughed and gave him a good ear scratch.

"Yeah, yeah, Daddy missed you too," Eryx cooed. Mr. Whiskers watched imperiously from atop his cat tower, tail twitching. Eryx shot him a rueful look. "Don't worry, I didn't forget you." The cat chirped smugly.

But even their antics couldn't distract Eryx for long. He made a beeline straight for the infirmary. The door was ajar, and he could make out the rumbling cadence of Alex's voice from within.

Eryx rapped lightly on the frame before pushing inside. Zac was sitting up in bed, still looking far too wan and exhausted, but smiling. Eryx thought his heart might burst from happiness.

In three long strides he was across the room, sweeping Zac into the gentlest of embraces. "You really scared us, kiddo," he murmured into Zac's hair. The solid reality of the boy in his arms chased away the last lingering shadows of fear.

Zac hugged him back tightly. "Missed you," he mumbled into Eryx's shoulder. They stayed like that a long moment, just holding each other close before Eryx drew back to look the teen over critically.

Alex came up on Zac's other side, affectionate hand ruffling his hair. "How're you feeling, tough guy?"

Zac managed a lopsided smile. "Been better. But Dr. Sloan says I should be okay." He bit his lip then. "I know you guys probably have questions…"

"Only if you're up for it," Eryx said gently, taking Zac's hand. As much as they needed answers, Zac's wellbeing came first.

But Zac shook his head. "No, you should know what happened." He gratefully accepted the glass of water Dion handed him, taking careful sips before beginning his story.

Eryx felt his stomach drop when Zac described Sven taking his blood during the kidnapping. One glance at Alex showed his jaw clenched in anger, no doubt thinking the same thing - that Sven could now mimic Zac's rare hemomancer abilities. This just got a lot more dangerous.

When Zac recounted his meeting with Absalom's spirit, Eryx listened in dismay. He'd hoped the ancient vampire wasn't still manipulating events, but clearly they had not seen the last of him. Absalom's desire to sway Zac to his side changed the game.

"Please, don't judge Absalom too harshly," Zac pleaded, looking between Eryx and Alex earnestly. "I know he's done terrible things in the past, but he explained it was only to survive back then. He seemed so…tired of all the violence and politics. He just wants peace now."

Eryx exchanged an uncertain glance with Alex. They both cared for Zac deeply, but this bond with the ancient vampire set off warning bells.

Zac correctly interpreted their hesitation. "I'm still me, I promise. Absalom and I are connected now, but I'm in control." His voice took on a note of steel. "And I intend to keep it that way. But he's not the monster you think. Working with him is our best chance to stop the Order for good."

Alex looked thoughtful, but Eryx still had reservations. He didn't fully trust Absalom's motivations, no matter how sincere he'd seemed to Zac. They needed to tread cautiously.

Sensing this, Zac met Eryx's eyes pleadingly. "Please, just trust me on this. Absalom is on our side now. Together, we can protect both human and supernatural worlds from Morvain's madness."

Eryx hesitated, then slowly nodded. It was clear Zac believed fully in what he was saying. And Eryx had to trust his son's judgment, even if he remained wary of Absalom's influence.

"Alright," he conceded. "We'll see where this new alliance takes us. But if he gives me any reason to think he'll betray us, the deal is off. Understood?"

Zac sagged a little in relief. "Thank you," he said earnestly. "I know in time you'll see that Absalom doesn't want harm to come to any of us."

Eryx hoped desperately that Zac was right. Because unleashing the ancient vampire's powers could save them - or doom them all. Only time would tell.

Thank you and Please Leave a Review!

Dear Readers,

As we come to the end of this wild and whimsical journey with the second book of Shadowguards, I want to take a moment to express my deepest gratitude. Thank you for joining us on this adventure filled with laughter, love, and a touch of the supernatural.

It's been an absolute joy to share this story with you, and I hope their antics brought a smile to your face and warmth to your heart. Writing their tale has been an incredible experience, and I'm so grateful for the opportunity to share it with all of you.

If you enjoyed our story, please consider leaving a review. Your feedback means the world to me, and it helps other readers discover our book and join in on the fun.

Thank you again for your support, your laughter, and your love. Here's to many more adventures together!

With heartfelt appreciation,
Ken Sanchez

About the Author

Ken Sanchez, the visionary behind spellbinding M/M romance-fantasy worlds where love and magic entwine in a mesmerizing dance. With a heart devoted to the art of LGBTQ+ romance and an unbounded imagination,

Subscribe to my newsletter:

✉ http://eepurl.com/iJMYvA

Also by Ken Sanchez

Echoes of Destiny (Shadowgaurds Book One)
Eryx, a gifted musician, channels haunting melodies that echo his forgotten godly lineage. When a sinister encounter alters his reality, he finds solace in an enigmatic guardian named Alex, whose alluring presence sparks an inexplicable connection.

Unbeknownst to Eryx, Alex is Hades, sentinel of the Underworld. As he guides Eryx through their intertwined destinies, an undeniable attraction forms, challenging the fabric of their worlds.

Amidst mysticism in contemporary New York, ancient prophecies resurge with encroaching darkness. Their bond becomes a beacon of hope as Eryx's ancestry awakens and their love deepens. The duo embarks on a quest that will test their resolve, unravel hidden truths, and decide humanity's fate.

Shadowguards is a gay urban fantasy that marries the ordinary with the extraordinary. Where music and shadows converge and the line between mortal and divine blurs, this spellbinding tale explores the complexities of destiny and the unbreakable ties that bind us.

Enchanted (Willowbrook Book One)
In the enchanting town of Willowbrook, a young man named Benjamin discovers a remarkable power—the ability to bring stories to life. When he encounters a reclusive Beast named Adrian, cursed to shift between a fearsome ice dragon and a human form that freezes everything he touches, their destinies entwine.

As Benjamin and Adrian navigate a treacherous journey filled with love, friendship, and the transformative power of stories, they must break Adrian's curse to save Willowbrook from an eternal winter. With the town's magical essence slowly fading, time is running out.

Discover a captivating tale of redemption, acceptance, and the enduring magic of true love. Uncover the secrets hidden within the enchanted library and witness how love can rewrite even the darkest of stories. Join Benjamin and Adrian in "Enchanted" and experience the magic within your reach.

"Enchanted" is a captivating gay retelling of a timeless legend of Beauty and The Beast.

This is a standalone and can be read in any order. Unlock the Magic Within, and Let Love Rewrite the Story.

Stormweaver (Willowbrook Book Two)
In the enchanted town of Willowbrook, where supernatural forces intertwine, a storm is brewing, threatening to shatter the delicate balance between magic and reality. Weather witch Dominic Reed seeks solace in his bakery, Glimmer, but his haunted past and tumultuous family dynamics refuse to fade.

Enter Christian Belgrade, heir to a vampire coven, whose scarred history and possessive nature are eclipsed only by his mysterious powers. When their worlds collide at Christian's club, a revelation unfolds, setting off a chain of events that will test their strengths, unravel their vulnerabilities, and force them to confront the shadows that lurk in the magical underbelly of Willowbrook.

As the connection deepens between Dominic and Christian, they must navigate the treacherous waters of Elder Eros Grim's vendetta and Dominic's malevolent stepfamily. Will love be enough to weather the storm that threatens to consume them, or will the secrets of their pasts tear them apart?

In this enthralling sequel to Willowbrook, immerse yourself in a tale of redemption, passion, and the enduring power of love. Stormweaver will sweep you away into a world where the supernatural meets the deeply human, leaving you breathless and craving more.

This is book two in the Willowbrook Series and can be read as a stand alone. This is also a gay retelling of Cinderella.